SUPER-DETECTIVE

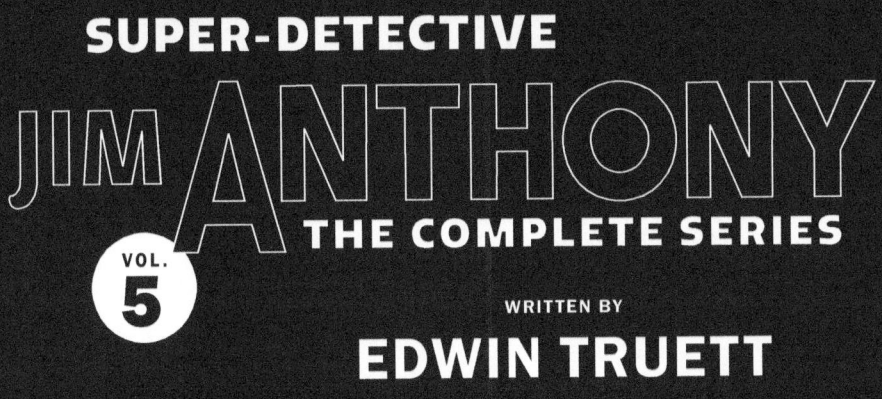

JIM ANTHONY

THE COMPLETE SERIES

VOL. 5

WRITTEN BY

EDWIN TRUETT LONG

AND

ROBERT LESLIE BELLEM & W.T. BALLARD

ILLUSTRATIONS BY

JOSEPH SZOKOLI

STEEGER BOOKS

2024

PUBLISHING HISTORY

"Mark of the Spider" originally appeared in the August 1942 issue of *Super-Detective* (Volume 3, Number 3). Copyright © 1942 by Trojan Publishing Corporation.

"Hell's Ice-Box" originally appeared in the October 1942 issue of *Super-Detective* (Volume 3, Number 4). Copyright © 1942 by Trojan Publishing Corporation.

"The Days of Death" originally appeared in the November 1942 issue of *Super-Detective* (Volume 3, Number 5). Copyright © 1942 by Trojan Publishing Corporation.

"The Caribbean Cask" originally appeared in the December 1942 issue of *Super-Detective* (Volume 3, Number 6). Copyright © 1942 by Trojan Publishing Corporation.

"Murder Between Shifts" originally appeared in the January 1943 issue of *Super-Detective* (Volume 4, Number 1). Copyright © 1943 by Trojan Publishing Corporation.

"Cauldron of Death" originally appeared in the February 1943 issue of *Super-Detective* (Volume 4, Number 2). Copyright © 1943 by Trojan Publishing Corporation.

Visit *steegerbooks.com* for more books like this.

TABLE OF

CONTENTS

MARK OF THE SPIDER

MANY A TIME JIM ANTHONY HAD SAVED HIS LIFE BY HIS ABILITY
TO PREDICT A CRIMINAL'S NEXT MOVE. BUT HERE HE HAD TO COPE
WITH A CAPRICIOUS WOMAN—NOW CRUEL, NOW TENDER. READY TO
KILL, TODAY—AND TOMORROW WILLING TO BETRAY A MURDERER...

BECAUSE HIS MOTHER HAD been a full-blooded Comanche princess, Jim Anthony, after the thing was over, might have preferred the American Indian expression, "The dropping of a leaf in a forest may turn the lives of four who dwell a thousand miles apart to the four winds."

Dolores Colquitt, his lovely fiancée, no mean student of the Orient, no doubt would have used the subtler Chinese; "Many strange threads make an inch of silk."

Tom Gentry, Anthony's genial pal, would have said simply, "It's a damned queer world, ain't it?"

The reactions of Trotter, or Gross, or of that exotic woman who called herself Lupe Carranza—as of all the others involved—would be unpredictable.

The whole thing really began in the backroom of a certain precinct police station in the city of New York which was notorious for its toughness. Gross was a small man, but tough, like so many of the male products of Hell's Kitchen. But with the glaring light beating down on him so relentlessly, so hotly, with his face battered and swollen, his lips puffed and thick, it was evident to all who watched that the end was near. Not that his defiant eyes showed it—but there is a limit to the endurance of the human body.

Trotter, of Homicide, the man who stood over him in his shirt sleeves, was a detective of the old school. He came up from pounding a beat, he believed in stool pigeons, and the use of force. Jim Anthony, millionaire detective, who stood back in the shadows grim with anger, was a strict proponent of the use of science. Often he and Trotter worked together but more often they were at daggers' points.

Trotter's face was red, perspiration gleamed on his forehead, his great chest heaved. He was nearly as tired as the little man whom he had been working on for the past two hours.

"For the last time, you little rat, I'll give it to you, and I want an answer!" Gross' eyes glared back doggedly. "You drove for Mansfield, just a plain chauffeure. He was a peculiar guy, lived all alone, except for you. The guy disappears, he's clear gone! You turn up with plenty of jack, and three months later when somebody thinks to wonder about this Mansfield, you don't know a damned thing!" The ominous sneer in Trotter's voice became tinged with a hint of triumph. "You still don't know a damned thing when we dig up a skull and a thigh-bone in the backyard!"

Anthony put in wearily, "You snatched him off the streets and clapped him in this backroom so quickly that you haven't even listened to the truth. I tell you, a woman's skull is a great deal less in capac-

"Don't kill him!" she cried. "We let Jim Anthony get
away—but this man is twice as valuable!"

ity than a man's; I even gave you the height of the woman from her
thigh, I—"

"Nuts! What the hell do I care about that stuff? I've got a killer here
and I'll make him admit that was Mansfield's body if I have to break
his own thighs. I—now what the hell do you want?"

The last was addressed to an entering detective with a cigarette
dangling unlighted between his lips. He bore a folded paper, said in a
bored manner, "It was a dame, Trotter. Four prominent anthro-what-
cha-macallits agreed. Anthony makes five."

Trotter didn't bother to take the paper. He glared at Anthony; he glared at the near collapsing Gross. He snarled, "Take him away to a cell, he ain't cleared even if it wasn't Mansfield."

But later it developed that Gross was freed. He drifted away from the dirty sidewalks of his youth, and not for two years did Jim Anthony so much as think of the man.

ANTHONY WAS A murder man of International repute. Not the murderer, of course, but the hunter of men, the seeker of killers. This was his major hobby, homicide, though an amazing mind and physical perfection, allowed him tremendous insight into fully half a hundred of the other ologies usually assumed by the college professors alone. Possession of one of America's major fortunes was always an advantage—for Jim Anthony charged no fees, and consequently was called all over the world on interesting cases.

He ran into the fat rat named Fago simply because one of the properties Jim had inherited from his father was the *Daily Star*. Newspaperdom and newspapermen had interested him from childhood. He could run the great presses, edit copy at the horseshoe desk with the white-headed old rewriters, or work a police beat.

Thus at night court, when two rather defiant kids of thirteen and fourteen had been brought in for possessing a gunnysack half filled with radiator ornaments, another strange thread was woven into the fabric.

They said they thought it was okay, because the fat man told them he'd take care of anything that happened. The fat man proved to be Fago. He was but a few inches over five feet in height, his baggy trousers were green with age, a derby hat several sizes too small sat atop his bald head. Instead of brows, great folds of fat, fishbelly white in color, overhung beady black eyes, almost obscuring them. His mouth was a gaping wide slot disclosing yellow jags of teeth, his nose was a mere afterthought, as if thrust there contemptuously by a maker more than a little ashamed of his handiwork.

Sure, Fago whined, he bought anything brought into him. Wasn't he in the junk business? But as for sending kids out to steal them ornaments and caps—nix, nix, not Fago! And he'd winked knowingly. The kids were sent to a reform school, Fago got off with a warning, for the time being, at least. Never, Jim Anthony thought, had he ever seen so contemptible a figure—like a white slug from beneath an honest manure pile.

His own investigation born of this native antipathy for vile things, disclosed some amazing matters. Fago wasn't only a junk dealer; he owned garages, filling stations, shady hotels, throughout New York! By spending a lot of time and money Anthony finally got him a two year sentence on a receiving charge.

A few weeks later, Fago had strutted into Jim's office, spat on the Persian rug, grinned malevolently and advised the young millionaire to stick to his own business. For one of the few times in his life Anthony really got mad—and yet could not hit the creature. Afterward he said it would have been like thrusting your hands deliberately into filth.

"Listen to me, Fago," he'd said, choking on each word, "if I ever so much as see you again, I'm going to step on you like the fat little slug you are."

Fago spat again, turned and waddled through the door. That night Jim said, to Dolores, and Tom, "You know I've bucked some tough ones in this business. But there was something in that fat devil's eyes that actually scared me—and he was too filthy to hit!"

They'd laughed at him. They'd always claimed fear was an emotion unknown to Jim Anthony. And afterward, all three of them were to remember his words.

LUPE CARRANZA FLASHED across the New York sky about that time.

She was wild and exotic, utterly physical, for when she did her bold dances on the handkerchief dance floors, beneath the fingers of the spotlight, there seemed to be no bone at all to her. She was flesh alone.

Her hair was the zenith in shiny blackness, her lips the acme of red provocativeness, and her body itself was tawny. Men saw her and wanted her. She danced perhaps three weeks… and then there was one millionaire play boy after another. She was really the match that touched off the fuse, for Tom Gentry wanted her, too.

CHAPTER II

FAGO'S CATCH

TWO ANGRY MEN FACED each other in the magnificently furnished living room of New York's finest penthouse. Both wore tails, and gleaming shirt fronts, but only one had on the tall silk hat necessary to the ensemble. The swarthy man, Jim Anthony, had tossed his contemptuously aside.

"I'm hoping I didn't hear you right, Tom."

Gentry was so angry his freckles were like moles on his white face. "You heard me right—and who the hell are you to make any remarks? I've got a right to my friends."

Anthony shrugged. "No doubt we all have our dirty linen, but we don't have to flaunt it in the public's face."

Dolores called from another room, "Be with you in a jiffy, fellers, I smeared my mouth."

"Never mind," called back Anthony, "I don't think we'll make this a party after all, just a couple of twosomes."

"Just what have you got against Lupe Carranza? My personal friends aren't good enough to be seen in the company of the great Anthony and his beloved? Come on, you're the guy that raised the objection, aren't you man enough to say it instead of merely hint it?"

"Damn right I'll say it! I can name you a half dozen men she's utterly ruined in the last few months. There's something slimy and nasty about her, something like leprosy! She's got the alluring beauty of the brightly spotted snake that lives for her own selfish lusts and desires, some of them physical, some of them material. She reminds me of that fat filthiness that calls himself Fago, only she uses bewitching physical beauty to cloak the impurity that's the real Lupe, just as Fago uses deliberately unattractive clothes and an oily, smirking manner to hide his own impurity and nastiness. She—!"

Lupe's voice broke in on them: "Thank you, Mr. Anthony. Then you might say this—ah, Fago was the name?—and I are sisters under the skin? I'd love to meet him!"

Anthony naturally was aghast. He had naturally supposed that she was not yet along, that they were to pick her up a bit later. Now the woman he had spoken of so hotly—and rightly—stood sneering at him in his own doorway. There was even something alluring about her sneer, as if she had practised it for many hours before a mirror.

She wore a long black evening gown with a silver lame wrap. As she swayed into the room toward Anthony, the wrap opened; it was the most daring and revealing gown he had ever seen. Deliberately she brushed Tom with her shoulder in passing, as if shoving him aside in contempt. She faced Jim with blazing eyes.

"Men do not speak like that to Lupe Carranza."

It happened all too swiftly, even for Jim Anthony, the athlete. Deep red fingernails left furrowed gashes on his cheek. A man slaps even an attacking child away, he does it instinctively, from reflex action. Yet afterward he swore to Dolores that his palm had merely slapped at her braceleted wrist.

She screamed, and fell to the floor.

Tom Gentry said, "Damn you, you hit her, the woman I'm going to marry!"

"Damn you!" grated Tom. "You hit her—the woman I'm going to marry!" His fist lashed out.

HIS OWN FIST smashed into Jim Anthony's mouth. Anthony didn't fall, he rolled with the punch, but it was yet hard enough to bring a red worm of blood from the corner of his lips down over his chin.

"Come on, damn you, come on," snarled Tom Gentry. Jim wasn't even looking at him. Rather he stared down at the woman who still lay on the floor. He'd slapped her wrist—yet the gown was torn down the front! And she smiled at him tauntingly and he understood her act.

To Tom he said levelly, "I can take you apart, my friend, but I wouldn't give her the pleasure of seeing it! Can't you see, you fool, that's the reason for the act, and the act proves what I said of her? What would she gain? Nothing but some perverted satisfaction from seeing two friends fight."

"Make it ex-friends," answered Tom slowly and deliberately. He helped the woman—now whimpering weakly—to her feet. "To hell with the big bold man that goes around slapping ladies down. Come on."

Anthony called after him, "I'm telling you right for the last time, Tom. Go with her and you're deliberately fouling yourself. I don't usually care for filth."

The angered voice flung over a retreating shoulder said, "Don't worry about it. If I never see you again, that will be soon enough."

For a moment Anthony stood there with twisted emotions. The blood dropped off his chin onto his white shirt bosom. Almost absently he dabbed at it with a handkerchief. The strange bloods of the fey Irish and the Indian mixed in his veins. Now they throbbed with a premonition of evil. He leaped for the phone, but it was a full two minutes before a sugary voice said, "Yes, please, Mr. Anthony?"

Anthony roared, "Tell that damned house detective to arrest Tom Gentry before he gets through the lobby!"

A gasp was his answer. "I—ah—to arrest *Tom Gentry?* You don't mean *Tom Gentry?*"

Jim groaned. By now Gentry would be gone, for the elevator was express from the penthouse, the phone service had been poor. "No," he finally snapped, "never mind doing that. Just find the house detective and tell him to arrest *you* and see that you get about twenty years in solitary!"

He slammed down the phone. Dolores had a drink ready for him but it was like so much water.

"Damn it," he muttered, "there's hell and high water in this. I feel it, I know it. That woman is death itself, the sort of woman that attracts violence even in the middle of a desert!"

JUST ONE HOUR and thirty minutes later the woman who called herself Lupe Carranza was behind the wheel of the white Packard convertible, Gentry's head on her shoulder. He was snoring a little, as their slumming tour had had many stops.

There was a cunningly vicious brain beneath that lacquered black hair and it was working now with fully as many cylinders, fully as much horse power as the big car possessed.

She turned into a narrow street leading downhill toward the water-front. Warehouses were on either side, but ahead of her, almost at the next intersection, she saw the neon lights of the spot she desired. She parked before it. Her arm slid around Gentry's shoulders, she shook him gently.

"Wake up little boy," she murmured and kissed him, thoroughly and completely. Little Boy awakened at once and cooperated. Men usually did with women like Lupe Carranza. "Here's another stop, little boy, help mamma out."

Little Boy helped Mamma out, though he was a little unsteady in so doing. She held his arm tightly, led him through the grimy glass doors. Inside, the dimly lighted joint was without other customers. There was dirty sawdust on the floor, the whole place smelled of stale beer. She did not even glance at the potbellied bartender.

"Sit here, little boy," she said lovingly, and placed him at a table, his back toward the door. She hesitated for a moment, then took off his hat. Already his head was lolling. Blithely she swayed toward the door marked "Little Girls."

Outside two men argued in the shadows. "They was to be four, damn it," said one, uncertainly.

"Nemmine," was the reply, "this is the car, and the dame damned sure was Lupe. Come on." They went in. Looked inquiringly at the potbellied bartender, who shrugged, as if a bit puzzled. Gentry's head was almost on the table. They went silently toward him, and a pair of blackjacks nailed him simultaneously. As if the movement were long practised, each placed a hand beneath an arm of the lolling man. The points of his shoes made odd little trails in the dirty sawdust as they dragged him through a rear door. The whole thing had not consumed sixty seconds.

Dropping their burden carelessly, one tapped on still another door, called, "Okay, boss, soup's on."

A man came through the door, shouldered past them. He turned the inert figure over with his foot. "You blasted fools," he snarled, wheeling on them, eyes blazing, "you got the wrong one. That ain't Anthony, that's his pal, Gentry. Where the hell is Lupe?"

Turning, he kicked Gentry viciously in the head.

"Quit it," cried Lupe Carranza from the door. "I couldn't get Anthony, but you got something better right there in your hands!"

For answer the man once more kicked Gentry in the head. The woman literally dragged him away before he could stomp the unconscious man to death, cursing him, screaming at him.

It was Fago.

CHAPTER III

MAN LOST

DUE MOSTLY TO DOLORES, Anthony did not come out into the open with his premonitions for two days. After all, she had seen Gentry smack him, and seen the blow pass unretaliated. That was bad enough, so why make it worse by telling her he didn't resent the bust in the mouth at all—knowing the sort of woman this Lupe Carranza was. Some men lose their heads over liquor, others over dope, others, like Tom Gentry, over women.

However he did secretly conduct a bit of an investigation as to the whereabouts of Tom's white Packard. The car was well known, Gentry was a reckless driver often hailed into the speed courts. But there was no such record for the night of the quarrel or afterward. The old Apple Woman on Fourth Street told him it had been parked before the unsavory Black Cat Café for some time, and that Mr. Tom had seemed very drunken. A checkup there, casual, of course, showed the couple had departed fairly early.

On the third day, Trotter, the homicide detective, dropped in, as he often did with the grin of the cat that has just swallowed the canary. After a lot of conversation concerning this and that, he said, "What's happened to your friend, Gentry? Haven't seen him about, not for a few days, anyway."

Jim shrugged, but his pulse beat quickened. He said something about a vacation.

Trotter blew a cloud of smoke from his two-for-a-nickel cigar. He looked at the ash reflectively. "How come you've been asking about him lately? That seems funny, after you practically slugged his lady friend and then ordered him never to darken your door again. What do you care where he's at?"

What was Trotter's interest in this? Trotter was *homicide!*

"Who told you about that?" He tried to make his voice sound casual. Trotter arose, picked up his hat, flicked ashes on the rug.

"Everybody in town is laughing about it. Quite a girl, Lupe. At the drop of a hat she shows where the brooch she was wearing bit into her flesh. Says it's a badge of honor from that great gentleman, James Anthony! Well, I got to go."

Jim was thinking: "What the hell—I never touched her!" He stood up while Trotter ambled to the foyer door where he once more turned. "If you find your ex-friend, Gentry, tell him I sort of want to see him myself. It was all right for him to dump his date and go back to that lousy dump. He shouldn't have smacked the bum with the bottle, though. And what I can't figure is why he took his car way out on the Concourse to a guy's empty garage that was out of town, jimmied the door, ran his car in and wiped off all the prints? Was he screwy or something? The guy just got back this morning and found hisself owner of a white Packard convertible. Well, I'll be seeing you, Anthony." He opened the door, started out, then as an afterthought, seemingly, thrust his head in, shaking it till his purple shaven jowls quivered. Sotto voce, he added, "Of course he was just a bum, the guy Gentry smacked, but he died."

The door closed behind him.

IT WAS ALMOST too coincidental. Hardly had the slight echo died away when the phone rang. He snatched it, said, "Hello, hello!"

"Why, it's Mr. Anthony himself! How nice, you're the very man I wanted to talk to and I was afraid you'd be so terribly busy that—!"

He had never heard her on the phone, had never heard her voice at all until three nights previously.

"And I want to talk to you, lady! Where's Tom Gentry, damn you?"

"What a strange coincidence! I was calling to ask you the same question! Charming fellow, but he drinks *sooo* much. Wasn't it silly of him to hide his car that way and wipe off his own fingerprints?"

What was in her very mocking voice that caused little shivers of something strangely akin to fear to run up and down his spine? Not just plain mockery, it was sheer relentlessness.

"Let's talk a bit of sense. Where was this spot where he was supposed to have hit the bum? I could find out from the police but as long as I'm talking to you—?"

"Yes, I heard about that, too." She gave him the address, near the river front. "But he took me home, darling, and went back alone. I wasn't with him. Funny you'd ask *me* for help, after all the things you called me. Comparing me to a man named—what was it? Fagon, Rago—no, Fago!"

"I'm not asking your help, damn you!" And he turned right around and asked it again. "Who owns this joint?"

"Why not come over and ask me personally, darling? I might show you my badge of honor, the scar left by my brooch when you hit me. It's—well, let's just say on my chest." Her giggle was sultry. "And what was it you asked last? Who owned the joint. Well, my dear, I have heard it was owned by a man named Fago. Shall I expect you over?"

Jim Anthony slammed up the receiver. Why was Trotter so interested? If Tom had hit a fellow in a drunken brawl, killing him, the charge could only be manslaughter. And as the woman had said, he wouldn't have hidden his own registered car in an empty house-holder's garage. Something decidedly rotten was taking place. Trotter realized it, was merely scenting around then. He'd more than enjoy seeing Jim Anthony involved in a bit of trouble.

HIS FIRST STOP was the house in whose garage the car had been left. The lady was very voluble in explaining how they had driven all the way back from Colorado and Henry gets so peeved when he drives far, and how he'd almost torn his hair out when he found some of the cheapskate neighbors had used their garage while they were gone. And that's about all she knew except you should have heard Henry telling the police on the phone! Some day high blood-pressure would—At this point Jim Anthony departed.

He wrinkled his nose at the smell of the joint. The potbellied barman evidently recognized him, for he swabbed the dirty bar with a dirtier bar rag and said it wasn't often Mr. Anthony got down this way. Sure, he knew all about what had happened. Young Mr. Gentry had been in earlier with a young lady and had come back later alone. Four or five of the boys had laughed at his clothes and he'd been plenty

"You said you'd make trouble for me, Fago, and you've done it. Now I'm going to step on you like the slimy worm you are!"

willing to fight! The poor old bum got hisself caught in the middle. Here, he caught the gleam of the five hundred dollar bill in Jim's hand.

It wasn't there long. Matter of fact, any of the boys might have hit the poor old guy. Only thing was, Mr. Gentry ran, making it look bad, and stayed ran. The bartender understood the coppers didn't aim to charge nobody, the bum not amounting to much!

The bartender gave him the names of the other fellers, after some deliberation. Sure, they all worked for the boss, for the same feller owning this joint owned a lot of joints. His name was Fago. Naw, he never came here.

At the East Sixties address a trim mulatto maid admitted him. Her voice was the carrying kind, evidently it penetrated the boudoir at least. For when she said would Mr. Anthony wait as Señorita Carranza was dressing, the *señorita* gave a little squeal of surprise, grabbed what was handiest and emerged.

What was handiest was a negligee. "Why, Mr. Anthony!" she said in that throaty voice of hers, running toward him. She extended both hands in greeting and the negligee fell open. There was a flash of tawny flesh, the flicker of trim, slim legs before she caught it together, laughing heartily. However, she didn't catch it quite high enough. She saw his eyes on the queer shaped mark above her breast.

"When you hit me," she beamed, "I was wearing a diamond brooch. Didn't it leave a funny scar? Sort of like a spider, isn't it?"

He felt like really hitting her. "Listen," he snarled, "I don't get this at all. I have no idea what the racket is. You know I never hit you, yet you bear down on it. The bartender down at that joint of Fago's says any one of four or five fellows could have killed that bum. Tom wouldn't have pulled the car stunt even if he was high as a kite. Where does that lousy Fago come in on it? Why have you—?"

"HERE'S WHERE HE comes in," said an obsequious voice, and Fago himself came out of the same boudoir. True, he was a bit better dressed than he had been when Anthony had last seen him, and he was without his derby. But the bulges of bone and fat still almost hid his eyes; the teeth were the same yellow jags in the black slot that served as his mouth.

Every muscle in Anthony's body electrified, then cringed away. "So here's the two of you together, the two of you so alike underneath your outer shells. You said you'd make trouble for me, Fago, and you've chosen this way to do it! But do you remember what I said I'd do the next time I saw you? I said I'd step on you like the slimy creeping thing you are."

His hand flew out, hurled the woman half across the room. Fago seemed to cower back defenselessly, whining, "Now, now, Mr. Anthony, when all I meant to do was offer my honest condolences. I know how much you thought of him and he of you, though Lupe says he was terribly vindictive concerning the ugly scar you left on her pretty flesh. Now, now, don't hit me. Haven't you seen the late evening papers?" He thrust a newspaper toward Anthony.

"Police late this afternoon advanced a theory that young Thomas Howard Gentry, best known as the companion of James Anthony, local millionaire detective, committed suicide in remorse concerning the death of one James Smith. Smith, hit by Gentry with a bottle in a barroom brawl, died in a local hospital. Parts of Gentry's clothing were found on an abandoned East River pier by three schoolboys. A suicide note was beneath the clothing, the handwriting authentically identified as that of Gentry. It stated that he could no longer face his own conscience. The body has not as yet been found."

CHAPTER IV

BADGE OF THE SPIDER

TOTALLY BEWILDERED JIM ANTHONY drove to headquarters and viewed the note. The newspaper was right, the hand-writing was undoubtedly Tom Gentry's. Jim had too many samples in his own possession to doubt that. The clothing was likewise his friend's.

Back at the penthouse Dolores tried to console him. "Tom was sensitive darling, you know that. He drank heavily, too. That no doubt explains the whole thing?"

He shook his head stubbornly. "That doesn't explain the car in the garage with the fingerprints wiped off. Nope, it was put there by someone else who didn't want his fingerprints found. It doesn't explain why the brawl occurred at a joint owned by Fago, when Fago is on intimate terms with the Carranza woman, and Tom was crazy about her. It doesn't explain the scar on her breast supposedly made by my fist blow on a brooch she wasn't even wearing. I merely slapped her wrist aside."

"And how would you explain his clothing and the suicide note in his own handwriting?"

"I've been drinking of that, Dolores. Fago is the type of man that hates with all his heart and soul. I told you once that he was the only man I ever saw that inspired fear in me, and I meant it. Sort of a fear of contamination. Now suppose Fago has Tom somewhere and forced him to write that note?"

She shook her blonde head. "We both know Tom too well for that. The little quarrel of the other evening would have blown over. He'd have cut his hand off before worrying you with something like that!"

They were still discussing the pros and cons of the situation when the phone rang. For a moment both stared at it fearfully, each thinking the same heartrending thing—the police had discovered Tom's body! Dolores put her hand on Jim's shoulder, arose and went to the jangling instrument.

"Yes? Who—?" Her eyes grew wide with disbelief, she held the black machine against her breast, breathing deeply, then extended it toward Jim. "It's—it's—!" He snatched it from her hand.

"Hello, who is—great God! Where are you?"

"Never mind," came the hoarse and haunted answer, "the line may be tapped. The police will never get me, I tell you! The suicide hoax will hold them for a while, but Jim, I need money, I need—!"

"You fool! Come up here at once, there'll be no charge! Are you out of your mind?"

"I killed him, they want me! I know. Get me ten thousand dollars now, Jim. Bring Dolores with you, let her be holding it. You'll see me in the shadows of the hedge at Parkett and McQuillan on the right hand side of the street. *Right away, Jim!*"

The phone went dead in Jim Anthony's hand.

"He's crazy," choked Dolores. "He's absolutely demented, the poor guy! All we can do is get the money and take it to him, then persuade him to come in! Why are you looking so strangely?"

"Was that Tom?" He was asking it of himself. "There was a sort of hoarse choked up effect, though I'll admit it sounded like him. But when you think how rational he's always been, would he pull a harebrained stunt like this mad merry go round?"

He seized her arm. "Come on, the cash is in the safe. If it's a frameup of some kind, we'll darned sure find out."

TRAFFIC WAS HEAVY, the distance was long. Once she asked how it could possibly be a frameup. "If someone held a gun on him, forced him to talk," he answered. That was what they were both hoping for, for the fear of unreasoning insanity was in their souls. At last they neared the corner of Parkett and McQuillan. A long box hedge sheltered the semi-estate lurking back on a little hill. The streetlight was out, the shadows thick.

But each saw the shambling, stooped man who ran toward the car. "Give it to me," he half snarled. "I knew you'd try to make me give up but I'm not going to do it, never, never! So I got a gun, Jim! I'll use it. Shut up, give me the money!"

His fingers snatched it from her lap, he thrust his head into the car. His right hand flashed. Dolores screamed a bit, flinched, jerking away. "That'll even up for what you did to Lupe," he snarled, leveling the gun. "Start driving!"

Jim put the big car in gear, drove perhaps twenty feet, conscious that Tom still covered him. There was a blinding flash of light, a shot combined with a roar of rage. Tom crashed through the hedge and the sound of his running feet soon disappeared.

She was like two different women—one cruel and hard, one frail and feminine....

"What is it? What is it?" screamed the excited newcomer. "Our paper got a tip that something was going to happen. It—hey, Tony, get a picture of this, quick. It's Jim Anthony and the Colquitt gal and this Gentry just put the same mark on her that Anthony put on the Carranza girl!"

THE FLASH WAS booming before the words were finished. The triumphant newsmen ran toward their own car parked half a block down the street. Too sick for words, utterly too sick for thought, Jim and Dolores sat silently in the deep darkness. There was no doubt in their minds, the man had been Tom. And only an utterly demented Tom could have pulled such a thing.

What could have crazed him? Perhaps the realization of what his quarrel with his life long friend would mean to him? Perhaps some drug given to him by that vicious woman? Had Fago, through the woman, and hence through Tom achieved his purpose of promised revenge? How else explain the newspaperman?

Dolores said, "Let me have your handkerchief, dear, it's bleeding."

She blotted the blood from the spot above her breast. The angry red scar was, in truth, exactly like that on Lupe Carranza.

Jim said softly, "This is only the beginning, Dolores. Only God knows what will happen next. He could have had an instrument made, were he crazy enough, to make such a scar. But I doubt it."

What did happen next were the shrieking tabloids the next day. Lupe Carranza obligingly allowed her photograph taken, to reveal the scar. The picture taken on the spot revealed a fresh wound on Dolores, revealed Tom Gentry, gun in hand, glaring into the camera! The caption was: "The Anthony Badge of Infamy?"

Below was the letter reproduced as written. It accused Jim Anthony of practically every crime and vice known to man while posing under the banner of criminologist! It went on to say that if Jim Anthony represented the acme of American detectives, Tom Gentry wanted only to be on the other side from now on! In other words he was casting the gauntlet. Let lawmen be on the alert for the badge of the spider! And it was in Tom's handwriting, signed with his name!

CHAPTER V

NEW CRIMES FOR OLD

IT WAS THE HARDEST problem that Jim Anthony had ever faced as criminologist, or psychologist. He had made a study of the various types of dementia, was accepted as an authority. Never had he come upon such a complete reversal of character, all apparently over nothing. The accidental pushing of a woman who was attacking him. It didn't add up, it made no sense whatsoever that he should deliberately go to the bad for such a small reason.

He placed his pieces about, mentally, as though they were on a chess board. The woman? She would and could be in it—for personal gain alone. Not merely money, though in such a woman the money avarice was dominant. Personally gaining something wanted by her, perhaps another woman's man. Or gaining sheer satisfaction out of ruining something or someone whom she knew was a much better person than she.

Fago was hard to place. Money assuredly. A place in the sun because he recognized his own sliminess. A sort of inferiority complex that made him want to ruin people to show them he had the power.

There was this about it—even if deranged, Tom was mad for the woman; she was in it. And Jim had seen Fago emerging from the woman's boudoir with his own two eyes. Hence the two were in it. But where was the big money to come from? The childish drivel given the newspapers about the spider mark being the "gang" mark was easy to see through. It was simply to roil up an already muddied situation in the public's eye.

There was one factor of danger, however, which he had failed to take into consideration. In laying his plans to recapture Tom before Fago and Lupe Carranza involved him in some desperately big scheme, he almost forgot Trotter, and Trotter's resentment of Anthony's success.

Now Trotter sat in the same chair he had previously occupied without bothering to remove his hat and laid his cards on the table.

"You and I, Anthony, have never liked each other, because we've disagreed over ways and means of attaining an end. We've worked together, however, and some people might say I owe you a lot. All right, I owe you a lot. But I'm still a detective of the old hard-boiled school. He's dangerous as all hell because he's a good man deliberately turned bad. They're the worst kind. I want him."

"What for?"

"For the things he may do in such a state of mind. I want him in my backroom for a few hours. Maybe he'll admit he shot McKinley, something, anything that we can lock him up for. I want him."

"You'd do it, too. I've seen you do it before. If it's Tom, then he's crazy—"

"And he still gets locked up. What do you mean—if it's Tom?"

"Some sort of double? Some clever imitative handwriting?"

"Nuts. That sort of thing works in stories. And farther, if you beat me to him, and try to hide or shield him, I'll ride you the same as if you was him. He's dangerous and I want him!"

"But he hasn't done anything yet!"

"He took ten grand of your money and he attacked Miss Colquitt. And what about the bum who was killed? That'll be enough to start on."

"He can have the money. I wouldn't file."

"You leave the filing to me," snorted Trotter, and swaggered out, cheap cigar cocked at an imposing angle.

FAGO DIDN'T COME to see him. With hint of triumph in his oily, whining voice, he suggested that he was very busy, and maybe Mr. Anthony better come to see him. His office proved to be a little shack

**"This'll pay you back for what you did to my girl!" he snarled—
and he smashed the spider-ring into her breast.**

of corrugated iron in the corner of a huge junkyard. Jim wasn't much
surprised to see Lupe Carranza seated on the corner of his desk in a
silk leg revealing manner, insolently smoking a cigarette.

"Your secretary?"

"Just filling in temporarily," she answered. "Sorry we haven't a chair.
There's the other corner of the desk."

"I can say it standing up. How much, Fago before you get him in
some real trouble?"

"How much? Him? Real trouble?"

"Don't stall. I managed to convey to you once just what sort of slimy,
scummy, creeping little piece of filth you were. I was lucky enough to
tell Miss Carranza the same thing. You're combining business with

pleasure in this thing. How much—before somehow or someway he really gets in bad?"

"If you mean your friend Gentry, I don't know nothing about him, Mr. Anthony. My honest opinion is that he's dead or something and some crooked gang has got a clever double to—!"

"That's drivel for childish minds. How much? A million dollars?"

Lupe Carranza whistled through red, red lips. "You do well by your friends, don't you, Anthony? And him smacking you around? A million is a nice thing."

Fago said, "I only wish to golly I had that boy. Me, a millionaire! I expect he'll end up doing something pretty bad, like getting involved in a murder."

Jim sickened. Here was Fago's triumph. Here was the height of the fat man's slimy career and he meant to enjoy every minute of it. He had the great Jim Anthony squirming under his thumb!

"Damn you, damn the both of you!" choked Jim.

"Tch-tch," clucked Fago, "imagine a feller like that Trotter getting him if he committed something sort of serious. And I can see one of Trotter's men trying to read a newspaper over across the street right now. Why do you suppose he followed you here?"

Anthony wanted to leap across the desk and swallow the man. But he had to take it. If Fago knew where Tom Gentry was, a dead Fago couldn't talk. And what he said about Trotter was all too true, as proven by Trotter's own warning.

Lupe Carranza slid down off the desk, revealing a few inches of each tawny thigh. She wriggled down into her skirt, adjusted the few folds over her breast. "Well," she said, "Fago, we'll have to run along. Tell you what, Mr. Anthony, we'll sort of inquire around town if anybody has seen Tom. He's sweet; I'd sort of like to see him myself, and a million is nice, too. Suppose you drop around tomorrow." She patted his cheek as she passed and laughed to see him shrink back as though she possessed a foul disease. The laughter wasn't nice.

Getting in his own car Jim noticed bitterly the taxi parked idly some half block down on the other side, saw Trotter's man reading the newspaper against a telephone pole. He called, "If you're tailing me you might as well ride with me, come on."

A little shamefaced the fellow got in. "What you doing with Fago?" he asked bluntly.

"Dealing in filth and foulness!"

The dick looked suspicious. "Hell, he sells junk and stuff."

"Right."

That night, timed to perfection, the Rialto's boldest robbery occurred. The Shelby Theatre had the season's hugest hit. As the crowd mulled out of the show at intermission it was done. Two sleek looking thugs with automatics did the actual work. A man with a tommy gun covered for them, grinning evilly. There was a little shooting outside, in which the tommy blazed merrily. A mounted policeman was shot off his horse, the slug catching him in the shoulder.

One of those golden spider ornaments that girls often wear on their collars was found in the office of the theater.

CHAPTER VI

FAGO DRAWS THE NOOSE

MORNING PAPERS WERE ON the street in phenomenal time proclaiming the first big robbery of the "Spider Mob" as led by Tom Gentry. The account of the quarrel between Gentry and the millionaire criminologist Jim Anthony was reviewed. Gentry's letter to the press was quoted verbatim, an account of his first ten thousand dollar robbery and the spider episode was given, with a proud picture of Señorita Lupe Carranza, very much cheesecake, shown. Anthony had managed with a bit of money to suppress his fiancée's picture.

The tabloids were inclined to romanticize Gentry as a man who saw the dirty side of detective work for so long that it turned his stomach. The more conservative sheets said sternly that this young menace must be put down before he became a killer.

It was all sickening to Jim Anthony, and incredible, too; although he was beginning to get an inkling of what had somehow occurred. But what if he did know positively how the thing had happened—it had happened—and what was Anthony to do about it?

What could he do with Gentry if he did get him, did succeed in keeping him out of Trotter's beefy hands? And—and this was the horrible thought—what if Fago did *not* have him under control some way. Perhaps he was seeing a way of making Anthony squirm, just as dozens of quack ransom notes are usually received by the friends and parents of one who has been kidnaped.

If that was so, and Fago was capable of it, damn him, then the thing was all on the legit! A cog had slipped in Tom's mind and he was really embarking on a career of crime, he really meant all that he said in that damned letter to the press.

AROUND THREE THE phone rang. He glared at it. Phone calls were apt to be unpleasant right now. At last he answered.

"Good morning, darling," mocked a husky voice. "You answered so quickly I suppose you're still up pacing the floor over the latest antics of your little ex-boy friend? Cute little trick, isn't he. Damn' near got that policeman plumb center. He needs a little more practise with that Tommy gun of his."

When she ran out of breath, he grated, "Damn you, why did you call here, just to gloat over me? I'm to meet you in a few hours anyway."

She laughed again. "Don't lose your temper. I sort of sympathize with you. I could picture you walking endlessly over the Oriental rugs in your priceless robe, just worrying! Cost doesn't mean anything to you, does it, darling?"

"If that's all—?"

"No. Why don't you come over and see me?"

He stiffened. What was this. "Is Fago there?"

"Of course not, foolish."

Did she mean she'd deal—?

"There's no way for me to get there without being tailed. Suppose you come over here. They won't be watching for you."

"That's an idea. Watch for me, wait for me and sigh for me until I arrive. Try to look nice for mamma, won't you?"

He was still pacing the floor when she arrived some forty minutes later. She was tailored for the delectation of mankind, her makeup was the acme of something or other, she was feminine perfection. But when she swayed toward him, he backed off, said, "Well, what the hell do you want? You must have had something in mind."

She shrugged, walked to a deeply upholstered divan and sank down, crossed trim shapely legs revealingly. "First, a drink. And hadn't you better play decent until you see what mamma has to offer?"

"Damn the woman," he thought and the thought was so vehement he expressed it. He mixed drinks to the accompaniment of her laughter. He sat down beside her unwillingly and winced when she laid long, shapely fingers on his knee.

"Like to talk about Tom?"

"Certainly. What did you think? God, how filthy you people are to let him do a job like that! Is he all right?"

"The last time I saw him he was making a perfect getaway. As for being filthy people!" Her eyes glowed. "And letting him do the job. Perhaps it raises the price. After all, he shot a man."

He nodded grimly. "I'd expected that."

HER LAUGHTER WAS mockery. "This is pretty hard on you, isn't it? Jim Anthony, the great law man, conniving against the law. All your adult life you've fought the criminal, followed him like a bloodhound with all your scientific piffle and puffle. What good does it do you now? Is it going to show you how to get away from Trotter? After all, in helping Gentry escape, you're a criminal, too."

He groaned. "Great God, don't you think I know it? This is the end of Jim Anthony, if I'm successful." He repeated the last phrase bitterly.

"I think you'll be successful. You know it's been fun being with Tom. He's really sweet, really nice." A pause. "But a million dollars is nicer."

He glared at her. "I could kill you for what you've done to him, whatever it is!"

She shrugged. "I thought we were talking about a million dollars."

"Where's Fago?"

"Out of town." Her eyes were meaning.

"You'd sell out on your own, double cross Fago?"

"What does that greaseball mean to me! I can get all the men I want, but this is the first chance I've ever had to get a round million dollars. Do we deal?"

"How do I know you've really got him. Is he in town?"

She shook her head. "Nope. I can give you the exact address where he is, however."

"For a million in advance," he sneered.

"Take it or leave it, in advance."

"I'll leave it," he snapped. "If you'd double cross Fago, you'd damned well double cross me. There's the door." He arose.

"Fago is going to put the torture to you. My way is the easiest, little boy blue."

"I can take a little torture with a little certainty at the end. From a woman like you I know exactly what I'd get—the double cross."

He opened the door of his closet—and there was a dead girl hanging on a wire hook.

Now she arose but she did not move toward the door. Instead he turned to find her so close to him that her breast almost touched his chest.

"No hard feelings? And how about another drink?" Her meaning was all too evident in her eyes.

ANTHONY WAS NO better and no worse than other men, he was no plaster saint. Blood that flowed in his veins could race hotly, emotions common to others were his as well. There was a heady scent about her, filling his nostrils, not a mere perfume, but an unnamable, mysterious something that belongs to all beautiful women. Her eyes, lids half lowered, were at once a challenge and an expectancy, deep brown, almost black, flecked with dancing little lights. Her lips were full, deep red, moist and parted.

He understood how a woman like this, utterly unmoral, could hold a man, could even hold a man like Tom Gentry. She swayed closer, an arm went about his neck, her fingers were like fire. Slowly he pressed her to him.

The phone rang.

It was like a dash of ice water. He shoved the woman away from him almost viciously, turned for the instrument.

It was Dolores. For the space of a few moments they talked, and at ending Jim Anthony said a strange thing. He said, "Darling, you'll never know how thankful I am you called. Good bye."

To Lupe Carranza, he said, "No use, my dear. No drink, no nice million, absolutely nothing. Should we say goodbye?"

When he closed the door behind her, he leaned against it and wiped perspiration from his forehead. He knew that had he kissed her, before she left the penthouse she would have had the money she wanted so much more than anything else in the world.

TROTTER HAD NEVER risen as high as he had through sheer stubbornness. Trotter was a shrewd policeman in spite of his bulldozing tactics. He had a fine knowledge of human nature, and put it to constant use. He knew that the shortest distance between two points was a straight line. He knew Jim Anthony.

Consequently, while a few thousand other policemen scoured the city for Tom Gentry, the next morning, Trotter planted himself in the lobby of the Waldorf-Anthony Hotel and waited for Anthony to make an appearance. He knew that if he stuck with Anthony long enough, the trail would eventually lead to Tom Gentry.

He did not notice the fat little man in the badly fitting clothing who read a paper in a deep chair across from the bank of elevators. Shortly before nine an elevator door slid back soundlessly and Jim Anthony, gaunt eyed from lack of sleep emerged among others. Trotter stiffened. The fat little man in the badly fitting clothing pushed through the emerging crowd, said in a whining voice to the operator, "Can I go to the penthouses on this car?" And when assured that he could, entered the car.

Anthony walked to the cigar counter for cigarettes, lit one, stood staring toward the street reflectively. Trotter prepared to follow. Anthony took half a dozen steps in the direction of the door, brought up sharply, snapped his fingers and whirled about. Apparently he did not see Trotter. Slapping at his pockets he hurried back toward the elevators.

Forgot something, said Trotter to himself, and sank back down into his chair.

FAGO WAS WAITING for Anthony before the door of the penthouse. "Good morning, Anthony," he smirked. "Clever, was it not?"

"Very clever," snapped Anthony. "But what's good about the morning?" He keyed open the door, stepping aside. Fago bowed, preceded him into the foyer. Jim lead the way into the living room, turned, said, "Well, let's get down to facts."

But Fago was moving admiringly about the room. "I have never been able to afford such elegance, Anthony," he said obsequiously, "may I not look around? And don't you sometimes offer your visitors a drink?"

Jim winced. What could he do? The man was holding aces back to back. He moved to the liquor cabinet, fixed a solitary drink and brought it back to the fat man. Because he had been so preoccupied, Anthony had sent the maids away when they came to clean that morning. Now Fago stood beside an ashtray, staring down at it with an odd smile on his face. He reached for a cigarette butt. It was slender, it was stained with a peculiarly colored lipstick.

"So," he said slowly, "she was here. Was it for pleasure, or was she going to sell me out?"

Anthony shrugged. "It damned sure wasn't for pleasure," he said. "The type doesn't interest me. I like to keep clean. To hell with all that! Since last night I suppose the price has gone up?"

"Not at all, Anthony!" Fago acted surprised. "You mentioned a price at my office that is altogether satisfactory. You have it, I suppose, in cash?"

"Certainly. But don't think you're playing a sap. That money isn't changing hands at all until I know for certain Tom is alive, that you have him. It would be like you to take my money then turn the poor deluded devil over to the police, simply to hurt me."

Fago seemed to consider it. "Yes, he agreed, "that would be rather like me, wouldn't it? Deluded devil, you called him? What makes you so certain Gentry is so deluded. Couldn't this all be his own plan. Isn't it probable that at last he saw through you for the sanctimonious hypocritical—!"

"That's enough. You can make me squirm, Fago; you have me where the hair is short. But tell me this. What's to prevent my throttling the life out of that ugly mass of flesh you call your body, doing it right here and now? What's to prevent my paying the damned woman after I've killed you?"

Fago didn't move away! His gash of a mouth twisted half humorously, like that of a gargoyle.

"Anthony, Anthony," he chided gently. "Do not underrate poor Fago! The woman doesn't know where Gentry is. She thinks she knows, true enough, but be very assured I did not take him to that particular place, knowing Lupe Carranza!"

SLOWLY JIM'S ARMS fell to his sides. He turned away, his shoulders sagging, mixed himself a drink, and drank it in silence before speaking once more.

"All right. You win again. But you're going to have to show me you have him."

Fago reached into his pocket, withdrew two white cards, which he extended. "Fingerprints?"

Anthony was rated among the best print men in the world. Prints were to him, like photographs. A solitary glimpse at the two cards proved them to be Tom Gentry's prints. But he shook his head stubbornly.

"You could have gotten them any place. I could test them in my lab, of course, for salt and perspiration. But you should be able to do better than that."

Fago nodded, again revealed the yellow-black stumps of his teeth in what passed for his smile. "I should have been very disappointed, Anthony, had you accepted them. As a matter of fact, they are mere copies. You have a violet ray?"

"Certainly." What was coming now? There was a hard shrewdness about this man that made him even more awe-inspiring, fearsome!

"Another card. Here on this little card, very carefully mounted, you will see three hairs from the head of Tom Gentry. Does it ring a bell?"

For answer Jim snatched the card from the man. Three blonde hairs were mounted on the card, as Fago had said. Without a word Jim left the room, entered the quarters occupied by his friend. His military brushes were neatly arranged with other toilet articles on a chifforobe. By working carefully, he managed to find two hairs long enough for his purposes.

HURRYING INTO THE room equipped as one of the finest criminology laboratories to be found in America, he soon mounted the two hairs on the same card with those brought by Fago. With trembling fingers he set the card in place.

At least he'd soon know something! He'd know whether he was being cruelly hoaxed or whether Fago really was in contact with Tom Gentry. He switched on the ultra violet rays.

Slowly the hairs flouresced, lost their blondeness, assumed a new and glistening tint. And the glow from each slender hair was exactly the same shade. With a sigh—of relief or fear—he turned off the lamp.

Fago said, "Well?"

"Take me to him, the million is yours."

"Not so fast, my friend, not so fast! It is not as simple as all that. I am a man of business ethics." Jim grinned derisively. "I am not at all able to guarantee that Tom Gentry will go with you willingly even when I place you in contact with him."

"Let me worry about that," said Jim, grimly.

"What do you intend doing with him? Get him out of the country?" He saw by Anthony's expression he was right and grinned in delight. "And of course Jim Anthony then will be a criminal. Too bad, isn't it, the way things happen?"

"Damn you," raged Anthony, "what happens afterward is my business! And if you meddle in it—afterward, understand—I'll follow you to hell to get you!"

"Now, now. Very well, I will give you a few instructions. I want in cash, before I leave this magnificent apartment, one hundred thousand dollars."

WITHOUT A WORD Anthony went into the other room. He returned in a moment with two packages of bills which he handed to Fago. Fago bowed, thrust them into an inner pocket.

"Three days from now I expect another hundred thousand—not here, but at an address I shall give you in St. Louis, Missouri."

"For the love of God, why? Why all the fol-de-rol?"

"Perhaps because I am a strange man. I warn you now that the payments shall all be in like amount, that each will be made in a different city and under different circumstances. Once the entire amount is paid—your friend is yours, to do with as you please."

Jim Anthony realized now what Lupe Carranza had meant when she advised him to deal with her, when she said that Fago would torture him.

Weeks, months of worry, having to trust this odious creature. Wondering every minute of the day if Tom Gentry was engaged in another crime, wondering if he were already in the hands of the police!

"And all the time you'll lead him deeper and deeper into crime, you and that damnable woman of yours! Hell, by the time you turn him over to me, he'll be public enemy number one. No, no, I can't do it. You smirking worm, it's more than anyone could do. Let's pay off, let's get it over at once!"

Fago arose, slowly. Very meticulously he adjusted his trousers, though it is doubtful if they had ever possessed a crease since leaving the factory. He took the two packets of bills from his pocket, laid them on a table.

"So sorry, Anthony," he said softly, and waddled toward the door. "After all he is your friend. And by the time the police get him, believe me, he will be wanted for murder and even worse. Of course you know the police will get him in the end. When I am through with him. Your friend!"

Friend? My God, more than friend! They'd grown up together, they'd been all over the world together, there were a million and one intimate experiences shared that made them closer than brothers, a thousand adventures, hardships, battles where they had fought back to back against hard odds, successes that were so much the sweeter because they were won together.

Friend? More! A thousand times more. And when this slimy creature got through with him, he'd be a murderer, the perpetrator of dozens of odious crimes, sought for across the face of the earth. It was bad enough now, but—ah, God, what else was there to do?

"Wait, Fago," he called.

The fat man turned.

"If I agree to any and everything you say, will you promise me that nothing else happens to him, that he doesn't get in any deeper?"

Fago seemed to ponder the question, tugging at his lower lip with grimy fingers.

"Anthony," he said judiciously, "Gentry is not crazy. You act as though he were a demented child, that he is simply led into these things. Believe me, that is not the case. He is a very vicious man. I can only promise you that I will do all in my power to restrain him during this—ah—period."

He shrugged, as if the thing were finished.

"You win," said Jim. "Pick up your money and give me the St. Louis address. I'll be there three days from now with another hundred thousand."

Fago waddled back toward the money on the table, triumph written across his ugly features.

CHAPTER VII

THE MYSTERY OF A WOMAN'S MIND

THOSE INTERVENING HOURS WERE hours of mental and physical torture. Physical, because there was nothing at which to strike back. Mental, because he could not determine the thing to do once he did get Tom Gentry into his hands.

Anthony was a fighter, a man of action. A thousand times he considered bringing his detective ability into play. He was positive he could, if given the opportunity, find Gentry himself, even though the police had been unable to do so. He knew he was being watched, not only by Trotter or Trotter's men, but by someone hired by Fago, for he didn't make the mistake of underrating the fat man. If it were only himself he'd fight back, matching his brains and physical powers against Fago's. But there was Tom to think of. Fago had only to drop a hint and Gentry would be picked up, wherever he was, by the police, which was the last thing in the world Jim wanted. He was like a tiger in a net. One false move and Fago blew the whistle.

All right, he asked himself, suppose I let Fago have his fun, suppose I take his torture over the required period and at the end get Tom. There was Fago's hint that perhaps Tom wouldn't be so willing to do what Jim wanted, that Tom had turned into a vicious man. If that was true, it could only mean that Tom had slipped a cog mentally. Jim thought of a thousand things, a thousand means, and discarded them one by one. Grimly he told himself that he'd hit his friend in the head, that he'd dope him, that he'd do anything at all to get him away to a refuge. Once in that refuge he'd use what medical ability he possessed to restore him to some semblance of normalcy. After that—what?

After that, if it had been Tom Gentry who shot the policeman during the Rialto holdup, he'd simply have to face the music. That is what Tom himself would want to do. The thing was to keep paying, keep playing Fago's game, in order to keep Tom from getting in any deeper.

Ah, that Fago, he was a sly one! He knew that mental torture was a million times worse than physical! He wasn't just torturing Jim Anthony, he was torturing, in his own estimation, all that Anthony represented, all that Fago never could be! And the fullness of his plan was not apparent until Jim Anthony was almost ready to leave for the rendezvous in St. Louis.

Trotter came up to the penthouse, took his usual seat.

"What do you suppose has happened to your pal?" he asked, casually enough. Cat and mouse stuff, thought Jim bitterly.

"If I knew," he answered shortly, "I'd go to him."

"I hear that's what you're fixing to do." It was like a bombshell!

"You hear—?"

"Um-hunh. A little birdie told me that you were fixing to take off in a very few hours to meet Gentry and get him out of the country. Said you were already packed and fixed to go. Mind if I look?"

"To hell with you," snarled Jim. "If you want to look around here for something or other, get yourself a warrant. If I've broken any law, arrest me. But don't come around here with your damned insinuations. I throw a little weight around this town, Trotter. As a matter of fact, I don't like your company at all. It would tickle me for you to leave now and not to bother coming back."

Trotter arose, sighing. "Well, it's your place, you can have in whoever you want." At the door he paused. "Aiding and abetting is pretty serious, Anthony." He opened the door. "This seemed like such a good tip, too! Tell you what, if you want to lay a bet, I'll give you six, two, and even you don't get out of the hotel without one of my men spotting you."

"I ought to take it. But I'm particular who I bet with. Beat it, you big tramp."

HE SANK DOWN
into a chair. Fago
again! Making
things all the tougher,
laughing like hell all
the time. Fago knew
Anthony's intel-
ligence, he wasn't
afraid of not getting
his hundred thou-
sand in St. Louis!
Not at all! But he not
only wanted to bleed
the money from
Anthony, he wanted
to make Anthony
fight to pay it. Jim
knew he'd have the
same thing to combat
all the way through.
He'd constantly be
evading the law itself
in order to pay black-
mail!

Fago could not be reached like an ordinary
criminal. For his motive was not greed for money,
but deadly hatred for one man—Jim Anthony.

Jim wasn't bragging when he said he threw a little weight in New York City. He threw plenty. In ten minutes he knew the exact locations of every policeman in the building. He canceled his plane reservation and made arrangements for a flight with a private pilot who was a very good friend of his.

Around eleven o'clock, timed to the second, it happened. A milk wagon was slowly passing the front entrance of the hotel, the driver seemingly half asleep at the wheel. A drunken driver careened down the Avenue, the policeman stopped him, leaned into the car to administer a bawling out. The drunk hit him with a blackjack, got out of the car to carry the fight farther.

A newspaper delivery truck rammed the side of the drunk's sedan, A cab shot out of nowhere and added to the tangle. The drunk had somehow obtained the policeman's gun, was waving it wildly. The cop was blowing his whistle frantically, a thousand auto horns were adding to the din. The milk wagon had just escaped the mêlée. The lobby sitters, including the detectives assigned by Trotter, were as interested as the milkman. One of the detectives departed to help subdue the drunk. The second did not even notice the man in white trousers and white jacket who miraculously shot out of the elevator at that moment.

No one seemed to notice him get into the milk wagon, to notice the milk wagon drive slowly away. But sometime later the same milk wagon drove up to a private landing field where a plane waited, its engine warmed and ready.

A man dressed in white got out of the milk wagon and ran toward the plane.

THE DELMAR ADDRESS in St. Louis proved to be a small, run-down hotel, with the desk at the head of the stairs. The clerk behind the desk, sucked at his toothpick and guessed he had a room. He made no move to take Jim's luggage, purchased at a stopover, preceded him down the squalid hall and opened the door to Room 25.

A cracked window shade obscured the only window. The clerk raised it, hesitated a moment, and brushed along the sill with his fingers. "Have to be careful of spiders," he said, snickering. Jim cast a sharp glance in his direction, but said nothing. He gave him a tip, the man departed, looking at him strangely.

Now what? Would he be contacted as Fago had claimed he would be? How, and by whom? Would there be more trouble with the police?

He crossed the room to the dresser—started back in surprise. A small gold spider-pin, from the five-and-ten cent store lay in the exact center of the shabby old cover. He looked at it grimly, opened each drawer and looked within. Only the top left-hand drawer held anything at all. And that was only a sheet of brown wrapping paper and some heavy cord. The door opened and the clerk reappeared. Jim wheeled. "Listen you punk, when you come in here, knock!"

"It's okay," sneered the man, "you'll like this. Your blonde girl friend sent a message to you. She'll be waiting across the street in the bar in twenty minutes anti she said be sure and bring the package."

"Blonde girl friend? Package. Oh, yes. My friend, why did you put this spider on my dresser? And why the remark about spiders at the window?"

"Nuts," said the clerk, and Jim watched him go helplessly.

A few minutes later he wrapped two packets of bills in the brown paper, tied it with the heavy cord and tossed it on the bed. He stretched out beside it, hands beneath his head, and tried to relax, only to find it utterly impossible. The bed creaked when he moved and he almost leaped off it.

Grimly he wondered how he'd be when the thing was over if already he was as jittery as this. Well, he could take it. But when the thing *was* over—he almost groaned aloud. When the thing was finished, there wasn't a thing in the world he could do about it! Fago would have a stronger hold on him than ever.

The clerk was still sucking at his toothpick when Jim passed.

IT WASN'T EXACTLY a bar, it was more of a bierstube, a large place with many tables and a place cleared in the sawdust floor for dancing. However, there was a bar, and that is where Jim found her.

She was blonde, all right, but the eyes were nearly black, and in spite of the tricks of makeup, Jim knew her at once. Gutturally, with the Teutonic accent so prevalent in some parts of St. Louis, she greeted him, bawled him out for being late and asked if he'd brought her package. She tossed it carelessly to the bartender, slid off the stool and raised her arms. It was Lupe Carranza.

"Now what the hell," he said in her ear, "is the meaning of all this? I don't want to dance. You've got the payoff; let's sit down and talk. How is he? Has he done anything else?"

"He's all right, and so far he hasn't gotten in any deeper." She seemed to wince away from his hand on her back, so noticeably that he moved it a bit higher up. There was something stiff and unyielding now beneath his palm. She smiled up at him a little bitterly. "The result of your telling Fago I tried to sell him out. They may heal up in a few weeks."

They danced silently for a few steps.

"Next stop, Kansas City," she whispered, and gave him an address. "Just one week from today. And listen to me, Jim Anthony! *Watch your step!* That devil will do everything he can to make trouble for you, trouble you're supposed to overcome. Because if you ever miss a payment, he'll see the police back East get Tom. And you can't have that!"

"Why should you warn me? Because of your back?"

"I wonder myself," she answered. "Maybe sometime you'll understand it. If Fago had any idea I told you what lay in store for you, I don't know what he'd do to me. He—!"

A heavy hand whirled Jim about. A red faced bouncer stood there. "Pal," he leered, "this is a respectable joint. You can't dance like that on this floor. And you, you little tramp, suppose you get your package and leave?"

She hurried toward the bar. The bouncer said, "You want to make something of it, mister?"

Jim held up his hands in protest. "Not a thing, chum, not a thing. I was getting a little tired of the lady myself. Didn't think much of her line of talk. Be seeing you."

On the sidewalk, he laughed to himself. That was one he hadn't fallen for. Suppose he'd taken the bouncer at his word. The result would have been a jail sentence, maybe of more than a week.

But where did Lupe fit in now? Why did she warn him of what was to come? The psychology of a hater of society like Fago, he could understand. The things that ran through the woman's mind, baffled him.

CHAPTER VIII

THE HUNDRED-GRAND BOX

IN LESS THAN THE eight weeks eventually consumed by the payments, Jim Anthony dropped from one-hundred and ninety-five pounds to slightly over one hundred and sixty. He would look at himself in the mirror and laugh, knowing that those few bulges left were not muscle, merely nerve. He drank little liquor, but immense quantities of coffee to keep himself awake; he took caffeine tablets.

He was the hunted as well as the hunter, and he found it the grimmest game in which he had ever engaged. Always he had to fight to pay, to match his wits and brawn against the cunning of the fat man, Fago. And Fago used the law, for the traps he laid for Jim were always such that trouble with the law would follow. It was cat and mouse with a vengeance.

There was Chicago, the fourth stop in the strange game. Jim was coming down the elevated stairs at a Loop stop, vigilant, alert as a hunted animal. He thought. Suddenly a man behind him yelped, "My billfold, my pocketbook, it's gone!"

The crowd seemed to tighten up, to mix and to mill. The man kept shouting shrilly. Almost automatically Jim knew what was happening, so constantly aware were his nerves. No sooner had his fingers brushed the unfamiliar bulge in his coat pocket than he went into action. He literally hurled himself through the crowd and down the steps, head over heels, bowling others over in his mad progress.

By the time his head had cleared a bit, and some obliging person had handed him back his hat, a policeman was on the scene. The anxious little man was dancing up and down, shouting at the officer.

"That's him, officer, that's him, he was right beside me. I thought I felt fingers in my pocket, and then he hurried away. Search him, officer, search him!"

Jim put an aggrieved air on his face. "Because I stumble and fall, I'm trying to make a getaway, eh? All right, officer, search me, I demand to be searched!"

The cop grinned and scratched his head. Up the stairs somebody called, "Here's the monkey's billfold on the step.

Red-faced, he-who-had-lost, looked inside the billfold, mumbled an apology and hurried away to lose himself in the crowd. The cop helped brush Jim Anthony off. That night the payment was made.

FAGO KEPT HIS word about no more crimes for Tom Gentry, and that, too, puzzled Anthony. Not that the spider gang didn't receive publicity! Every major crime committed throughout the country during that period was laid to Tom Gentry and his vendetta against law and order. Every petty crook took to leaving a spider of some kind at the spot of his crime. Gentry's picture appeared in a hundred papers over the country. If a bank in Kansas was robbed, the whole state shrieked, "Gentry! The Spiders!" During a payroll holdup in California hysterical witnesses were found who could positively identify the leader of the bandits as Tom Gentry. He was wanted in every state of the Union!

All of this made Jim more determined than ever to play the hand out. The strangeness of it often made him laugh. Fighting frame-ups now in order that eventually he would be a criminal himself. It was grotesque, and no one but a man with a brain, twisted and warped could have conceived such a plan.

AS SOON AS the door of a hotel room was safely locked behind him, Jim went to work. He searched the room as minutely as only a trained detective can search. He knew he could overcome this by demanding a certain room, a certain number, but by now it had resolved into a grim sort of game between himself and Fago. He was going to outwit the fat man. He was going deliberately to walk into traps and break them open!

Trotter said, "You win, lady. If you ever did that before a jury,
they'd turn the guy loose and give him a medal."

But Omaha, Nebraska, was the grimmest of all! He took the room the sleek clerk assigned, closed his own door and found that it was one of connecting rooms. For a moment he wondered about this, like a forest animal might ponder a strange woodfall that had not been present the last time he passed.

He tapped at the door. There was no answer. From his pocket he drew two slender pieces of steel, and in less than a moment had picked the lock. Cautiously, soundlessly, he opened the door. The room was empty, the blinds drawn. Puzzled more than ever, he closed it again, his eyes roving around the room.

His closet door stood open the fraction of an inch. He crossed hurriedly, threw it open and started back in horror. There was a woman in his closet! A young woman, once beautiful, nearly nude. She hung to a hook by a short length of picture wire, and her contorted face was terrible to see.

He forced himself to touch the flesh, found it cold. She had been dead some hours. Now what? If he went to the phone, horrified, and called the police, there would be much questioning, much running here and there! He had, perhaps, an hour to make his payoff. Of course he would not be accused of throttling the woman, he could too easily prove the time of his entrance. But the delay, that was the thing.

Grimly he took the cold, beautiful body from its resting place. He carried her across the room, through the door and into the next room. He forced himself to wire her in the closet exactly as she had been wired in his. Returning, he relocked the connecting door. Threw off his coat and hat and used a towel to wipe away the cold sweat!

Ten minutes later the phone rang. A clerk wanted to know if Mr. Anthony had found his room quite satisfactory. Mr. Anthony assured him politely that everything was fine. The clerk seemed a bit puzzled, but Anthony clicked the phone.

IN MEMPHIS THERE was Trotter. Jim opened his door to step into the hall, and Trotter's bulk filled it. "Going out, Anthony?" he asked. He started to step in. Jim's reflexes were now as fast as those of a cat. His left hand shot out to seize Trotter's lapels, he jerked him into the room, crashed a right against the ponderous jaw. Trotter sagged into his arms.

When Trotter snapped out of it, he glared malevolently at Jim, mumbled something through his gag. Anthony said, "I had to do it, Trotter. I guess a little birdie told me to, the same one that told you where to find me. Now if you take it easy, I'll phone the hotel to come and untie you. As soon as I'm through with my business."

Trotter's hot gaze cursed him. Anthony shrugged, picked up what was apparently a box of candy, and left the room. A few minutes later he dispatched a messenger with the candy to a certain address. There was one hundred thousand dollars in the box.

CHAPTER IX

CHAMP CHUMP

SAN ANTONIO, TEXAS, THE ninth payoff, and not a sign of a trap. It worried him, more so than if he had had to match wits with a dozen clever framers. The payoff was made peacefully—and the final payoff was to come just one hundred and fifty miles south, in three days rather than the usual week. He wondered why the three days. A chance glimpse of a placard in a window showed. The day would fall on George Washington's Birthday, and Laredo, Texas, combined with Neuvo Laredo, Mexico, held high carnival.

There would be thousands of tourists, a bullfight, a *Noche Mexicano*, a ball, all attended by visiting functionaries of State from both sides of the Rio Grande River.

He rode up in the elevator at the appointed hotel, wondering what, if any connection, this fiesta had with his own affairs. He put the key in the lock, twisted the knob, opened the door perhaps an inch and froze, every nerve tense and expectant. He smelled cigarette smoke, a fragrant sweetish variety not his own.

A voice called softly, "Come in, come in, I've been waiting for you." He opened the door, turned on the light. Lupe Carranza smiled at him from the depths of an easy chair, her legs crossed as attractively—and as revealingly—as ever. He closed the door, locked it.

"How did you get in here?"

"Fifty dollars to the bell captain," she said cheerfully. "It's okay, I merely want to talk to you. I'm not going to make any passes."

He tossed his hat on the bed, lit a cigarette and sat down.

"You've changed since St. Louis," she said. "Lost weight, all nerved up. Fago has noticed it too. He says we must treat you more cautiously than ever, that the starved and hungry tiger is a beast to be fooled."

He laughed. "I'll enjoy seeing Fago. It's nice knowing I didn't fall for any of his frameups."

She nodded. "He thinks you are the second cleverest person in the world. The first, of course, is Fago."

"Tom is all right?"

Her eyes gleamed, she smiled—not like the seductress she was, but like an ordinary woman. "Tom is fine," she said. She arose and walked to the dresser frowning, ground out the cigarette in the tray.

What's wrong with her? wondered Jim. She seemed out of character, she didn't seem the woman he had known and hated so greatly before. Wisely he waited, knowing from her actions that she had come here determined to tell him something, and could not make up her mind whether to do it or not.

Over her shoulder she said, "It was nice of Fago to keep Tom out of more trouble, was it not?"

"He has a reason I suppose, though I can't figure what it could be. Would you mind telling me how he can control Tom, if Tom is the unmanageable fellow I'm to believe he is?"

She whirled, her eyes blazing, breast rising and falling in anger. "How can you say that of him? He is never unmanageable. He is sweet and kind, I will tell you that!"

Jim nodded slowly. He was understanding something now.

"You think after the last payment Fago means to play fair? Will Tom go with me willingly?"

She giggled. "If I tell him to. Tom thinks you are a chump, Jim Anthony!" She shook her head. "Poor fellow."

"I don't get it. Why should he think I'm a chump, Lupe?"

"Because he has beaten you out of nine hundred thousand dollars by a ruse and means to make it a million eventually. He calls you his world's champ chump."

THE ONLY ANSWER to that was bewilderment. Eventually, "Is his mind as badly gone as that, is he a complete moron?"

"His mind is as good as yours," she snapped.

It was Jim's turn to shake his head. "He couldn't be doing this willingly, I'll stake my life on this."

"But he is! Willingly chumping you. Do you still mean to stick by in spite of that?"

"I'll stick. There's an answer, there has to be. After the last payoff we'll know."

"There's the rub. Has it occurred to you, Jim Anthony, that he hasn't done anything very bad?"

"He shot a policeman. Trotter will pin more than that on him, if he ever gets hold of him. There are a dozen different places where he was supposedly identified doing crooked work."

"But if there was a witness to show he was somewhere else at the time of the crimes. Me, for example."

Bitterness came into his eyes. She hadn't changed after all!

"How much?"

She walked across the room and slapped him across the mouth. "Don't say that to me again," she blazed. "You are a greater fool than I thought. Let me get this business over with and leave you! Listen closely. It is not like Fago to turn him over to you without a final fling. I think he has devised something, something big, in which Tom is to be the kingpin. Something that will make him wanted so badly that even you cannot hide him! I do not know what, but I do know it has something to do with General Gonzales, who is to represent officially the Republic of Mexico at the fiesta.

"When and if I learn what this is, I shall get word to you and you must be ready to act at once. Do you promise?"

"There is nothing else to do but promise. Whether he thinks I'm the world's champ chump or not, Tom Gentry is still my friend, will always remain my friend. I want to save him from himself, as well as from Fago."

At the door she turned, laughing a little. "It does sound odd to you, doesn't it? Tom thinking he is chumping you. Shall I tell you why?" Jim nodded. "Because he doesn't think he's Tom Gentry at all! He thinks he's a forger named Henry Harrison, a perfect double for Tom Gentry. He thinks Gentry is dead! And he actually believes, in his own heart, that he conceived this entire plan for mulcting you out of a million dollars. I only hope to God something can be done for him after this is over—if it is ever over!" She left him gaping, open mouthed.

Gentry dead? Champ chump? Harrison the forger? His own plan? There was only one answer to that, one way to figure.

Amnesia!

CHAPTER X

FIESTA OF DEATH

LAREDO, TEXAS, FEBRUARY 22ND. Streets were gaily festooned with streamers of flags, resplendent in holiday attire. Tourists gazed with awe at the orange trees in the plaza, bought cheap *serapes* and curios supposedly made in Mexico, sampled Mexican candies made of yams and pumpkins, drank too much and generally had a good time.

Jim Anthony had preceded less than half a block from the station when he heard a startled expletive from behind him. He turned, saw a grinning face and an outstretched hand. Anthony's memory for faces and names was proverbial.

"Hello, Gross," he said, "how have you been? Been two or three years since I saw you!"

Gross pumped his hand vigorously, beaming from ear to ear. "And I'll never forget what you did for me that time, Mr. Anthony. About one more round and that big bull Trotter would have had me admitting I torpedoed the Lusitania. Hey—wait a minute."

He fingered Jim's tweeds doubtfully, looked him over from head to foot. Wonderingly, Jim waited.

"I might ask you what's the idea, Gross, but I guess you'll tell me soon enough."

Gross looked quickly about, stooped as though to tie a shoe. The words came up to Anthony but faintly. "Step across the street to that bar and sit down at a rear table. I'll join you in a minute."

Trap? There had been genuine gladness and gratitude in Gross' face. Jim decided to chance it. And a moment later the ex-easterner joined him.

"You know a guy named Fago, a fat guy?"

"Slightly. Why?"

"He's having you tailed. I'm it."

"You're what?"

"The tail! I'm supposed to check you all day and turn in hourly reports. Lay off that monkey, he's mean!"

Jim laughed aloud. "He's been having me tailed for two months, Gross, so one more day won't matter in the least. But I hope it's the last day." He arose.

Gross wrinkled his brow. "Tell you what, Mr. Anthony. You go anyplace you want, and I'll tail you, but when I call the fat slob I'll tell him you was someplace else!"

Anthony laughed and slapped the little man's back. "It doesn't matter in the least, Gross. Do your job, draw your money. I'm going up to the Hamilton Hotel now, so tail me all you please. We'll get a chance to talk later."

AT THE HAMILTON, to his surprise, he found that a reservation had been made for him days before. Which, considering the number of visitors, was a good thing, for rooms were at a premium. The tap at the door was, of course, to be expected; the identity of his visitor was a complete surprise.

Fago stepped in beaming. He looked no different from what he had back in New York, except that he wore a battered fedora rather than a derby. He seated himself, beamed around the room, said, "Well, Anthony, we've had a nice little affair, haven't we? I see you've lost some weight?"

"Oh, not much," answered Jim, determined to play it out. "I'm just about down to my normal fighting weight."

Fago chuckled in appreciation. "How did you like the little pastimes I arranged for you, Anthony?"

"Some were fair. Others a child could have evaded. I got to where I deliberately walked into them to see how smart I was." He yawned elaborately.

"The affair of the dead woman was nice quick work, Anthony. I had trouble obtaining a body." The fat man sighed. "If I could just have had a nice, warm, bleeding corpse there, it would have been much better."

Jim agreed that it would have been much better.

"I suppose you've come for your money?" Fago nodded. Fago got it. "You've done very well, Fago. A million dollars, I'll have no kickback at all, and you've had your fun."

Fago chuckled, hating the smooth-talking man with his eyes. He had hoped to come into the room and see a beaten, cringing, pleading man, haunted by his past and fearful of what the future was going to bring. Instead he found Anthony still arrogant, more than a little scornful, and absolutely self assured.

"Don't you think it was okay of me, nice of me, to arrange the final payment here in Laredo, Texas?" His answer was a bland shrug and smile. "Over there lies Mexico," went on the fat man. "And after all, Gentry hasn't done much. You'll be safe—pretty safe."

"We'll be safe enough, Fago. Now, when do you turn him over to me?"

"That wasn't the agreement! I said I'd see to it that you talked to him alone and tried to persuade him to—shall we say flee—to safety. Tonight, I take you to him myself, I promise you that. I'll call for you here at the hotel, my dear Anthony, at exactly eight thirty."

Jim nodded. Almost nonchalantly he said, "I suppose you know what happens if you cross me?"

"Yes, indeed. Promptly at eight-thirty."

Hardly had the door closed behind him when the phone rang. It was Gross. "Hey, Mr. Anthony, you remember the guy that was beating my head off, that feller Trotter? Damn my eyes, he's sitting in the Hamilton lobby where he can watch the elevators, trying to cover up with a newspaper! What's he doing down here, they got something else dug up about me?"

Anthony laughed. "No Gross. Trotter's tailing me."

There was a moment of silence, then, "My golly, Mr. Anthony, you must be hot as a firecracker! Did Fago come up to your room?"

"Yes. Gross, no matter what happens, are you for me?" The answer was all that he could expect. Jim went on: "Tonight Fago and I are going for a ride somewhere at eight-thirty. Someway, somehow, I want you to stick close behind. If it looks to you like I need some help—we're going to meet some people, one man at least—I want it. And sort of keep an eye on Trotter."

Leaving the elevator, he spotted Trotter, his face well covered by a newspaper. It amused him, and at the same time made him cautious. He'd have to take care of Trotter. Tonight was the night!

THE PARADE WAS greatly like other parades, floats, student bands and organizations, except for the fact of the presence of many colorful officials from Mexico. He asked a bystander to point out General Gonzales, remembering Lupe's words. The General was a pompous, much bemedaled and gold braided old fellow with a mustache of grey which he twirled constantly. He didn't look so dangerous to Jim Anthony.

Afterward Jim went back to the hotel and went to bed. This was the showdown, this was the last strand of silk in the fabric, he'd need all the relaxation he could get. The note was sent up about seven.

"I don't know what is going to happen. General Gonzales is an old admirer of mine. I have a rendezvous with him at Palomar Courts and I think F is also bringing you there. I don't get it. But be on the alert."

AT EIGHT-THIRTY ON the dot, Fago arrived. To Jim's relief he did not see Trotter at all going through the lobby, nor when they entered Fago's car. "Where are we going?" he asked.

"To a place named Palomar Courts, Anthony. You must remember that Gentry considers himself a very much wanted man. I think he will show up sooner or later at these courts. Matter of fact, I'd like you to observe them closely. Very quaint, liked for their primitiveness by all the tourists. You see while they have all modern conveniences, they are constructed of adobe, they even have thatched roofs."

The fat man chattered incessantly, but Jim Anthony scarcely heard him. He was wondering if Trotter had not noted their departure, if Gross was managing to follow successfully, what he could say to Henry Harrison, forger and blackmailer, to persuade him he was in reality Tom Gentry, that he could hardly forge his own handwriting, and that the scheme was not his, Gentry's, but Fago's. And a most diabolical scheme hatched in a monster's brain it was!

Palomar Courts was all that Fago had said, quaint and typically Mexican. The fat man pulled the car to a stop not far from one of the cabins. Before it, was parked an enormous limousine bearing the Mexican insignia. Inside, Anthony knew, Lupe Carranza entertained her old admirer, General Gonzales. Now what—?

On and on went Fago's talk. Jim's mind reverted to amnesia. Most of it was curable, he knew. That resulting from accidents was usually caused by pressure on the brain that a good surgeon could remove. The more common variety—caused by worry and trouble—was a bit harder to manage, but he placed Tom in the first category.

"—and Tom Gentry usually shows up around these courts about this time—!"

It flashed over Jim like a bolt from the blue. Tom Gentry, Henry Harrison! Henry Harrison loved Lupe, Lupe loved him, it was evident from her actions the last time he had seen her. And Henry Harrison would arrive at Palomar Courts to find the woman he loved with another man! This was it! This was the last phase of the demoniac scheme devised by this fat monster beside him.

He turned and crashed his fist against a fat jaw. Out of the car he leaped like a cat. And at that same precise moment saw Tom Gentry walk across the moonlight toward the cabin, a gun dangling in his hand!

Damn Fago! He'd arranged it to make a murderer of Tom Gentry-Henry Harrison. And a killer under any name! He kept well to the shadows as he sped after Gentry. Now Gentry paused at the door, listening, listening. Nearer and nearer crept Anthony. He heard the mad curse emitted, saw the hand raised to fling open the door.

JIM ANTHONY LEAPED. The force of his leap carried the two men forward. He heard a crash, heard wood splintering. Then Gentry was silent beneath him, the door was flung open by a furious General Gonzales, a frightened Lupe Carranza behind him. She it was who pushed the sputtering General aside. But it was Jim who lifted the inert figure and carried it to the *serape* covered couch. Tom Gentry was bleeding from a wound in the head.

Afterward he wondered why he did it, and the only answer was that he was afraid the fat dog would revive and escape. But Jim went back to the car and dragged Fago into the house. He was amazed to find the General himself working over Tom Gentry.

Pompously the general explained, "I am one of the finest doctors in all of Latin America, my friend. This young lady says this man and you are friends of hers, and friends of hers are friends of mine. We will need no stitches, we will—and what do you want, sir?"

"Me?" said Trotter, in the doorway, gun in hand. "Why, I thought I'd drop in and pick up a few friends of *mine*. Hello, Anthony, how's Tom Gentry?"

Fago stirred and sat up. He, too, was covered by Trotter's gun.

Trotter said, "Well, an addition to our little group. What are you doing here, Fago, and I might ask you the same, *señorita*."

Fago said, "I knew Gentry was coming here tonight, Mr. Trotter. I was going to capture him if possible and turn him over to the authorities."

Jim started toward him; Trotter's gun waved him back. "All right," said Anthony, "I'll tell you all about it, Trotter."

When he had finished, Fago said, "That is a lie! You'll have a hard time proving any of it!" And Jim realized he would.

"I'll prove it," put in Lupe Carranza in a low voice. "I took Tom Gentry to one of Fago's taverns almost two months ago. I was supposed to add Mr. Anthony to the party but was unable to do so."

"Why Anthony?"

"Because Fago has been obsessed for two years with a hatred of Jim Anthony. Not that Anthony once caused him some trouble, but just—I don't know—I think it was because Anthony represents all that Fago can never hope to be. Brains, breeding, ability, money!"

"At the tavern Gentry was blackjacked by a pair of Fago's thugs."

"Just a minute, lady. Gentry took you home and came back and hit an old man with a bottle," said Trotter. "We—"

"Talk to that bartender! He'll sell his teeth. He'll tell the truth. The bum was deliberately killed long after Tom Gentry lay in a basement room. Fago had kicked Tom in the head twice—"

"Ah," said General Gonzales, beaming, "that explains those odd contusions." He seemed quite pleased.

"We'd originally meant just to hold Gentry for a few grand from Anthony, knowing Anthony would gladly pay it. But when Gentry snapped out of it, he didn't know who he was! Couldn't recall his name or anything else! Fago is smart, I'll warn you of that. Maybe you can't hang this on him. But he convinced Gentry that his name was Henry Harrison, that he was a forger and an exact double for Tom Gentry. He told him he'd fallen downstairs."

SHE PAUSED FOR breath, her face clouded. "I'll admit," she threw back her head defiantly, "that I helped. I played the part of the sweetheart of Henry Harrison, God help me. We convinced him, between us, that he had a marvelous plan for taking the millionaire, James Anthony, for a million bucks. Because we worked on him so hard, even showing him the typewritten details, he finally believed it. He used to admit to me sometimes that he'd lost his memory, but I convinced him it would come back. Now you have it, and the whole thing was a plan of Fago's—and mine—to use a man with amnesia, playing the part of himself, to make a million. You can't blame poor Tom Gentry!"

Fago smiled. "A more fantastic story I never heard. Do you agree, Lieutenant Trotter?"

"It's true," cried Jim. "It all fits in with what I've told you, don't you see?"

Stubbornly Trotter said, "Whether he was Gentry or Harrison, he still shot a cop in New York."

"He didn't!" Lupe cried. "He was still shaky when that happened. We were afraid to commit mass murder! That tommy-gun was loaded with blanks! I'll even give you the names of the other two thugs!"

Trotter shook his head. "But he was there!"

"Under duress," half screamed Lupe. "I made him do it. Look at me!" The thin negligee revealed every line of her flawless body. Proudly she stood before them, unashamed, fighting, fighting—

It was the general who said, "Phyrne before the Tribunal."

Trotter only got red in the face. He said, "Lady, if you ever took all that before a jury, they'd free the guy and give him a medal and a pension. But just the same, to me, he's a crook. How about all these other spider jobs?"

"He's been with me constantly since that night!"

Anthony put in, "If we can ever get his brain in shape he'll be the first one to want to face a charge in New York, Trotter."

"And how do you expect going about connecting me with all this? Isn't it the lady's word against mine?" That from Fago.

At that moment it happened.

THERE WAS A crash, a splintering of thin beams, the tearing of thatch. Something fell through the roof and landed on Trotter's head. He went down. The gun went off. Fago screamed and whirling, fell. Out of the wreckage scrambled Gross, voluble in explanation.

Five minutes later Trotter was still out from one of the beams. General Gonzales arose from his knees, saying, "I do not think you will ever take this fat man into court. He is very dead."

Gross was looking at Trotter. He said, "You think he's pretty unconscious?" Jim agreed that he was. Gross kicked Trotter, where men Trotter's size should always be kicked.

The general was a gentleman of the old school. He clicked his heels together, saluted Lupe Carranza. "And I am very happy to report to a brave woman, a wonderful woman, that I, Raul Jose Maria Gonzales can very easily relieve the pressure on the brain of her lover, so that he will reassume his normal identity!"

Tears streamed down her face. She turned to Jim Anthony. Someway, somehow she found her way blindly to his arms. And he did not mind holding her at all. She was a different woman now from the Lupe he had known. All the filth and slime seemed to have gone from her, to have been somehow purged from her by her willingness to sacrifice everything for Tom Gentry.

"I guess," he said gently, "I better do what I can to revive Trotter. Gross, Gross?" But at the name Trotter, Gross had faded into the night, wisely and well.

HELL'S ICE BOX

DEATH BECKONS TO JIM ANTHONY IN HIDDEN VALLEY,
LURING HIM TO SINISTER DEPTHS WHERE EVEN THE
DEVIL HIMSELF WOULD NOT DARE TO GO.

THEY HELD ANOTHER TRIPLE funeral in Haunted Valley that morning. Three similar plain wooden coffins were lowered into three identical graves in the little cemetery at the outskirts of town. And the trio of men being laid to rest were alike in yet another respect.

All had been miners. And each had died swiftly, horribly, under the flaming touch of phantom fingers—a touch that shriveled human flesh past all recognition, leaving it seared and hideously blackened like so much overcooked meat.

Jim Anthony did not arrive in time to attend the services. It was mid-afternoon when he had his conference with Eric Meline, chief engineer in charge of the Haunted Valley copper mines, at the latter's isolated hillside house.

"Well, Mr. Anthony, there it is below you," Meline's voice was weary, embittered. "Haunted Valley. A superstitious mining town. And a mine everybody said couldn't be reopened."

"But you did reopen it. Successfully."

"Yes, only to run into this damned mysterious sabotage!" the engineer made a sour mouth. "I don't know who is interfering with the work, or what they hope to gain. But I do know that one of the most important ore-producing projects in the country is being strangled!"

Jim Anthony lifted an eyebrow. "The local police?"

"They've failed! The State cops did no better. We've even had Federal agents here. And still murder follows murder. Here I am, responsible for keeping the mines operating; responsible for the thousands of people below us in that valley. And I'm powerless to protect them, to check the spread of this damnable terror!"

"So now you've sent for me."

"Yes. You're one of our largest stockholders. That gives you a vital interest in making sure the mines remain in operation. But it goes deeper than that. I know your reputation as a detective. If anybody can stop this horror, you can."

Jim Anthony's smile was at once modest and grim. Sportsman, multimillionaire, athlete, and criminologist, he had been pitted against some strange situations in his time; but none had ever matched the sinister conditions he found confronting him here in Haunted Valley.

Two years ago he had investigated this mining deal and subsequently invested in it. The possible profit had not motivated him, for he already enjoyed more income than he knew what to do with. But the whole idea behind the reopening of the abandoned copper property had captured his imagination.

The entire hillside quaked with
that blast behind them.

Then, yesterday, he had received this appeal for help from Eric
Meline and had flown west immediately in his private plane, with his
friend Tom Gentry. Leaving the freckled aviator at the hotel down in
the mining town, he had rented a horse and ridden up here to consult
with the haggard, worried chief engineer.

MELINE'S ISOLATED RESIDENCE was glassed clear across the north side. In the heavy winters, shutters like an extra wall were put up for protection and warmth. But now, with the hot haze of summer rising from the valley, the windows were thrown wide open. There was a steady breeze blowing, pressing against the two men as they stood looking down at the valley far below.

The wind ruffled the pages of a mining journal which lay on a small table; and then, with sudden gusty force, lifted the framed photograph of a girl and slammed it to the floor. Eric Meline stopped talking, turned, gently retrieved the smiling picture. There was no glass to protect it, and his blunt fingers brushed lightly across the photo's surface. He stood for an instant, reading again the scrawled message that was inscribed in the lower corner.

"Dad. I love you. Beth. Vassar College, '42."

His face, square and hard and weathered by sun and rain until the skin was like leather, softened as he replaced the picture on the table. But as he rejoined Jim Anthony at the window, this softness vanished. His expression matched the jagged hills that made a panorama of ugliness as far as the eye could reach.

Across that high land, the devil must have walked behind some gigantic jerking plow. The heavy earth had been furrowed and torn apart until it stood in misshapen clots and shattered rocks along the full length of the ragged range.

The wounded land had bled its hundred colors from these cuts; had streaked the mountain slopes with greens, blues, reds. It was a scene to make a city man gasp; but to Jim Anthony it whispered a message which few could hear. His American Indian blood, inherited from his mother, a princess of the Comanche tribe, rose to meet this whispered challenge.

And, too, his queerly developed sixth sense caught a feeling of evil, a foreign and malignant intrusion that had nothing to do with the region itself. Something sinister had come into the valley from outside, insidious, throttling, slimy.

Anthony and Meline were alone in the house. In the deep distance they could see the huddled cluster of buildings that marked the mine's main shaft. The structures were of unpainted wood—bleached like dead skeletons by wind and weather.

THE CHIEF ENGINEER'S grey eyes were steady as he surveyed the scene; but his fingers trembled a little as he removed his pipe from between clenched teeth. "I don't know Mr. Anthony," he muttered. "It's a big thing for one man to fight. Even a man as capable as you. But if you fail, Haunted Valley is doomed."

"The valley means a lot to you, doesn't it?" Anthony's smile was grave.

"It means a lot to the world. Let me tell you the full story. I may repeat things you already know; but I'd like you to have a clear picture."

"That is why I came," Anthony said.

Meline drew a deep, weary breath. "Years ago, that mine down there was the biggest copper producing property in the world. Until they struck water; so much their pumps couldn't handle a fraction of it. Then the mines were closed. They stayed shut down for twenty years."

"And Haunted Valley became a ghost town," Anthony supplied. "Deserted by all except the legendary Indian spirits who'd given the place its name."

Meline nodded. "When the present war began, a number of the old company's stockholders tried to interest me in reopening the mine. It seemed useless until I talked to a young chemist friend, Steve Bannixter. He mentioned a system used in the building of a dam in the northwest."

"I remember," Anthony said. "They had trouble with a sliding bank. So they held it in place by running refrigeration pipes in the loose earth and freezing it solid."

"Right. Now, my friend Bannixter had developed a cheap chemical refrigerant. He suggested that we lower pipes in the mine's flooded shafts and tunnels. Then we could freeze the water in the passages, and the rock walls as well—to a depth of several feet. That would halt further water-seepage."

It had been this experiment which had piqued Jim Anthony's scientific mind and caused him to invest in the property. Now he inclined his head. "You did a good job."

"The credit belongs to Steve Bannixter," the chief engineer said. "And if it weren't for these mysterious killings, we could be running at full capacity today; turning out the copper so badly needed for America's war effort. As it is, though..." his voice trailed off bitterly.

Anthony studied him. "Do you suspect Nazi agents of these murders? A sabotage scheme?"

"I'd sooner let you form your own opinion after you've talked to the members of the operating syndicate this evening."

"How many are in the syndicate?"

Meline checked them off. "There's Lew Jefferson, president of the Haunted Valley Land and Cattle Company. And Fargo Lane, mayor of the town. Old time westerners, both."

"Who else?"

"Michael Murdock," the engineer said. "Head of one of the biggest mining corporations in the world. His company has more money invested here than anyone else except yourself. And finally there is Willis Todhunter, the Wall Street broker. You know him, naturally. Your stock was bought through his office."

Anthony nodded. "A good man. I didn't invest just because he was handling the stock issue, though. I knew of you by reputation. I was interested in seeing if the freezing plan would work."

"It worked, all right," Meline said glumly. "Too well—since it brought these damned Black Ghosts down on us!"

Jim Anthony thrust out his hand. He had a feeling that he had learned all there was for the engineer to tell him at present and now he was eager to go down into the valley, study the mining town at close range.

"Thanks for the information," he clasped the engineer's palm. "I wanted to meet you before seeing the others. You'll be at the conference this evening?"

"Yes, of course."

ANTHONY WENT OUT to his horse, mounted, turned the animal toward the precarious trail leading downward to the valley. He had ridden perhaps ten minutes when the explosion came.

It wasn't a loud report. The sound seemed muffled, buried—and all the more sinister for this reason. The wind picked up its echoes; carried them away from the town below. But Jim Anthony both heard and felt the thudding shock. Glancing up, he choked out a startled exclamation.

Above him, Eric Meline's hillside house was tilted where its foundation had been blasted loose. Then, abruptly, the structure seemed to fold and collapse, while the engineer stood helplessly at his window. And as the building plummeted, the entire side of the cliff slid with it.

Anthony's reaction was automatic. An avalanche of earth and rocks and rubble roared down at him; would engulf him in another instant. He reined his horse toward the protecting lee of a mammoth boulder.

But the fear-crazed animal reared, bolted. There was but one thing to do, and Anthony did it. He allowed himself to be thrown. Catlike, he landed on his feet; crouched behind the jutting boulder. Then the landslide struck, carrying all before it. The plunging horse disappeared with a shrill whinnying scream.

And Anthony clung to his boulder—the one solid object in a world of smashing chaos.

At last the din subsided and he straightened up, his clothes torn, his muscular torso bruised and lacerated by the rocks that had swirled around him. And as he peered upward with dust dimmed eyes, he saw a man in the distance, silhouetted against the horizon, coiling a length of wire around a detonator box.

Presently this far-away figure vanished over the rim.

CHAPTER II

BLACK GHOSTS

JAKE GORCHIKOFF'S PARENTS HAD come from the old country; but in spite of his accent and broad Slavic features, Jake himself was one hundred percent American. Years of toil underground as a hard rock miner had bent his shoulders, bowed his legs and thinned his greying hair. But he still had the strength of an ox and the courage of a lion.

That is, he had a lion's bravery in the face of ordinary perils. Ghosts were something else again, though. Particularly black ghosts that killed with the flaming touch of their finger-tips. A man had a right to be scared of things like that!

Just now, Jake was working on the fifteen hundred foot level of the Haunted Valley mine along with two other drillers. This was one of the old galleries, started in the days before water had flooded all operations to a halt.

With that water now frozen solid, the scene was like a weird and frigid hell. An Arctic temperature prevailed; and raw electric bulbs were strung at spaced intervals along the tunnel's ceiling, casting harsh illumination upon walls and floors which glittered with a myriad diamond-like facets. The crystals were not diamonds, however. They were particles of ice, refrigerated by hidden pipes.

Jake and his two companions were using air drills on the face of a stope, boring powder holes. All three men presented an eerie appearance in their specially made heating suits—thickly padded one-piece garments which covered them from ankles to neck, with cowl-like hoods for their heads such as Eskimos wear.

These suits were patterned after those used by aviators in the upper stratosphere. They contained networks of resistance wire, on the same principle which is employed for electrical heating pads and blan-

One look at the mayor and Jim recognized
the type—Western gambler!

kets. You plugged a cord from your suit into the nearest socket receptacle, and it kept you warm against the frigid underground chill.

Jake Gorchikoff and his fellow workers looked like creatures from Mars as they labored with their air drills. The machine-gun clatter of the jackhammers drowned all other sounds; and it was only some hidden instinct that made Jake look around and see the black ghost creeping toward him.

He knew it was a black ghost because he had heard other men describing these weird visitations in recent days. The figure was thick, lumbering, clad in a padded costume similar to the heating suits worn by the miners—except that it was solid black and its cowl was a complete hood, totally obliterating its wearer's features save for eye-slits.

A spate of fear inched through Gorchikoff's marrow. He yelled a warning to his companions, but they couldn't hear him above the din of the compressed air drills. He dropped his own drill, turned, started to run.

His soles skidded on the icy floor and he lurched, struggled for balance. Then his feet gripped and he increased his frantic pace, staring back over his shoulder as he catapulted out of the gallery.

The thing he witnessed was horrible beyond description. The black-clad shape was closing in on the two other miners. At the last instant they turned; saw their doom approaching. They tried to shrink away, to find some avenue of escape. But they were in a trap. Their exit was blocked by the black ghost.

Jake's eyes bulged as he saw that sinister figure extend a pointing finger. Then, from its' finger-tip, an arc of blue fire spurted. It lighted the whole drift with fiendish brilliance, as a lightning bolt might strike. And the miner at whose face the finger was pointed seemed to shrivel inside his heating suit—seemed to collapse like a deflated balloon as he folded over and fell.

The second miner cowered, screamed. Again the black figure pointed; again the blue flame arced. But Jake Gorchikoff didn't wait to see the man fall.

He spurted toward safety, knowing that he himself had eluded death by the slenderest of threads.

THE TOWN OF Haunted Valley boasted a weekly newspaper, the *Mining News*. Editorially independent, it was actually owned by the New York *Star*—which, in turn, was owned by Jim Anthony, who had inherited it from his father along with other vast holdings.

Jim Anthony never did things by halves. When he had first heard of the refrigeration experiment to reopen the old copper mines in Haunted Valley, his quick brain had realized that if the plan succeeded, the valley would by a rich source of news in which the outside world would be interested.

He had wanted his New York *Star* to have full coverage. Therefore, when he bought stock in the mining venture, he also gave orders for the *Star* to purchase Haunted Valley's only weekly paper and send out a competent man to run it.

The editor thus chosen turned out to be a wiry, two-fisted young *Star* reporter named Don McCorkle. He had done a good job, too. Jim Anthony's faith in him had been well justified, for McCorkle was covering Haunted Valley in expert fashion. The task was not an easy one, though. Booming as it had never boomed in the wild old days, the town was a sprawling, brawling, hell-roaring mining camp that seethed with action every hour of the day and night.

It took an aggressive fighter like McCorkle to handle such a berth. This afternoon, however, the wiry little newspaperman was worried—and he didn't mind admitting it.

He was seated in his office at the front end of the elongated, shed-like building which housed the *Mining News;* and he was talking to Tom Gentry, the freckled aviator who was Jim Anthony's closest friend.

"I don't like it," he was saying to Gentry. "Mr. Anthony has been gone too long. He should have come back from his visit to Eric Meline before this. It's almost sundown!"

Gentry grinned. "Don't worry about the boss. He can take care of himself. Nothing's happened to him."

Even as the aviator spoke, there was a faint sound at the side door of the office. McCorkle stiffened. He was no coward; he'd risked his neck in the pursuit of news more than once. But things had been happening recently in Haunted Valley that would rasp any man's nerves raw.

While Gentry stared at him in amazement, he yanked open the top drawer of his desk; produced a flat automatic. Then he catapulted to the side door; flung it wide.

THE MAN WHO swayed over the threshold was big, handsome, battered. He smiled a tired, thin-lipped smile as he entered. "Put away the hardware, McCorkle."

Tom Gentry yelped: "Jim! *Jim Anthony!* What the devil happened to you?"

Anthony shrugged. He was weary, yes; but now that he'd reached his goal, his astounding vitality was beginning to overcome the fatigue that filled him.

"Wait until I wash some of this dirt and blood off me," he said. "Then I'll tell you."

"There's a shower in the back," McCorkle offered.

Anthony nodded, availed himself of a quick, bracing cold spray. Then, dressed again and feeling as fit as ever, he went back to Gentry and McCorkle.

"Eric Meline is dead," he announced grimly. "His house collapsed in a rock slide. The avalanche almost caught me but I got out alive; walked all the way back to the valley. My horse was killed."

The rattle stopped as Anthony's shot blew the snake's head off. But the man underneath would never move again.

"Rock slide?" Don McCorkle stared at him. "But that cliff under Meline's house was solid! He was too good an engineer to be fooled on a foundation—"

"Any rock will crack if you use enough dynamite," Anthony retorted tersely.

"But we didn't hear any explosion!"

"The wind carried the sound the other way, probably. It was a blast, just the same. I saw the man who did it. He was too far off for me to know what he looked like; but he came over the rim behind the house and he went back the same way, taking a plunger box and wire with him."

"Good God! McCorkle whispered. "Meline murdered! Chances are they hoped to kill you at the same time."

Anthony's dark eyes glittered like a falcon's. "Very likely. But they failed. And now I intend to pay them in their own coin, whoever they are." His gaze bored holes in the wiry little newspaperman. "I want you to tell me every thing you know concerning the happenings here in Haunted Valley. I've read the reports you wired east; but I want it from your own lips."

"Sure," McCorkle began pacing the floor with quick, nervous strides. "To start with, this town has sprung up like a mushroom since the mines reopened. The big payrolls have attracted every gambler and criminal who could get here. I don't know much about the old west; but from all accounts, Haunted Valley is more wild than Tombstone or Deadwood or Virginia City in their palmiest days. A rip-snorting boom town."

"I can see that."

"And yet it isn't just a mining camp. In some respects it's a modern city with modern conveniences: electricity, plumbing, a police force, a mayor. The miners themselves are a tough bunch—with good reason, considering the conditions they work under."

"Conditions?"

"They've nicknamed the mine tunnels Hell's Icebox because of the freezing units. They swear even the devil couldn't work continuously underground here. I agree it's a nasty job. You can't blame them for drinking and gambling and carousing when they're off duty. Even so, they could have stood the gaff if it hadn't been for the Black Ghosts."

Jim Anthony's black brows drew together thoughtfully. "I'd like your version of these Black Ghosts."

"Well, as a class, miners are superstitions. And Haunted Valley is supposed to be full of Indian spirits. When these murders started, the killers were seen in the old drifts—figures wearing black outfits something like our regular heating suits, but hooded, masked. Their touch brings death. It's only natural that the workers would begin thinking of something superhuman."

"That is true," Anthony agreed. "And as a result, the miners are in a turmoil, eh? Many of them refuse to work?"

McCorkle started to say yes; to explain that the miners were now running at less than half capacity for want of skilled labor. But his words were never uttered, because just then a heavy pounding sounded on the office door.

By instinct, the newspaperman hefted his automatic before he answered that desperate summons. Then he opened the door and a man shambled in; a grey-haired man, shoulders bent, legs bowed by years of toil. The newcomer's eyes were glassy, protuberant; his broad Slavic face as pale as watered milk.

"Jake!" McCorkle exclaimed. Then he turned. "This is one of the mine foremen. Jake Gorchikoff."

Anthony reached out, touched the man. "What's wrong?"

In thick, choked accents the miner sputtered: "Dose damned Plack Ghosts! Dey struck again! Killed two my friends! Me, I no go pack in dat mine for million tollars! And I tell everybody I know, you betcha! I tell 'em get to hell out of Haunted Valley in damned pig hurry!"

CHAPTER III

FIERY DEATH

FIERCELY JIM ANTHONY WHIRLED on Tom Gentry. "Tom, you keep this fellow here. Don't let him out of your sight or he'll be spreading panic all over town."

"Sure, Jim," the freckled aviator drawled. "But where are you going?"

"Down in the mine to help remove those corpses—and have a look at them!" Anthony snapped. "Come on McCorkle. I'll be needing you."

Followed by the wiry little editor, Anthony sprinted out of the newspaper building. In McCorkle's rattletrap car they headed for the mine shaft a mile away.

Dusk was thickening as they gained their destination. And already a mob had gathered there; a restless, surging, uneasy mob, but a quiet one—for a blanket of fear had fallen over these miners, hardbitten though they were. Evidently Jake Gorchikoff had told his story before going to the office of the *Mining News*, and now there would be hell to pay.

Alighting, Anthony and McCorkle whispered: "Here's a couple of guys you ought to meet."

"Introduce me, then."

The newspaperman approached a stubby, chunky, middle-aged man whose head was as bald as a billiard ball and whose seamy features were wrinkled from squinting into many suns.

"I'd like you to know Jim Anthony, sir," McCorkle said. "Jim, this is Lew Jefferson, president of the Haunted Valley Land and Cattle Company."

"Ka-humph. Anthony, hunh? Glad to meet you." Jefferson's rumbling voice was like deep thunder; a voice built for a man twice his size. And he carried himself with a certain arrogant assurance—the kind that comes with self-made success. This was natural enough, since he owned most of the land in Haunted Valley; including the site of the town itself.

"And this," McCorkle went on, "is Fargo Lane, our mayor. He doubles in brass as chief of police, too, since our last chief quit the job and left town."

Fargo Lane shook hands with Anthony. He was tall, and his old fashioned black broadcloth swallowtail coat made him seem even taller. He wore a black string tie, a broad-brimmed black Stetson, a black mustache and goatee. The total effect was that of an old time western gambler.

Which, as a matter of fact, he once had been. Reforming, he had turned to cattle and presently to politics. Now he packed a lot of weight if it became necessary. His face held unmasked power; his eyes were as cold and unwinking as a snake's. A bad man to have for an enemy, Anthony decided.

"Both these gentlemen are on the mine's operating committee," McCorkle finished his introductions.

Jim Anthony surveyed them gravely. "That makes us all partners, in a sense. Are you willing to go with me, then, down in the mine?"

"Ka-humph!" the stubby Lew Jefferson rumbled. "What for?"

"To bring out the two murdered drillers."

Fargo Lane tugged at his goatee. "We'd need help. And there isn't a living soul down there now. The whole shift walked out when they heard the news."

"I can call for volunteers."

Lane's unwinking eyes hardened. "You seem to be taking plenty of authority, Mr. Anthony. I'd say this is Eric Meline's job, not yours."

"Eric Meline is dead."

A thunderous exclamation leaped from Lew Jefferson's throat. *"What—?"* he roared.

Anthony nodded. "He was murdered."

Fargo Lane's lips held the suspicion of a sneer. "By the so-called Black Ghosts?"

"By a dynamiter," Anthony said evenly. "And now, as heaviest stockholder, I'm declaring myself in charge. Unless you want to challenge me, of course."

The former gambler dropped his truculent manner. "All right. Your aces top my hand. I'll go down with you."

"Ka-humph. So will I," Jefferson rumbled.

"Counting McCorkle and myself, that makes four. Two for each corpse," Anthony said. "That's enough. Let's go. We won't need to wear heating suits; we'll be back topside before the cold bothers us too much." And he led the way into the shaft house; stepped onto the crude elevator platform.

The others joined him, with McCorkle volunteering to guide them when they went below. The wiry little newspaperman was no stranger to the lower tunnels. When the old workings had first been refrigerated and reopened he had been taken on a complete tour of shafts and galleries to gain material for a news story. Hence, he knew the mine well enough. He should have felt no uneasiness as the cage dropped.

He did feel uneasy, though. And he cast a curious glance at Jim Anthony.

But the millionaire detective's expression betrayed no hint that this trip into the frozen depths was in any way foreign to his ordinary routine. When the platform came to a sudden jerky stop at the fifteen hundred foot level, he was first to walk out into the square station hollowed from living rock. His sole concession to possible danger was the blue steel automatic that appeared abruptly in his fist as if by magic.

"Tell me the way, McCorkle," he said quietly.

The reporter pointed in silence; and a heavier silence lay upon the brightly lighted tunnel, all the more eerie because of those bright lights here in the deserted bowels of the earth. A steady fiery glitter sparkled from ice particles in the walls, and the footfalls of Anthony's party resounded hollowly as they moved grimly forward on their corpse-hunt.

"This would be a nice time for the Black Ghosts to strike," Fargo Lane remarked. "Br-r-r, it's cold!" A glint of frost was on his mustache and imperial, giving him a peculiarly Satanic appearance.

Anthony ignored him; quickened his own pace. "Here we are!" he muttered, spotting the working face of the drift dead ahead. Then he tensed. "Who in hell—?"

THERE WERE TWO huddled forms on the gallery's icy flooring, shrunken and shriveled in their heating suits. A vague odor of roasted flesh came to Jim Anthony's sensitive nostrils. However, it was neither the dead men nor the sickish smell that made him stiffen. It was something else.

Someone was leaning over the sprawled corpses; someone who suddenly straightened up and stared at the newcomers.

"Hey!" he said mildly into the menace of Anthony's narrowed eyes and steady gun. He was a slender young man, the studious quality of his face emphasized by horn-rimmed glasses. A smile, ingratiating yet bewildered, came to his lips. "Hey, point that away from me, will you?"

Anthony kept him covered. "Who are you? What are you doing here?"

"Me? I'm Steve Bannixter. Chemist. Couldn't persuade anyone else to come down with me and have a look at these poor devils, so I came alone."

Don McCorkle stood on tiptoe, whispered into Jim Anthony's ear. "Bannixter's okay," the wiry little reporter said. "You'd do well to trust him."

Anthony lowered his automatic. "Very well. But you shouldn't have taken such a risk by yourself, Mr. Bannixter."

"Why not? Somebody had to," the young chemist retorted. "I don't mind a spot of danger."

"Admirable, but somewhat foolhardy," Anthony smiled. And he leaned down to examine the two corpses.

These were the first victims of the Black Ghosts he had seen. And as he stripped each one out of its heating suit, he made an angry mouth. The bodies were seared, scorched by intense heat—as if some giant flame had reached up from hell to consume terrified, living human flesh.

"Ka-humph! Good God!" Lew Jefferson's voice thundered weirdly in the tunnel. "This is damnable!"

Anthony came erect. "I agree with you. Damnable, but not supernatural. I think I see how our Black Ghosts operate."

The others stared at him. "You know how these men were killed?" McCorkle gasped.

"Yes. They were electrocuted."

"You mean their heating suits short-circuited?"

"No. The suits operate on an ordinary light current with an effective voltage of one hundred and ten to one-fifteen and very few amperes flowing. The charge that killed these men was a lot bigger."

"But where would the extra current come from if it isn't in the line?" Fargo Lane demanded skeptically.

"I can't tell you—yet. But I intend to find out," Anthony said coldly. And even as he spoke, the gallery was plunged into solid darkness.

The lights had gone off!

In the blackness, Jim Anthony raised his gun and his voice. "Stand where you are, all of you! Don't move!" He used a Hindu trick he had learned long ago; dilated the pupils of his eyes by an effort of will. Ordinarily, by this means, he could see in the dark where normal vision could not.

Now, though, it gained him nothing. The blackness was absolute and impenetrable. He had only his super-keen hearing to rely on; and he detected a sound that brought anger swelling into his throat. One of the party was darting away!

"I said stand still!" he commanded. "I mean it. I shall call your names. I want you to answer. McCorkle?"

"Here, Jim."

"Fargo Lane?"

"I haven't left."

"Lew Jefferson?"

"Ka-humph. Present!" the stocky, bald man's voice was a rumble of thunder.

"Steve Bannixter?"

There was no answer from the slender, studious-looking young chemist. He was gone. His were the footfalls Anthony had heard.

CHAPTER IV

GHOST THREAT

SILENTLY JIM ANTHONY CURSED himself for his failure to bring along his little black kit—which, among other things, contained a small but powerful flashlight of his own special design. Rarely was he without the kit; but this time, when he needed it most, he'd left it behind.

As he fumbled into his pocket for a match, with the marrow-chilling temperature of the tunnel making his fingers clumsy, a queer thing happened. The overhead string of lights began flashing weirdly on and off.

Intermittently they blazed and winked out with a curious, irregular rhythm. And Anthony immediately recognized the meaning of those alternating flashes. They were blinking a message in Morse code—a message to Anthony himself!

Swiftly he spelled out the dots and dashes: *"Jim Anthony. Get out of Haunted Valley if you want to stay alive."*

Then, with a final flicker, the incandescent bulbs glowed to steady life. And as illumination returned to the gallery, young Steve Bannixter came pelting into view, carrying two tubular objects.

Anthony regarded him sternly. "Where've you been?"

"To an emergency cabinet in the next cross-tunnel. I figured we'd need these flashlights," Bannixter answered readily. "Guess I was wrong, though. Current seems okay again."

His explanation sounded plausible, especially since he had the flashlights he claimed to have gone for. It was reasonable to assume that he was telling the truth; that he alone had known where to find the electric torches in the darkness and had taken it upon himself to fetch them.

On the other hand, he'd been absent when the overhead bulbs blinked their warning message. Could it be that he knew the location of a master switch that might be alternately opened and shut to create flashes in Morse code?

There was no way of telling, at present. Jim Anthony pretended to dismiss the matter, since evidently nobody but himself had interpreted the warning message.

"Let's get these two bodies out of here," he commanded. "Before we all freeze to death."

IT WAS AN hour later when the operating board of the Haunted Valley copper mine met in a room on the third floor of the bank building owned by Lew Jefferson. Originally a two-story affair, an additional floor had been added by the bald, chunky land baron when the ghost town got its new lease on life.

This newly added upper floor was not yet fully completed. A pleasant odor of fresh lumber and paint pervaded the directors' room, and the illumination was supplied by a number of Coleman gasoline mantel-lanterns strung from the rafters, since electric lines hadn't yet been run up this far.

The yellowish light glared down on the faces of the men at the long plain table, revealing them to be white and strained by inner tension. At the head of the board sat Jim Anthony by right of his superior investment in the mine. Narrowly he studied the faces before him.

Jefferson was mopping his hairless pate. Fargo Lane stroked his black goatee and met Anthony's stare without blinking. There was a vacant chair where Eric Meline should have sat; but the engineer would attend no more board meetings.

Then there was a man whom Jim Anthony had last seen in New York months ago. He was the investment broker, Willis Todhunter, who had floated the mine's new stock issue. There was a meekly quiet, grocery-clerk quality about Todhunter. He seemed colorless in both complexion and manner, the kind of man you might meet a dozen times a year—without the slightest impression being made on you.

Next came Don McCorkle, not as a member of the board but as a working newspaperman reporting the conference. And finally, another vacant chair opposite McCorkle.

"Wonder what's keeping Murdock?" the wiry little editor muttered. "He's usually prompt."

"Murdock?" Jim Anthony repeated. Then he remembered what Eric Meline had told him. Michael Murdock was head of one of the largest mining corporations in the world; his company had a bigger stake in Haunted Valley copper than any other investor save Anthony himself.

"Ka-humph!" Lew Jefferson rumbled. "I say let's get on with the business at hand. We've got a quorum without Murdock."

Fargo Lane quit stroking his goatee. "And just what is the business at hand?" he inquired sardonically.

"The Black Ghost murders," Anthony said. "As a stockholder in the mine, you realize the importance of keeping the work going. As mayor and chief of police, yours is the responsibility for maintaining order. What's being done to that end?"

The former gambler smiled mirthlessly. "That puts me sort of under the gun, doesn't it?"

Anthony sensed the man's poorly concealed animosity. "Yes," he said frankly. "It does."

"Well, mister, I'll lay it on the line. Our police force is small. Conditions in this town stink. There's more gamblers and crooks and shady ladies in Haunted Valley than in any other city our size in the country. My cops have all they can do to keep an eye on the joints and dives without horning into these so-called Black Ghosts."

"Meaning you haven't even investigated the killings?"

"Meaning we did, and got nowhere—the same as the State and Federal dicks. The same as you'll get nowhere, too."

Jim Anthony caught the hidden challenge and accepted it. "I wouldn't be too sure," he advised softly. "Meantime, suppose the miners get out of control? What if there's panic, a riot?"

"Then I'd say run for cover. My cops couldn't handle it."

A squeaky, rabbitlike protest came from the colorless broker, Willis Todhunter. "Good gracious! Couldn't you wire for the militia?"

"The state militia has been taken into the United States Army," Fargo Lane sneered. "There's a war going on."

"And war demands copper," Anthony snapped. He started to add something, but the words were never spoken—because just then the room's door burst open and a freckled, panting man came pelting into the room.

HE WAS ANTHONY'S aviator friend, Tom Gentry. "Jim!" he caterwauled. "Hell's boiling over!"

"What do you mean?" the millionaire detective sprang to his feet.

"Well, you remember that mine foreman, Jake Gorchikoff? You left me guarding him so he wouldn't spread panic all over town. I kept him under wraps like you said. But then—"

"Where is that stock?" the Black Ghost demanded.

"But then what?"

"A guy barged in; said he was looking for you. Young fella, wears glasses. Chemist, he called himself. Told me his name was Steve Bannixter."

"I know Bannixter. What about him?" Anthony asked.

"He claimed he'd spotted one of the Black Ghosts right here in front of the bank building and took a shot at it. Said there wasn't any doubt he connected—but the damned ghost didn't even twitch when the bullet hit. Kept on going; vanished."

"When was this?"

"Half an hour ago, Bannixter said. Maybe more. Anyhow, while he was telling me, Gorchikoff listened—and then took a powder. Lammed when my back was turned."

"And now?"

"And now this Gorchikoff guy is stirring up trouble. Telling all his pals how the Black Ghosts have finally come up out of the tunnels to kill everybody. A mob's gathering, and they look plenty mean."

Jim Anthony's dark eyes flashed. This made twice that Steve Bannixter had turned up unexpectedly, with his appearance immediately followed by sinister developments. Down on the street you could already hear a distant surf of voices coming closer—the mutter of the mob. That droning noise held an ominous quality, a portent of trouble.

Fargo Lane toyed nervously with his goatee. "Judging by the sound, there must be five hundred miners coming. Maybe more. My cops can't stop that many. We're in for grief."

A shrill squeal of fear came from the mouselike Willis Todhunter. "Then why doesn't somebody do something? I should have stayed in New York! Things like this can't happen on Wall Street. I—I—"

Anthony quelled the investment broker with a swift look. "I suggest you take it easy. You're not hurt yet."

"But—but we own the mine. Suppose they hold us responsible for what's happened?"

"We are responsible," Anthony retorted. "And I'm shouldering that responsibility." He turned to his freckled aviator friend. "Come on, Tom, let's face this out."

Don McCorkle spoke. "What will you do, promise to shut down the mine?"

Anthony didn't answer the newspaperman's question. Instead, with Tom Gentry at his heels, he made for the door; went out to the corridor.

To reach the street it was quicker to use the rear staircase of the remodeled bank building instead of the front one. Anthony and Gentry plunged toward these back steps, the aviator lighting the way with his pocket torch.

And then, as they gained the head of the seldom-used stairs. Gentry stiffened. "Jim!" he gasped. "Look!"

There was a man sprawled before them; a well dressed, portly man whose face was blistered and blackened; whose hands resembled overcooked meat. He was dead; struck down by the same flaming horror which had slain so many miners below ground.

Jim Anthony swiftly searched the tailored coat for papers of identification; found them. Then he realized why there had been two vacant chairs at this evening's meeting of the Haunted Valley board of directors.

One chair had belonged to the murdered chief engineer, Eric Meline. The second had marked the place that should have been occupied by Michael Murdock, head of the world's biggest mining investment syndicate. But the man had been absent.

For a good reason. This dead man was Michael Murdock.

CHAPTER V

MYSTERY AND A MOB

TOM GENTRY'S FRECKLES STOOD out like red copper pennies against the sudden pallor of his face. "My God, he looks like he'd been roasted alive!"

"He was, in a sense. He was electrocuted, the same as those poor devils of miners."

"But Jim, look. He wasn't wearing a heating suit connected to live current. Hell, there ain't any electricity up here yet! Then how—?"

Anthony shook his head. "I have a theory, but I've got to prove it first." As he spoke, the growling surf of vocal sound became louder in the street below. The mob was nearing the bank building.

"Here comes trouble, Jim!" the aviator whispered.

"Right. And it must be stopped. That's my job. Meanwhile, I want you to go back to the board room—"

"And leave you to face that mob alone? Nix!"

"I can look after myself. You do as I say. Tell the board of directors about Michael Murdock, here. Have Fargo Lane guard the body; after all, he's acting chief of police. Move, now!"

Gentry turned, obeyed. And Jim Anthony sprinted downstairs into the night; took up his stand in front of the building while the oncoming miners advanced like a human tidal wave. The mob's vanguard, twenty abreast, surged relentlessly forward.

"Stop!" Anthony called. And there was a superlative quality of authority in his upraised voice; the tone of one accustomed to command—and to obedience.

The mob wavered, slowed, came to a shuffling halt.

Anthony surveyed them. "Well, men?"

A miner detached himself and stepped forth, shoulders bent, legs bowed by toil, thin grey hair rumpled. He was the foreman, Jake Gorchikoff; and with shouts, outcries, his fellow workers made him their spokesman.

"You talk for mine owners?" he demanded.

"Yes. I *am* one of the owners."

"Then I tell you what we want, py damn. You clean out Plack Ghosts plenty quick or we take over mine, plast it shut with dynamite! We take over town too, tear inside out, see? There won't pe no more Haunted Valley!"

Anthony drew himself erect, his splendid height towering over the mob. "Very well, men. You've had your say. And your demands are justified. The Black Ghosts will be cleaned out, I give you my word. The word of Jim Anthony."

That name had a startling effect, for there were few even in this remote region who had not heard of the millionaire detective's unbelievable exploits. An audible murmur went up.

Anthony pressed his advantage. "Now go to your homes, all of you. There will be no more flame-deaths among you." Secretly he wondered if he would be able to keep this promise; but in his heart there was a grim determination.

And the men believed him; displayed their confidence in the magic name of Anthony by breaking up raggedly and dispersing in little groups that wandered off into the night.

WHEN THE FINAL stragglers had gone, Anthony returned to the bank building's third floor. Here he found his fellow stockholders grouped in the rear hall, holding lanterns as they formed a circle around Michael Murdock's seared corpse.

It was Todhunter who spoke first. "Wh-what about that mob?" the colorless investment broker shrilled. "Did—did you—?"

"I sent them away. They won't make any more trouble—for a while. But there's no telling what may happen if these mysterious Black Ghosts continue their killing."

Fargo Lane hunched his shoulders. The former gambler seemed

The chartered plane arrived, bringing the two girls into a jeopardy they couldn't escape.

no longer antagonistic. There was a hint of fear in his unwinking eyes now; and even his mustache and goatee had a dispirited droop.

"Well, Anthony," he muttered, "I take off my hat to you. If you can put down a riot you can do anything. You can call on me for any help I'm able to give."

"All I ask is a free hand," the bronzed, hawk-like criminologist said. "I'm fairly familiar with conditions, now. Eric Meline told me a lot before he was dynamited; and I've learned the rest of it through observation and by talking to you men. Come on, Tom," he added to Gentry. "We've got work to do."

Together they went from the building, leaving Fargo Lane to take care of necessary formal police procedure such as sending Murdock's body to the morgue for autopsy. As for little Don McCorkle, he scurried off in the direction of the *Mining News*, speaking of getting out an extra.

As Anthony and Gentry made for their hotel, the freckled aviator hazarded a question. "Where will you start, Jim?"

"With a phone call to New York," was the terse answer. And a few moments later, in the privacy of his room, Anthony put in his long distance call.

It was the familiar voice of Gibbons, managing editor of the Anthony owned New York *Star,* that presently came back over the wire. "Yes, Jim?"

The millionaire detective gave him a brisk resume of all the happenings in Haunted Valley. Then he ended with: "I want you to contact my brokers. Have them go into the market when it opens tomorrow morning and buy Haunted Valley stock."

"Buy?" Gibbons exclaimed. "But when this riot news breaks, that stock will hit bottom! Especially with the chief engineer dead, and Michael Murdock."

"All the same, buy all that's offered. And I want a report on who else buys—and who sells. Got it?"

"Got it, Jim," Gibbons said. "Good bye and—good luck."

As he rang off, Anthony's keen ears detected a slight sound at the door of his hotel room. Like a flash he whipped out his automatic; sprang lithely to the door and yanked it open. Then his dark eyes widened.

"Well, Mr. Jefferson!"

The chunky land baron was mopping his bald brow with a handkerchief. "Ka-humph! Wanted to see you a minute, Anthony. Trust I'm not disturbing you," his voice was muffled thunder.

"Not at all," Anthony said quietly. But he wondered how long the man had been here at the door; how much of the telephone conversation he might have overheard.

JEFFERSON ENTERED, HIS manner somehow furtive. "Got some information for you. Might throw some light on Eric Meline's death, if not the others. Haven't had a chance to tell you before."

"Yes?"

The bald man lowered his rumbling voice to a whisper. "Last week Meline drew up a will."

"You think he expected to be killed?"

"Ka-humph. Don't know. Maybe. He was chief engineer. He saw others die. Man can't tell what's going to happen, these days! Anyhow, he made this will. Named me administrator without bond. Nice compliment, that."

"Quite," Anthony agreed. "But then, you were his friend."

"Sure. Ka-humph. Certainly. All the same, there's a damned funny provision in the will. I don't like it a bit. Every dime Meline owned was invested in Haunted Valley copper stock. Left the whole works to his daughter, Beth."

"What's so strange about that?"

"Nothing. But if Beth dies unmarried and without issue, you know who inherits?"

"No. Who?"

"That young chemist. Ka-humph. Steve Bannixter, that's who! Gets everything if the girl dies." By this time Jefferson had forgotten to whisper. His voice was thunderous again; you could hear it a figurative block away.

Jim Anthony scowled. Bannixter again! Could he possibly have dynamited Eric Meline's cliffside house in order to put himself a step closer to the copper stock inheritance?

The idea seemed fantastic, on the surface. Because unless the chief engineer's daughter also died, Bannixter would gain absolutely nothing. *Unless she died....*

Anthony drummed the situation over on his mind. It was difficult to conceive of the young, studious looking chemist plotting the murder of the girl as well as her father. Moreover, she was somewhere in the east, at college, according to the inscription on the photograph Meline had rescued when the wind knocked it to the floor.

And you can't kill a person over a distance of two thousand miles, when you're in Haunted Valley and your intended victim is back at Vassar!

Then, too, the theory didn't mesh with what was happening in the mine itself. If Bannixter was scheming to inherit the copper stock, he wouldn't try to sabotage the property by means of these Black Ghost visitations. That would defeat his own purpose—for if the mine shut down, the stock would be worthless.

Just the same, the chemist would bear watching. His actions had been queer, although plausibly explained. Jim Anthony decided to withhold judgment for the present.

He thanked his chunky visitor for the information. "Keep me in touch with anything else that turns up, Mr. Jefferson. We've got to work together, all of us."

"Ka-humph. Certainly. Well, I'll be seeing you."

After the man had gone, Anthony went to Tom Gentry's room at the other side of the hall. "Let's go calling, Tom."

"Where?"

"On some electrical supply stores." Together they left the hotel; but scarcely had they walked out of the main lobby when a voice called: "Mr. Anthony. Jim!"

IT WAS DON McCorkle, a smudge of ink on his face where he'd been helping set type for an extra edition of the *Mining News*. That extra edition was forgotten now, "I've got something to tell you!" he panted as he raced up.

Anthony waited expectantly.

"Meline's daughter just got into town on a chartered plane," the wiry reporter said. "And your fiancée came with her. Dolores Colquitt."

A startled frown creased Anthony's broad forehead. The presence of Beth Meline could only complicate matters, not to mention the possible jeopardy into which she was thrusting herself. As to Dolores, he could think of no explanation for her arrival; he only knew that Haunted Valley was no place for her, the way things stood now.

Even as he thought about it, a shot barked viciously from the dark alley alongside the hotel—and Tom Gentry let out a gasping grunt of pain.

CHAPTER VI

EYES THAT WATCH

ANTHONY PIVOTED, GRABBED AT his freckled friend. "Tom! You're hit!" There was a neat torn spot on the upper left sleeve of the aviator's coat, and he kept slapping at it; rubbing the flesh beneath. "I'm okay. The bullet barely nicked me. More like a burn, is all. Stings like hell."

Don McCorkle was quivering with excitement. "That slug must have been meant for you, Jim! Figure the angle; the way we were all standing—"

The wealthy criminologist was not listening. He had already bunched his sinews, hurled himself toward the alley. It was unlighted save for a thin knife of illumination that came from an exit of the hotel, little used but now slightly ajar.

In the faint glow a man was floundering around on all fours, shaking his head dizzily and trying to push himself upright the way a boxer does at the count of nine. He was a colorless, unobtrusive looking person with a dazed expression on his meek face, like an injured grocery clerk.

"Willis Todhunter!" came bursting from Anthony's lips as he leaned over the investment broker and helped him to his feet. A glassy stare was his only thanks.

"Want to go back to New York," Todhunter mumbled. "Not safe here. Never should have left Wall Street...."

Anthony shook him. "Snap out of it. What happened?"

"Huh? Oh. Yes. I remember now. I was coming out of the hotel by the side door. I thought I heard a shot. Then somebody rushed past me, knocked me down. I think I got kicked on the head." He rubbed a bruise at his temple.

Anthony left him; went belting through the alley. It gave access to the next street, which was fairly well populated with a cross section of Haunted Valley's night-time strollers: riff-raff, percentage girls on the make, miners sauntering from one saloon to the next. Nobody was running, though. You couldn't see anyone who looked as if he might be trying for a getaway.

Lips compressed, eyes bleak, Anthony retraced his course into the alley; again faced Todhunter. "What did the guy look like, the one that knocked you down?"

"I don't know. It happened too fast."

"Was he tall? Or chunky? Young? Or middle-aged?"

"I didn't see him. He clipped me and I went down. I d-don't like this town, Mr. Anthony. It's too rough!"

"It's all of that," the millionaire agreed grimly. "The quicker you leave, the safer you'll be. And I know a couple of young women I intend giving the same advice to. Better go to your room and stay there."

THEN HE LEFT the man and went out of the alley; rejoined Gentry and McCorkle.

"Find anybody, Jim?" the freckled flyer asked.

"No. How's your arm?"

"It's okay."

"Then I think we'd better go see Dolores and the Meline girl. I must persuade them to beat it—if I can." Anthony turned to the newspaperman. "Where are they staying?"

McCorkle furnished directions. It seemed that Eric Meline had owned a residence in town as well as his cabin on the cliff. It was this town house to which the slain engineer's daughter had gone. The address was just a few blocks distant.

Jim shot, but too late to save the land baron from the Black Ghosts' roasting.

"What a layout!" Tom Gentry said a few minutes later when he and Anthony reached the residence. Awed, he blinked at the faded splendor before him.

Surrounded by an iron-railed yard, the house was a survival of Haunted Valley's former greatness; a rococo relic of architectural bad taste, covered with gingerbread ornamentation now sadly in need of paint. Despite its run-down condition, though, it still possessed a gloomy dignity.

Dolores Colquitt opened the door to Anthony's knock. "Jim!" his lovely fiancée exclaimed in delight. And for a moment she nestled fragrantly in his embrace.

Presently he released her; stared at her soberly. "Why did you come, Dolores?"

"Beth asked me to. She was looking for you, and I told her you'd left New York to come out here. So she prevailed on me to charter a plane—"

"You know Beth Meline, then?"

"But of course, darling. For several years." Then she added: "Wait. I'll go get her."

Anthony and Tom glanced about the massive library in which they found themselves. The walls were paneled, dark; the ceiling high and mottled by shadows from a time-dulled crystal chandelier whose light was insufficient for so large a room. The effect was somber, brooding.

But the place seemed to take on a brighter air when Dolores returned with Beth Meline in tow. Beauty brightens any surroundings; and Dolores' startling loveliness was matched by the wistful, fragile beauty of the murdered engineer's daughter.

"This is Beth Meline," Dolores said. "Jim Anthony. Tom Gentry."

Beth's smile was wan, unhappy. Her hair seemed to have been spun out of refined gold, and her shimmering blue negligee served only to intensify that golden quality and the pale, translucent purity of her complexion. Tears hinted themselves in her blue eyes as she came forward.

THE GLANCE SHE gave Tom Gentry was only casual and passing; but the aviator gulped ecstatically to think she had even noticed him. He couldn't seem to keep his hypnotized gaze away from the sleek curves of her hips and the swelling sweetness of her firm breast where it was outlined by the clinging silk negligee. He was fascinated by the faint, rhythmic surges that stirred it with her breathing.

Then he snapped himself out of it. This jane wasn't for him, he told himself. Her entire attention was for Jim Anthony; that was all too obvious!

"Thank you for looking me up so soon," she murmured gratefully to the wealthy criminologist.

"Not at all," Anthony said. "But why have you come here to Haunted Valley? It's no place for a girl—especially with all this trouble brewing."

"I came because I had to. You see, two days ago I received a letter from my f-father. It worried me so much, I finally decided to visit you in New York and have a talk with you."

"But in the meantime, I'd left."

"Yes," she said. "Then I ran into Dolores and asked her to charter a plane. It wasn't until we were halfway across the continent that we got a radio flash about dad being… d-dead." For an instant her voice broke.

Dolores slipped an arm around her waist. "Now, Beth. Mustn't go to pieces," she soothed the younger girl.

"I know. I'm trying to be brave. But it's all so… horrible! And the letter my father wrote to me… as if he had known what was g-going to happen…!"

Anthony said quietly: "May I see the letter?"

She delved under the negligee; pulled a folded sheet of paper from her rounded bosom. A hint of her fragrance still clung to the paper as Anthony read it.

The murdered engineer had written:

"…things are going from bad to worse here. The killings continue, and my own investigations have led nowhere. I have one suspicion, but it is almost too fantastic for belief. Meanwhile, I myself may be in danger. Should anything happen to me, I want you to make contact at once with James Anthony at the Waldorf-Anthony Hotel, New York. Persuade him to take up the investigation, if you can.

Love, Your dad."

WHEN HE FINISHED reading the note, Anthony's eyes were glowing with a weird light. "So your father knew he was marked for murder. And after he wrote you this letter, he decided to contact me personally."

"Y-yes, it looks that way," Beth answered wearily. "But they k-killed him in spite of everything…."

"He'll be avenged, I promise you. Right now, though, we have your own safety to consider. I want you and Dolores to leave here right away."

The blonde girl's eyes widened into azure lakes. "But I can't do that. At least not until I've seen Steve."

"Steve who?" Anthony rapped out sharply.

"Why, Steve Bannixter, of course. We're engaged."

This news came as a shock to the smitten Tom Gentry, who had been wondering how he might get better acquainted with this golden haired angel. Tom's disappointment showed in his face.

Anthony, too, was startled; but for a different reason. Beth, if she really loved the young chemist, would only be antagonized to learn that her intended husband was under suspicion. Loyalty to Bannixter might cause her to work against Anthony, rather than with him.

Therefore, it would be better to keep those suspicions dark for the moment. Anthony summoned a smile. "So you're engaged to Steve. He's a lucky fellow!"

The girl blushed. "Thank you."

"But all the same, I wish you'd reconsider and get out of Haunted Valley for a while. You may be in danger."

"Danger—?"

"Of death."

Her breast rose and fell swiftly. "Who would—?"

"I can't tell you that, yet. I may be wrong about it, as a matter of fact. Anyhow, if you take my advice, you'll go."

She shook her head stubbornly. "Not until I've seen Steve." She added: "I've got to know what he thinks about dad's d-death. Whom he suspects. What he's doing to track down the killers. He was dad's closest friend, you know."

Anthony realized the futility of arguing with her. "Have you contacted him yet?"

"No. There's no phone in this old house."

"Very good. If you won't leave town, then promise me one thing. Stay tight here; don't go out until I say okay. I'll try to find Steve and send him to you."

"I promise," Beth agreed, looking somewhat puzzled.

Anthony turned to Dolores. "Keep a close watch. Don't let anyone in unless you're sure who it is." Then he kissed her and left the old residence with Tom Gentry at his heels.

IN THE OUTER darkness the freckled aviator mumbled discontentedly. "I meet Miss America in person, and what happens? She's already tied up with some other jerk!"

"Bannixter may be a good man. Eric Meline seemed to think so. Meline gave him full credit for the mine-refrigeration idea—and left him quite a fortune in case Beth should die before they could be married."

"You don't say!"

"Yes," Anthony nodded. Then he tensed. "Take it easy! Keep on walking toward the street, but look over toward that clump of bushes by the house."

Gentry stared. "I don't see any thing." This was because he didn't possess the visual acuity of his millionaire friend; the Hindu trick of seeing in darkness.

Anthony whispered: "Three men are crouching over there. Hiding. Watching the residence. Come on, let's get 'em!" And he uncoiled himself into surging motion.

The shadowy shapes saw him coming. They burst from their concealment, vaulted the iron fence and went sprinting down the side street.

"Stay here!" Anthony commanded Gentry. "Guard the girls. My hunch was right; they're in danger!" Then be plunged in pursuit of the three vanishing men.

CHAPTER VII

INTO THE TRAP

THEY HAD ALMOST A full block's start on him; but they lacked his superb speed, his stalwart stamina, his tremendous endurance. Even so, he closed the gap but slowly; for he was running on silent strides, keeping to the shadows in order to make his quarry think they were not being followed.

Presently they slackened their speed, glanced back. Anthony lunged sidewise into an areaway just in time to escape being noticed. When he peered out, he saw that the trio were merely jog-trotting now. By and by they slowed to a brisk walk. It was evident that they thought themselves out of danger.

But Anthony continued to trail them implacably, as unnoticed and as noiseless as one of his Indian ancestors stalking game in the forest. He was making no effort to overtake them now. It was not part of his plan to close with them here on the street. His fey Irish blood had developed within him a hypersensitivity to impressions, a keen sixth sense which told him that these three men were mere underlings to the unknown criminal responsible for the reign of dark terror in Haunted Valley.

Therefore he decided upon surveillance rather than capture— hoping they might lead him to some rendezvous where he could come to grips with their murderous leader.

And his strategy bore fruit. Up ahead, the trio kept going in the direction of the town's lower end. Presently they disappeared up a narrow stairway alongside the entrance to a shoddy saloon.

Anthony angled across the street, observing the building from the shadows. After a few minutes he saw a light slash into life at one of the second floor windows, to be immediately shut off by a drawn shade. He smiled grimly to himself, knowing that he'd run his quarry to earth.

The saloon itself was a mean affair, nothing like the flashier joints on the main stem. Very little noise came from the interior, and there were no drunken loafers hanging around the entrance. In a little while Anthony stole across the street and investigated the stairway.

Nobody stood guard at the bottom, and there was no light in the hallway above. He hesitated a brief instant; then ascended the steps as soundlessly as a wraith.

At the top he was confronted by a new problem. There was a closed door barring his further progress, and when he tried the knob, he discovered it to be locked.

This was just a temporary check, though. From an inner pocket of his coat, Anthony drew his prized steels. A moment's manipulation by his deft fingers and the door's bolt silently slid unlatched.

HE SWUNG THE portal open a bare inch and peered into the solid darkness beyond—a darkness, however, which was not complete enough to baffle his dilated pupils. Before him stretched a long hall, like a hotel corridor, with rooms opening from it on either side.

On catlike tread he moved forward, came to a right-angle turn and perceived a thin ribbon of light issuing from beneath a door. Swiftly orienting himself, he realized that this was the room at whose window the light had briefly gleamed when he observed the building from the street below.

Cautiously he placed an ear against the door's panel. Although the woodwork was thick, heavy, Anthony's superb concentration enabled him to distinguish what was being said within the room in spite of the low, guarded tones being employed.

Three men were talking. "Everything's going okay," one said. "Quit being jittery. Another couple of bump-offs and you couldn't make a miner stay in this valley if you handed him seven million bucks."

A second voice, nervously brittle, answered: "It's this guy Anthony that worries me. I wonder if it was him that spotted us casing that old house?"

"Maybe," the first man retorted. "So what? We shook him off, didn't we?"

"Yeah, but I've heard about him. He's a tough customer."

A third voice chimed in sardonically. "He'll need all of the toughness he's got when one of the boys burn him down." Then, in a speculative tone: "Is the boss comin' here?"

"You know he ain't. He never goes no place where there's danger."

"You're telling me! I'd like to see him just once. I'd sure like to know who he is."

In the corridor, Jim Anthony frowned. It looked as if he had drawn a blank by trailing this trio of thugs. Not only was there no chance that their mysterious boss would come here; but apparently these men didn't even know the identity of the fiend they were serving!

The first voice chuckled inside the room. "You'll have your chance to see him when we meet in the tunnel."

"How come? He'll have his mask on, like always."

"All you gotta do is grab the mask off his face—if you've got the guts."

"And have him burn me?" there was shocked fear in the exclamation. "Not me! I don't crave to get croaked."

"Me neither, pal. I want to stay friends with the boss. You know something?"

"What?"

"I betcha we'd be sittin' plenty pretty if we could snatch this Anthony guy and turn him over to His Nibs."

"Yah!" came a scoffing jeer. "Fat chance!"

The frown which had creased Jim Anthony's forehead in the dark corridor suddenly faded out. The conversation's trend had given him an idea; a possible means whereby he might discover the identity of the leader of the Black Ghosts.

TRUE, THIS SCHEME would involve serious personal peril. He realized that he was dealing with a gang that had already committed countless killings; men who certainly wouldn't hesitate to add another to their list of victims.

But Anthony had made a career out of what had started as a mere hobby: the hunting of criminals, the tracking down of murderers. In the course of that career he had risked his own life numberless times before—and he was willing to do it again if it would bring him face to face with the mysterious arch-plotter who was directing the sabotage of Haunted Valley.

He considered the problem swiftly but thoroughly. His principal task would be to permit himself to he captured with the least chance of his captors killing him in the process. The men inside that room were nervous, on edge. They had proved this by running away from the Meline house. Their trigger fingers might react instinctively, without thought.

Well, that was the gamble he had to take. And he could reduce the odds by means of a certain subterfuge. He grasped the doorknob, more or less expecting it to be locked. It wasn't, though; so he eased it with infinite slowness, making no sound.

Then, suddenly, with a mighty smash, he shoved the door inward. Following this, he pretended to dive over the threshold—and he faked a clumsiness of foot as he moved. He pretended to trip; and then he toppled headlong, face forward, so that his long body was perfectly prone on the floor.

The fall seemed to have stunned him, for he didn't move as the three occupants of the room surged to their feet with guns jerked and aimed. But no shots were fired, for to all appearances Anthony was inert and helpless. He even groaned a little.

He heard a rasping command. "Lay where you are, chum. If you move you get drilled to hellangone, see?"

Anthony's only answer was another groan.

"Fan him for a gun," were the next words he heard. Then he felt himself being frisked, and his automatic was lifted from inside his coat. Then he was rolled over, roughly, so that he lay sprawled on his back.

"Jeest!" one of the three men gasped in amazement. "You guys know who this is?"

"Naw. Who?"

"Ain't you never saw his picture in the newspapers? Cripes, a fortune just dropped in our laps. This is Jim Anthony!"

CHOKED OATHS OF consternation sounded as the thugs realized the importance of their captive. Anthony kept his eyes closed, but he could visualize the expressions on all three faces; first amazement, then slowly dawning glee.

"But where the hell did he come from?" a voice cried.

"He musta followed us from that house we was watchin'!" came a shrewd answer. "I betcha he was leanin' against this door here, and it wasn't quite latched. So he falls in the room."

"What about that door at the head of the stairs? You was supposed to lock it when we come in. How'd he get past it?"

"Who cares? Maybe I didn't throw the bolt all the way. And so what? We got the guy. That's the main thing. You was sayin' a minute ago how you wished you could snatch Jim Anthony and take him to the boss. Well, you get your wish."

Anthony feigned returning consciousness. He blinked his eyes, quivered, tried to sit up. "Wh-where am I?"

His three captors were grouped around him, alert and ready to shoot if he made a wrong move. Now, for the first time, he had an opportunity to study them.

They were brutal, coarse-featured men; all three of them. Unintelligent, but all the more dangerous for that reason. Cunning, with the devious shrewdness of the born criminal. The kind of men who kill for pay; hired gunsels, the scrapings of the underworld. The murderous tools of some unknown master-mind!

Two of them leaned down, yanked Anthony upright. He swayed as if his legs had turned to rubber, and he made his expression completely blank.

"Wh-where am I?" he asked again, dully.

"You're at the side door of hell, pal, that's where you are! You've butted into somebody else's business once too often—and you won't never do it no more."

"But I—I—"

They shoved him into a chair. "Button your trap or we'll bat your teeth down your throat."

"Are you going to—to kill me?" he tried to make his voice sound fearful.

"Damned right But not here. That'd leave us with a stiff on our hands and no place to get rid of it. When you go outa this joint, it'll be under your own power, see? Until we get to where we can croak you nice and comfortable."

Then a length of cord was produced and Anthony was expertly bound to the chair.

CHAPTER VIII

HELL'S ICE-BOX

ONLY BRIEFLY WAS JIM Anthony puzzled by this procedure of being trussed hand and foot. Through scraps of grunted conversation dropped by the three thugs, he soon understood the reason for all that was happening.

They were not scheduled to meet their mysterious leader until later. Meantime, the whole night lay before them.

One of them slipped from the room; returned with three bottles of whiskey and a deck of cards. Then the trio settled down to kill time at stud poker, using matches for chips and taking occasional swigs of liquor.

The endless hours dragged. It was well toward dawn when one of the players threw down his cards in disgust. "Hell! I just thought of somethin'!"

"Yeah? Like what?"

"Well, we was supposed to grab off that Meline dame, remember? Only we got scared away."

"Aw, quit worryin' about it. The boss won't bawl us out for fallin' down on that job. Not when we bring him this Jim Anthony guy."

"But that's just the point. Here we've had Anthony under control all night. We coulda gone back and snatched the jane without no trouble at all."

"Bigahd, you got somethin' there! Maybe we still got time to take care of it— Jeest! Why ain't you lugs been lookin' at your watches?"

"Huh? Whatcha mean?"

"I mean we're already late for our meetin' with His Nibs! We got so interested in that damn' card game we forgot to keep tabs on the time!"

"Then we won't be able to grab the wren?"

"Not now! We gotta get goin'! Come on, move!"

All three leaped into motion. They unfastened Anthony; kept a gun at his spine as they prodded him from the room. His expression was apathetic, listless; but his brain was seething with anticipation. Soon, now, he would be conducted into the presence of the man he was after; the leader of the Black Ghost gang. It was the thing he had been waiting for.

DOWNSTAIRS, THE STREETS of Haunted Valley were silent and deserted as the first dirty grey streaks of dawn marred the eastern horizon's blue velvet darkness. Anthony was steered into an unlighted alleyway, his captors cursing as they stumbled over the rough paving. Forward the compact group moved, until the alley itself ended.

Here the town of Haunted Valley straggled to its outskirts and petered away in scattered shacks, ramshackle cabins. Beyond lay the sloping foothills, with a weed-choked path dimly marked by infrequent travel. Anthony's mind measured the minutes with uncanny accuracy as he shuffled forward.

By checking that elapsed time with the number of steps he took, he could gain a fairly correct estimate of the distance covered. And, since he knew the direction of his journey, he'd have little difficulty in locating this same course again if it became necessary.

And if he lived!

The three thugs were not entirely stupid, however. They must have considered some such possibility; for presently they halted long enough to tie a blindfold around Anthony's eyes. Now he was no longer able to see his surroundings.

He could sense the slope of the ground, though. And he guessed where he was being taken. He had been walking for at least a half hour; perhaps even a few minutes more than that. Therefore, he was somewhere near the mine. And yet, when the trail twisted back upon itself, it seemed that he must be headed away from the main shaft.

In consequence, he concluded that there was probably an old tunnel or drift which ran from that main shaft to an opening on the side of the hill. Confirming his deductions, he was suddenly commanded to halt.

"Almost the end of the line for you, smart guy," a voice remarked unpleasantly. Then there was the sound of metal rasping against rusty metal: a key being fumbled toward the lock of some sort of door that seemed made entirely of iron or steel. Oiled hinges whispered as this portal was swung open, and a breath of dank, warmly moist air swept against Anthony's cheeks.

Again he was prodded forward, his sensitive hearing acutely attuned to the echoing footfalls of his companions and himself. He knew that he was in a subterranean passageway, but the temperature was not frigid, as it was in the main sector of the mine. Instead, it was clammy and fetid.

Progress was slow, especially at one point where the flooring seemed to be wooden and somehow springy, resilient. Here, too, Anthony heard a curious buzzing and hissing sound which presently receded behind him as he went onward.

Then, at long last, his captors brought him up short. One of them turned off the flashlight that had been used to guide the way through the underground maze as another whipped away his blindfold and flicked an electric switch.

ANTHONY BLINKED AS raw incandescents glowed harshly overhead. He was in a square chamber hewn from the solid rock; a room fitted with a rough table and a few crude chairs. There was a fragment of paper on the table, and one of the thugs spotted it immediately.

"Damn! We missed the boss. Here's a note from him!"

"What's it say?"

"He's sore. He expected us to have the Meline jane here when he showed up. But there wasn't nobody here at all. Jeest, we'll catch hell for this!"

"Yeah, unless we go get the doll right now. That'll fix it."

"Maybe. But what about this Anthony guy?"

Three pairs of hard, cruel eyes turned on Jim Anthony. And in spite of his iron nerve, a little shiver ran down his spine as he faced that ruthless inspection. These were cold, calculating killers; men who didn't know the meaning of mercy.

One thug spoke harshly. "Wish we had some of them heaters here. I'd burn him just for the fun of watchin' him shrivel."

"But we ain't got none. And we ain't got time to play around. Besides, if we was to burn him, the boss might not never believe it was Anthony."

"Yeah, that's true. Well, what'll we do, put a slug through his conk?"

"Nix! You know the rule. No shootin' in this part of the mine, never at no time. Somebody might hear it in them frozen tunnels and come snoopin' around, maybe find out about how we're usin' this old drift."

"Hell, there ain't nobody workin' in the mine now. They all got scared out."

"All the same, the rule is no shootin'. It sticks. But look. We can tie this guy up and shove him in one of the ice tunnels. He'll freeze to death before long. And he'll look like himself when the boss checks up."

"Swell idea!" And all three crooks closed in.

It was Anthony's first impulse to resist. He had permitted himself to be captured in order to confront the man he was after; the brains of the Black Ghost mob. In this he had failed, and he saw no sense in remaining a prisoner.

But the thugs seemed to sense his thoughts, for one of them smashed him viciously on the skull from behind, without warning. The blow didn't knock him unconscious; but he was stunned enough to sag for an instant. That instant was sufficient for his enemies to rope his wrists and ankles.

It was while they were at the task that he called his splendid recuperative powers into full play. Then he was lifted bodily and carried to a rusty iron door, like a big bulkhead studded by rivets. The door was unlocked, opened, and Anthony felt himself being carried into the tunnel on the other side.

A SOLID WALL of sub-zero coldness impacted upon him; gnawed at his very marrow. And he understood at once why those other passageways had been warm, fetid. All the mine's old exits had been carefully equipped with hermetically sealed iron bulkheads when Eric Meline and Steve Bannixter had started their project to freeze the water which flooded the lower levels. These bulkheads would seal in the cold, and prevent the wasting of costly refrigeration on galleries no longer productive.

But Anthony was now in a tunnel section where the freezing temperature was still maintained, although it had an appearance of abandonment in the rays from a flashlight carried by one of the thugs. Apparently the copper ore had been exhausted out of this drift a month or so ago, and all work had then been stopped here.

Consequently when the Black Ghosts began their murderous operations during the past couple of weeks they had felt secure in making their secret headquarters in the warmer passages and galleries beyond this particular tunnel's bulkhead door. No miners would be working anywhere near their hideout, which they could enter from the hillside opening. And they had full access to the mine itself by means of this more recently abandoned passageway.

Eventually it, too, would be sealed off to save refrigeration; but that had not yet been done. Hence it made a perfect set-up for the death they were planning for Jim Anthony.

They lugged him forward through the frigid gallery, dumping him presently onto a pile of loose rock and rubble. A gag was thrust into his mouth. "Not that yelling would help you," came the jeering taunt. "Nobody would hear you but the devil, and he don't give a damn!" Then the trio left him there, taking the light with them. Anthony was alone in the chill darkness, with only his thoughts for company.

CHAPTER IX

SNAKES IN HELL

HE SQUIRMED AS THE icy air seeped through his clothing to numb his sinews. It would only be a question of time until this numbness crept into his very brain, he realized. Then he would fall into that sleeplike coma from which there would be no awakening.

If he intended to do anything about freeing himself, that effort must come before the chill robbed his muscles of their tremendous strength. Already his fingers were beginning to stiffen.

He tested the ropes which held his wrists, trying to get all the stretch possible. The attempt was futile. But at least it restored some of the circulation to his hands and arms; and then he set to work in deadly earnest.

By jack-knifing his body, he was able to get his fingers on the cord that was looped about his ankles. He plucked at the cruelly tight knots, which would never have yielded to any ordinary strength. In fact, there was a while when Anthony began to think that even his own superlative muscular development would prove unequal to the task. The cold had robbed him of a measure of his dexterity, and his doubled-up position was both awkward and painful.

He persisted, though. He kept at it, long past the time when all feeling had fled from his hands. A certain slippery quality of the rope told him his fingertips were bleeding; and still he worked. He had to get free, he kept telling himself. Those thugs were on their way to kidnap Beth Meline—and they might perhaps capture Dolores Colquitt as well, if for no other reason than the fact that the two girls were together.

Tom Gentry, of course, had been left to guard them. But Tom, for all his courage, would be outnumbered three to one. He must have help. The help which only Jim Anthony could give!

And so Anthony struggled at his fetters, while the freezing atmosphere congealed his veins. In solid blackness he worked on the knots—and at last they gave way.

His ankles were free!

He swayed drunkenly to his feet, panting from his exertions. Then, moving blindly, he found the tunnel's wall. A jagged edge of stone jutted under his searching fingers, sharp enough for the purpose he now had in mind.

Desperately he began sawing his wrist-ropes back and forth against the rough projection, oblivious to the pain that arrowed through him when he missed connections and the jagged rock rasped upon his raw flesh, tiny droplets of blood oozed from these gashes in his wrists, but he paid them no heed.

He kept sawing away; and in the end, the last frayed strand of rope snapped apart.

TEN SWIFT TIMES he clapped his palms together, until a measure of feeling returned to his lacerated, frost-numbed fingers. The sharp splatting sound bounced curious, thin echoes back at him from the unseen passage walls; and he got a sudden idea from this natural phenomenon.

It was impossible—for even his eyes to discern anything in these tunnels so completely devoid of the slightest vestige of light. But he could hear. And he remembered how the pilots of steamboats in inland Alaskan waters sometimes guided their craft through impenetrable fog by taking advantage of certain acoustical laws.

The system was simple enough. These steamer captains tooted their steam whistles, then listened for the bouncing echoes. By judging the time it took for the echoes to return, a pilot could know exactly how far he was from the mountainous shore. Thus he would steer a safe channel course.

That same method came to Jim Anthony's aid now. He started walking; clapped his palms every few steps. And his super-keen hearing measured the swift echoes which returned from either side, so that he could move forward at a brisk pace in solid darkness with no risk of smashing into walls or obstructions.

Time! That was the element he needed. Time to escape from this frigid, stygian underground trap; time to reach Beth Meline's house before it was attacked!

Onward he strode, guided solely by his ears. Presently the echoes of his clapping took on a different quality, and he knew he was approaching some sort of dead end.

That would be the iron bulkhead door, of course; the doorway to those warmer galleries beyond, where the Black Ghosts held their rendezvous with the arch criminal who employed them. Would there be any of the gang in that farther tunnel now? Would Anthony walk straight into their waiting hands?

He had to risk that possibility. He extended his arms before him, feeling now for the bulkhead. At last he encountered it and felt its clammy, icy surface very carefully for a handle of some kind. He shivered when he considered the possibility that his captors might have locked the door from their side....

Well, he still had his faithful steels in a secret pocket of his coat. With them, he could pick any lock ever devised. And as it turned out, he found no necessity to use them. Under his pressure the bulkhead swung silently open.

As he moved it, though, he had a queer feeling that it was the wrong door; that it was narrower than the one through which he had been carried a while ago.

But at least it was an exit; and a gush of warm, moist air rushed out to greet him, informing him that he'd reached an unfrozen gallery—regardless of whether or not it was the one in which those thugs had slugged him and tied him up.

He shut the bulkhead behind him and clapped his way forward once more. When he had traveled at least two hundred yards, the echoing splats again took on a different quality; as if the passageway had widened into a rectangular chamber.

Here Anthony paused, allowing warmth to soak into his flesh. Then he found one wall and, by feeling his way, made a complete circuit of the subterranean room. Presently his groping fingers encountered the one thing he'd hoped to find.

A light-switch!

HE FLICKED IT, and blinding brilliance rewarded him. The instant his eyes became accustomed to this glare, he stared about him. An amazed, muffled cry leaped to his lips.

This, definitely, was not the chamber where he'd been bludgeoned. As his sixth sense had told him, he had mistakenly opened a different bulkhead; had entered an old cross-tunnel. And by a stroke of Anthony luck, he had stumbled into a terrifically important discovery!

There were high shelves all about him, and upon these shelves he saw numbers of black heating suits. In many respects they were similar to those worn by the copper miners; but in addition to being black, they also had full masks attached to their cowls, and they seemed heavier, thicker.

This, then, was the room where the Black Ghosts donned their weird garb before setting forth on their errands of murder.

Anthony sprang to one of the shelves, yanked down a suit and scrutinized it intently. The shoulders, back and legs were thickly padded and curiously lumpy. He ripped some of the padding open and whistled soundlessly at what he saw.

Each small lump was a flat drycell battery. There were hundreds of them, each carrying a potential of a volt and a half—and each connected in series to the next by an intricate network of wiring. In other words, any one of these black heating suits was a powerful battery capable of discharging perhaps three thousand volts; maybe more.

Anthony fully realized that the resistance of the average human body is around fifty thousand ohms, and that a man can safely withstand only a fraction of an ampere. But if you came in contact with a charge such as these black suits could produce, the effect would be instantly fatal. Driven by the enormous voltage, this much current would kill—and it would also sear and blister, as those murdered miners had been cooked by the mere touch of the electrode with the insulated handle which was attached to each black garment.

No wonder that pointed electrode had seemed like a finger of fire! No wonder the Black Ghosts could strike wherever they went, without need to plug their suits into a power line! No wonder Michael Murdock had been roasted to death on the newly added top floor of the bank building, where there was no electricity at all!

Nor did the fantastic truth end there. Each black suit was equipped in front with the woven metal material used for bullet-proof vests, thereby protecting its wearer from throat down to knees against gunshots.

Anthony scowled, remembering Steve Bannixter's story about encountering a Black Ghost outside the bank building and firing a shot that had no effect. In the light of present knowledge, the young chemist's claim might possibly be true. Maybe he had seen the murderer of Michael Murdoch emerging from the building. Maybe it had been Murdock's killer that Bannixter had shot at! The thing sounded plausible, now.

But who had designed these black heating suits? What fiendish brain directed the killers who wore them?

These, and a hundred other questions swirled through Jim Anthony's mind during the few precious seconds it had taken him to examine the padded garment. Then he realized he had no more seconds to waste. He must escape from the mine—quickly!

An ugly thought struck him. Thus far, his luck had held. But suppose he encountered some of the murder gang as he searched for the exit? Would he dare stop and give battle, when time was so valuable?

There are occasions when subterfuge is the better part of valor; and this was one of those occasions. A daring plan came full-blown into Anthony's mind; and he acted upon it swiftly. He slipped into a Black Ghost, closed the zipper fastening. From another shelf he grabbed a .38 revolver and a flashlight out of a box piled full. Then he lumbered clumsily toward the passage which led at right angles from the chamber.

This short cross-tunnel soon took another right angle turn; and presently it widened out upon a square room which Anthony immediately recognized. This was where the three thugs had bashed him over the head, tied him up.

Now he had his bearings!

From here, he needed only to follow the long gallery which eventually led to the hidden hillside exit. A sense of frantic urgency prodded him onward. As nearly as he could calculate it, almost an hour had fled since he had been dumped in that frozen stope and left to die. It had taken him that long to free himself and to find his way to this point.

An hour! In that length of time, the gunsels could have gone to Beth Meline's house and back again.

"But not with Beth and Dolores!" he whispered. "If they had kidnaped the girls, they would bring them here. I'd see them as they came into the tunnel. It can't have happened—yet!"

He kept going, his speed hampered by the awkward rig that encased him.

And now, dead ahead, there was a peculiar sound; a continued buzzing, hissing noise such as he had heard when he was first brought into the passageway with his eyes blindfolded. Sweating in the tunnel's dank heat, weighted down by the heavy black costume, Anthony flashed his torch-beam before him.

"Good God!" he gasped.

He recalled having come over one section where the flooring had seemed to be wooden and springy. Now he saw the reason, and it held him spellbound for an instant. Horror crawled through him, mingled with red rage.

There was a pit across the full width of the passage, where in some early day the miners had begun to sink a shaft, only to abandon the project when it was but ten or twelve feet deep. Now, to bridge this chasm, narrow planking had been placed from one side to the other. When you walked on the planks, they were springy under your feet; and if you happened to make a misstep, you would topple into the shaft itself.

Not that the fall would be fatal. *But the entire bottom of this yawning hole was alive with rattlesnakes!*

THEY WRITHED AND rattled and hissed in coiled masses when Anthony sprayed light down on them, as if someone had combed the countryside for the vicious reptiles and tossed them all into the deep trap.

And trap it really was. The cunning brain behind the Black Ghost killings had also devised this weird pitfall. Should any interloper accidentally happen into the tunnel and attempt to explore it in the darkness, he would inevitably tumble into the gruesome reptilian snare. Poison fangs would make short work of him, if that happened!

The thing was hellishly clever. Only in this warm section of the mine could it he worked; for in the refrigerated galleries, the rattlesnakes would become torpid, dormant, harmless. But here they were concentrated destruction.

Jim Anthony had faced crime and criminals in many forms; but he had never encountered as ruthless and fiendish a killer as the one he now hunted. Gripping himself, he walked across the narrow planks with sure-footed strides, wondering how he had ever made it when blindfolded. It was with a distinct feeling of relief that he reached hard rock flooring on the far side and increased his pace.

The exit was not far away now, he knew. And the sun would be almost an hour high. Suddenly, straight ahead, he saw a glimmer of yellow daylight which told him that the hillside mouth of the drift was open, its iron door ajar.

And then, as he approached it, this light was abruptly blotted out by a weird, cumbersome figure. It was a Black Ghost that stood guard at the entrance!

Anthony gripped his gun; gave silent thanks for the impulse which had caused him to don a similar costume. Thus disguised, he might get past that sentry without being challenged. Boldly he strode forward.

A muffled oath came from beneath the other figure's masking hood. "Hey, what are *you* doin' here? You know we was ordered to keep out of the mine while that Meline wren and her girl friend are bein' held here along with the freckled guy."

Sickened rage welled into Anthony's heart. He was too late! Dolores and Beth and Gentry had already been kidnaped, brought into the mine! But they could not have entered through this particular tunnel or Anthony would have seen them; could have made an attempt to rescue them from their captors. Therefore, he realized the murder gang must have still another secret entrance and underground hideout in addition to this one.

The black-clad sentry went on talking. "There'll be searchin' parties huntin' them people soon. That's why we ain't supposed to be bargin' around the works. Too risky."

Anthony schooled his voice to a growling mumble. "Okay, okay. I'm leavin', ain't I?" Then he essayed a casual question. "Where is His Nibs holdin' them janes and the aviator?"

The instant he uttered the words, he knew he'd made a mistake. The sentry peered at him through eyeslits in his mask. "That's a hell of a funny thing for you to ask. Who are you? Let's have your number."

"Six," Anthony hazarded quickly. It was another blunder.

"Six, huh? That's my number, damn you! You're a phoney!" And the guard raised his dread, insulated electrode; pointed it. In another instant, a crackling blue arc of death would flame from its metal tip.

Anthony's razor-sharp reflexes jumped him sidewise. But even in this moment of peril he remembered that the front of his assailant's black suit was bullet-proof. So he fired at the man's unprotected knee.

His slug kicked the Black Ghost's leg out from under him and the man went down, twisting, yowling. As he fell, his death dealing electrode jammed under him and hellish fire erupted from it. Before Anthony's very eyes the man shriveled and cooked and died, his seared flesh issuing wisps of nauseous smoke from inside the black suit.

Anthony shuddered despite his iron nerves. Then, swiftly, he peeled himself out of his own costume and plunged from the tunnel into the clean brightness of the morning.

CHAPTER X

FRUITLESS QUEST

WITH NO KNOWLEDGE OF any other secret entrance to the copper workings, Jim Anthony realized the uselessness of conducting a single-handed search for Dolores, Beth and Tom. He might hunt all day for a hidden passageway without finding it. Such an exit could be here on this hillside or it could be on the slope of some other foothill—of which there were dozens.

One thing was certain. The prisoners were not in this sector of the mine. To locate them would be a task for many searchers, not just one. Help must be enlisted!

It was a good mile downhill to the valley, then upward again to the mine's main shaft house. Anthony sprinted every step of the way with the trained ease of a cross-country runner and the speed of a specialist in the hundred yard dash. But when he finally reached the cluster of bleached buildings which marked the principal diggings, he found them silent and deserted.

In the sinister stillness he turned, began racing in the direction of town. The pace he set for himself would have brought collapse to a lesser man; and even Anthony was winded as he came in sight of the *Mining News*.

He burst into the office. "McCorkle!"

The wiry little newspaperman was on duty after a sleepless night. "Jim! Where've you been? What's happened?"

Anthony outlined the situation in terse phrases. He finished with: "So we've got to form searching parties. That mine must be combed until we find Tom and the girls. They may have been left to freeze, as I was!"

"I'll phone Fargo Lane and tell him to meet us at the shaft house with some of his picked cops," McCorkle answered. And he dialed his telephone.

When the call had been made, Anthony spoke again. "I'll need maps of the entire mine. Not only the galleries now in use, but the abandoned ones. Can you sketch them?"

"Not from memory. But Steve Bannixter can." Once more McCorkle used his phone.

Within ten minutes the studious looking young chemist dashed into the newspaper office. "Is something wrong?"

"Plenty," Anthony growled, repeating what he had told McCorkle a few minutes before.

Bannixter's eyes widened behind his horn rimmed spectacles. "Beth... kidnaped? My God! Why, I called on her just last night. She was okay—"

"This happened shortly after dawn," Anthony said. "Now get busy on those map-sketches."

The chemist fell to work. It was a time-consuming task, for the mine's tunnels and cross-tunnels and galleries extended over a distance of scores of acres underground, with stopes and chambers at dozens of levels. Even a rough approximation of the layout was complicated to draw on paper.

AS HE WORKED, Bannixter talked.

"I'm marking where all the main tunnels lead; where they join the old workings. As you've already discovered, the main shaft isn't the only entrance to the mine."

Anthony nodded grimly.

The chemist continued. "When we began operations, we closed off the old haulage tunnels with iron bulkheads. One of those haulage tunnels is the one you were taken into. But there are more. I'm indicating them on this map."

An ugly possibility struck Anthony, and he gave voice to it. "While we're searching the mine from the main shaft, Dolores and Beth and Tom might be whisked away through one of those old tunnels! That means we must divide our party into as many groups as there are exits, so that all escape will be blocked."

"Good idea," Bannixter said as he finished the complicated sketches. It had taken him almost three quarters of an hour to complete them;

and his facial muscles twitched with taut-drawn nerves. "Let's move!" he pleaded frantically, springing to his feet. "We've got to find Beth!"

He was either sincere or a damned good actor, Anthony told himself. "Okay. On our way. Come on, McCorkle."

In the newspaperman's rattletrap car they sped to the main shaft building, over the road which Anthony had traversed afoot not long ago. At the mine they found Fargo Lane waiting with a picked force of his local policemen, heavily armed.

The former gambler stroked his goatee nervously. "You give the orders, Anthony. It's your deal."

This relinquishing of authority could be interpreted in two ways. Maybe he wanted to show his willingness to follow Jim Anthony's lead; or perhaps he was disclaiming responsibility for anything that might happen.

It didn't matter. Anthony barked crisp commands as he handed out heating suits. He dispatched one group down the main vertical shaft and sent other searching parties to the various unused tunnels which opened out upon several hillsides in the distance.

For himself he saved that particular tunnel with which he was personally familiar; the one where he had been a prisoner. "You and I will tackle that one, McCorkle," he told the wiry editor. "Let's go."

It cost them many precious minutes to gain the hillside entrance. McCorkle gasped when he saw the charred corpse of the Black Ghost who had died by his own electrode. "God! I can still smell his cooked flesh!"

"He deserved what he got," Anthony rasped, snapping on his flashlight. "Be careful when we come to the snake-pit."

Onward they traveled. "Say," McCorkle exclaimed presently. "We should have brought heating suits for ourselves. When we go into the refrigerated section—"

"I thought of that. We'll wear Black Ghost outfits to keep warm, but without the masks. That way, the other searchers won't mistake us for enemies."

"You know where to find those rigs?"

Anthony led the way into a crosscut. "Right here," he flashed his light around a square chamber. Then he said: "Damn!"

"What is it, Jim?"

"The Black Ghost suits. *They're gone!*"

McCorkle tensed. "You mean the murder gang may be prowling around in the mine right now? Hell, we'd better not go any farther. Not without reinforcements!"

"We can't wait for reinforcements. Dolores and Beth and Tom must be found—quickly. Cold or no cold, Ghosts or no Ghosts, I'm going into Hell's Ice-Box!"

The wiry little newspaperman grinned crookedly. "Lead ahead, boss. I'm with you till hell freezes over—which it has."

And so they went past the weather-tight bulkhead and entered the frigid region beyond.

HOW LONG THEIR search continued, or how much territory they covered, Anthony could never afterward clearly remember. He followed his map-sketch as closely as possible; investigated every ore shoot, every stope. But he found no trace of Dolores and her fellow captives. He found nothing but shiny ice that glistened moistly under the light, and shallow puddles which splashed beneath his tireless feet.

At long last he saw a flickering gleam ahead; shouted a hello. Then he and McCorkle joined up with Steve Bannixter and his party.

The chemist's features were white with despair. "I've checked with the other groups," he said tonelessly. "They all report the same thing. No luck! I tell you, Beth isn't in the mine. She can't be or we'd have found some trace of her...."

Anthony surveyed the younger man bleakly. Bannixter seemed broken, beaten. And he seemed justified in his claim that Beth Meline and Dolores and Tom weren't anywhere underground. If all the tunnels had been covered, then the prisoners were obviously not here.

"All the searching parties followed your map-sketches thoroughly?" Anthony asked.

"Yes."

In that case, the quest had failed—unless Bannixter's drawings had been incomplete, either by accident or design. Suppose one or two tunnels had been omitted from the sketches by faulty memory, ignorance or... on purpose?

Anthony rejected the thought, temporarily. There was no way he could prove or disprove the question at present. "We might as well go topside," he said; and the words were so many stab-wounds in his own heart, for they spelled his admission that he'd failed in his effort to rescue Dolores Colquitt, the girl he loved—and Tom Gentry, his best friend.

He splashed forward through miles of tunnels to the landing station of the main shaft; boarded the elevator cage with his weary companions. And when they were finally lifted to the top, the sun's rays slanted redly.

It was late afternoon.

CHAPTER XI

VENOM TRAIL

BUT TO JIM ANTHONY, failure was unthinkable. Three lives were at stake, but for the moment he had reached a blind alley. He knew, now, that there was only one way to find out where Dolores and the others had been taken. That would be to discover the master brain behind the Black Ghost mob; the arch-criminal himself. If this could be done, pressure might force the man to reveal where he was holding his captives.

Identifying the chief plotter seemed a hopeless job, though. As McCorkle drove Anthony back to town, the situation looked as black as the electrical costumes worn by the murder gang. This outlook was intensified by the appearance of the town itself—for the streets were almost deserted.

Anthony alighted from the rattletrap car in front of his hotel. "I'll see you later," he told the newspaperman. Then he went into the hotel lobby, to be confronted by its lugubrious proprietor.

"I guess Haunted Valley's washed up," the man said dolefully. "Half the miners have pulled up stakes. The rest will be gone by morning. This'll be a ghost town again."

Going upstairs to his room, Anthony digested the information. It explained the silence, the deserted streets. He scowled as he picked up the phone by his bed and put through a long distance call to Gibbons, managing editor of his New York *Star*.

"Anthony talking," he said presently. "How much Haunted Valley stock was my broker able to buy?"

"Practically none, Jim," came the surprising answer. "I know it sounds screwy. With the mine's troubles smeared across every headline in New York, you'd think the bottom would drop out of the market on that stock. Instead, some guy named Paul Richmond has been buying up every share that's offered."

"Paul Richmond? Never heard of him. Who is he? Who's he acting for?"

"I can't find out. Nobody in his office will talk. Richmond himself grabbed a plane an hour after the market opened; headed for Haunted Valley. He ought to be there now."

Anthony hung up; stared at the wall. Then he lifted the receiver again, got the desk. "Have you a Paul Richmond registered?"

"Yes. Came in about an hour ago by plane. He's in 209. Want me to ring him?"

"Never mind." Anthony moved across his room in the gathering dusk; picked up the small black kit that was a major part of his equipment when working on a case. Then he went out into the corridor; strode softly to the door marked 209. He knocked.

HE THOUGHT HE heard a scurrying sound inside, but he couldn't be sure. In any event, nobody responded to his tap. He tried the knob but it was locked. That called for the use of his valuable steels.

They made short work of the latch. Gently he pushed the door inward; peered through the thickening gloom. What he saw caused the short hairs to prickle at the nape of his neck.

The room was a chaos of looted luggage and rummaged bureau drawers. Across the bed lay a thin, consumptive-looking man whose face was mottled, whose eyes protruded horribly. There were two tiny punctures in his neck, at the jugular vein.

And there was a rattlesnake coiled on his chest!

THE REPTILE RATTLED as Anthony approached; bared its fangs to strike at him.

He drew his gun, shot its head off.

Then he leaped to the open window opposite the door. Its curtains were blowing inward, driven by the hot desert wind. A thick coating of dust had been disturbed on the outer sill, as if by the passage of a large object; and the hilly ground rose rapidly behind the hotel structure so that this second-floor room was but a few feet above ground.

An active man would have had no difficulty entering the room and dropping out again. And it was evident that somebody *had* entered, for it was almost impossible that a rattlesnake could have got into the building by itself. Someone had brought it!

The door punched open and the hotel proprietor barged over the threshold, panting. "Hey, did I hear a shot up here?" Then he saw the dead snake and the equally dead man. "Good God—it's the guy you asked me about! Paul Richmond, the one that just registered less than an hour ago! How'd that snake—?"

"A plant to throw us off the trail," Anthony answered grimly. "This was a premeditated murder."

"You mean somebody tossed the rattler at him?"

"No. He was slugged unconscious; you can see the bruise on his temple. Then, unless I'm badly mistaken, he got two hypodermic injections of poison. The killer made a slight error, though. He spaced the punctures too wide apart. They wouldn't fit a set of snake fangs."

"But great heavens, who'd dream up such a stunt?"

"A murderer who wanted this particular death to look natural—if snake-bite can be called natural." As Anthony spoke, he extracted two vials of chemicals from his black kit; poured a few drops from each into a water tumbler.

He then got a small wad of absorbent cotton from the kit and moistened it with his mixed chemical reagents. He dabbed at the twin red punctures on the slain man's throat. "I was right," he said softly. "There's no discoloration-reaction. Whatever this poison was, it definitely wasn't rattlesnake venom."

"I don't get it," the hotel man said.

"The motive was robbery. The killer was someone Richmond knew well enough to allow him to come close, within striking distance. Richmond didn't guess he was going to be slugged."

"God, I wonder who it was and what he wanted?"

Anthony made a bitter mouth. "I'd like to know that, myself. You can see the luggage has been frisked. If the killer got what he was after, I'm up against another blind trail."

"Wait a minute!" the hotel man exclaimed. "When Richmond registered, he gave me a brief case to put in the safe. You suppose it might have something?"

Hope leaped into Anthony's hawklike eyes. "Come on! I want to see that brief case!"

DOWN BEHIND THE lobby desk, the proprietor opened his safe and handed the bulging leather bag to Anthony. Unfastening its catch, the millionaire criminologist spilled out a thick sheaf of stock certificates—Haunted Valley mining stock which must have belonged to a large number of persons, judging by the names to which the shares had been issued.

This, then, was some of the stock Richmond had been quietly buying up, even before today. But why? And why had the man flown here to Haunted Valley to keep a rendezvous with death?

Anthony snatched for the desk phone; dialed Lew Jefferson's office at the bank building. "Mr. Jefferson?"

"Ka-humph. Yes. Who's this?" came the rumbling answer.

"Jim Anthony. I've got to see you."

"But I'm on my way home this minute. Got a dinner guest."

"Then I'll come to your house. Have you a copy of the Haunted Valley stock book? If so, take it home with you. I want to examine it."

"Ka-humph. All right. I'll look for you."

THE CHUNKY LAND baron's residence was almost as old and ornate as the one from which Beth Meline, Dolores Colquitt and Tom Gentry had been kidnaped. It stood on a knoll, surrounded by a clump of pines grotesquely twisted by constant wind.

Jim Anthony entered, to be met by Jefferson and his dinner guest, the rabbit-like broker, Willis Todhunter. They both seemed vaguely uneasy.

Jefferson mopped his bald pate. "Ka-humph. What's this about the stock book?"

"I want to check it against these shares." Anthony produced the certificates from the murdered Richmond's brief case. Then he set to work, comparing shares against book.

Presently he looked up. "You can take any name on these certificates, and you won't find it entered in the stock book!"

"But—ka-humph—but what—

Anthony pulled some vials from his little black kit; spilled their contents into an ash tray. He dabbed some of the resulting liquid upon one share after another. "Every certificate is a forgery!" he announced.

The stubby land baron paled, and his thunderous voice seemed to lose its rumble. "I don't understand! If the stock isn't listed on the company's books it's no good. No dividends would ever be paid on it, so who'd bother to counterfeit it?"

Anthony made no effort to explain. Instead, he asked a question. "Has anyone offered to buy your holdings?"

"Ka-humph. Why, yes. How did you know? A man named Richmond phoned me an hour ago—"

"How did he get your name?"

"He said Fargo Lane told him to contact me."

Anthony's black brows drew together at this mention of Haunted Valley's combined mayor and police chief. He wondered if that murdered man, Richmond, had been working as purchasing agent for the reformed gambler.

Even as the puzzle seethed through Anthony's mind, a terror-stricken yelp came from Willis Todhunter. The colorless investment broker had been casually standing near a window, and now his face held panicky pallor as he pointed toward the outer darkness.

"Shapes—coming toward the house—everywhere—closing in on us—Black Ghosts—!" he screeched.

With one swift movement, Anthony drew his gun and shot out the room's lights. Then he leaped to the window, his eyes attuned to the night.

Todhunter's cry had been true. At least eight or ten lumbering and black-clad figures were deploying toward the residence, with their death-dealing electrodes extended. Already two of them were battering at the front door.

The investment broker squealed shrilly and ran for cover as a mouse might dart toward its hole. He vanished into the darkness of the rear of the house. Simultaneously, Anthony grabbed at Lew Jefferson's arm.

"Upstairs with me!" he commanded the land baron. "It's your one chance. My bullets can't stop those fiends."

"Ka-Humph! My God, you think they're after me?"

"Why else would they come to your home? Get moving!"

The bald man stumbled to the stairs, guided by Anthony's sureness of vision despite the absence of lights. But halfway to the second floor Jefferson stumbled, lost his footing. He fell like a rotund, bouncing ball; landed in the lower floor just as a surge of Black Ghosts smashed in.

ANTHONY WATCHED FROM the head of the steps, powerless to prevent what happened. He snapped a couple of shots downward and had the satisfaction of seeing two ghostly figures topple with bullets through their brains—for their masking hoods were no protection against gunfire. It was only their bodies which wore armor.

Even so, others piled in. And blue arcs of flame licked forth from their electrodes to roast the land baron before he could get on his feet. He died instantly.

Anthony knew there was no more he could do. His own life would be in jeopardy if he remained here. But if he escaped, there was a slender chance that he might trail the murder mob when they left this house. They might unwittingly lead him to their new hideout—and to the place where Dolores, Beth and Tom were being held captive.

With that hope in his heart, he sprinted along the upper hallway until he came to a bedroom door. He entered, and his vision pierced the darkness to discern a dormer window jutting outward like a nose on a sharply chiseled face.

From his black kit he drew a long length of fine line, not a great deal thicker than bell-wire but immeasurably stronger. It was a special rope, braided for Jim Anthony a long time ago by his Indian grandfather, old Mephito.

Swiftly he fashioned a curious sort of loop over the windowsill and laid out his line. Then he clambered out; descended hand over hand until his feet silently touched the earth. A dexterous twist freed the rope's upper loop, so that the whole length fell into his hands. He coiled it, stowed it away in his kit and then crouched down, waiting.

He had a hunch that the game was drawing to its conclusion.

CHAPTER XII

DEATH'S HIGH TIDE

IN HIS OWN MIND, Jim Anthony knew the identity of the murder gang's leader. But that was less important now, than rescuing Dolores and Tom and Beth Meline. They came first!

Narrowly he watched the Jefferson residence; and presently his vigil was rewarded. Nine black, ghostly figures filed from the house and skulked past him, so close he could have reached forth and grabbed them one by one.

Instead, he fell in behind them as silently as a marching specter. They headed into the foothills, toward a region where no mine outlet had been shown on Steve Bannixter's sketchy map. Then, abruptly, they seemed to vanish as if the very earth had opened up and swallowed them.

Anthony waited a good ten minutes to make sure this wasn't a trap into which he was being lured. Satisfied at last, he approached the spot where he had last seen his quarry.

His heart leaped as he beheld an opening in the hillside, a lateral passageway concealed by underbrush. On noiseless strides he entered the black maw. Warm dampness closed in around him as he moved. Deep ahead, dim light flickered. He made for it.

The glow emanated from a crosscut gallery. Here the Black Ghosts were congregated, only they weren't Black Ghosts now. Removing their costumes, they proved to be merely a motley assortment of thugs— including the three who had tried to kill Jim Anthony by leaving him to freeze.

He could hear their muttered conversation. "Cripes, I hope we wash up this job soon. I'm gettin' fed up!" one said.

"Don't worry. The show's about over. The town will be empty in another day. Wonder what the boss's angle is?"

"Hell, that's easy. Too much stock for the mine."

"Yeah? So what? And what's that got to do with them two cupcakes we snatched, or the freckled guy?"

"I wouldn't know. His Nibs said leave 'em in that ore shoot to croak. I didn't ask no questions. I just lugged 'em back past here and dumped 'em like he told me."

JIM ANTHONY WAITED to hear no more. He might have stopped to confront these hired killers and capture them at gun's point, but that, too, could wait. Silently he sped past the cross-cut where the thugs were talking; arrowed into the downward-slanting darkness of the passageway.

At last the lateral tunnel leveled off and he risked a beam from his electric torch. It revealed a shoot to his left, where a blind gallery had been stopped up in previous years. A slanted hole led upward, with a ladder laying under it.

He braced the ladder into position, crawled up the slanted shoot. And as he flashed his light, he heard faint sounds above him; writhing sounds, muffled moans, as if someone might be attempting to shout through a gag.

A last burst of speed brought Anthony into a square-hewn and long-abandoned chamber. His heart leaped as he saw three bound forms on the rubble of the floor.

"Dolores!" he choked. "Tom! Miss Meline!"

He sprang to his lovely fiancée first; whipped away her gag and slashed her fetters. Then he performed the same service for Beth and Tom.

Dolores swayed into his arms. "Jim! I knew you'd make it before it was t-too late!"

His embrace crushed her almost savagely, and he thrilled to the sweet yielding of her bosom upon his chest. Then, reluctantly, he released her. "You're okay?"

"Y-yes, now that you're here."

He surveyed Tom Gentry and the Meline girl. They, too, were unharmed save for the rigors of their long confinement. "We had better get out while we have the chance," he told them in a grim voice. "Before the ghost gang accidentally finds out that their plans have gone haywire."

Beth Meline touched his arm, timidly. "How can I ever thank you for… everything?"

"You needn't bother. Not until I've put your father's murderer behind bars. Do you know why you were kidnaped?"

She nodded. "One of the Black Ghosts tried to make me tell where my f-father's stock was located, so I could be forced to sign it over. I refused to t-talk. I thought it might give me a chance to live longer. As for Dolores and Tom, they were captured with me because they t-tried to protect me."

"I thought as much," Anthony grunted as he guided them down the slanted ore shoot to the lower tunnel. And then, just as they reached the lateral, a terrific blast sounded.

The entire hillside seemed to quake, and a blast of air came surging through the passage, almost knocking them down. Tom Gentry bellowed: "What the hell was that?"

"Wait here," Anthony commanded, "I'll go see." He vanished, to return a moment later, his face a bleak mask. "Somebody dynamited the tunnel exit. The whole gallery is caved in, blocked with fallen rock."

"You mean we can't get out that way?" Dolores gasped.

"No, and neither will anyone else. I have an idea that the head of the Black Ghost gang is about through with his work. He didn't need his thugs any longer, so he buried them alive. Their hideout fell in on their heads."

Beth Meline whimpered. "Then w-we're trapped…!"

"Not necessarily," Anthony retorted. "Maybe we can reach the main part of the mine if we follow this tunnel in the other direction, away from the dynamited entrance. Come on, we'll try it." And he herded them forward with his flashlamp.

IT SEEMED AGES before they reached an iron bulkhead door. But the sight brought a relieved exclamation from Anthony's lips. "Beyond that bulkhead is the refrigerated part of the mine—and safety!" he added buoyantly.

Then he opened the bulkhead.

He was braced for the shock of frigid temperature. And the cold air came; but not with the sub-zero chill he had anticipated. His sixth sense came alert, warning him that something was wrong. He couldn't decide what it was, though.

Forward he guided his friends, their footfalls making tiny splashing sounds. From what Anthony remembered of Bannixter's map, this must be somewhere around the twelve hundred foot level. The main shaft should be half a mile ahead.

Little trickles of water dribbled from the rock walls, and the usual facets of sparkling, diamond-like ice particles were no longer glittering in the reflection of Anthony's flashlight. He scowled; then, abruptly, he realized what was wrong.

"The refrigerating system!" he rasped. "It's not working—hasn't been working for hours!"

"What do you mean?" Gentry stared at him.

"I noticed puddles of water all afternoon when I was searching for you. The freezing apparatus must have been tampered with even then. Melting had already started. And now—"

"And now what, Jim?" Dolores asked.

"And now all the ice is practically gone. Water's seeping into the mine again."

"You—you aren't trying to tell us—?"

"We'll have to face it," Anthony answered bitterly. "There's a subterranean river under this mine, flowing thousands of gallons a minute. That's what flooded the workings twenty years ago. And now that the refrigeration has stopped, the mine will be flooded again."

"In other words," Dolores looked at him steadily, "we're all trapped. When the water level rises this far, we'll drown."

CHAPTER XIII

GHOST'S PAYOFF

RESOLUTELY JIM ANTHONY REFUSED to accept that inevitability. "Maybe we still have a chance!" he shouted. "Come on!" And he urged his companions to a sprint.

After a desperately long time they reached the main shaft and came to a stop, panting, at the square-hewn station where the elevator platform would drop to a landing when you sent a signal to its operator up in the shaft house.

The platform didn't appear now, though, despite Anthony's repeated signals. He even fired three shots upward, hoping to attract attention; but nothing happened.

Below, in the deeper reaches of the shaft, a swift gush of water could be heard flowing, rising. Anthony picked up a piece of rock, dropped it into the black abyss. Almost at once came a responding splash. The underground river was free of its frozen chains; water was pouring from every lowermost crack and crevice in the mine. It would be but a few minutes before the mounting tide rose in the shaft to reach this tunnel level.

"Well," Tom Gentry said with his customary courage, "I guess this washes us up—and I *do* mean *wash*. It's been nice knowing you people."

Dolores nestled in Anthony's arms. "Somehow it won't seem so bad to d-die if you're with me, Jim."

"Who said anything about dying?" he growled. "We're not licked yet—Tom! Lend a hand."

"Yeah, Jim?"

"These mine timbers over here. This loose lumber. We're going to build a raft. I'll rope it together with my special line." And Anthony opened his little black kit to extract the long, stalwart coil of thin, braided rope.

Gentry blinked at him. "You're crazy! But—sometimes a crazy guy has good ideas." Grinning, he jumped to help his millionaire friend.

It was a forlorn hope, but the only one. Apparently the power was off all over the mine, so that the elevator cage couldn't operate. Therefore, the sole chance of salvation lay in floating upward on the rising waters by means of this raft which Anthony and Tom were throwing together.

They toiled in grim haste; and finally the job was completed. Anthony smiled bleakly. "May as well sit down and rest, all of us. This is going to take a long time."

His prophecy proved correct. According to his estimate, the flood was rising about a foot every ten minutes and they would have twelve hundred feet to go before they reached the top of the shaft. Two hours of floating, more or less!

Of course, as they rose, the lateral tunnels running outward from the main shaft grew shorter; this made less space for the water to fill. So the tide would swell upward more swiftly, the nearer it reached the surface.

Anthony's keen eyes saw the first black liquid surface as it appeared and overflowed the elevator station platform. "Okay, Tom. We launch our ship now. Step aboard, girls. Careful. Only thing we need to watch from now on is that we stay in the shaft proper and don't drift into one of the tunnels."

Gentry chuckled. "Keep your light burning and I'll see we don't get sidetracked!"

Then they were floating, and the flood bore them upward.

IT WAS AN hour and a half later when the rising water gushed over the top of the shaft, bearing Anthony's raft with it. He leaped to solid ground with Dolores in his arms, while Tom carried Beth Meline to safety.

A crowd had gathered about the shaft house, drawn by those signal shots Anthony had fired from below. Now they milled forward, their faces weird and strained in the light of swaying lanterns.

Beth Meline spotted somebody. "Steve! Steve Bannixter!" she cried as she stumbled wearily into the young chemist's waiting arms.

Whereupon Tom Gentry was heard to mutter something that sounded like: "Nuts!"

And then Jim Anthony drew his automatic; moved toward Fargo Lane. The former gambler was nervously tugging at his goatee, and his eyes popped as if he were seeing an apparition. "Anthony—I was afraid you were dead—!"

"I'm very much alive. And I'm ready to place a formal accusation of murder against the leader of the Black Ghosts."

"Wh-who is he?"

Anthony pivoted toward the edge of the crowd, where the wiry McCorkle was standing. He didn't aim his gun at the newspaperman, though. Instead, he said:

"Raise your hands, Willis Todhunter!"

The colorless investment broker went white. "What—wh-what's this?"

"Your game is up. From the very start, you had no confidence in the scheme to freeze the mine and reopen it. But the plan had received tremendous newspaper publicity, which would make it easy to sell stock. So you undertook to float the issue."

"Certainly I floated the issue! But—"

"But you also sold more stock than the company's capitalization called for," Anthony said grimly. "You forged thousands of dollars' worth of certificates and disposed of them to unsuspecting investors. If the freezing system failed to work, those investors would never ask why they didn't receive dividends. They would write off their stock as worthless, and the money they had paid for it would line your pockets."

"You—you—" the little broker shrilled.

ANTHONY SILENCED HIM. "Unfortunately for you, the refrigeration idea was successful. The mine went into production. And the investors who had bought counterfeit stock would soon wonder why their dividends failed to come through."

Todhunter's knees began to buckle.

"So you had to do something about it," Anthony went on. "You decided to sabotage the mine, put it out of business. Your Black Ghosts killed just enough miners to drive the others away. Then you also began murdering the members of the operating board, to make sure the property would shut down."

"No—you can't—"

"By depressing the market value of the stock, you were able to buy back the phony shares you had issued, at a fraction of the price for which you had sold them," Anthony continued his reconstruction. "Then you got another idea. Why not buy up the genuine stock too, for a few cents on the dollar, and reopen the mine again after the excitement died down? That way, you would reap another fortune."

The broker just stared.

"Your stock purchasing agent was a man named Paul Richmond, who flew here to Haunted Valley today for a conference with you—

and to hand you what certificates he'd been able to pick up, thus far. Perhaps in recent weeks he had tried to chisel himself into the deal; or maybe you were afraid he might blackmail you, later. Anyhow, you were prepared for his arrival. You killed him in his hotel room with a poisoned hypo and set the stage to make it look like snake-bite."

"You... even found that out?" Todhunter gasped. It was his unwitting confession of guilt.

Anthony nodded. "I know the whole story, including why you had Miss Meline kidnaped, and why you dynamited your crew of Black Ghosts when you were finished with them. I wouldn't be surprised if Eric Meline had suspected you, which was why you blasted his hillside cabin."

"He—I—"

"I realized you were the brain guy tonight when your Black Ghosts attacked Lew Jefferson's house. Jefferson was murdered, but you went scot-free. Moreover, you were the only possible person who could have profited from the counterfeit stock. Anyhow, it's ended. You'll hang."

"No!" the little criminal screamed. He turned and started to run.

FARGO LANE WAS chief of police, and he knew his duty. He made a lightning draw and shot the broker through the heart.

Anthony nodded his approval. "Good job, Mr. Lane. I must admit I suspected you for a while, until I learned the truth. Am I forgiven for my suspicions?"

"You are. And you can have my right arm any time you want it!" the former gambler smiled through his mustache and goatee. "But right now our job is to get the freezing equipment working again, so the mine can be cleared out and put back in operation—Hey, Bannixter, can you handle it?"

The young chemist said of course he could. "But not this minute. I'm busy." And he returned to the more important business of kissing Beth Meline.

Tom Gentry sighed disconsolately. "Hey, Jim. Dolores. McCorkle. Must we stand here and watch that mush all night, or can we go somewhere and get a drink?"

So the four of them went and got a drink. They raised a silent toast to the men who had died—and to the Haunted Valley mine which would soon again be producing copper for America's war against the Axis.

THE DAYS
OF DEATH

JIM CAME INTO THE CASE BECAUSE AN INNOCENT FRIEND
WAS ACCUSED OF MURDER. BUT IT WASN'T LONG BEFORE HE
KNEW HE HAD DISCOVERED SOMETHING BIG... AND THE NEXT
DEATH MIGHT BE HIS OWN—OR THAT OF THE GIRL HE LOVED

YOU WOULDN'T HAVE GUESSED Jim Anthony's American Indian ancestry on the afternoon that he and his freckled aviator friend, Tom Gentry, walked into the lobby of the San Francisco hotel in which they were staying.

At the moment, Anthony looked more like a vengeful and high-caste Hindu than the descendant of Comanche warriors, for a bandage swathed his head like a turban, its whiteness standing out in sharp contrast to his strong, sun-tanned features.

When the genial Gentry had first seen the bandage, he'd gone into a mild attack of hysterics.

"Ain't you something?" he chortled. "If that palm tree had been a little harder, the emergency hospital docs would probably have fixed you up to look like a complete model for a Red Cross first aid class!"

Anthony hadn't shared his friend's merriment. The anger that filled him was too intense. In his own mind he was certain that the sedan which had sideswiped his powerful roadster, knocking it into the palm tree, had done so intentionally.

Nor was his wrath diminished by the knowledge that while the offending driver had been a white man, the sedan's tonneau had been full of Orientals—Japs, he suspected.

He couldn't be sure of this, though, since he'd caught only a fleeting glimpse of their yellow faces as their car swerved into him and sent him crashing against the tree trunk.

Luckily, Anthony had been observing the wartime speed regulation of forty miles an hour when the thing happened. To this, he and Gentry owed their lives.

But it infuriated him that the sedan had got away from the scene without even stopping to see what damage they'd caused to his specially-built roadster, which he kept on the west coast for use on his infrequent visits here.

He scowled now as he thought about it; continued to scowl as he crossed the lavish hotel lobby, approached the desk and asked the clerk for his key.

The man cleared his throat nervously. "Er, Mr. Anthony, sir, I, er, ah—"

"Yes?" Anthony grinned despite himself, for the clerk's fluttery manner bordered on the ridiculous.

"There is a young woman in your suite, sir. A rather remarkable young woman, if I may say so."

Immediately, Anthony thought of his lovely fiancée, Dolores Colquitt. "In my suite?"

"Yes, sir. She said she had to see you on a matter of tremendous importance. I finally admitted her to your rooms, sir. She was, er, ah, attracting far too much attention here in the lobby, sir."

"How was she attracting attention?"

"By her appearance, sir. Everyone was staring."

Tom Gentry thrust his oar into the conversation. "What's the matter with her appearance? She get two heads or something?"

"Oh, no, nothing like that! It's just that—well, anyhow, I thought it would be all right to—"

"Looks like I'm just in time, baby!"
He smacked her on the jaw.

Jim Anthony cocked an eyebrow at his aviator friend. He knew that Dolores Colquitt wasn't due to arrive from Los Angeles until the following morning, by train, since all airliners in the coastal area had been temporarily grounded by order of the Fourth Interceptor Command.

Therefore he felt sure the girl who was now waiting for him couldn't be his fiancée. Even if Dolores had come north ahead of schedule, she wouldn't have waited in the lobby. She would have gone on upstairs to her own suite which Anthony had reserved for her.

There seemed a hint of mystery in the desk clerk's manner—and Anthony disliked mysteries. In fact, he spent a good portion of his time unraveling them; for in addition to being a multimillionaire, he was one of the world's greatest scientific criminologists.

He didn't question the clerk any further, though. Instead, he accepted his key and moved toward the battery of elevators on the far side of the lobby, with Tom Gentry at his heels. A modernistic cage sped them silently upward.

Presently, with matching silence, Anthony unlocked and opened the door of his suite.

THE LIVING ROOM windows overlooked the city in the direction of the Embarcadero and the bay beyond. A chair was placed by one of these windows, its back to the door; and there was a brunette girl sitting there, staring at the view.

"You wanted to see me?" Anthony said quietly.

His visitor jumped as if he'd prodded her with a knife. And when she turned, Tom Gentry emitted a soft, admiring whistle. Anthony himself had a hard time keeping his expression under control, for the girl was the most startling creature he had ever seen.

Her face was a smooth ivory oval and her brows were plucked to make thin, high arches over her almond eyes. Her mouth was a scarlet passion-flower and her small, delicately formed body was clad in a clinging frock of heavy Chinese silk trimmed with jade buttons, a frock so tightly fitted that it revealed every tempting nuance of her figure.

As Gentry put it later, she was just about the mostest of the bestest. And when she smiled timidly, her mask-like doll's face came alive with vivacious beauty.

"Mr. Anthony!" her voice was husky, vibrant. "Thank goodness you've come!"

Gentry gasped and sat down on the arm of the nearest chair, as if he couldn't stand the shock of her loveliness. But Anthony held himself in check; gave no sign that he was affected. He was busily trying to determine the girl's nationality.

Her hair was like spun black jet, but its silky texture looked more Caucasian than Asiatic. Her eyes were slanted, yet she had the straight aquiline nose of an Occidental. Her milky complexion was ivory rather than white, although her speech held no trace of accent. One thing contradicted another.

Anthony finally decided she must be Eurasian; and, having seen her, he could understand why the desk clerk downstairs had wanted to get her out of the lobby. Her exotic beauty could disrupt any man's routine.

She drifted toward the wealthy criminologist, for the first time noticing his bandaged head. "You've been hurt!"

"You ought to see the palm tree," Tom Gentry said, unwilling to remain longer ignored. "There wasn't enough left to make a box of toothpicks."

She rewarded the freckled aviator's boyish grin with a wistful smile. "Really?" Then, nervously plucking at an insecurely sewn jade button of her dress, she shifted her glance back to Anthony. "I hope your injury isn't t-too serious. I have desperate need of you."

"What is it that's so urgent?" he asked.

"It concerns your intended meeting with William Soong."

Anthony repressed his surprise. Nobody was supposed to know what he was doing on the west coast. How, then, had this Eurasian girl got hold of the information?

He parried her statement. "I expect to say hello to Bill Soong while I'm here, yes. But principally I'm taking a short vacation."

"You needn't fence with me, Mr. Anthony," she kept pulling at one jade button after another. "I know why you've come to San Francisco. And I know something else, too."

"Such as?"

"Bill Soong will not meet you tonight. He has disappeared—and the police are hunting him for murder!"

CHAPTER II

TANGLED THREADS

JIM ANTHONY STIFFENED AS he stared at the girl. "Murder?" he exclaimed harshly. "That's fantastic. Bill worked with me as a laboratory assistant for two solid years—all the time he was attending post-graduate classes back at Columbia. He's no killer!"

The girl's control was visibly slipping. "The police seem to think otherwise, although they've kept their suspicions from the newspapers thus far."

"But what's it all about? Who—?"

"They believe Bill murdered his employer last night," the Eurasian girl said dully.

As she spoke, she came even closer to Anthony. Looking down at her, he realized how exquisite she was; and her subtle perfume drifted to his nostrils, made his pulse beat faster. He restrained a sudden impulse to touch her; and his effort was so obvious that Tom Gentry's eyes narrowed as he watched.

Then the tall, sun-bronzed criminologist recovered his poise. "What connection have you with Bill Soong?"

"We w-were to be married next month."

"Then you must be Lotus Toy!" Anthony regarded her with new interest.

His former laboratory assistant, the American-born Chinese, William Soong, had written him many lyrical letters about this girl. But none of those letters, Anthony realized now, had done full justice to her beauty.

As she acknowledged that she was Lotus Toy, the wealthy detective shifted his active mind to another phase of the puzzle confronting him. He was remembering a certain mysterious telegram which Bill Soong had sent him only a couple of days ago.

The wire had been couched in vague terms, hinting that Soong had stumbled upon a matter of grave importance which he wanted to discuss personally with Anthony. Between the lines of the message there had been hidden fear.

Intrigued, Anthony had flown west at once in his own private plane, piloted by Tom Gentry. He had hoped to make it a pleasure trip, since Dolores Colquitt was vacationing with friends in Los Angeles.

He had phoned Dolores long distance, asking her to join him in San Francisco over the week-end. By that time, he had thought, he'd have finished whatever job it was that Bill Soong wanted him to investigate.

But here was the unexpected. Soong was missing; was being hunted by the police on suspicion of murder!

The thing whetted Anthony's interest. His occult sixth sense, inherited from his Comanche princess mother, told him that the young Chinese student was innocent of any such crime. His friendship for Soong filled him with a desire to prove this innocence.

Possessor of one of the world's largest fortunes, Jim Anthony had for many years devoted himself to the solving of mysterious crimes.

MANY FACTORS ENTERED into his success as a man-hunter. Rich beyond avarice, he never had to worry about financial considerations. His tall, sleek-muscled body was trained to complete physical perfection. Superlatively educated, his mind was an edged tool that sliced through puzzles the way a scalpel might cut a knotted string. And he'd developed an extraordinary skill in the use of every known type of weapon, ancient and modern.

No wonder, then, that Jim Anthony's name was one to send terror into the heart of any wrongdoer!

Now he smiled gently at the Eurasian girl, Lotus Toy. "Bill Soong must have told you he'd wired me."

She nodded unhappily. "Yes. He said he had sent for you on a matter of terrific importance. But he wouldn't let me know what it was. He said the information was d-dangerous...."

Anthony frowned thoughtfully. He might have had something to work on if Soong had only confided more fully in the girl.

As it was, there seemed no way of finding out what had been troubling the Chinese student except by locating him and talking with him. Since he was hiding out from a murder accusation, this looked pretty remote.

"What about the killing?" Anthony asked.

"Bill hadn't been able to land a regular laboratory job when he came home from college," Lotus Toy answered. "So he accepted temporary employment as chauffeur and house boy for a woman named Sarah Beaumont. She's the one who w-was murdered."

Even as Jim felled Elayne's
attacker, she screamed and ran.

"What makes the police think Bill did it?"

"There's a cabaret dancer, Elayne London, who has an apartment directly under Sarah Beaumont's suite. She saw Bill go upstairs. So did the doorman—"

"What time was this?"

"Seven-thirty last night. A few minutes later, a shot sounded. The doorman heard it and investigated. He found the Beaumont woman in her living room with a b-bullet through her heart. And Bill was g-gone."

Tom Gentry snorted. "That don't prove he bumped her!"

"No, b-but several tenants in the building testified they had heard him arguing with Miss Beaumont earlier in the afternoon. Or anyhow they heard loud voices, like a quarrel."

"What's your own opinion?" Anthony asked gravely.

She pressed her band against the swelling roundness of her alluring breast as if to stifle the pain there, then went back to her nervous habit of plucking at her frock's green jade buttons. "I know Bill isn't guilty. My heart tells me so. You must clear him, Mr. Anthony. You've g-got to!"

"I'll do my best. First, though, I'll have to know all the details. You say you haven't the slightest idea what was bothering him; what made him wire me?"

"N-no… except that he'd been acting strangely ever since that importer disappeared."

Anthony's voice sharpened. "What importer?"

"A Japanese named Taoki Komura who'd been very kind to Bill," the girl explained.

"You say he disappeared?"

She nodded. "When all west coast Japs were rounded up to be interned for the duration of the war, Komura couldn't be found. It was rumored that perhaps a branch of Tokyo's Black Dragon Society might have liquidated him."

"Why?"

"Because he wasn't in sympathy with their espionage activities and fifth column work. He was loyal to this country. Or anyhow, that was the theory."

"But his body wasn't found?"

"No. And it worried Bill a good deal. Still, I can't see how Komura's disappearance could have any connection with the death of Sarah Beaumont last n-night."

Jim Anthony's lips curved in a thin smile.

"Lots of things are connected that don't always show on the surface," he said enigmatically. He was thinking of his own recent accident, and the sedan full of Orientals which had forced him off the road—deliberately.

Was it possible, he wondered, that the thing had been done in an effort to remove him from action? Could it be that somebody feared the investigation he might make?

As yet, the pattern was shapeless and indistinct in his mind; but he sensed a sinister undercurrent here—a mystifying recurrence of Asiatic names and yellow faces. Maybe it was coincidence, but he didn't think so.

He decided to call at police headquarters, see what he could learn there.

CHAPTER III

GUY WITH A GUN

INSPECTOR NYLAND WAS A big man, a hard man, with twenty long years of San Francisco police work behind him.

He knew of Jim Anthony's reputation in criminology, of course; there wasn't a homicide official in the United States who hadn't heard about the millionaire detective's astounding exploits. All the same, Nyland was of the old, tough school which didn't take a great deal of stock in the scientific efforts of non-professional crime investigators.

Nor did he attempt to conceal his impatience now, as Anthony queried him here at headquarters.

"What's your interest in this Bill Soong?" he asked his sun-bronzed visitor.

"A personal one. Bill's a friend of mine. He worked for me in my lab, back east. And he's not the killer type."

"You're wasting your time," Nyland said bluntly. "If he didn't murder the Beaumont woman, why did he lam?"

"That's what I'd like to find out, damn it."

"I wish you luck, then," Nyland grunted. "But I don't think you'll get very far." He busied himself with some papers, dismissing Anthony from his mind as well as from his office.

Anthony made his way from the building; rejoined Tom Gentry and Lotus Toy outside. As he piled into the rented U-drive sedan in which he'd left them waiting while he interviewed the police official, he frowned thoughtfully.

The Eurasian girl saw his frown and guessed its meaning. "So you didn't learn anything from Nyland."

"No more than you've already told me. We do know the police haven't nabbed Bill as yet, though."

"That's something," Tom Gentry said. "What happens next?"

"I'm going to see this dancer, Elayne London—the one who's supposed to have seen Soong go up to Sarah Beaumont's apartment just before the shot sounded." Anthony looked at Lotus Toy. "Can you tell me where to reach her?"

"Yes. She works in a downtown cabaret. The Club Lorenz."

THAT NIGHT, IMPECCABLY clad in full evening attire, but with his head still swathed in the white bandage that looked like a Hindu turban, Jim Anthony entered the Club Lorenz. Again he chose to play a lone hand, leaving Gentry and the Eurasian girl in the rented car outside.

The cabaret occupied the ground floor of one of the old buildings perched on a steeply tilted side street angling off Market. It wasn't a prepossessing place, but it seemed to cater to a nice patronage—if you could judge by tonight's clientele.

There was a small dance floor entirely surrounded by tables, all of them occupied. At one end of the room an orchestra purveyed sweet swing from a tiny stage, and near this platform there was a cocktail bar.

Anthony made for this, looking for all the world like a tall, distinguished Rajput potentate. A white-coated barman eyed him curiously, as if wondering whether or not he could speak understandable English.

"Your order, sir?"

"Double brandy." When it came, the millionaire detective's long, clever fingers creased a ten dollar bill lengthwise; deftly palmed it into the barman's hand. "For you, pal."

"How come?"

"I'm looking for a dancer named Elayne London. How do I get to her dressing room?"

"You don't. It's against the rules."

"Whose rules?"

"Pomeroy's. He's the owner. He'd raise hell." The bartender cast a casual glance toward the other end of the polished mahogany, indicating the man he meant.

Anthony's glance was equally casual, but he missed nothing of Pomeroy's appearance.

The cabaret proprietor was short, wiry, compact in an expensively tailored tuxedo. He had shrewd little eyes that darted constantly about the place as if checking up on everything that went on. Now and then, between sips of plain charged water, he would twist the spiked ends of his small waxed mustache.

Waiting until the man looked away, Anthony did tricks with another ten-spot, masking the movement by lighting a cigarette from a match proffered by the barkeeper.

"Making twenty all told," he told the white-coated dispenser of drinks. "Pomeroy needn't know anything about it."

The barman hesitated, then bent forward with a towel as if to wipe a spot of moisture off the polished woodwork.

"See that door? You go through it. There's a hall to the left. Elayne's room is second from the end."

Anthony nodded, finished his brandy without undue haste, and started to turn away. Whereupon Pomeroy spoke clearly from the other end of the bar.

"You forgot to pay for your drink," the café owner's voice was neither truculent nor apologetic. He was merely stating a fact. "One double brandy. Dollar and a half."

JIM ANTHONY'S JAW dropped as he shoved two ones across the counter. He was almost certain that Pomeroy hadn't been looking in his direction, yet the fellow had called the turn as if he'd had eyes in the back of his head.

Not that it mattered. "Keep the change," Anthony told the barkeeper, who looked a bit worried. Then, as the cash register jingled, the wealthy criminologist strolled off.

This time he made very sure Pomeroy wasn't watching him. Once he was convinced of this, he ducked through the rear doorway into the deserted hall beyond.

Reaching the second dressing room from the end, he tried the knob. It turned. He pushed the door inward; stepped across the threshold.

"Miss London?" he said softly.

The dancer gasped, jumped, spilled the makeup kit she'd been using.

She pivoted to face Anthony, and he saw fear slithering into her eyes; noticed the surging turbulence that stirred her voluptuous white breast in the spangled mesh cups of a costume brassiere.

Other than the brassiere she wore nothing but a pair of very brief, skin-tight satin panties sparkling with rhinestones. Her hair cut in page boy style, was bleached to a bright platinum blonde shade; and her features were just a bit on the coarse side, although pretty enough. She was tall and lithe, had the long, muscular legs of the professional dancer.

Gradually the fear on her face changed to sullen resentment. "What's the big idea, barging in here without knocking? How'd you know but what I might be undressed?"

Anthony repressed a smile. If ever a girl had been undressed, this one was. She didn't seem to think so, though. Evidently the spangled bandeau and panties conformed to her conception of modesty.

"Sorry if I startled you," he apologized. "My name's Anthony. The police tell me you're a witness against Bill Soong."

She grew tense, and he saw the color draining from her heavily rouged cheeks. The reaction, he decided, was abnormal. This girl knew something; more, perhaps, than she'd told the homicide men. Else why should she be edgy, nervous?

"I made my statement," she lipped. "What of it?"

"I'd like to hear it again, direct from you, if you don't object."

"Why?"

"I'm interested in the case for personal reasons."

She surveyed him; seemed to like what she saw. "What are you, a fly cop in disguise or something?"

"No. Just an ordinary citizen with a gashed scalp. Automobile accident," he added. "Now, about Bill Soong."

"We-ell, okay. No harm in telling it again, I guess. It was pretty warm last evening. I had my apartment door open and I saw the Chink go up the stairs. Then, in a little while, I heard the shot, it came just as I was starting over here to work."

"What time?"

"About seven-thirty. I was already in the hall, going out. I passed the doorman in the lower hallway. He asked me if I'd heard anything and I told him yes, but I thought it was just a backfire from some car.

So he went upstairs and I went out. I didn't know until later that the Beaumont woman was dead."

"Was there one shot or two?"

Her eyes wavered uncertainly. "Why… just one, I think."

"Look," Anthony said, stepping toward her. "You're not coming clean with me, sister. You're holding back. What's scaring you?"

"Who says I'm scared?"

"It's plain enough." He reached out, touched her bare shoulder. "You can trust me."

FOR AN INSTANT, it looked as if she might be going to give in to him. In fact, when his palm contacted her smooth skin a little tremor seemed to go through her. Her breast rose swiftly.

Then she backed off, suspicion growing in her stare. "Wait a minute! You're the guy that phoned me this afternoon and offered me five grand to powder out of town by sundown or be killed, aren't you?"

Anthony stiffened. This was a new development—a damned amazing one.

"So there was a threat and a bribe to get you out of San Francisco!"

"You ought to know. It was your voice I heard over the wire. Now lay off me or I'll tell the cops about it."

The bronzed criminologist smiled thinly. "That's what I think you'd better do, baby. Put on a dress and we'll run down to headquarters. Inspector Nyland will be interested."

Her bluff called, Elayne London pouted sullenly. "To hell with you and Inspector Nyland. I'm not going anywhere. I got a dance to do. It's almost time."

"Time for a showdown, yes," Anthony grabbed her and hauled her toward the other side of the little dressing room, where her street clothes hung from hooks in the wall. "Get dressed. Unless you want me to take you as you are."

She squirmed against him. "Let me g-go!"

"Yeah, mister. Let her go."

Anthony released the girl; whirled in his tracks. His cabaret proprietor, Pomeroy, was standing at the doorway with an automatic in his steady fist.

CHAPTER IV

GUNSEL'S THREAT

HIS GUN WAS TRAINED at Anthony's bandaged head. It was a
.38 Colt, the kind that could blow the top of a man's skull clear
across the room.

"I run a respectable joint, see?" the café owner said, tweaking the
spiked ends of his mustache with his free hand. "No rough play with
the hired help."

"Rough play, hell!" Anthony retorted. "I want this girl to go to police
headquarters with me, is all."

"You a dick?"

"I'm Jim Anthony."

Pomeroy looked impressed. He didn't lower his automatic, though.

"Mister, you could be the king of Peru and I still wouldn't let you
maul any wren that works for me. Besides, it's time Elayne was doing
her stuff out front. There goes your music cue, kiddo," he added to the
girl. "On your way."

The scantily clad dancer scurried from the dressing room; vanished.

Anthony measured Pomeroy. He could have broken the little man
in half, gun or no gun; but there were probably a dozen husky waiters
within easy call, trained to deal with unruly customers. You wouldn't
get very far, starting a fracas in a place like the Club Lorenz.

Besides, more flies can be caught with honey than with vinegar.
Anthony shrugged his deceptively broad shoulders and grinned
boyishly.

"No hard feelings," he said. "Maybe you'll let Miss London go with
me after she finishes her dance."

"That's up to her, mister. If she wants to, okay. If she don't, you
better not start anything. Now scram. Customers—aren't allowed in
the dressing rooms."

Anthony wandered forward to the bar; bought another double
brandy. Elayne London was cavorting in the blue glare of a spotlight,
sinuously twisting her lithe form to the subdued music of the orches-

tra. She was plenty good at her specialty. And she had the figure to go with it.

Presently she bowed to the applause, blew kisses at the patrons and made for the rear door. Anthony started after her, then halted; narrowed his eyes.

A hulking man in a worn blue serge suit had stopped the platinum blonde dancer by grabbing her wrist. Now he said something to her.

She paled, tried to wrench free. None of this by play got any attention from the audience, for a team of tap dancers were now the center of attraction in front of the orchestra dais. The back of the cabaret was clothed in shadows.

But Anthony saw what was happening, and he sprinted past the bandstand; sank his fingers into the shoulder of the hulking man in the blue serge suit.

"What do you think you're doing, bub?"

The guy swore bitterly and aimed a punch at Anthony's bandaged head. Anthony parried it; countered with a jolting uppercut which dropped his adversary like a poled steer. Elayne London opened her rouged mouth; screamed shrilly. Then she ran.

He sent the fellow flying over his head, then chased after the dancer.

WAITERS, BARMEN, AND bouncers were closing in from every direction. Anthony started after the fleeing girl; followed her down the rear hallway.

But she didn't dart into her dressing room. Instead, not even stopping for a topcoat, she arrowed through a back door into the alley behind the cabaret.

Somebody tackled Anthony, tried to climb his spine. He hunched himself, sent the fellow flying neck-over-teakettle, then resumed his pursuit of the dancer.

He gained the alley, raced to the street. He was just in time to see one cab pulling away from the curb, to be followed immediately by a second taxi—the last on the rack.

Anthony wasted no time staring after the two cabs. Turning, he loped toward his own parked U-drive sedan and found Tom Gentry prancing up and down beside it.

Of the brunette Eurasian beauty, Lotus Toy, there was no sign.

"What the hell happened?" Anthony rapped out.

"Almighty damn, I never saw anybody move so fast!" the aviator yowled. "I'm sitting here with Lotus when we see an undressed cookie come barging out of the alley and grab a hack. Then Lotus says the wren is Elayne London and tells me to trail her cab. But I can't, on account of you took the sedan's ignition key. So Lotus rushes over to the second taxi and starts out on her own. You saw them pulling away, didn't you?"

Anthony nodded, made a sour mouth and went back into the cabaret by its front entrance, with Gentry at his heels. Pomeroy, the proprietor, met them just inside.

"Look, mister, do me a big favor," Pomeroy said. "Get out and stay out. You and trouble are twin brothers."

"Okay," Anthony said. "But let me take that big lug in blue serge with me. The one I knocked over."

Pomeroy's grin was bleak, unfriendly. "Help yourself, chum—if you can find him. I had the boys dump him in the alley. Maybe he's still there. You sure hit him hard enough to keep him stiff a while."

Pivoting, Anthony strode out. He and Gentry searched the alley, from one end to the other. But the man in the blue suit was gone.

THE APARTMENT HOUSE which had been Sarah Beaumont's home was an old brick building half a dozen blocks west of Van Ness. Once it had been a sumptuous private residence, but the current owners had cut it up into suites, four on each floor.

The liveried doorman, who said his name was Finney, was still on duty when Jim Anthony and his freckled friend went there a bit later to ask him some questions about the Beaumont woman's murder. "I'll tell you all I know, sir," he said politely. "It won't be much, though."

His voice, like his face and manner, was without personality. He wore the visor of his military cap rather far down over his eyes and the tunic collar of his topcoat up about his chin.

To Anthony, there was something vaguely familiar about Finney, but he couldn't quite recall where he'd seen him before. Perhaps it was just that the man was so typical of his kind.

"After Miss London left the house, I went upstairs to the Beaumont apartment," he said. "The door was partly open. I knocked on it but nobody answered, so I walked in. Miss Beaumont was there on the floor with a bullet through her."

"Can you remember the time?"

"Around seven-thirty, maybe a little after. Miss Beaumont was dead, of course. Shame, too. She was awful pretty. Seemed to have plenty of money. She could've lived in a better place than this if she'd wanted to, I guess. Her sister stays at the Ridgeway Tower, and you know how swanky that is."

Which was about all Finney had to tell. He wasn't sure whether there had been one shot fired, or two. But what difference did it make? Everybody knew the Chink houseboy had killed her. That was what people got for hiring Chinamen in the first place, he added in a tone of disapproval. "There's plenty of white guys that'd be glad to have the work."

ANTHONY THANKED HIM, tugged at Gentry's arm. They headed back to their hotel—and, when they reached their suite, they found a visitor waiting for them in the corridor. It was Inspector Nyland from headquarters.

"So you decided to come back," he said.

Anthony stared at him. "Why shouldn't I?"

"Well, if I'd tried to bribe a witness and then threatened to kill her unless she left town, I might think twice before showing up around here," the inspector said sarcastically, stepping into the living room. "But the hell with that! Where's Soong?"

Anthony made an impatient gesture. "Would I have come to your office asking about him if I knew?"

"Maybe you found out since then. You admitted you're a friend of his. But get this, Anthony. Your money and influence won't save that murderous yellow guy when we lay our hands on him."

"So you think I'm trying to save him by bribing and intimidating witnesses," Jim said softly. "To be specific, the witness named Elayne London. She must have phoned you and tried to put me in the grease."

"She did, a little while ago," the homicide official grunted. "She says you called her this afternoon and offered her five thousand bucks to leave town by sundown or get bumped. Then, tonight, you tried strong-arm stuff in her dressing room."

"I strong-armed her in an effort to take her to headquarters and make her tell you of the attempted bribery, was all."

"Oh, yeah?" Nyland drawled his disbelief. "That don't make a lick of sense. You'd be double-crossing yourself."

Anthony shook his head. "Wrong, Inspector. I tell you I'm not the one who tried to scare her."

"Says you."

Tom Gentry lost his temper. "What this lug needs is a couple teeth kicked down his throat, Jim. And I'm just the guy that can do it. He reminds me of Lieutenant Trotter back in New York. Too damned big for his badge."

"Don't bother," Anthony told his red-haired and red-tempered aviator friend. Then be turned back to Nyland. "What time does this Elayne London say she got the bribery call?"

"About three this afternoon, she told me."

"Then she's either lying or making an honest mistake. Maybe the man's voice sounded like mine over the wire, but it happens that I was in an emergency hospital at that time, getting my injured bead bandaged after an auto accident near Palo Alto."

Nyland blinked. "Are you leveling?"

"Call the Bay Shore traffic patrol. Check their records. We were driven off the road by a sedan full of yellow men."

"Chinese?"

"I'd be more inclined to say they were Japs, although all the Japs in this area are supposed to have been evacuated. Anyhow, I can tell you this much. They hit me deliberately."

Nyland stared at the wealthy criminologist. "But why?"

"I didn't get a chance to ask them," Anthony smiled savagely. "But somehow I've got a hunch they wanted to put me out of action for a while—or permanently."

Again Nyland asked: "Why?"

"Maybe to keep me from contacting Bill Soong. You think Bill disappeared because he murdered the woman he worked for. *I* think he vanished for another reason."

"And that reason?"

"He'd wired me to come see him here in San Francisco. He had stumbled into some mystery that he wanted me to investigate."

"Do you know what the mystery was?" Nyland asked.

ANTHONY SAID NO, bitterly. "If I knew, I wouldn't be sitting here waiting for something to develop. Hell, I've even lost contact with Soong's fiancée, Lotus Toy. The last I saw of her, she was tailing that blonde dancer out of the Club Lorenz."

"Bigahd, the way you tell it, you make it sound straight," Nyland turned toward the door.

"It is straight."

"Maybe so. But I still think Soong killed Sarah Beaumont. And I'll keep on thinking so until you prove I'm wrong."

"I'll prove it," Anthony promised grimly. "Sooner or later."

The police official scowled. "Help yourself. But remember, I won't stand for any monkey business. This is San Francisco, not New York. You won't get away with anything here." Then he lumbered from the room, muttering to himself.

Tom Gentry opened a bottle of brandy, poured a drink for himself and one for Anthony.

"You sure brought that guy around in a hurry. I was just set to put a dent in his bridgework."

"Oh, Nyland's okay. Allowing for lack of education and training, you've got to admit that most cops do a pretty fair job, except they get in the habit of following the obvious."

As he defended the homicide inspector, Anthony raised the pony of brandy to his lips. He never drank it, though, because just then a knock sounded at the door.

"Come in," Gentry called.

The door opened and a thin, furtive man stepped over the threshold with a gun in his bony fist.

"Freeze," he said in a tubercular whisper. Then he looked all around the room. "Okay, boss, it's clear. Nyland didn't leave none of his coppers here."

From the corridor, another visitor stepped into the suite. He was the Club Lorenz proprietor, Pomeroy.

"Hey, what the hell?" Tom Gentry yelped angrily.

Pomeroy fingered his spiked mustache. "You shut up," he showed his tee tit to the freckled aviator. "It's your friend Anthony I'm going to talk to."

Jim Anthony raised an eyebrow. "What about?"

"About your sweetie. Dolores Colquitt. I got her under glass, down in Los Angeles."

CHAPTER V

DEATH'S DANCER

THE WORDS STRUCK AT Jim Anthony's heart like a physical blow. "You *what?*" he snarled.

"I got your sweetie under glass," Pomeroy repeated. "It was like shooting fish in a barrel. First I phoned your hotel here and found out you'd made reservations for her. The clerk told me she was due tomorrow morning, by train."

"Go on," Anthony said through white lips.

"Well, that meant she must be leaving Los Angeles tonight on a sleeper. So I long distanced some pals of mine down there. They had Miss Colquitt paged at the railroad station; told her there was a message for her—from you. She fell for the gag. Walked into the snatch as pretty as you please."

The millionaire criminologist balled his fists, took a step forward. "Damn your soul," he said.

"Take it easy, bud," Pomeroy's tubercular gunsel advised. "I shoot any guy that takes a poke at my boss."

Anthony froze. Even if he and Gentry jumped these two men and disarmed them, it wouldn't do any good. Not if it proved true that Dolores had been kidnaped.

"What's your game, Pomeroy?" he said grimly.

The cabaret owner's voice was deadly serious. "You've been poking into the murder of Sarah Beaumont. Why?"

"Because the cops have accused an innocent man, Bill Soong. I like Soong. He's a friend of mine. I want to clear him."

Pomeroy toyed with his mustache. "That's what I thought. Were you ever wrong, Anthony?"

"Occasionally. Not often."

"You're wrong this time. Soong's guilty. I string along with the cops on that."

"You're entitled to your opinion," Anthony said.

"I'm entitled to Soong, too. I want him. I mean I want him personally, before the law gets him."

The wealthy detective stared. "Meaning what?"

"Meaning I loved Sarah Beaumont and the Chink killed her. You understand, Anthony? He bumped the only woman I ever cared for. I want to pay him for that. Having the law send him to the gas chamber wouldn't help me. I've got to give it to him myself, in my own way. I want to see him squirm."

Pomeroy spoke in a dry, harsh monotone that held a vindictive, almost insane quality. Anthony shuddered when he pictured what would happen to Bill Soong if he ever should fall into the cabaret proprietor's vengeful hands.

"Why tell me all this?"

"Because you're the great Jim Anthony. If anybody can locate the Chink for me, you can."

"You think I'd work for you on a thing like that?"

"Not for dough, no. You got all the money you need. But I got Dolores Colquitt. She's okay, understand. She hasn't been hurt—and she won't be, if you play ball."

"You want me to hand you Soong in exchange for Dolores, eh?"

"You catch on quick."

"Suppose I can't find him?"

"You will, if you love your girl half as much as I loved Sarah Beaumont." The wiry little man turned to his gunsel. "Come on, Rudolph. We're through here."

They went out.

TOM GENTRY GRABBED at his tall, sun-bronzed friend's shoulder. "You going to let him get away with it, Jim?"

"Not if I can help it. But Dolores is on the spot, remember. I can't make a direct move as long as that holds true."

As he answered the aviator, Anthony was reaching for the phone. Now he dialed the editorial department of the San Francisco *Star,* which was supposedly an independent newspaper, but which in reality was controlled by the New York *Star,* owned by Jim Anthony himself.

He contacted the city desk. "Jim Anthony speaking."

The city editor's awed reply indicated that he knew he was talking to the man who paid his salary. "Yes, sir! What can we do for you?"

"I want everything you've got in your morgue files on that woman who was murdered last evening, Sarah Beaumont. Clippings, photographs—everything. While you're at it, get me a dossier on a man named Pomeroy, owner of the Club Lorenz. Send the stuff over to the hotel by messenger."

"Yes, sir."

"And one more thing. There's a witness in the Beaumont case, a dancer, Elayne London. I want—"

The city editor's voice crackled with excitement. "Then you must've heard the news!"

"What news?"

"The London jane was found dead in her apartment. Knifed. I got the flash not ten minutes ago."

Jim Anthony said: "Good God!" and rang off; turned to Gentry. "Let's get going, Tom. Elayne London has been murdered!"

THERE WERE A number of police cars drawn up in front of the converted apartment structure when Anthony and Gentry arrived. For one building, this seemed to be doing pretty well in the murder line. In a little more than twenty-four hours, two women had met death here.

Shoving through a crowd of reporters and uniformed officers, the detective sped upstairs, followed by his freckled friend. At the door of Elayne London's apartment, their way was barred by a bluecoat—until Inspector Nyland looked out, spotted them and motioned them inside.

The platinum blonde dancer's body was being lifted into an oblong wicker basket. In death, the London girl's rouged features seemed less coarse than they had appeared at the Club Lorenz; and there was a

As they lifted the girl's body into the basket, Nyland scowled:
"So the Chinaman came back and killed again, eh?"

wistful smile on her lips, as if she might be merely asleep and dreaming of something pleasant.

The illusion was harshly broken, though, by the raw stab-wound in her left breast, where the medical examiner had peeled away her spangled costume brassiere.

Nyland scowled at Anthony. "So the Chinaman came back and killed again. Killed this girl because she'd testified against him."

"You think Bill Soong did this?"

"Who else? But he won't get away this time. I've got every exit from the city blocked."

Anthony nodded. "Naturally. What about fingerprints on the murder knife?"

"We can't even find the knife, damn it."

Jim didn't comment on this. His trained eyes were quartering the room, and his mind was on an ugly possibility.

Sometimes a knife is a woman's weapon; and there was a green jade button on the carpet near the threshold of the flat, just inside the door. Into his memory there flashed a picture of the Eurasian girl, Lotus Toy, and her subconscious habit of plucking at the buttons of her frock when nervous or disturbed.

The round, flat flake of jade on the floor had undoubtedly come from Lotus Toy's white silk dress. Which meant that she had been here recently—and in an overwrought condition.

Which wasn't too surprising, since she had followed Elayne London from the cabaret. But what had happened when Lotus confronted the dancer?

Had she pleaded with the platinum blonde woman to change her testimony concerning Bill Soong? Had the dancer refused? Had Lotus then pulled a knife and stabbed her?

ANTHONY REJECTED THIS theory. It was as difficult for him to picture the exotic girl as a killer as it was for him to believe Bill Soong guilty.

Yet the jade button was here; and it hadn't come by itself. Elayne London was dead. She and the doorman had been the only witnesses against Soong....

... The doorman!

As Anthony thought of the liveried flunky, he cursed himself silently. Not often did he make a mistake, but he suddenly realized that he'd pulled a boner this time.

He pivoted, shot a question at Inspector Nyland.

"Where's Finney?"

"Finney?" the police official blinked. "Oh. The doorman downstairs. Damned if I know. He wasn't here when I came. He must've gone off duty for the night."

"Then he didn't discover the kill?"

Nyland shook his head. "Not this one. He reported Sarah Beaumont's murder last night in the apartment up above. But we got a bleat on this London girl's death from somebody else."

"Who?"

"A dame named Renee Beaumont. The sister of the jane that got killed last night."

"What the hell was she doing here?" Anthony exclaimed.

"She was going up to go through her dead sister's effects and get the apartment ready for sub-letting. She says she passed this door, saw it open and sort of glanced in as she went by. That was how she noticed Elayne London's body."

"Where is this Renee Beaumont now?"

"Still upstairs in the flat over this one."

"Mind if I go up? I'd like to ask her a couple of questions," Anthony said.

"Help yourself. You won't find her alone, though. She brought a guy with her, some magazine writer or something. Don Baxter was the way she introduced him to me. Funny looking bozo, all bent over like he had arthritis of the spine."

Nodding, Anthony left the flat. Trailed by Gentry, he went up a flight of stairs; knocked on a door.

A man opened it and looked out. Inspector Nyland had been correct; the fellow *was* funny looking. His torso twisted forward at a grotesque angle, as if he were bowing to unheard applause. This caused him to cock his head back when he looked at you, so that his body took on the general shape of the letter S.

But it was his face, rather than his physical deformity, that made Jim Anthony go tense. Unless he was badly mistaken, this was the man who'd forced him into that palm tree today; the man who'd been driving that sedan full of Orientals!

CHAPTER VI

TRIAL OF THE LOTUS

FOR AN INSTANT, ANTHONY** had a vengeful urge to grab the man, accuse him of hit-and-run driving, and turn him over to the cops downstairs; bring charges against him.

But he stifled the impulse. After all, he couldn't prove any such accusation now; and, moreover, he preferred to make sure of his ground before acting. The highway crash might have been accidental rather than intentional.

On the other hand, had it been deliberate, it meant that the twisted man was an enemy. To come right out and say so would gain Anthony nothing. In fact, it would put the fellow on his guard.

So Jim decided to pretend he didn't recognize the man with the crooked back. Instead, he smiled with affable politeness.

"Mr. Baxter?" he inquired.

"Yes."

"My name's Anthony. Is Miss Beaumont here? I'd like to speak to her if I may."

From within the room, a woman's modulated voice exclaimed in seeming delight. "Not the famous *Jim* Anthony?"

Then the twisted Baxter opened the door wide, beckoning Jim and his aviator friend into the room. Whereupon Gentry emitted another of his long, admiring whistles.

Renee Beaumont was superb. That was the only word to describe her. Not that she was actually beautiful, or even pretty. She was too tall for that. But she carried herself with a regal sureness, a magnificent poise which matched the perfection of her silver lame evening gown and the meticulous coiffure of her brown hair. Emerald pendants dripped from her ears at the ends of tiny, fragile gold chains, and there was a single unrimmed glass fitted to the left eye.

ANTHONY HAD SEEN many women in Europe wearing monocles but he couldn't recall one on this side of the ocean. Renee Beaumont belonged in pre-war Nice or Monte Carlo: and her companion should

"Look!" she gasped: then
shuddered into his arms.

have been at least a grand duke, rather than this twisted Don Baxter
with his crooked spine.

"Not *the* Jim Anthony?" she repeated, coming forward.

"Afraid so. And this is my friend, Tom Gentry."

She extended long, tapered fingers to the aviator, who seized them
and held them as if reluctant to let go. Later he told his sun-bronzed
friend that the thrill had sent live steam squirting out of his toenails.

But it didn't last long, because she disengaged her hand and turned
to Anthony.

"I know of your reputation, Jim. You don't mind if I call you Jim?" she purred. "And I've often hoped to meet you. What brings you here? Are you investigating the terrible thing that happened to poor Elayne London downstairs?"

"In a way," he admitted. "I'm more interested in the murder of your sister, though."

"My step-sister," she corrected him gently. "Sarah was an adopted child, poor dear." She dropped her monocle, dabbed her eyes with a lace handkerchief, polished the monocle and replaced it deftly. "But how could her death possibly interest you? She'd be *so* flattered if she were alive!"

"I'm interested because the police have accused Bill Soong. He used to work for me in my lab. I like him."

Across the room, Baxter cocked his head back on its thin, wry neck. "The police are damned fools. Soong didn't shoot Sarah. He wouldn't. He had no reason to."

"I wish you'd tell that to Inspector Nyland. Being a writer, you might convince him," Anthony said.

Renee Beaumont smiled. "Don's not a writer. He's an editor. He runs the *Return to Reason Magazine*. Perhaps you've seen it?"

"No," Anthony said, which was a lie. He was well acquainted with the publication. Then he added: "What do you think, Miss Beaumont? Do you disagree with the police, too?"

"Completely. Bill Soong wouldn't harm a fly. The man they ought to arrest is that nasty little ex-gangster, Pomeroy."

"The cabaret owner?"

"Yes," her voice took on a frigid vengeful quality. "Pomeroy was in love with Sarah. She tolerated him only because she was so bored. She treated him like dirt, most of the time."

Here was a new angle—definitely!

As Anthony digested the information, Tom Gentry broke out with a sudden thought.

"Hey, look!" he exclaimed. "Both Elayne London and that flunky doorman, Finney, testified they saw Soong come upstairs here before the shot was fired. But maybe they made a mistake. Maybe it was Pomeroy they saw!"

"That's possible," Renee Beaumont agreed eagerly. "I hadn't thought of it, but it could be."

"Then maybe Pomeroy got scared the London girl might change her testimony, put the finger on him. So he tried to bribe her or frighten her into leaving town. She balked, so he killed her tonight."

The tall, monocled woman was in complete accord with this reconstruction. "You've got it, Mr. Gentry!"

"The police may not think so," Anthony said grimly. "Nyland has made up his mind that Soong's guilty."

"But Soong *can't* be guilty!" Renee Beaumont protested. "He'd had the day off and told my sister in the morning that he was going down to San Jose. If he made the trip, he couldn't have come back at the time of the… murder," she seemed to dislike using the word.

Anthony looked at her. "Have you told that to Nyland?"

"Yes. He just laughed. He says Soong's disappearance is as good as a confession of guilt."

The criminologist scowled. "That disappearance is what sticks in my craw. And speaking of disappearances, did you ever know a Jap named Taoki Komura?"

FOR AN INSTANT it seemed as if Renee Beaumont might be going to faint. The monocle dropped from her eye, the color leaked out of her cheeks, and her knees buckled. Then she recovered her cool poise; smiled apologetically.

"Please forgive me. My heart… I have these seizures once in a while…."

Anthony had studied enough medicine to know she was lying. It wasn't a heart attack that had shaken her. It had been fear—pure, crystalline fear induced by the Jap's name.

She was a remarkable woman, though. When she spoke again, it was in a voice as steady and normal as if nothing out of the ordinary had occurred.

"Taoki Komura?" she said. "Yes, I knew him. He imported lovely things from the Orient. My sister and I often bought from him. Poor fellow, I wonder what really happened to him?"

The twisted Baxter cocked his head back, made a bitter mouth. "They say the Black Dragons got him. I don't believe it. The F.B.I. wouldn't let an outfit like that operate in this country."

"Let us hope you're right," Anthony turned toward the door as he spoke. "And here's hoping we're right about Bill Soong's innocence, too. Come along, Tom. We've got work to do."

Gentry didn't seem too pleased to leave Renee Beaumont's dazzling presence. Later, downstairs, he said as much.

"That jane's got class, Jim. All my life I've been dreaming of meeting a woman like that."

"You're always dreaming of meeting a woman. Any woman."

Gentry grinned. "This one's different. She's for me, Jim. I go for that monocle stuff."

"Do you also go for phony heart attacks?"

"What do you mean, phony?"

"I watched the pulse in her throat. It accelerated, but there was no syncope. Her heart's okay. I just scared hell out of her when I mentioned Komura."

The aviator blinked. "You're nuts!"

"So I'm nuts. I'll tell you something else. Baxter is the guy who drove that sedan into us this afternoon."

BACK AT THE hotel, Anthony found a big envelope from the *Star* awaiting him. He opened it; sat down to read.

The file was fat on the Beaumont girls. They'd been more than prominent in San Francisco's café society; and in addition to the clippings, the *Star's* city editor had typewritten a brief *precis* of their careers.

Anthony's photographic memory digested the written pages and then he looked up at Gentry.

"Better start dreaming about some other charmer, Tom. It says here that Renee's engaged to Don Baxter."

"So what? I've been engaged to a dozen wrens, but you ain't seen me ankle down the middle aisle yet, have you? Engagements don't mean anything. Who the hell is Baxter, anyhow?"

Anthony's brow furrowed.

"I know more about the magazine he edits than I know about him. It's full of anti-war, anti-British propaganda. I wouldn't be surprised if Brother Baxter had been getting a few dollars from the Nazis before we threw Hitler's bully boys out of the country."

"Or the Japs," Tom Gentry said it idly, but Anthony dropped the papers he'd been reading; jumped to his feet. His reaction made Gentry stare. "Now what've I said?" he asked penitently.

"You may have handed me the key to this whole thing, Tom."

"Hunh?"

"The Japs. Of course, the Japs! Let's go back a minute. Bill Soong graduates from Columbia, leaves New York and comes back home here to San Francisco. He gets a job as chauffeur and house boy with Sarah Beaumont."

"Well?" Gentry waited.

"Sarah Beaumont knows a Jap importer named Taoki Komura, who becomes friendly with Bill Soong despite the fact that Chinese and Japs are natural enemies. Then America gets into the war. Komura disappears before he can be evacuated with the rest of the Japs in San Francisco. Bill Soong starts worrying over something; asks me to fly west and see him."

GENTRY RUBBED HIS jaw. "Yeah. Then Sarah Beaumont is croaked and Soong lams. You and I get here; take a ride out the Bay Shore. We're crowded off the road by a car full of Japs driven by a guy named Baxter, who's engaged to the murdered Sarah Beaumont's step-sister. Did Baxter know you were to meet Soong? Was he trying to prevent the meeting? That's the question."

"No, Tom. The question is: What dangerous knowledge had Soong stumbled on?"

"Okay, I'll bite. What was it?"

"I'm not prepared to say, as yet. But I'm beginning to think it cost Sarah Beaumont her life. And the life of that dancer from the Club Lorenz, Elayne London."

"You ain't forgetting Dolores has been snatched, are you?"

"I'm not forgetting," Anthony's voice was bleak. "But the man who had her kidnaped, the cabaret owner, Pomeroy, must be handled with kid gloves—for Dolores' sake. I've got to unravel the rest of the puzzle before I get around to him."

"And where do we start?"

"By hunting up the apartment house doorman, Finney."

"What's he got to do with it?" Gentry demanded.

"He happens to be a mistake I made; a neglected identification that I didn't realize until later. *He's the guy in the blue serge suit, the one who came to the night club and started trouble.*"

"No!"

"Yes. You see, it was sort of shadowy by the orchestra stage when he tried to stop the London girl and talk to her. I didn't get too good a look at his face when I popped him."

The freckled aviator frowned. "So you didn't tab him when we saw him later in the apartment house doorway, huh?"

"Unfortunately, no. He was wearing his livery by that time, with the cap pulled down, the collar up. All doormen look pretty much alike, anyhow. You're inclined to dismiss them as a type rather than as individuals."

"So now you want to ask him what he wanted to see Elayne London about, is that it?"

Anthony nodded, picked up the phone and called the city editor of the *Star*, from whom he elicited the doorman's home address. Then he and Gentry went down to the street, piled into a taxi and got going.

Presently they drew into the cheap residential street where Finney lived. As they neared the address, Anthony noticed another cab parking in front of the doorman's shabby little bungalow. A girl emerged from this other cab; a diminutive girl whose white silk frock stood out against the night's darkness.

"Tom! Did you see that girl?"

"Yeah," Gentry's low-pitched voice held bewilderment. "Damned right I saw her! Now, what the hell do you suppose Lotus Toy is doing here?"

CHAPTER VII

FLUNKY'S FINISH

THERE WAS NO DOUBT about it. The dainty feminine figure clad in white silk was the Eurasian girl, the missing Bill Soong's fiancée—and she was vanishing in the gloom, pelting toward the rear of the doorman's cottage.

Anthony ordered his cabby to proceed to the end of the block. Here he and Tom Gentry alighted, told the hacker to wait for them. Then they stole silently back along the quiet street, with Gentry doing his best to match Anthony's noiseless stride. The latter moved like a wraith, for all world like an Indian brave hunting game in the primeval forest.

Gaining the house, the wealthy criminologist studied it for a brief moment. It was dark, deserted looking, as if it had stood vacant for a long time; or as if its tenant had made no attempt to keep up the yard or the building's exterior.

"Lotus went around to the back," Gentry whispered. "Do you suppose she's inside now by the kitchen door or something?"

"We'll soon see." As he said it, Anthony produced his prized steels from a concealed pocket within his coat. With silent skill he applied them to the front door lock, manipulating them until the lock's bolt-slid soundlessly from its keeper. Steady pressure then forced the door inward. The two friends moved over the threshold into sinister darkness.

Ahead of them, a flashlight beamed momentarily, then winked out. Anthony's eyes narrowed. If Lotus Toy had come here to have a meeting with Finney, why was she so cautiously using a flash? What was the reason for her apparent stealth?

Well, he'd damned soon know the answer, he promised himself. Employing a trick he had learned in India, Anthony, by a conscious effort of will, distended his pupils until his vision was enabled to penetrate the blackness. Seizing Gentry's elbow, he steered his companion forward.

They passed through a small dining room into a kitchen. Despite the lack of light, Anthony perceived the confusion here; the dirty dishes piled in the sink, the disorderly housekeeping. It was obvious that Finney lived alone, looked after himself and didn't do too good a job of it.

There was a swinging door that gave access to a short hallway. Beyond this, the flashlight blinked again; winked out. Anthony followed its brief beacon; saw Lotus Toy coming out of a bedroom, unsteady on her feet. He sped silently toward her, grabbed her.

"Okay, Lotus. Start talking," he said grimly.

THE EURASIAN GIRL uttered a tiny scream, struggled in his embrace, tried to break free. Her exotic fragrance was like an intoxicating drug in his nostrils, and he felt the frantic heaving her breast made against his chest. He'd have been less than human not to get a thrill out of the contact.

Then, somehow, she managed to release one hand, the one that held the flashlight. She snapped the beam at Anthony; drew a sobbing sigh of relief.

"Y-you!" she moaned. "Oh-h-h, th-thank God!"

"For what?"

She clung to him, welded herself against him as shudders went coursing through her flesh. "In there… that bedroom… it's horrible…!" she choked.

Tom Gentry took the flashlight away from her and directed its ray into the room she indicated.

"Jeest!" he made gulping noises in his throat. "Jim, take a look!"

Anthony had already seen. On a mussed bed law the sprawled figure of Finney, the apartment house doorman, with his shirt stained crimson from a stab-wound that pierced his heart.

"WH-WHY ARE YOU looking at me th-that way?" Lotus Toy whimpered. "You don't think *I* k-killed him…?"

"I'm waiting for you to tell me," Anthony's tone was level, neither accusing nor exonerating.

The Eurasian girl shivered. "I didn't do it. I swear I didn't. You've got to believe me!"

"Take it easy, hon," Tom Gentry tried to soothe her. "Jim ain't going to feed you to the wolves. Just come clean with him, is all. I'll stand by you."

Her almond eyes were grateful. Then she turned back to the sun-bronzed criminologist. "I—I'd better start from the beginning. You know I took a cab and followed Elayne London when she ran out of the Club Lorenz—"

"Yes, I know. Why did you do that?"

"I sensed something wrong when I saw her get into that other taxi with n-nothing on but her costume. I wondered what she was running away from. I had to find out. So I acted on impulse; trailed her."

"And?"

"She must have known she was being followed, I guess, because her driver twisted and turned through half of the streets in San Francisco. We crossed Market, went south of the Slot, then back again and out Kearney, over the hills and turns toward China Reach, past the Presidio and back toward town. Then something happened, a traffic signal or something, and we lost her."

ANTHONY NODDED. "I can understand why she shook you. She was scared. She'd had a phone call offering her five thousand dollars to get out of town by sunset of today or be killed."

Lotus Toy's slanted eyes widened. "Th-that's the same threat Finney received!"

"What? How do you know that?"

"He t-told me so, himself."

"Let's keep this thing straight," Anthony fought for calmness. "Go back to where you lost Elayne London's cab."

"Well, I had my driver cruise around a while. Then, by accident, we spotted her taxi but she wasn't in it. I hailed her hacker and asked him where she'd gone."

"What did he tell you?"

"He said she'd got out of his cab after shaking me. He loaned her his own topcoat because she was practically undressed. And she paid off with a small diamond ring from her finger. That was all he knew."

As the driver lurched aside, Jim seized the wheel, still firing at the kill-car.

Anthony paced the room. "In a topcoat, she could go anywhere without attracting notice. What did you do?"

"I th-thought she might make for her own apartment, so I went there. But instead of going upstairs right away, I stopped to talk with the doorman, Finney," the Eurasian girl glanced toward the man's corpse and shivered.

"It checks," Anthony said. "By that time, he'd recovered from the knockout I'd dealt him at the cabaret. He'd had time to get back on his job. And meanwhile. I'd been there to question him—not recognizing him as the man I hit in the night club."

Lotus nodded. "So he told me."

"What else did he tell you?"

"Well, I started in by asking him if he was positive it was Bill Soong he saw go upstairs just before Sarah Beaumont was murdered. He said yes, he was sure of it. But of course he couldn't swear it was Bill who had fired the shot."

"Anything more?" Anthony asked.

"He explained why he'd gone to the Club Lorenz to see Elayne London. He'd got a phone call offering him five thousand dollars to leave town, with a threat of death if he stayed. He knew that Elayne and himself were the only two witnesses against Bill Soong, and he wanted to ask her if she'd had a similar threat."

"But he never got a chance to ask her," Anthony mused. "When he accosted her in the cabaret, she got scared. I butted in, messed things up."

"Yes. And now comes the terrible part," Lotus faltered. "Finney and I decided to go upstairs to the dancer's apartment and see if she might have come in the back way without being noticed. We found her door ajar and she w-was dead on the floor...."

The millionaire detective scowled. "Whereupon you nervously pulled a jade button off your frock before running out.

"I d-did?" her mouth opened in dismay. "Oh, my God! Then the police will be looking for me—!"

"NOT NECESSARILY," HE reassured her. "They won't know where the button came from. Meantime, what brought you here to Finney's house?"

"Well, when he saw Miss London's body he got scared; figured he might be next. He refused to talk to me anymore; said he was going to get out of town."

"He ran out on you?"

"Yes."

"But you weren't finished with him," Anthony hazarded. "You spent some time, learned his address and came here, only to find him dead."

She nodded.

"Okay," he told her. "I believe you. Now let me ask you about this Jap, Taoki Komura. At the hotel this afternoon you said his disappearance had worried Bill Soong."

"That's right. But I wouldn't know why."

"Were you acquainted with Komura yourself?"

"No. All I know about him was what Bill told me from time to time. He was kind to Bill—always tipping him five or ten dollars for running little errands."

"Such as?"

"Well, like taking manuscripts over to Don Baxter's magazine."

"Komura wrote articles for that propaganda sheet?"

"I think so. That's what I understood."

Anthony's eyes glowed. The puzzle's pieces were beginning to fall into place, to take shape and form.

"Now let's talk about Soong," he said. "Do you know anything about the trip he was supposed to make to San Jose?"

She seemed surprised. "How did you find out about that?"

"Never mind. Just answer my question."

"There's not much to tell. He had the day off; phoned me he was going to San Jose on business. He was supposed to leave that afternoon."

"But instead, he apparently didn't go. He came back to Sarah Beaumont's apartment that evening around the time she was shot. Then he dropped out of sight," Anthony supplied.

The Eurasian girl's eyes moistened. "That seems to be the way of it. But I don't know what kept him from making the trip; what brought him back to Miss Beaumont's flat. I—I never heard from him again." She swayed weakly, wearily.

Anthony caught her and supported her. "Forgive me for running you through the wringer this way. You're worn out. I'll take you home. You need rest."

"I can take her, Jim," Tom Gentry offered too eagerly.

The criminologist smiled. "She needs rest, not recreation. I think you'd better go back to the hotel and wait for me; receive any messages that might come."

"Aw-w-w, nuts!" the genial aviator said with feeling. He obeyed orders, though. He knew better than to argue, once Anthony's mind was made up.

So Anthony escorted Lotus Toy to her home on Grant Avenue, at the fringe of Chinatown, and then returned to his hotel suite. Here he found Gentry practically pop-eyed with excitement.

"Almighty damn, Jim!" the freckled flyer exclaimed. "Wait'll you hear the news!"

"What news?"

"The cops have located Bill Soong!" Gentry said.

CHAPTER VIII

DEATH IN THE DITCH

A **SINKING SENSATION SLUGGED** Jim Anthony in the pit of the belly. He was thinking of Dolores Colquitt, the girl he loved. That cabaret proprietor, Pomeroy, was holding her as a kidnaped hostage to be released only in exchange for Soong. But what would happen to Dolores now, with Soong in custody?

"He's been arrested?" Anthony gasped.

Gentry shook his head. "Hell, no. That's the screwy part. He couldn't have murdered Sarah Beaumont last evening, anymore than he could've killed the dancer and the doorman—tonight."

"Why? What are you driving at, Tom?"

"Soong's been in a San Jose hospital since yesterday afternoon," the aviator answered. "He's got a waterproof alibi!"

"You're sure?"

"So Inspector Nyland said when he phoned a while ago. Nyland sounded sore as hell, which proves he must be convinced."

"Just what did he tell you?"

"It seems Soong was in an auto smash that knocked him unconscious. He didn't have any identification papers, so the hospital people didn't know who he was until he came to this evening and mentioned working for Sarah Beaumont. Then they put two and two together, called the cops."

Anthony paced the rug. "Soong with an alibi! By God!"

"Yeah. And that monocled babe, Renee Beaumont—she phoned us, too. She's heard the news from Nyland, and she's on her way down to San Jose. She wants you to come, if you will."

"Damned right I will! Maybe we can catch a ride with Nyland."

"No. He's left by this time."

"Okay. You get on the phone," Anthony clipped out. "Arrange to have a car and chauffeur waiting for us in thirty minutes. Maybe you'd better call the coffee shop, too. Tell them to have some bacon and eggs and coffee waiting for us."

"It's good to see you alive," Jim said,
and the muffled voice came back:
"There's not much left of me."

While Gentry carried out these instructions, Jim took a quick
shower, and the fatigue vanished like magic from his muscular body.
Dressed, he rejoined his freckled friend; debated whether or not to call
Lotus Toy and tell her the news. He decided against this. She might
want to go along with him to San Jose, and he preferred not to take her.

Downstairs, he and Gentry spent exactly seven minutes wolfing
hot coffee and food. They were at the hotel entrance just as the sedan
they had ordered pulled up at the curb.

"San Jose Emergency Hospital," Anthony told the chauffeur as he settled back in the tonneau beside Gentry. Then he closed his eyes, catnapping, rebuilding his amazing vitality.

Tom, though, was not content with a catnap. Soon his head began to loll forward and his breathing became an audible snore. He lacked his sun-bronzed friend's splendid reserves of strength, and the constant strain of the past few hours had sapped his vigor to a low ebb.

Dawn was breaking as the car whispered through silent, deserted streets toward the Bay Shore highway. This, too, was devoid of traffic save for an occasional slow-moving truck. The driver let his speedometer clock up to forty-five; and the fresh, salt-tangy air coming off the bay brought Anthony awake.

They passed San Mateo and he could see the unused race track which had been made into a reception center for internees. It made him think of Taoki Komura, the Jap who had vanished.

Am I on the right trail? Anthony asked himself. Had the missing importer any connection with this series of murders? *Soon I will know,* he thought. Again he closed his eyes, and the sedan's steady swaying was a cradle lulling him to rest.

THE SUDDEN BITE of hastily applied brakes yanked him wide awake. Instinctively he grabbed for one of the upholstered hand-holds to keep from being thrown to the floor.

Tom Gentry almost skidded off the seat. "Hey, what the devil goes on?"

Up front, the chauffeur was fighting his wheel and trying to stay on the highway; swearing bitterly and fervently at the big sedan that was edging him toward the ditch.

Anthony stared at the offending car and yelled a sharp warning, for a ray of early morning sun had glinted upon the nickeled barrel of a revolver.

"Look out!" he rasped at his chauffeur, ducking and dragging his own automatic from its armpit holster. With his free hand he knocked Tom Gentry to the floor—just as a vicious volley blasted slugs from the other machine.

Anthony's driver yipped, clapped a hand to his shoulder, and sagged sidewise, driven down by a bullet's hammering impact. His wheel, abandoned, began to twist.

Jim Anthony realized that the car would crash in another instant; and he reacted with reflex swiftness. Straightening up, he pumped lead at the machine that was pushing them off the road. With his other hand he reached forward past his wounded chauffeur, clutched the steering wheel, twisted it furiously to the left.

There was a grinding, rending sound of metal meeting metal as the two cars locked fenders. Anthony fired at the other sedan's driver; and he didn't miss.

The man jerked, slumped. Completely out of control, the attacking car veered off to the far side of the highway. It hurtled horribly through a fence protecting the ditch, leaped the ditch itself and went smashing into the concrete pillars of a vacant service station with cannonball velocity.

Anthony didn't have time to watch this, though. He was trying to steer his own machine by reaching across the front seat. Presently he contrived to worm his way forward, settle under the wheel. Then, panting, he applied the brakes.

"Almighty damn!" Tom Gentry gasped. "I thought you weren't going to make it!"

The detective got into reverse; backed the sedan to a point opposite the spot where the other car had come to a shattering halt. He alighted, gun in hand; ran toward the wreckage, ready for instant action. But action wasn't needed now. Both the wrecked car's occupants were dead. The driver had perished from Anthony's well-aimed slug. His companion, who still had the nickel plated revolver clenched in his lifeless hand, had been crushed when the engine had been driven back into his lap by the force of the collision with that concrete pillar.

Anthony studied their yellow faces, knew they had been Japanese. Then he went around to the driver's side, peered in, took a long look at the sedan's ownership registration certificate which was affixed to the steering column in conformity with California law.

The car was registered in the name of one Edward Pomeroy, and his address was the Club Lorenz.

CHAPTER IX

SOONG!

OVER BY ANTHONY'S CHARTERED automobile, Tom Gentry was putting a bandage on the wounded chauffeur's shoulder. It was only a makeshift, torn from the man's own shirt, but it seemed to suffice. At least Gentry had stanched the flow of blood, and the chauffeur was conscious.

"I'll be... okay, sir," he was saying as Anthony came up. "Just a... little nick, I guess."

"Nick, hell! That slug tore a piece of meat out of you as big as a beefsteak!" the aviator growled. "Hey, Jim, see if I've done this job all right."

Anthony inspected the bandage, approved it. From his pocket he extracted a flat, black leather kit—a miniature replica of the larger kit he carried when investigating cases nearer home. This one was more compact, portable; but it contained a variegated assortment of materials he might find useful in conducting a crime-hunt.

He opened the container, withdrew a vial of pellets, spilled four into his palm and gave them to the chauffeur.

"Swallow these. They're sulfanilimide tablets. Cut down risk of infection from your wound."

Then, making the man comfortable on the rear seat, the criminologist and Gentry examined the damage to their car. Its left front fender was crumpled firmly against the tire and the running board had been torn off.

With the help of the jack handle they bent the twisted metal away from the tire's tread. As they worked, Gentry panted a question.

"What about those guys in the other jalopy?"

"Dead. Both Japs. I think it's the same car that ran us off the road yesterday, although Baxter wasn't driving it this time."

"The hell you say!"

"Yes. And here's something else. The registered owner is Pomeroy of the Club Lorenz cabaret."

The aviator's eyes bulged. "Jeest, that certainly ties him into the mess, doesn't it?"

"We'll take that up later. Let's get this fender fixed and roll on to San Jose. Our chauffeur needs attention and I'm anxious to see Bill Soong." As he said it, Anthony heaved on the bent fender. His magnificent strength lifted the metal with a rending sound—and tore it completely away from the tire.

THERE WAS QUITE a crowd in the visitors' room at the hospital when they walked in. Renee Beaumont sat in a far corner, looking very pale and attractive in black, her sinuous feminine figure attracting no more attention than did the monocle she wore in her left eye.

Like a twisted letter S, the arthritic Don Baxter bent over her solicitously, talking in a low tone. On the other side of the room stood Inspector Nyland and a couple of men from the San Jose police department.

There were newspaper reporters, too, and cameramen. They all turned when Anthony and Gentry appeared, and flashbulbs blazed white brilliance as the photographers snapped the famous investigator.

Renee Beaumont flowed to her feet and moved forward, her every movement a poem of fluid grace. She extended a cool, indolent hand.

"Jim Anthony!" she purred. "I'm glad you got here. I didn't want to go in and see Bill until you arrived. After all, he worked for you longer than he worked for my sister."

Then Nyland came up, his face red, his voice almost apologetic.

"Damnedest thing I ever saw," he grumbled. "Here I had a solid case worked up against the Chink, two witnesses, and we find he couldn't have killed Sarah Beaumont because all the time he's been right here in a hospital bed!"

"You don't have two witnesses," Anthony corrected him.

"Okay, one, then. The dancer girl, Elayne London, is dead—but there's the doorman."

Anthony dropped a verbal bombshell. "Finney's dead, too."

"What?" the homicide official roared apoplectically.

Jim told of discovering the doorman's corpse, omitting nothing except Lotus Toy's part in the affair. There was no use involving the Eurasian girl, he decided.

Nyland listened in helpless bewilderment. "But what does it all mean?"

"That's what I hope to find out before long. And before somebody else makes another attempt to get rid of me!"

"Still thinking about your car accident yesterday, eh?"

"No. I'm thinking about my car accident today on my way down here." And Anthony summarized what had happened.

Nyland's stupefaction might have looked almost funny—under less grim circumstances. "Damn!" he muttered. "Then you were leveling when you said there was something behind all this!"

"Sure he was leveling," Tom Gentry said sourly. "You think a man like Jim Anthony goes around kidding dumb cops?"

Nyland was so stunned he let the insult pass.

THEN ANTHONY ASKED the homicide official to take him to the doctor who'd attended Bill Soong's injuries. They went into the hospital office, and Nyland presented a white-coated surgeon, Dr. Loring Herkimer.

Herkimer was elderly, pleasant, capable looking. "I've heard of your work, Mr. Anthony. It will be a pleasure to tell you anything you want to know."

"How badly is Soong hurt?"

"Internally, not at all. Some traumatic abrasions of the torso, but nothing serious. His face, though, was considerably damaged."

"To what extent?"

The surgeon spread his hands. "You might say I had to reconstruct his features. From what he told me, he had accepted a ride from a passing motorist whose car then crashed into a pole. This driver was apparently uninjured, for he left the scene and hasn't been seen since. But Soong went through the windshield."

"Another auto accident!" Anthony frowned. "The pattern keeps repeating… Soong was gashed by the glass?"

"Badly. It severed the masseter muscle from the left ear almost to the nostril, requiring six sutures. The mentalis was cut, along the lower lip above the point of the chin. The nasolabialis was slashed, the right buccinator laid open from the mandible to the corner of the eye. Too, the frontalis muscle was exposed completely across the forehead."

Gentry whistled. "Sounds like you had to patch him up with an electric welder!"

"It was quite a job of hemstitching," the surgeon confessed modestly. "And to make it worse, we had no idea what he'd actually looked like originally. So we just did the best we could. I'm afraid even his own mother wouldn't recognize him, though, when the scars heal."

"May I see him?" Anthony asked.

"Yes, if you don't excite him too much. He's still pretty weak, of course; suffering from post-operative shock. The poor devil's heart wouldn't stand a general anaesthetic, so I had to use local injections of novocaine and adrenalin. It must have hurt like hell."

The detective digested this, then followed the surgeon out of the office, accompanied by Gentry and Inspector Nyland.

Anthony fell into step alongside the homicide official; asked him a question.

"This driver who picked Soong up and gave him a ride and then vanished after the accident. Have you any idea why he should drop out of sight?"

"Sure. He was driving a stolen car. Don't ask me why a guy in a hot heap would stop to pick up a Chink hitch-hiker. But you can see why he ducked out after the smash-up."

In silence, Anthony pondered what Nyland told him. Then Renee Beaumont and Don Baxter joined the little group; rode an elevator up to the second floor.

The surgeon, Herkimer, thought it wouldn't be good for Soong to have so many visitors. So Anthony and the attractive Renee were the only two who entered the injured man's room.

ON THE BED, the accident victim lay restlessly. His head and face wrapped mummy-like in white bandages with only one eye showing through a slit in the encircling gauze, he peered feebly at his callers.

"Mr. Anthony!" his voice was weak, muffled, but he managed to inject a note of glad surprise into it.

There was a yellow hand plucking at the covers, and Anthony pressed it with both his own.

"Hello, Billy. It's good to see you alive. We were beginning to wonder."

"I'm alive all right. It takes more than a windshield to put me in the graveyard. But I'm sorry you had all the worry. And... even sorrier about Miss Beaumont's death...."

His one visible eye turned toward his murdered employer's attractive step-sister, and blinked in sympathy.

Renee said: "Thank you, Billy," in a choked voice. "Th-thank you very much."

"And how's New York?" the injured man asked Anthony.

"Dandy. I saw a friend of yours the other day. Remember Mary Low whose old man ran that laundry on Pell Street? She was asking about you."

"Mary," you felt that there was a grin under the bandages to accompany the reminiscent tone. "We had some swell times together, Mary and I."

"I'll say you did," Anthony agreed. "You got away with murder, Bill."

"But she won't know me after this. The doctor says I'll hardly know myself."

"Then you'll be safe if you ever come back to New York," Jim Anthony chuckled. "Mary's old gent was looking for you with three shotguns when you left, I hear. But we mustn't talk too long now. I'll see you again in a day or so, unless I'm called back east."

"You think you will be?"

"I'm afraid so. I'll keep in touch with you, though." Anthony turned from the bed, took Renee Beaumont's arm. Together, they left the room.

"You're nice, Jim," she said in the corridor. "Only a nice person would take such an interest in a former employe, even to his love affairs. I never knew Soong was such a gay blade."

"Neither did I," the criminologist answered enigmatically.

CHAPTER X

DEAD END

IN HIS HOTEL SUITE, Jim Anthony was busily engaged in fitting a compact electrical apparatus into an expensive leather briefcase when a knock sounded at the door.

He answered it himself, since Tom Gentry was downstairs in the lobby looking over the noon editions of the newspapers.

Anthony showed no surprise when a gun poked at him and the tubercular little hood named Rudolph walked into the room, followed by his boss, Pomeroy, owner of the Club Lorenz.

Pomeroy had a *Star* in his hand, folded to show the big black headlines. "What's this about the Chink being found in a San Jose hospital?" he demanded. "Some gag you cooked up?"

Ignoring the gun held by the cabaret proprietor's bodyguard, Anthony went back to his brief case and closed it before answering.

"It's true," he said. "He was in an auto accident and pretty badly smashed up."

"But hell, how could he have killed Sarah Beaumont if he was in the hospital at that time?"

"I told you before that Billy Soong didn't kill her," Anthony said quietly.

Pomeroy's shifty eyes glittered. "Then who did?"

"I'm not prepared to tell you—yet."

Under the spiked mustache, Pomeroy's mouth made an ugly slitted line. "Listen, wise guy. These pals of mine down in Los Angeles have still got your girl. Try crossing me and see what happens to her."

"I'm not crossing you," Anthony said evenly. "When I can show you Sarah Beaumont's murderer, I will. But get this straight. If you or your friends harm one hair of Dolores Colquitt's head I'll hunt you down and break you in half with my naked hands."

The cold, toneless fury of the threat made Pomeroy go pale in spite of his gunsel guard.

"I've got nothing against you personally, Anthony. Or Miss Colquitt, either. But I want the dirty rat that killed Sarah."

"You'll have your chance," Jim promised. "Meantime I want to know something. Do you own a 1940 Buick sedan, Roadmaster series, license number 77-B-D-568?"

Pomeroy tensed. "Why, yes. But what—?"

"Where is that car?"

The man said uncertainly: "The last I knew, it was in the garage back of Sarah Beaumont's apartment. I loaned it to her. I've got three others, and to tell you the truth, I'd forgotten that Buick until this minute."

"You may as well forget it completely, then, unless you had it insured. It's wrecked between San Mateo and San Jose. When I saw it early this morning, there were two Japs in it. Dead," Anthony added, watching Pomeroy's face closely.

The cabaret owner's expression showed blank amazement. "Japs? I thought they were all in concentration centers."

"They're supposed to be," the investigator admitted. "But I think you'll find a few of them haven't been caught yet. The two in the Buick will never bother anybody again, that much is sure."

"But how'd they get the car?"

"If I were ready to tell you that, I'd be ready to tell you who killed Sarah Beaumont and why. Maybe this afternoon I'll be in a position to talk. I don't want Dolores held any longer than necessary. And remember, if any harm comes to her—"

"Play square and it won't," Pomeroy growled. "Cross me and all hell won't save her." He jerked a nod at his gunsel, and they left the suite as furtively as they had come.

IT WAS MID afternoon when Tom Gentry noticed his tall, sun-bronzed friend dressing with special care.

"Going somewhere, Jim?" the aviator asked.

Anthony nodded. "Before I left Renee Beaumont at the hospital at San Jose, she invited me to call on her this afternoon for cocktails and a chat."

"Swell! Wait'll I change my shirt. I've got a yen for that babe."

"Sorry, Tom. You weren't included in the invitation." Then, picking up his brief-case and grinning at the freckled Gentry's obvious disappointment, he left the room with his turban-like bandage making him resemble a handsome and rather jaunty Malayan maharajah.

Downstairs, he summoned a cab. "Ridgeway Tower," he told the hacker. Then he settled back, after casting a single glance through the rear window. A somber black

She ran her hands over him. "No weapons," she reported.

limousine pulled into the traffic stream behind him, keeping a discreet distance away.

Anthony's lips parted in a grim smile. Pomeroy was tailing him!

Renee Beaumont occupied the pent-house apartment of the Ridgeway Tower, and she personally opened the door to his ring.

"Jim," she purred. "How nice of you to come. I was afraid you might forget poor little me, what with all the things you've probably got on your mind."

It would be damned difficult, he thought, to forget a woman as striking as Renee. The lavish good taste of her apartment was duplicated by the well-chosen expensiveness of the lounging pajamas she was wearing. They were of heavy, shimmering black satin, the trousers softly outlining her shapely legs, the jacket clinging like poured oil to her breast. A startling white gardenia was pinned to her perfectly coiffed hair, she was smoking a cigarette in a long ivory holder, and the monocle was affixed to her left eye as if it had grown there.

Anthony put his brief-case on a chair; faced her with undisguised admiration. Her tallness matched his own, almost, so that he could look full into her eyes.

"I never forget anyone who intrigues me," he said.

"And do I… intrigue you?" She said it softly, like a challenge, yet he had an impression that she was secretly mocking him.

His gaze swept her sleek figure. "You intrigue me very much," he told her frankly.

Laughter tinkled furrily in her throat, like bells muffled in ermine. "I think you must be impressionable," she tantalized him with deliberate coquetry in her voice, her glance, the supple and sinuous movement of her body as she undulated closer to him. "You look almost as if you'd like to… kiss me."

"Perhaps I would," he said. "If you could convince me of one thing."

"And that?"

"Make me believe you had nothing to do with the murder of your step-sister," he growled.

RENEE BEAUMONT RECOILED as sharply as if he had slapped her across the face. The monocle squirted from her eye, the cigarette dropped out of her hand unnoticed on the thick, costly carpet. An acrid odor of scorched wool drifted up from the ruined rug, unheeded.

"Wh—what did you say?" she panted.

"I accuse you of killing your stepsister. Or was it your friend Don Baxter who actually fired the shot?"

She just stared at him.

He went on, conversationally. "It must have been rather a bad surprise to the two of you when Soong walked in just as you were murdering Sarah. Especially after you'd so carefully arranged an errand that would take him to San Jose."

"Are you insane?"

"No, not that I know of. On the contrary, I think I'm just sane enough to see through your whole set-up. Yours and Baxter's. Too bad he failed to kill me when he forced me off the road yesterday afternoon.

Too bad his Japs also failed this morning. As for now, I suppose you invited me up here to feed me a poisoned cocktail or something, eh?"

"You're playing the tune," she said coldly. "You seem to know the music."

"Most of it," he agreed. "For instance, that's not Bill Soong we saw in the San Jose hospital. He was coached to pretend to recognize me, but he made one bad slip that proved he was an impostor."

"Really?"

Anthony nodded. "When I mentioned a Mary Low, he fell for it. But the *real* Soong wouldn't have, because there's no such person as Mary Low. I made her up. You see, Bill Soong was very much in love with a Eurasian girl named Lotus Toy here in San Francisco. All during his years in New York he never even looked at another woman."

"So you have proved that the accident victim is not Soong," Renee Beaumont purred. "Then who is he?"

"At a guess, I'd say he's the missing Jap importer, Taoki Komura."

FROM BEHIND THE detective a new voice spoke, harshly, gutturally. "You're a smart fellow, Anthony. Much, much too smart for your own good—or for ours. Turn around and keep your hands high."

"Hello, Baxter," the sun-bronzed detective said even before he slowly pivoted to look at the man. Then be lifted an eyebrow, for Baxter was no longer twisted as if by arthritis of the spine. That had been a pose, a sort of disguise. The fellow now stood upright, uncrippled, and he was surprisingly tall. He seemed muscular, too; strong enough to look out for himself even if he hadn't been clenching a Luger automatic in his fist.

He spoke to the woman. "Frisk him, Renee."

She obeyed, running her hands expertly over Anthony's clothing. "No weapons," she reported.

Jim made a bitter mouth. "Would I have done myself any good, carrying a gun?"

"No," Baxter said. "I had you covered all the time."

"That's what I thought. You're damned thorough, Baxter."

"Thorough enough to remove a man that gets too inquisitive! Before I kill you, though, suppose you tell me just how much you know."

Anthony bowed sardonically. "To begin with, you run a Nazi-Axis propaganda sheet and the Beaumont girls were working with you in the pay of the Jap government, under direct orders of Taoki Komura—

who, incidentally, conducted his importing business as a blind. Actually, he's with the Black Dragon Society; or that would be my guess. Maybe he's head of its California branch."

"Keep talking. You're going good."

"Well, everything was fine until all Japanese were ordered evacuated. Komura didn't want to go to a concentration center. So you had to cook up a scheme to give him freedom for action in espionage and fifth column work."

"You know what the scheme was?"

ANTHONY NODDED. "HE had to assume a new identity. Since he's a yellow man and couldn't pass as a white, you chose to have him become an apparent Chinese. Then he'd be free to come and go as he liked."

"So?" Renee Beaumont purred.

"So it was arranged that Komura would assume the identity of Bill Soong. He was Sarah's house boy; that made it all the easier. Komura cultivated Soong, studied his mannerisms, his voice, his background. That was to perfect the subsequent impersonation when the time came."

"Go ahead. What else?"

"But Soong got suspicious and wired me," Anthony said. "You must have found out about this; which was why you tried to kill me on the Bay Shore highway yesterday. Meantime, though, you had gone ahead with your other plans."

"Such as?"

"You despatched Soong on an errand to San Jose. The idea was to kidnap and murder him when he got there. In turn, Komura would go through a fake accident, having his face slashed with broken glass. When the plastic surgeons repaired his features, he planned to impersonate the genuine Soong and be free to continue his espionage and propaganda work."

"Clever, eh?" Baxter grinned crookedly.

"Damnably. But your plans slipped somewhere. For some reason, you were forced to shoot Sarah Beaumont."

"Yes. She lost her nerve when she realized the real Soong was to be killed. She threatened to spill to the police. That means liquidation in this game," Baxter spoke the confession as casually as a man might tell of stepping on an insect.

Anthony inclined his head. "And then, just as you fired a shot through Sarah's heart, Soong himself came into the apartment and caught you red-handed."

"The fool Chink had forgotten his bill-fold and identification papers," Baxter's tone was still casual. "The very papers Komura should have had for his impersonation."

"I thought it was something like that," the millionaire criminologist said. "Soong came back to get his papers, which was just too bad. You probably slugged him, took him out the back way and disposed of his corpse somewhere. But by that time it was too late to get Soong's wallet to Taoki Komura, who'd already gone through with his fake accident in San Jose."

Renee Beaumont drawled a remark. "Komura didn't really need the papers, anyhow."

"No, I guess not," Anthony agreed. "Everything seemed to be working okay—until you learned that the dancer, Elayne London, and the doorman, Finney, had both seen the genuine Soong go upstairs just before that shot was fired. So now Soong was accused of Sarah's murder."

"That messed it up," Baxter admitted.

"DAMNED RIGHT IT did! Soong was dead by this time, of course. You'd killed him. But the cops didn't know that. They were hunting him. And how could Komura dare impersonate a man who was wanted on a homicide charge? That might be dangerous. Even with his hospital alibi, Komura was in a jam—because Finney and Elayne London were in a position to smash that alibi. They had seen the real Soong at the time he was supposed to be having his accident in San Jose. He couldn't be in two places at once. Therefore, the man in San Jose would be unmasked as an imposter."

"What was the answer, wise guy?"

"The answer was to bribe those witnesses out of town," Anthony said. "And to murder them if they refused to leave. Which you did. You also had those two Japs try to murder me on the highway this morning. They used a car which Pomeroy could easily get from her garage. They failed to kill me, though."

"But *we* won't fail," Renee Beaumont snapped. "We'll sink you in the bay, the same as we did Soong. Before we do, I'd like to know something."

"What?"

"How did you guess it was Komura in the hospital at San Jose this morning? What made you suspect him and pull that trick Mary Low question on him?"

Anthony smiled. "The surgeon said he was forced to use novocaine because the man's heart wouldn't stand a general anaesthetic. I knew the real Soong's heart was sound. Therefore, the person they operated on had to be somebody else. Komura seemed the most likely bet."

"Fair enough, mister. Get set. This is your finish." Baxter tightened his finger on the Luger's trigger.

Before he could fire, though, the door of the penthouse burst open and Pomeroy, the cabaret owner, catapulted into the room, a gun bellowing and jumping in his fist.

"I heard it all, damn you!" he yowled. "You killed Sarah—the only woman I ever loved!" And he sent three slugs bashing into Baxter's chest.

Baxter staggered, went down. As he toppled, his Luger vomited at Pomeroy. Gun-thunder blended with gun-thunder in the room as the night club proprietor hit the floor. Then, in sudden silence, Renee Beaumont screamed shrilly and made a dash for the door.

TOM GENTRY WAS just coming in. "Looks like I'm just in time, baby," he said. He grabbed her, hit her on the jaw, knocked her all the way across the room.

Anthony stared at him. "Tom—!"

"Yeh. I got tired wondering what kind of tryst you were keeping," the aviator rubbed his freckled chin. "So I decided to see what cooked. I sure found out," he added.

Anthony raced over to where Pomeroy lay on the rug, coughing red froth from his punctured lungs. "Pomeroy!" he shook the café owner. "Pomeroy, can you hear me?"

"Yes…"

"Listen. I found the killers for you. You've had your revenge. Do you remember your promise?"

"Give me… pencil… paper…"

Gentry produced an old envelope and a fountain pen; shoved them into Pomeroy's fist while Anthony supported the man. Then the pen made scratchy, uncertain sounds as it scrawled a wavery message.

Finished, Pomeroy signed it. "Give… to Rudolph… my… gunsel… he'll phone… friends in… Los Angeles… Dolores Colquitt will… be free… in twenty minutes…"

He coughed again, twitched spasmodically, and lay ominously still. He had gone to join his beloved Sarah in death's long sleep.

Jim Anthony loped for the door; barked a command over his shoulder.

"You call Inspector Nyland, Tom. I'm going to see about Dolores."

"Sure, but—but jeest, Jim, what about all this mess? Suppose Nyland asks me questions I can't answer?"

"There's an electrical recording machine in my brief-case. I had it switched on the whole time. Play it back for Nyland—he'll hear Baxter's confession, and Renee's." Then the millionaire criminologist was gone.

THE CARIBBEAN CASK

IT WAS A CASK THAT COLUMBUS HAD THROWN INTO THE SEA
AND WAS PURPORTED TO CONTAIN A PERSONAL MESSAGE
ADDRESSED TO THE KING OF SPAIN. TO JIM ANTHONY IT WOULD
HAVE BEEN OF COLOSSAL INTEREST—EVEN IF TOM GENTRY'S
AND DOLORES' FATE WEREN'T DEPENDENT ON HIS FINDING IT.

WITH DISBELIEVING EYES, JIM Anthony stared at the big black headlines which disfigured the front page of the New York *Star*. There was no real reason why he should doubt the accuracy of the headlines in question, since he was the paper's owner and publisher— and he knew full well that the *Star* was not in the habit of faking news.

All the same, he could scarcely credit this present Page One banner line. And his stupefaction must have been mirrored in his expression; for the girl at his side, his lovely fiancée, Dolores Colquitt, sensed his tension and demanded to know its cause. "Is something wrong, Jim?"

For answer, he passed the newspaper to her. "Take a look at this."

Dolores quickly scanned the heavy type, and a gasp made her alluring breasts surge tautly under the clinging bodice of her frock. "But— but there must be some mistake!" she protested in a stricken voice. "Tom couldn't possibly be held on a charge of murder!"

"A lot of things are possible," Anthony made a bitter mouth. "Remember, we've been away a full two weeks. Almost anything can happen in that length of time."

The girl was not convinced. "If what the *Star* says is true, then surely Tom would have got in touch with you. He could have called you."

"Maybe the police wouldn't allow him to use the phone," Jim Anthony hazarded. He settled himself under the wheel of his sleek convertible coupé, meshed the gears and eased the big machine at a tangent from the curb, heading toward the city.

As he drove, his sun-bronzed face with its high cheek bones and aquiline nose gave him a remarkable resemblance to his American Indian ancestors, all the more noticeable now that those dark features were set grimly in an impassive mask of thought. Silently he pondered the headlines which had disrupted the afternoon's pleasant serenity:

NOTED AVIATOR HELD IN ATTORNEY'S DEATH
Tom Gentry Faces Murder Charge

A traffic cop, headed the other way, recognized the expensive convertible and its driver; touched his hat in salute as he zipped past on his motorcycle. It was a little thing in itself, that respectful gesture; but it illustrated what a well-known figure Jim Anthony was in New York.

WEALTHY BEYOND THE dreams of most men, possessed of a superb build and an equally superlative education, Jim had inherited a newspaper, a swanky downtown hotel, and a vast amount of other important property from his Irish-American father. From his mother, a Comanche princess, he drew the Indian blood of which he was so inordinately proud—and the stolid calmness that made him stand out in any gathering.

With all his force he hurled the keg at the man's leering face.

With such a background, he might well have become one of the world's gayest playboys; for his properties were efficiently managed by capable employees, and he could have ignored everything except the pursuit of pleasure. Instead, he had chosen to turn to the study of crime and the tracking down of wrongdoers; and, as a result, by careful study and preparation, he had made himself a criminologist of international repute.

Now, as he sent his big car purring along under the legal war-time speed limit, he told himself he must once more call his uncanny talents of detection into play. His weird sixth sense whispered that peril lay ahead; that he faced a grim battle to save his best friend, the freckled, happy-go-lucky aviator, Tom Gentry.

FOR TWO WEEKS, Anthony and his fiancée, in company with a select party of friends, had been enjoying the woodland vistas at Jim's hidden lodge in the Adirondacks, the Tepee. They had tried to persuade Gentry to join them; but the genial aviator had insisted on remaining in town, saying that he had certain business which needed his attention.

Anthony had made no effort to pry into the nature of this mysterious business; but now he wondered if it could have some connection with Tom's present trouble. The millionaire criminologist was preoccupied as he dropped Dolores Colquitt at her home, bade her good-bye, and turned the convertible toward police headquarters on Centre Street.

Of old, he knew Gentry's penchant for getting into jams; and in this case he hoped desperately that the difficulty wouldn't prove as serious as the headlines indicated. Parking, he hurried into the grim building and, through force of habit, made directly for the office of Lieutenant Trotter of the homicide bureau, at the far end of the hall.

Anthony and Trotter were not exactly friends; they'd had too many battles in the past. But there was a mutual respect between them that served in the place of friendship—although Trotter sometimes tempered this respect with open animosity. Now the burly homicide official looked up.

"Hello, Anthony," he grunted around the chewed fragments of an unlighted cigar. "I wondered how long it would be before you showed up—"

Uninvited, Anthony sank into a chair and narrowed his dark eyes to glittering slits. "You've been expecting me?"

"Naturally," Trotter sighed. "Every damned time that screwball pal of yours deals himself into a jackpot, you come barging down here with bells on. But this is one time when you won't do him any good."

"Why not?"

"Gentry's bought himself a peck of very sour apples," Trotter growled. "And he'll eat them, core and all. We've got the goods on him up to the hilt!"

Jim Anthony's voice was a soft purr with steel beneath. "You might have let him contact me, at least. I deserved that much consideration after all the favors I've done for you."

"Let him?" Trotter sounded aggrieved. "*Let* him? Why dammit, I practically got down on my prayer bones, begging him to get in touch with you or a mouthpiece or somebody."

"He refused?"

"Flatly. I tell you the poor dope is off his chump. He sits in his cell and won't open his face, won't try to help himself. He just smiles like a billikin."

"May I see him?"

Trotter stood up. "You're damned right you can see him. I'd have phoned you myself only I didn't know where to reach you. I like Gentry, see? He's screwy, but he's a nice guy. I don't want to send him to the hot seat without giving him a chance to fight back."

"The hot seat," Anthony said. "As bad as that?"

"Yeh. The man he browned was a slimy shyster named Walter Wetzel. They had some kind of deal brewing, I don't know exactly what; but there was a lot of money involved, apparently. Anyhow, this Wetzel was having a little party night before last, it being his fortieth birthday. He got a phone call, excused himself and went out. He walked up an alley, there was a shot, and when the neighbors found him he was croaked."

Anthony leaned forward. "And just what makes you believe Tom fired that shot, lieutenant?"

"We found his rod nearby. Registered to him. He don't deny it belongs to him."

"Any fingerprints?"

"Plenty, but blurred." Trotter took some glossy photographic enlargements from a desk drawer; fanned them out for inspection. "They're all Gentry's dabs except one, and that's so smudged we can't tell much about it."

Anthony scrutinized the prints, paying especial attention to the one which was not Tom Gentry's. Faint though it was, he engraved it indelibly in the index files of his remarkable memory. Then he said: "Does the murder bullet match the rifling of Tom's gun?"

"It does."

"And you think it was Tom who phoned Wetzel, lured him into that alley?"

The homicide lieutenant scowled impatiently. "That would be my guess. But how the hell can I make sure? I tell you he won't talk."

"I'll make him talk," Anthony said quietly.

Trotter growled: "If you can, you're a better man than I am." And he signed a pass, rang for a turnkey.

CHAPTER II

BLONDE TROUBLE

TOM GENTRY NEEDED A shave. Aside from his sprouting crop of whiskers, though, he showed little or no effects from his two day stay in jail. He was sprawled lazily on the iron bunk, casually reading about the murder of Walter Wetzel, when Anthony was admitted to the cell.

He dropped the newspaper and sat up cheerfully. "Hi, pappy. Have a good trip?"

Jim nodded. He was accustomed to the freckled aviator's unpredictable moods, but he had never before seen his friend so completely oblivious to peril. Under the circumstances it seemed unnatural.

"Are you okay, Tom?"

"You bet. I've got dough enough to pay for special grub and smokes, and I can have all the reading matter I want. The quarters are a little cramped, but who wants exercise? Great place for a rest cure, jail. An ideal vacation spot. I ought to try it oftener."

The millionaire criminologist blew up. "Quit it, you idiot! From what Trotter says, you're in a bad fix. By rights, a man in your position should be wringing and twisting."

"Trotter talks through his hat. I've got nothing to worry about. Nothing at all. I can walk out of here any time I feel like it. Wait and see."

"You seem to forget a guy named Wetzel was murdered."

"I haven't forgotten," Gentry answered. "But I'm not losing any sleep over it. He had the makings of a first class rat. It's a wonder to me he lived to be forty. Somebody was bound to kill him sooner or later."

"Were you that somebody, Tom?"

"No."

"Can you prove it?"

"Later, sure. Right now she don't dare talk. She'd be exposing herself to danger; and you'd miss out on something mighty damned big. But in a few days—"

"*She!*" Jim Anthony pounced on the word like a hungry jungle tiger. "I might have known there'd be a woman in it somewhere. Any time you get behind the eight ball, it's dressed in skirts. You're like a fence-running tomcat!"

GENTRY, GRINNING, TOOK this as a compliment. "Maybe so, Jim. But from now on I'm a one woman guy." A far-away look came into his eyes. "I've found the only girl in the world, pappy. She's gorgeous. When you see her—"

"Which will be damned soon," Anthony snapped brusquely. "I want her name and address. Right now."

Gentry surged to his feet. "Nix. You can't walk in on her and start throwing your weight around."

"The hell I can't."

"I mean you mustn't. She'll get me out of this mess as soon as I say the word. I ain't quite ready yet, is all."

"Why aren't you?"

"I told you. It might put her in danger. Anyhow, she and her brother need time to find the Cask."

Anthony blinked. "What Cask?"

"Never you mind. You'll see what it's all about when the time comes. I can't explain any more, just now. All I'm asking you is, lay off Susan Claire for the present."

"Ah. So her name is Susan Claire."

A blush spread over Gentry's genial face, making the freckles stand out like copper pennies. "Why can't I learn to keep my big mouth shut?" he groaned. "Now you'll trace her and spill my beans from hell to breakfast!"

"I won't spill any beans," the sun-bronzed criminologist said, frowning. "And I promise you I won't let anything happen to this girl—if she's on the level."

"Can I depend on that?" Gentry asked earnestly. "And can I depend on you not to say anything to the cops about her until I give you an okay?"

"Yes. Now tell me where she lives."

THE APARTMENT BUILDING faced Central Park from the west. A silent elevator whisked Jim Anthony up to the fourteenth floor, disgorging him into a long and richly carpeted corridor through which you could have driven a herd of elephants without making any noise. Anthony came to a door discreetly numbered 1492, and pressed the buzzer button.

Nothing happened, so presently he pressed it again—harder this time. It didn't do him any good, though. Nobody responded, even when he gave up ringing and started knocking. Either Susan Claire wasn't home or she didn't want visitors.

Eyes narrowed, lips compressed to a thin line of resolution, the wealthy investigator drew his prized steels from their concealed pocket in his coat and applied them to the door's latch. No lock had yet been built that could withstand Jim Anthony's manipulation of those famous steels, and this one was no exception. There was a click, and the door swung open.

Anthony stepped in, soundlessly.

Inside, the apartment was precisely what he had expected to find. The furnishings were standard quality such as you'd see in any of the better uptown buildings, and the big living room over-looked the park. But there were no personal belongings scattered around to indicate permanent occupancy—and this appearance of temporary usage was emphasized by an open suitcase on the chaise lounge, half packed as if in readiness for a fast getaway.

Anthony loped toward the suitcase to inspect it. But before he reached the divan, he heard a sound behind him. He stiffened, pivoted, stared.

A DOOR HAD opened at the far side of the room, and beyond it lay a bathroom. Now a girl was standing on the threshhold, draped in a wet Turkish towel; a lissome blonde girl who must have just stepped from the shower without stopping to clothe herself. Droplets of water glistened on the warm ivory skin of her shoulders above the wrapped towel, and there was anger in her brown eyes as she met Jim Anthony's gaze.

Also, there was a .28 automatic in her right fist.

"Well!" she said in a brittle voice, and there was a gun in her fist.

"Well?" she said in a brittle voice.

For an instant, Anthony was speechless. Not with surprise at being caught in the role of an intruder, but with admiration for the girl whose gun menaced him. The clinging towel outlined the proud firmness of her torso, the supple slenderness of her waist, the lyric flare of her feminine hips. Silken tendrils of golden hair escaped the green bathing cap which shaped itself to her patrician head; and her face, despite its lack of make-up, was outrageously beautiful.

It was a competent face, too; a self-assured face, challenging and piquant and thoroughly unafraid.

She spoke again, calmly, dispassionately. "Who are you? And what are you doing here? Talk fast, mister."

"So you're Susan Claire," the millionaire criminologist said. "No wonder Tom raved about you. You're exquisite."

Suspicion deepened in her brown eyes. "Tom who?"

"Why, Tom Gentry, of course."

"You know him?"

"He's my best friend."

A subtle change stole into her voice, her manner. "Then you must be Jim Anthony!" she said swiftly, apologetically. And she lowered the threatening automatic.

The movement of her arm caused the towel to slide downward, and, blushing, she yanked the damp material back where it belonged as the wealthy criminologist said: "Yes, I'm Jim Anthony."

"But—but I thought my door was locked—"

"It was. Locks don't bother me, though, when I want to talk to somebody."

She gave him a long, steady stare. "I can guess what you'd like to talk about. Wait here while I put something on." Whirling, she ducked back into the bathroom and closed the door after her—but not until Anthony caught a fleeting, thrilling glimpse of undraped curves where the towel didn't reach....

THE INSTANT THE door clicked shut, Anthony sped noiselessly to that open suitcase on the divan. Deftly his long fingers explored the piece of luggage; and when he finished, nobody could possibly guess the bag had been searched. Every single bit of its contents had been replaced with mathematical precision.

Not that the search paid many dividends. What Anthony learned was important merely by inference. All the clothing in the suitcase was expensive, in good taste; but every label had been carefully removed. Obviously the golden-haired girl didn't want her background traced; which meant that the name she was using, Susan Claire, was quite probably an alias.

By the time she returned to the living room, Anthony was at the window which overlooked the park far below. Hearing her, he turned. She had exchanged the bath towel for a robe of shimmering blue silk that was much more becoming than the towel and almost as revealing. Her dulcet figure was liquidly graceful under the rippling azure cloth and her smile held seriousness.

"Now we can talk about Tom," she purred. "First, tell me why he sent you here."

Anthony shook his head. "He didn't send me. I had the devil's own time getting your name out of him. He sits in jail like an idiotic clam; refuses to help himself. He told me you would clear him at the proper time."

The girl's eyes looked startled, worried. "Has he mentioned me to the p-police?"

"No. And he made me promise I'd keep your name out of it before he gave me your address."

She relaxed. "Good! I knew I could rely on him."

"But don't be so certain you can rely on *me*," Anthony said curtly.

"Wh-what do you mean?"

"I mean I'm not going to twiddle my thumbs while Tom Gentry faces a murder rap. I came here to hear your story; and it had better be good. Otherwise I'll turn you over to Lieutenant Trotter and let him sweat you."

"But you p-promised—!"

"Promises given to fools and imbeciles don't count. And in the hands of a beautiful woman, Tom's the biggest fool alive. He may be willing to risk the hot seat for you, baby; but I won't let him."

She pouted, her scarlet lips making a kissable rosebud of temptation. "When you talk that way, you scare m-me."

"You'll have good reason to be scared unless you can explain your connection with the death of that shyster, Wetzel."

Her delicate shoulders quivered. "I swear I'm not involved in that m-murder, Mr. Anthony!"

"Then how can you clear Tom?"

"By giving him an alibi. He was here in this apartment with me the night Wetzel was k-killed."

A glitter came into Anthony's dark eyes. "Good God! So it's as simple as that! The crazy jerk is just trying to protect you from scandal!"

"No." She made a pleading gesture. "It isn't scandal we're afraid of. It's something worse."

"Such as what?"

"My personal safety. If I come out in the open and furnish Tom with an alibi, certain people will learn where to find me. The Queen would stop at nothing to get what she wants."

"The Queen? Who is she and what is she after?"

"She's after the Cask," Susan Claire answered in a whisper. "She and her followers think I have it. Or at least they believe I know where it's hidden."

ANTHONY SEIZED HER by the wrists and pulled her close. "I'm fed up with listening to this double-talk," he growled. "Gentry mentioned a Cask when I saw him in his cell; now you bring it up again and add a Queen to it. A Queen with followers. What's it all about?"

"I c-can't tell you unless Tom says it's okay." For an instant she trembled against the millionaire criminologist, with the fragrance of her hair drifting to his nostrils.

A tingling thrill lanced through him at this brief, intimate contact with her nubile body. Then he pushed her away, gently. "All right. If it takes Tom's okay to make you talk, we'll get that okay."

"How?"

"You and I will go down to Centre Street and see him. Climb into some clothes, sister. Make it snappy."

She studied him; seemed to recognize the finality of his decision. Then, nodding, she grabbed up her suitcase and scurried into an adjoining boudoir.

ANTHONY WAITED SIX minutes; seven. Then, scowling, he crossed to the closed door of the bedroom and grasped the knob; found it locked. He rapped but received no answer.

Swearing under his breath, he used his steels on the latch; shoved the door open and entered the room, peered around. Susan Claire wasn't there. Neither was her suitcase. Another door across the boudoir gave direct access to the outer corridor. It was ajar, mutely indicating the path of her escape.

Anthony lunged toward this second exit As he moved, he miscalculated his clearance between the bed and the bureau; struck the bedstead a glancing blow, with force enough to move it several inches on its casters. And when it rolled aside, it disclosed a corpse on the floor.

CHAPTER III

VOODOO KILL

IN FROZEN FASCINATION, JIM Anthony stared at the dead man who had been concealed under the bed. Clad in a cheap suit of dark blue serge, the corpse lay on its back, horribly impaled through the heart by a curious, needle-sharp blade not much bigger than a long old-fashioned hatpin.

Judging from the brownish coagulation of blood around the wound, the fellow must have been murdered some while ago. Anthony substantiated this by flexing the left wrist of the corpse and finding it stiffened with rigor mortis. And as he made the test, he came upon another discovery.

Clutched in the dead man's hand there was a tiny object which rolled free when Anthony dropped the clammy wrist. A sudden exclamation formed on the millionaire detective's lips as he eyed the thing.

It was a miniature wax doll, hardly two inches in length; a doll with features hearing an uncanny resemblance to the face of the murdered man. A small, black-headed pin impaled the tiny figure, exactly the way a longer and sharper weapon had been plunged through the heart of the doll's human counterpart.

Jim Anthony needed nobody to tell him what this represented. During his world travels, he had spent considerable time in the Caribbean islands, especially Haiti; and he knew of the voodoo rites practised by the natives there.

When a witch doctor wanted to wreak disaster upon an enemy, he made a miniature wax figure of his victim and then mutilated it while mouthing incantations. Thus, whatever damage was done to the doll was supposed to happen also to the person in whose image the figure had been created.

Which was all right, perhaps, when you encountered it somewhere in the Haitian jungle. But to find such a symbol of black magic clutched in a murdered man's hand on the fourteenth floor of a New York apartment house… well, that was something else! Anthony's strange sixth sense began to stir, tolling a warning knell deep in his subconscious mind.

GRIMLY THOUGHTFUL, HE considered the puzzle into which he'd plunged. First, Tom Gentry stood accused of killing a crooked attorney named Wetzel. But Tom was innocent; he had an alibi in the golden-haired Susan Claire.

Susan, though, was an enigma in her own right. She dared not come forward with Tom's alibi, for fear a certain "Queen" might find her. This so-called Queen and her followers were allegedly hunting a mysterious Cask.

Who was this Queen? And who was the dead man under Susan Claire's bed? Had Susan known the corpse was here, all the time she was talking to Jim Anthony? Had she calmly bathed, perhaps washing this man's blood off her dainty hands when Anthony had first entered the apartment?

It was difficult to picture the blonde girl as a killer. She looked like an angel; a very kissable angel. But Anthony had encountered other women whose innocent smiles masked murderous impulses, and he knew that beauty and guilt frequently go together.

Questions teemed through the wealthy criminologist's mind; but the silent boudoir mocked him, offering no answers. He bent forward over the corpse on the floor; examined the pockets of the cheap blue serge suit. But someone had been there ahead of him, apparently, for the pockets were empty.

Balked in this, he looked at the label inside the coat and learned that the garment had been bought in New Orleans—if that meant anything. He had a hunch it *did* mean something in connection with the miniature doll transfixed by a pin. The doll spelled voodoo. Voodoo spelled Haiti. From Haiti, the natural port of entry into the United States would be New Orleans.

That much of the jigsaw puzzle fell into place with little effort; but the larger, grimmer mystery remained. Two murders had been done, both unsolved, and Tom Gentry was accused of one of them. Tom's blonde alibi had vanished, leaving the second slain man behind her. Had she been afraid Jim Anthony would discover the corpse in her boudoir, or had she run away because she feared a different kind of danger?

On impulse, Anthony drew a flat black kit from under his coat. Out of the kit he brought a prepared glass slide, which he used for taking fingerprints. He made an impression of the dead man's fingers on the glass slide, dusted the prints with a special powder and held the glass up to the light. Sudden tension gripped him as he studied the results of his experiment.

"Good God!" he whispered to himself. "The same prints that were on Tom's gun! *I've found the guy who shot Wetzel!*"

THAT CONCLUSION WAS obvious; but proving it to the police would be another thing entirely. Dead men don't talk, and this man in blue serge was very dead indeed. Perhaps he was Wetzel's killer, but would Lieutenant Trotter believe it?

Probably not, Anthony thought

The dolls were of wax, and they were uncanny in their resemblance to their models.

as he stowed the glass slide away in the black kit and replaced the kit under his coat. He realized he should phone Trotter and tell him of these new developments; but intuition warned him that such a course would only complicate matters.

Once the police began muddling into the mess, they'd naturally start a search for Susan Claire. Susan might then drop out of sight completely, thus wrecking Tom Gentry's hope of establishing his innocence. The thing to do was locate Susan; force her to alibi Gentry. After that, the cops could be told about the murdered man under her bed—and she could do her own damned explaining!

Jim Anthony would have no compunctions about throwing the blonde girl to the wolves if, by doing so, he could save Gentry from the electric chair. And, having reached this decision, he silently left the apartment.

As he closed the front door after him, he noticed the metal numerals on its panel: 1492. That was odd coincidence, he thought. 1492 was the year in which Christopher Columbus first discovered the New World, landing on the island of Santo Domingo. And mysterious Haiti, home of voodoo and black magic, occupied the northern half of that same island!

Like the music of a song popular a few years back, the puzzle went round and round, and came out—nowhere!

DOWNSTAIRS, ANTHONY PILED into his convertible and sent it whispering toward the Waldorf-Anthony Hotel, where he made his residence in the penthouse apartment. As he drove, he was deep in thought. He must find Susan Claire, he kept telling himself. He must find her and make her talk.

And meantime he must not allow Tom Gentry to learn that he had scared the girl into running away. Tom, being infatuated with her, would do anything to protect her—even if it meant shouldering a murder rap.

The thought plunged Anthony deeper into preoccupation, so that he failed to notice the cab which was following him as he drove through the late afternoon traffic. Nor did he pay any heed to the tall, hook-nosed man who trailed him across the lobby of the Waldorf-Anthony a little later. It was not until the millionaire criminologist entered his personal automatic elevator that he saw the hook-nosed man crowding into the cage with him.

"Sorry," Anthony said politely. "You've made a mistake. You want one of the elevators across the lobby. This is a private car to my penthouse."

The man pulled a gun. "I haven't made any mistake, Mr. Anthony. Close the door and press the button. You and I have got some talking to do."

"Really?" Anthony said softly. And although he could have broken the fellow in half with his bare hands, he obeyed orders with a counterfeit meekness. By feigning fear of that drawn revolver, he might learn something important.

Presently the whirring cage drifted to a stop at the rooftop level, and the door automatically slid open. Ahead loomed the foyer of Anthony's apartment, into which the two men strode without speaking.

Then Hook-Nose, looking around, lipped: "Anybody else here? Servants, maybe?"

"No. I gave my staff a vacation when I took my trip to the Adirondacks. Since they weren't expecting me to return so soon, they're not here now."

Hook-Nose took his word for this. "Okay, friend. In that case we can get down to brass tacks. Where's the Cask?"

"I don't know," Anthony answered truthfully. "And I haven't the slightest idea what Cask you're talking about."

"That's a lie. The Queen doesn't like liars, Mr. Anthony."

"Ah. So you're from the Queen."

"Correct."

"And she wants the Cask."

"Sure she wants it. It belongs to her," Hook-Nose said. "If you've bought it, you're holding stolen property. The Queen can make plenty of trouble for you."

"By any chance could she make this kind of trouble?" Jim Anthony purred. And as he spoke, his fists flashed out like twin striking cobras. One knocked the man's gun aside. The other collided with the fellow's jutting jaw.

Hook-Nose went down and stayed down. He fell like a sack of oats, as if there weren't a whole bone left in his tall body. And as he dropped sprawling on the floor, a tiny object rolled from his coat pocket; came to rest at Anthony's feet.

It was a doll; a miniature but perfect wax replica of the golden-haired Susan Claire.

CHAPTER IV

VOYAGER'S CASK

JIM ANTHONY REGARDED HIS handiwork without the slightest alteration of expression. His first move was to stoop and pick up the little doll, paying no attention to the man he had knocked unconscious. Thoughtfully he inspected the tiny figure with its exquisitely modeled features and genuine yellow hair. There was no doubt about it; the miniature figure definitely represented the Claire girl.

But there was no pin thrust into the waxen breast; nor had the doll been otherwise mutilated. Which might mean anything or nothing. A voodoo image of Susan Claire indicated that she was in danger; but since the image was undamaged, this might be interpreted to the effect that the girl herself had not yet been harmed. There was no way of knowing for sure, though.

Anthony pocketed the figurine and bent over Hook-Nose; lifted him as easily as one might pick up a sleeping child. He carried the man into an adjoining room, dumped him on the couch and began searching him.

There was a billfold, well filled with American currency as well as Haitian banknotes. There was a passport from the Dominican Republic, identifying Hook-Nose as Olav Ericsen, a citizen of that little nation. And finally there was a note written on a sheet of expensive white paper which bore an extremely curious crest.

Anthony studied this crest minutely. He was familiar with Burke's Peerage and the *Almanach de Gotha;* but to the best of his knowledge he had never before seen this particular coat of arms. The embossed outlines of a woman in a clinging robe stood upright upon two snakes whose tails were twined together as a support for her sandaled feet, while the snakeheads curved up and outward, fangs bared. The woman wore a sort of crown, over which a motto-legend was lettered in Latin. Translated, the motto read: "Step cautiously upon death."

As for the note written below, it was in scrawled French—irregularly slanted and difficult to translate. Mainly it seemed to be instructions to the hook-nosed Olav Ericsen, bidding him to locate a certain girl and not let her out of his sight until he recovered *the Cask.* Those two words were underlined for emphasis.

All of which merely added to Jim Anthony's mystification. A scowl twisted his bronzed features as he tried to fit these new pieces into the puzzle. And then, even as he started pacing up and down the room, a buzzer sounded behind him.

HE WHEELED, WENT to a concealed niche, picked up his phone. "Yes?"

"There's a gentleman down here in the lobby to see you, Mr. Anthony," the desk clerk reported.

"Sorry. No visitors."

Hook-Nose fell like a sack of oats.

"But he says it's very important, sir. Concerning Mr. Gentry, he asked me to tell you."

Anthony stiffened. "That's different. Send him up." Ringing off, he pelted back to the unconscious Hook-Nose, lifting him into a rear bedroom and trussing him, gagging him with strips of adhesive tape. This done, the millionaire detective returned to the penthouse foyer just in time to see a man emerging from the automatic elevator.

The newcomer was young, almost boyish except for the worry in his brown eyes. "Mr. Anthony?"

"Yes."

"Thank you for letting me come up. Speaking as one bibliophile to another, I've long hoped to meet you and talk to you about your famous collection of rarities. But I never thought I would come to you under circumstances like these. I'm Brion Claire from New Orleans," he added, extending an engraved business card which proclaimed him a dealer in rare books and manuscripts.

Anthony's lips tightened. "Claire. Brion Claire. Are you related to Susan Claire?"

"Yes, sir. I'm her brother."

"Well, by God, now maybe we'll get somewhere!" Anthony rasped. "Where's your sister?"

"At my hotel, sir. And that's why I've come here to see you. I felt that you had an explanation due."

The wealthy criminologist made an angry mouth. "It's damned near time somebody started explaining! Two men have been murdered and my best friend is in jail—"

"*Two* men?" Claire cut across Jim's words. "Then... you must have found the b-body in my sister's b-bedroom!"

"I found it, all right."

"I suppose you n-notified the police?"

"No."

"Thank God!" the younger man wet his lips. "It was fear of the police that made Susan lose her head and run away. She was all ready to go to Centre Street with you to see Tom Gentry wh-when she noticed the corpse."

"Hadn't she known about it before that?"

"No, sir. But she realized what a spot she was in. She was afraid you might accuse her, have her arrested. That's why she got panicky, sneaked away, came to me. Evidently the man had been k-killed earlier in her room, while she was out...."

"It sounds plausible," Anthony said, without indicating how much of the story he believed. "But what about this Cask a certain Queen seems to be hunting?"

SUSAN CLAIRE'S BROTHER started pacing the room. "Have y-you ever heard of the Caribbean Cask, sometimes called the Cask of Columbus?"

"Of course I've heard of it," Jim Anthony's eyes narrowed imperceptibly. "What collector hasn't? It was supposed to have contained a message from Columbus to the King of Spain."

"Not just supposed to," Claire said. "It did contain such a message. Or rather, it *does*—for the Cask still exists, Mr. Anthony. Exists in exactly the same form in which Columbus threw it into the sea, four hundred and fifty years ago!"

He stopped and watched Anthony's face, as if expecting the millionaire criminologist to exhibit surprise. But Anthony was well schooled in concealing his thoughts, and he concealed them now. His expression was as impassive as that of a Comanche warrior in the primeval forest.

Brion Claire hesitated, then continued. "According to the story which Columbus himself told when he finally returned to Spain, he'd set sail for home after discovering the New World; but shortly after this homeward voyage began, his little fleet of three ships encountered a violent storm off the coast of Haiti. The *Santa Maria* was wrecked, lost. The *Nina* and *Pinta* were damaged; became separated in a second storm."

"Right," Anthony nodded. "Your facts are historically accurate thus far."

Claire went on: "Columbus feared that neither vessel would survive to make port and carry the news of his great discoveries. So he wrote out a complete report of his findings; wrote it on parchment in his own hand, mind you! He then coated the parchment with wax and wrapped it in a sharkskin bearing the official seal which the King of Spain had given him. Between the wrappings, he enclosed a notice that if the finder would forward this to King Ferdinand and Queen Isabella, there would be a reward of a thousand gold ducats."

"Which was never claimed," Anthony said.

"That is correct, sir. Columbus embedded the entire package in soft wax, placed it in a wine Cask, sealed the Cask and consigned it to the ocean. As it turned out, he needn't have bothered, for his two remaining ships arrived safely in Spain and he reported his discoveries in person."

Anthony inclined his head. "The Cask bearing the Columbus manuscript was never seen again, according to historians. Probably sprang a leak and sank."

"That was the belief," the younger man smiled wryly. "But a priest at the Spanish court prophesied that the manuscript would eventually come to light in a year whose numerals were the same as the year of the New World's discovery, 1492. By a very simple transposition you have the current year, 1942."

Jim Anthony's eyelids flickered. "Funny I never heard that part of the story before. I'm familiar with the rest of it; but the prophecy is new to me."

"It was new to me, too, sir, until I ran across it in an old Spanish book of the period," Brion Claire admitted. "It interested me tremendously, and I began studying the ocean currents in the vicinity of where the Cask was dropped overboard. There's a certain phase of the Gulf Stream off the coast of Haiti which has wrecked many vessels there; and it occurred to me that if the Caribbean Cask had been washed up anywhere, it would be the beach of that island from which Columbus sailed."

"Logical enough," Anthony agreed. "Then what?"

"WELL, MY SISTER and I set out to test the theory. We both speak French; and we thought if we asked enough questions, made friends with the natives, we might learn something about such a Cask."

"And—?"

"We learned plenty!" Claire's mouth made a bitter line. "I mean we learned about some things I wish we hadn't! Do you know anything about voodoo, Mr. Anthony?"

"A little." Jim didn't tell his visitor that he had made a special study of the subject in connection with his researches into criminology.

"Then you won't laugh at me when I tell you the circumstances under which we finally found the Caribbean Cask," Claire's voice sounded almost fearful.

"You found the Cask of Columbus?"

The younger man nodded. "Yes, with the wax intact, stamped with the King of Spain's seal! Think of it. A Cask containing one of the most fabulous documents in all history—Christopher Columbus' own handwritten report of his discovery of the New World. Imagine the value of such a thing; what it would be worth to a museum, or a private collector like yourself!"

"Fabulous," Anthony agreed. "You could price it at half a million dollars, maybe more. If it were authentic, of course."

"It's authentic, all right," Claire spread his hands emptily. "I wish I could show it to you."

"Why can't you?"

"That attorney, Walter Wetzel, had it in his possession," Susan Claire's brother answered sourly. "Then he was murdered. And the Cask has disappeared."

CHAPTER V

VOODOO THREAT

ANTHONY LOST HIS STOIC composure for a brief instant. He strode close to Brion Claire. "What in God's name would a shyster like Wetzel be doing with the Caribbean Cask? Did it belong to him?"

"No. It belonged to my sister and myself, if you can say that anything which has been cast up by the sea belongs to anybody. I bought it and paid for it in Haiti."

"Then how in hell did Wetzel come to have it?"

The younger man made an appeasing gesture. "I'll explain that in a minute. But first let me tell you what Susan and I found in the Haitian jungle, miles from the coast. You can't possibly understand anything that's happened until you know about the voodoo priestess who calls herself Queen Lele." He shuddered visibly as he pronounced the name.

"Queen Lele, eh?"

"Yes, Mr. Anthony. If ever there was a she-devil, it's Lele! She's a white woman; a giantess. And her power over those Haitian natives is fantastic. She holds them in virtual slavery—because of the Cask."

The millionaire criminologist stared. "What's the Cask got to do with it?"

"She had it set up on a sort of shrine, a voodoo altar, deep in the jungle. Her native followers worshiped the thing; considered it a symbol of the Devil—a token from hell. I don't know whether Queen Lele believes that, herself; but I do know the Cask was the source of her witch doctor authority. She was its high priestess."

"And you stole it from this shrine?"

Claire shook his head. "Not exactly. I bribed a half-caste named Raoul LaFie to sell it to me. Then Susan and I brought it into the United States; smuggled it past the customs officials. From New

Orleans, we came here to New York with it. Then, somehow, Queen Lele learned that we were the ones who had it. She and her cut throat companions trailed us...."

"Where did Wetzel enter the picture?"

"He was our attorney," Claire explained. "I turned the Cask over to him for safe keeping when I learned Queen Lele was after us. You see, Wetzel was acquainted with Tom Gentry."

Anthony said softly: "Ah. So now we come to Gentry!"

"Yes, sir. Wetzel knew Tom. And through Tom, we hoped to contact you. You're one of the country's greatest collectors of historical manuscripts and rare books. I wanted to sell you the Cask if I could."

"But Queen Lele caught up with Wetzel, murdered him and took the thing back; is that it?"

The younger man shrugged helplessly. "That's what we think. She killed him or had him killed. But as for the Cask, we don't believe she found it. We think Wetzel must have hidden it somewhere; because Lele and her gang are still hunting it. If they'd got it from Wetzel, they would have left New York by this time."

"And what about the dead man in your sister's room?"

"Haven't you guessed? He was Raoul LaFie, the one who sold us the Cask in the first place; the one who fled with us from Haiti. Queen Lele must have caught up with him today while my sister was out of her apartment. If Susan had been there at the time, they'd probably have k-killed her, too...."

JIM ANTHONY HAD the sensation of hearing a story out of the Arabian Nights; but there were three cold facts to remind him that this was reality, not a fable. Wetzel was dead. Tom Gentry was being held for the murder. And a second man had also been slain, his corpse hidden beneath Susan Claire's bed.

"Why have you come to me now?" he asked his visitor. "What do you expect me to do?"

"I don't know, really. Susan and I want to help Gentry. And we want the Cask. But we're scared of the Queen; scared to go to the police and tell them the truth. The whole thing's in such a tangle that I... I... well, I'm putting myself in your hands. If anybody can pull us out of this jackpot, you can."

Anthony's smile held no mirth. "The only jackpot I'm interested in is Tom Gentry's. Your sister is his alibi on the Wetzel kill. If you expect my help, you'll have to play ball my way."

One sight of the man's feet, and panic seized her.

"And what way is that, sir?"

"Bring Susan here to me. She'll be safe in my protection—and I'll have her on hand in case I need her testimony."

"It's a deal, Mr. Anthony. I'll go get her right away." The younger man turned, went to the elevator, entered it. The cage drifted downward.

The instant the sliding door had closed, Jim Anthony plunged to his telephone; flashed the desk downstairs and got the Waldorf-Anthony house detective on the line. "Doherty? There's a young fellow coming down from the penthouse. He should be getting out of the elevator right now."

"Right. I can see him from here."

"Tail him. Doherty. Don't let him out of your sight."

"Okay, chief. But look. You've got another visitor coming up. He just walked into the cage. It's Lieutenant Trotter and there's fire in his eye."

THIS WAS AN understatement, for when Trotter appeared in the foyer of Anthony's living quarters he was livid with rage. Fists balled, he approached the millionaire detective.

"You damned double-crosser!" he roared. "I ought to slam you in a cell to take Gentry's place!"

"To take his place—?" Anthony's sixth sense drew an ugly interpretation from the words.

Trotter snarled: "You heard me! I played the game straight, and what did it get me? The lousiest trick one guy ever pulled on another! I suppose I deserved it, though, for trusting you."

"Calm down and tell me what you're driving at."

"As if you didn't know!" the homicide official's lips parted in a sneer. "You sent one of your lawyers to Centre Street to see Gentry. Naturally I figured he was on the up-and-up, coming from you. So I gave him a pass to Gentry's cell. And the next thing I knew, the guy bops the turnkey unconscious and springs your freckled pal right out of jail!"

Anthony tensed. "You mean Tom's gone?"

"Yeah. Gone. Leaving this on the bunk." And Trotter extended a tiny wax doll; a perfect miniature replica of the genial aviator.

A cold premonition inched through Anthony's marrow. He snatched at the wax figure, stared at it. Then he faced his raging visitor. "You've got to believe me, Trotter. I had nothing to do with Tom's crush-out. I didn't send any lawyer to Centre Street."

"Ah, nuts!"

"It's the truth. And this doll spells danger for Tom Gentry. It means he's been kidnaped!"

"Don't feed me that fertilizer," Trotter rasped. "The guy's right here with you. Drag him out. I want him."

"I tell you he isn't here! He's been abducted. He's in peril. And I've got to do something about it!"

"You're damned right you'll do something about it. But quick. I've taken all the monkey business I intend to take from you, Mr. Jim High-And-Mighty Anthony. You have your pal back in my office by midnight tonight or I'll make this town too hot to hold you, understand?"

WHEN TROTTER HAD left, the wealthy criminologist pivoted and sped to the rear bedroom where he dumped his first caller, the hook-nosed man whose identification papers bore the name Olav Ericsen. He knew that this Ericsen was an emissary from Queen Lele; he likewise knew that Tom Gentry had been snatched by another of the Queen's cohorts. The doll left in Tom's cell proved this. To rescue the devil-may-care aviator, Anthony realized that he must find and confront the voodoo priestess; and the surest and quickest way to accomplish such a meeting would be through Olav Ericsen.

So he pelted to his hook-nosed captive, leaned over him and ripped away the adhesive strips which taped and gagged the man. "Up on your feet, rat!"

There was a swollen bruise on Ericson's lantern jaw where Anthony had hit him, but he had long since regained consciousness. "Hey, take it easy!" he complained querulously. "What's the idea?"

"The idea is you're going to take me to your Queen."

"Yeah? Suppose I don't want to?"

Jim Anthony's sun-bronzed features took on such an expression of sheer, cold ferocity that his prisoner cringed. "If you don't want to, it'll be just too bad for you."

"How come it will?" the man tried to bluster.

"Have you ever seen a scalping victim?" Jim drew a knife from his pocket as he spoke. "It's not a pretty sight. Your skull glistens raw and red, with the bare bones showing."

"Gawd!" Ericsen whimpered as the truculence drained out of him. "You w-wouldn't—jeest, I believe you really would! Don't look at me that way, Mr. Anthony. Nix on that s-scalping stuff! I'll take you to Lele."

"Good. Let's go," Jim grunted.

NIGHT HAD FALLEN when they reached their destination. Queen Lele's house was a narrow brownstone affair, three stories high, wedged between its two neighbors like the filling of a sandwich. Olav Ericsen keyed the front door open and led Anthony through a long, dark, old fashioned hall to a steep staircase.

Walking like a hypnotized man, he conducted the millionaire criminologist up to the second floor. Here he swept aside the heavy black curtains which cloaked an arched doorway, and shambled into one of the weirdest chambers Jim had ever seen.

The walls were draped in dark velvet, the windows were masked, and the only light came from a flickering flame before what appeared to be a black altar hewn of some wood resembling ebony. Mystic, cabalistic symbols were carved and embossed upon the altar's pedestal, and the air was pungent with incense.

Seated on a gilded throne behind the altar was a woman whose startling appearance made Anthony catch his breath. She was a giantess; and yet she was perfectly proportioned. Barring her size, you might almost have called her beautiful.

Her hair was blue-black, her complexion tawny, her features patrician. She was clad solely in a toga of rich white satin, caught across the left shoulder by a sparkling pin of brilliants made in the shape of two intertwined snakes. The other shoulder was bare, creamily white, and the swell of a high breast was visible where the robe fell away.

With inscrutable dark eyes she surveyed the two men who now came toward her. "You may go, Ericsen," she said in a resonant contralto voice that matched her bigness.

Then, as Hook-Nose scuttled off, her dark eyes came to rest on Jim Anthony. "So you have come to return my Cask."

Never before had he met anyone who was able, by her mere presence, to weave a mesmeric spell which gripped his senses and made thought fantastically difficult. He shook off the feeling, exerted every ounce of his splendid control as he struggled for psychic mastery of the situation.

"No," he said evenly. "I haven't got your Cask, Lele."

Her dark eyes flashed as she caught the subtle mockery in his tone. "*Queen* Lele!" she flung at him imperiously. "Remember that, Mr. Anthony. It will pay you to be respectful."

"Respect must be earned, Lele," he deliberately ignored her command. "And I repeat, I haven't got your Cask."

"I don't believe you. You've had traffic with my enemies. I know they came here to New York to sell you my Cask. Now I think you have it—or know where it is."

He smiled. "Contradict me all you like. It won't get you anywhere."

"I do not contradict; I command. And I command you now. The Cask is mine; I want it and I intend to have it. I demand that you bring it to me. You have until noon tomorrow to obey. Otherwise..." her voice trailed off threateningly.

WHICH MADE THE second deadline ultimatum to be hurled at Anthony during the past couple of hours. The other one had been laid down by Lieutenant Trotter, who had given him until midnight tonight to produce Tom Gentry.

Trotter's edict carried more weight with the millionaire investigator than Queen Lele's, for hers might be pure bluff. She didn't seem to be bluffing, though. Her manner was that of a card player who holds aces back to back.

"How can I bring you the Cask by noon tomorrow when I don't even know where it is?" Anthony asked quietly.

She made an impatient gesture. "Excuses and arguments weary me. I will have none of them. I want that Cask!"

Jim's lips split in a taunting smile. "You've got your geography wrong, Lele. Your orders may be obeyed without question by your Haitian slaves. But this is New York—and I take commands from nobody."

Her deep voice sank to a thrusting whisper which reached out toward him like a deadly rapier. "You will take commands from me, Mr. Anthony. In your own way you are a remarkable man. You possess talents that you have developed to complete perfection by long training and a splendid mind."

"Thank you."

"Therefore," she ignored his sarcastic interruption, "I insist that you bring me my Cask. If you haven't got it, find it! I can think of no one more fitted than yourself for the job."

He bowed. "You flatter me."

"It is not my intention to flatter you. Nor do I offer you money for your services. I know money has no interest for you, because you already have more than any one man will ever require. No financial fee could possibly hire you."

"Right," he admitted. "You can't hire me."

"Oh, yes I can, Mr. Anthony. You will find my Cask and return it to me; for in exchange I am in a position to offer you something that has more value than any coins that were ever minted. I offer you the safety of two persons who are nearer and dearer to you than anybody else in the world. I offer you their lives."

A cold slime of intuition slid through Jim's marrow. He remembered the little wax doll which had been left in Tom Gentry's empty cell. Tom meant more to him than anybody else in the world except a certain girl; the girl who was his intended bride. Dolores Colquitt…!

There was a dry, metallic taste in his mouth as he stared at the enthroned giantess behind the ebony altar. "You haven't got her. You—"

"Yes, Mr. Anthony. At this very moment, Dolores Colquitt is my… shall we say *guest?* Let us hope that you will not make it necessary for her to become the bride of the Gods of Death. It will rest with you and your ability to bring me the Cask. And remember, I also have Tom Gentry in my keeping."

CHAPTER VI

CASK QUEST

FOR AN INSTANT ANTHONY'S impulse was to hurl himself forward and wrap his powerful fingers around the thick white column of Lele's flawless throat; to throttle her until she revealed where Dolores and Tom were being held captive.

It took all his powerful will to restrain that raging desire; and the hands at his sides hardened into knotted fists, clenched so tightly that the nails bit into his palms like so many blunt knives.

The pain restored some of his stoic poise; and in another instant he was in possession of his voice. "So that's your bargain. I produce the Cask and you return my friends."

"Unharmed," she nodded arrogantly. "If you get the Cask to me within the time limit."

"If the thing's in New York, you'll have it," Anthony promised grimly, although he hadn't the slightest idea how he would make good. "But I warn you. Charms and voodoo and black magic won't do you a damned bit of good if you harm Dolores or Tom Gentry." And he turned toward the door.

"Wait," Lele said.

He pivoted, looked at her. "Well?"

"I am not impressed with heroics, Mr. Anthony. I am interested only in deeds. The Cask must reach me intact, unopened. This will give you a better idea of what Gentry and Miss Colquitt are up against if you fail." And she held up a box.

It was approximately the size of a regulation shoe box, and it contained two dolls. They were just large enough for Jim Anthony to recognize them from where they stood; to see that they were astonishing likenesses of Tom and Dolores.

"As clever as the one you made of Susan Claire," the millionaire criminologist breathed harshly. "The one which Olav Ericsen dropped in my penthouse when I slugged him."

"Quite so, although the Claire girl is no longer important. This is what I wanted you to bear in mind." Her pointing finger indicated two pins suspended over the little waxen heads hanging from threads like twin miniature swords of Damocles. The points barely touched the tiny dolls.

"To emphasize your threats, eh?" Anthony said.

"You may put it that way. The pins will remain as you see them now, except that with each passing hour they will come a fraction closer to these tiny heads. Are you familiar with rites of voodoo, Mr. Anthony?"

He nodded.

"Good! Then you realize that time is the important thing. Long before your noon deadline tomorrow, the pinpoints will be touching the skulls of these dolls. And even a touch will mean agony to Miss Colquitt and Tom Gentry. Should you fail to bring me the Cask by noon, the pins will be driven into these waxen heads—and your friends will die."

Again Anthony could sense no hint of bluff in the big woman's voice. He knew he must do her bidding as long as Dolores and Tom were her captives.

Lele spoke again, with flat finality. "Remember, I have eyes and ears everywhere. So do not think of calling on the police for help. Even if they searched, the lawmen would find no trace of your friends here—except, perhaps, as corpses. Now you may go."

MANY TIMES, SINCE dedicating his life to a battle against crime, Jim Anthony had been confronted by danger; but as he left Queen Lele's house he had a feeling that this was the most menacing nightmare into which he had ever plunged—menacing, not to himself, but to Dolores and Tom. Their safety was at stake; which meant far more to him than any personal jeopardy. Their very lives depended upon his success in finding the Caribbean Cask.

And he didn't even know where to start looking!

That is, he felt a species of bewilderment as he emerged from the brownstone house; but it lasted only a brief moment. Then, as his superlative intellect grappled with the problem, something occurred to him: a remembered lie which perhaps answered the whole ugly riddle. When you erect a structure upon falsehood, and then take the untruth away, your construction inevitably collapses. And Anthony had suddenly recalled this vital key!

His strap watch glowed luminously, indicating ten o'clock. That startled him, for he had spent more time in Queen Lele's weird throne room than he'd imagined. In two more hours it would be midnight, at which time Lieutenant Trotter had demanded Tom Gentry's return to jail.

Well, Trotter would just have to wait. Tomorrow noon was a more important deadline; the one set by Lele for the delivery of the Columbus Cask. "And she'll get it!" Anthony whispered to himself as he piled into his big convertible.

Heading toward the Waldorf-Anthony Hotel, he drove faster than was prudent in New York's wartime dim-out. But he had no thought for prudence, now. He had to find the Claires, quickly. Both the blonde Susan and her brother contended they didn't have the Cask; but at least they'd had it in their possession until they turned it over to Walter Wetzel, the shyster who was subsequently shot. Therefore, Susan and Brion Claire had to be questioned.

IN THE LOBBY of the hotel, Jim was relieved to find Doherty waiting for him. He seized the burly house detective by the shoulder. "Did you find them? Did you trace that young fellow I told you to shadow?"

Doherty looked offended. "Have I ever fallen down on a job yet, boss?"

"No."

"So I didn't fall down this time. I tailed the guy to some cheap theatrical hotel. He picked up a jane there, a swell looker with yellow hair, and the both of them came back here to see you."

"By God. They're here now, are they?"

"Nope. They acted disappointed when they found you'd gone out. So they went back to their own hotel."

"You mean to tell me you walked off and left them uncovered?" Anthony made a bitter mouth.

"Hell, no. The house dick over there is a pal of mine. He said he'd keep an eye on them for me. If they start to leave, he'll phone me and then tail them."

The wealthy criminologist relaxed. "Good work, Doherty. I should have known I could depend on you. Now listen. This is a matter of life or death. I'm going over there to see them. But if anything should slip—if I miss them and they come back to look for me here—hold them. I don't give a damn how you work it; but hold them."

"Right, Jim."

Anthony went back outside to his car; slid under the wheel. It was not until he had covered a couple of blocks that he became aware he was being followed.

At first he thought it must be Queen Lele's emissaries who were on his track; but after swinging quickly around a couple of corners and doubling back, he slowed down and got a glimpse of the two men in the car behind him. They were plainclothes detectives from Trotter's homicide squad!

Her body disappeared into the water with scarcely a splash.

Jim's mouth firmed to a grim gash across the bronzed handsomeness of his features. So Trotter was having him shadowed in the hope that he would lead those headquarters dicks to Tom Gentry! It was a typical Trotter trick. And yet Anthony was almost positive that he hadn't had a police escort when he made his visit to the voodoo priestess, Tele.

This was natural enough, though. Jim had left the hotel so soon after Trotter's call that there had been no time to prepare for a shadowing job. Consequently, Trotter must have made arrangements to have the Waldorf-Anthony covered in case the millionaire criminologist should come back.

Yes, that was it. These plainclothes men must have picked Anthony up no more than a few moments ago. And now they would hang on like bulldogs. He realized that much, from past experience.

But past experience also told him something else. He could shake his unwanted escort if it became necessary; and he decided that it was necessary this very instant. The time element was riding his broad shoulders, weighting him down. Already a half hour had passed since Queen Lele's ultimatum. And each passing minute brought the time nearer when those sharp little pins would begin descending toward the tiny wax images of Tom Gentry and Dolores Colquitt....

HE TURNED THE next corner, jammed his throttle all the way to the floor boards, sent the sleek convertible surging ahead like a whispering meteor. Its sudden impetus pinned him to the back of the seat—and reminded him of other pins entering wax that resembled human flesh—

With squealing brakes he stopped in front of a Turkish bath which he and Gentry occasionally frequented. Parking the convertible conspicuously at the curb, he hurried down the dingy marble steps to the basement entrance and strode inside, grinning.

He needed no fortune teller to predict that within a very few minutes, police would be thundering down those same steps, fully expecting to find the missing Gentry in one of the steam rooms. They'd be disappointed, though.

The former fighter who operated these baths, and the gym in connection, came forward as Anthony appeared. Socker Carney was quite a character, proud of his ancient ring record but even prouder of his secret membership in Jim Anthony's fabulous "Organization"—an undercover legion of loyal valiants, the individual members of which could be found in every strata of New York society. They ranged from beggars and bootblacks and newsboys all the way up to captains of industry and men of outstanding professional attainments; and they were leagued together for one purpose only: to help Anthony fight crime.

Now Socker extended a calloused, welcoming hand. "Hiya, Mr. Anthony. You ain't been around in quite a while. Must be on the wagon or something, hunh?"

Jim's smile was rueful. "Right, Socker; and I'm still on it. A little wagon that travels through here a mile a minute. And goes out the rear exit of your Turkish bath."

The former pug's eyes were heavily overhung with scar tissue and one ear was swelled to a stupendous cauliflower; but his wits hadn't been addled by the blows he had taken in his ring career. "Gotcha," he grunted. "Somebody's after you. Who? Can I slug 'em?"

"Hardly. They're cops. They're nosing into my business and they'll be along any moment. Better for you if you haven't seen me, Socker."

"So I ain't laid eyes on you. G'wan straight through. Follow the heating pipes. It's a kind of tunnel, brings you out in a basement across the street. There's an exit in the alley. You can't miss."

Anthony waited for no added instructions. He found the metal door which opened into the steam-pipe tunnel and slipped forward into darkness. The passageway itself was low, forcing him to bend double as he ran; and heat from the pipe-brought sweat streaming into his widened eyes. The only light was just a faint glow from the far end of the tunnels, but the millionaire criminologist was not bothered by darkness. Employing a Hindu trick he'd learned from a yogi in India, years before, he dilated his pupils by a conscious control of optic muscles and nerves, so that the gloom became as clear to him as a lighted room would be to an ordinary man.

PRESENTLY HE REACHED the tunnel's end; loped silently into the cellar of a building across the street and found its promised exit into a rear alley. In the alley, though, he found himself temporarily stymied. Radio prowl cars were drawn up before the Turkish bath opposite, and the entire block was surrounded by a cordon of cops.

Anthony crouched down, merging himself with the night. Time snailed by, moment after endless moment. A glance at his wrist watch told him that more than an hour had passed, now, since he had left Queen Lele's house.

An hour gone from the precious hoard of minutes she had given him in which to deliver the Caribbean Cask! Jim's heart hammered painfully as he again thought of Dolores and Tom, captives of the voodoo priestess—and of the little wax dolls with the pins descending—

"I can't stay here and hide all night!" he whispered harshly to himself. And he turned, sped noiselessly to the far end of the blind alley; scaled a fence that separated him from someone's back yard.

Ten minutes later he was four blocks away from the Turkish bath, free of pursuit and hailing a passing taxi.

CHAPTER VII

THINK FAST, MR. CLAIRE!

LUCKILY, THE THEATRICAL HOTEL was exactly as Doherty had described it, a tawdry little structure peopled by down-at-heel actors who could find work only on the subway circuit, pitchmen who made a meager living in the doorways of vacant stores, and the usual collection of con artists who had turned Broadway into a flamboyant copy of a county fair midway. The shabby lobby was notable mainly for a few sickly potted palms and a house detective whose square-toed brogans and derby hat, proclaimed him to be the man Jim Anthony wanted to see.

He came toward the millionaire criminologist, recognizing him and greeting him with a deferential nod. "Those parties you want are in 810 and 812," he whispered importantly. To be of assistance to the great Jim Anthony made this a red letter night in his life.

Anthony slipped a bill into the man's ready hand and moved to the single elevator. The house dick followed him, somewhat anxiously. "I'll be in the lobby if you need me, sir. Hope you won't make too much of a beef. They run a quiet house, here. Or anyway, they try to."

"There won't be any beef," Jim smiled. He stepped into the elevator cage and it lifted him jerkily to the eighth floor, groaning as it ascended.

In the corridor he hesitated; stole a glance at his strap watch. Almost another half-hour gone! And he was starting on a quest that seemed as hopeless as the proverbial search for a needle in a haystack...!

That metaphor was not a pleasant one, for it reminded him too sharply of the little pins closing down on the heads of the tiny dolls which represented Dolores Colquitt and Tom Gentry. Wincing at the thought, he made for the door of Room 810 and knocked.

NO LIGHT MADE a line under the door, and he wondered for an instant if the hotel detective had made a mistake. Maybe Susan Claire and her brother had managed to slip from the building unnoticed....

Then, abruptly, he heard the reassuring sounds of somebody moving within the room. A girl's nervous voice quavered: "Who's th-there?"

"Jim Anthony. Open up, Susan."

She pulled the door inward, without switching on the room's light; stood at the threshhold with darkness for a backdrop and the hallway incandescent bringing out the golden sheen of her hair. Silken pajamas clung with revealing candor to her nubile curves, outlined the symmetry of her hips and the lilting swells of her breast.

Reminiscent of Anthony's first meeting with her, she again had an automatic in her dainty fist. She lowered the weapon at once, though. "I—I couldn't be certain it was really you," she apologized meekly. "Come in."

He entered, closing the door after him while the girl fumbled for the wall switch. By accident she brushed against him in the gloom, her yielding charms warm to his touch; then she clicked the switch and drew back as light glowed above.

Anthony surveyed her. "Where's your brother?"

"In the n-next room."

"Get him, please."

She went to the connecting door; opened it. "Brion."

Young Claire appeared, saw Anthony and looked startled. "I wondered when we'd see you again, sir. I took Susan up to your penthouse, but you weren't there."

"I was interviewing Lele," Jim answered grimly.

"You—you've actually met the Queen?"

"Yes. And I learned plenty. She sent one of her henchmen to Centre Street; had him pose as my representative. The trick worked. They got Tom Gentry out of jail."

Susan Claire tensed. "Then Tom's f-free—?"

"No. He's more a prisoner now than he ever was. Lele's holding him captive."

"But wh-what does she w-want with Tom? He hasn't g-got the Cask!"

Anthony made a sour grimace. "I know he hasn't. And that's why I'm here. I must find that damned thing before noon tomorrow and deliver it to Lele."

"Wait a minute, sir," Brion Claire blinked. "You say that's why you're here. I don't quite understand."

"I'll put it bluntly, then," Jim said. "You brought the Cask to New York, hoping to sell it to me. Well, here's your chance—and I won't even quibble on the price."

"But—"

"I have at least a hundred thousand dollars cash in my hotel vault, maybe more. I have nearly another hundred thousand in diamonds and other jewels. Not to mention negotiable securities on hand and available before the banks open tomorrow. Call it about a quarter of a million, all told."

The younger man's jaw dropped. "You're making us an offer for the Caribbean Cask?"

"Yes. And if that's not enough I'll add more when I can get to my bank in the morning. But the quarter of a million is ready now—on delivery of the Cask."

"How can we sell it to you when we haven't got it?" the girl pushed herself in front of her brother.

"I'm asking you to get it. Now."

"Your hurry seems a little strange, Mr. Anthony."

"Not when I tell you Queen Lele demands the thing in exchange for Tom Gentry—and for my fiancée, Dolores Colquitt."

Susan drew a deep, startled breath. "Oh-h-h, I didn't understand! You mean she kidnaped them and wants the Cask as ransom? Is that it?"

SHE TOUCHED HIS arm as if to console him. "But that's terrible! It isn't your fight, Mr. Anthony. We dragged you into this, my brother and I. We're responsible…"

"I don't want sympathy. I want the Cask."

"You could have it—if we knew where to find it."

"We've got to find it," the millionaire criminologist retorted grimly. "I want you to tell me everything you can concerning this Wetzel, the man you gave it to for safe keeping. Then we'll start back-tracking."

Susan and her brother traded swift glances, and it was the young man who cleared his throat. "Well, I've already explained how I came

As he tried to steady himself,
the girl caromed into him.

to entrust it to him. He knew Tom Gentry, and we'd hoped to contact you through Tom."

"Yes. Go on."

"But Wetzel refused to play ball with us unless we placed the Cask in his charge. After he had it, though, we didn't like the way he acted. He was sort of dictatorial, as if he were in command of the whole deal."

Anthony, pacing the carpet, lighted a cigarette and nodded through an exhaled cloud of smoke. "Then what?"

"We got suspicious of Wetzel, so my sister took an apartment in the same building where he lived. That was the apartment where you met her this afternoon; on the same floor with Wetzel, as a matter of fact—although he didn't know anything about it. We made very sure of that."

"Well?"

"Susan watched Wetzel's quarters in the daytime and we engaged a private detective to keep it under surveillance nights, with orders to follow Wetzel or anyone else who might come out carrying a cask-shaped package. We knew the thing was in Wetzel's apartment, for we saw him take it in. But nobody ever saw it being brought out."

"What about the night Wetzel was killed?"

"Our man saw him leave the building. But he didn't have any bundle with him."

Jim Anthony crushed out his cigarette. "Then the Cask must still be in the shyster's apartment!"

"No," Susan Claire said. "It isn't."

"What makes you so positive?"

She blushed. "I stole a pass-key from the maid and searched his rooms, after I heard about the m-murder. I found nothing."

"Could Wetzel have hidden it in some other suite before his death?"

"We thought of that," Brion Claire said. "We hired a man to pose as a furniture estimator, and he went through every apartment in the building. It was useless. We then searched the basement, the store-rooms—every nook and cranny from the cellar to the roof. The Cask had vanished."

Anthony scowled. "You say you searched from cellar to roof. You mean *including* the roof?"

The Claires looked at each other, then back at the wealthy criminologist. "No, not the roof," young Claire admitted. "How could anything be hidden on an open roof?"

"I don't know. But if you're telling me the truth, it would seem the roof is the only place that's left. By a process of elimination, that's where we'll find the Cask—unless it's been destroyed."

Anguish came into Susan Claire's voice. "Destroyed? A manuscript worth half a million dollars? A priceless document that is part of history itself? I—I couldn't bear to think of such a thing!"

"Nor can I bear to think of my own stake in the game," Jim Anthony said heavily. "A stake greater than any half a million dollars. The lives of two of the sweetest people in the world depend on my finding that Cask. Come on. The three of us are going on a roof top treasure hunt!"

CHAPTER VIII

RANSOM DIVE

MIDNIGHT HAD COME AND gone when their cab pulled up before the apartment house facing Central Park which had been Walter Wetzel's home. Due to the dim-out, vehicular traffic was thin and there were few pedestrians abroad at this late hour. Dismissing the taxi, Anthony led the Claires toward the building entrance.

A shadow detached itself from a doorway across the street and came forward. "Thought I recognized you, Mr. Claire. Ain't nothing stirring. I haven't seen a soul take a package out of here bigger than a book all evening. How much longer you want me to keep this stake-out?"

Claire's voice sounded dreary. "I guess we won't need you any more, Hughes. You may as well go home."

The man sighed with relief, turned and trudged off up the deserted sidewalk.

Anthony watched him for a full minute, then approached the apartment-house door. He was fumbling for his steels when the blonde girl nudged him aside. "I still have my key, Mr. Anthony." Then, after she had turned the lock: "You w-won't force me to go into *my* apartment, w-will you? I can't bear to th-think of that murdered man under the bed... "

"He's beyond making trouble now. But you needn't think anything about him, one way or the other. The Cask is the important thing." Anthony gestured her into the automatic elevator, allowed her brother to go next, then followed them. He pressed the button for the top floor.

The cage lifted them skyward in silence. Emerging into the top corridor, they hesitated; looked around. "I wonder how you get on the roof?" Brion Claire whispered.

"We might use the fire escape. But there ought to be an inside stairway somewhere," Anthony answered. And there was. Its heavy metal door was locked, though, and the millionaire detective was compelled to utilize his uncanny skill with the famed steels.

Susan and her brother watched him wordlessly, but their calmness was counterfeit. Anthony could sense the excitement seething through them as he worked; and despite his own iron control, he felt his own blood pounding.

AT LAST THE bulkhead swung open, and he led the Claires up a flight of concrete steps; pushed another fire door outward. Thus they came to the flat, graveled rooftop.

A coping, almost waist high, ran completely around the expanse before them; but over it they had a clear view of the city with the sea beyond. Anthony had seen this same sight many times, but now there was a difference. Where thousands of brilliantly colored electric signs had once splashed the night with checker-board motley, there were now only rows of buildings lighted uncertainly by the distant moon.

Turning from the weird scene, Jim's superb eyes began surveying the roof for possible hiding places. These were few, and apparently they concealed nothing. Young Claire was quartering the graveled surface, peering behind chimneys and into corners with the alertness of a retriever striving to pick up an elusive scent. Presently he returned, glumly shaking his head. "It just isn't here!"

"What about the water tank?"

"I hunted all around it, sir. You saw me."

Anthony stared at the huge cylindrical tank which rose in the exact center of the roof to make a black blotch against the sky. "I didn't mean around it," he said. "I meant inside it."

"But—but the tank's filled with water!" Susan exclaimed.

"So is the ocean. Yet the Cask of Columbus was consigned to the ocean and survived. Would a tank of fresh water be greatly different?"

Brion Claire stiffened. "My God! The wax was in perfect condition when I last saw the Cask. I wonder—"

"We're wasting time," the millionaire criminologist rasped. And he loped toward the tank with the Claires at his heels.

There was a rusty iron ladder running up the side of the huge water container, ending at a platform on the tank's brim, perhaps thirty feet above the roof. Susan Claire drew up; shuddered. "I'm almost scared to climb it!"

"You needn't. Your brother and I can do whatever is necessary," Jim told her quietly.

She drew a deep breath; squared her lilting shoulders. "No. I risked my life for six weeks in the jungle. I've been dodging the Queen and her cut-throats ever since, all for the sake of the Cask. And I won't back out now!"

Even as she spoke, she began climbing the ladder hand over hand. As she ascended, Anthony could see her tapered legs flashing in the moonlight, melting upward into thighs as perfect as carven ivory. No damned wonder Tom Gentry had fallen for her, he mused thoughtfully. She had everything. When a man like Jim Anthony could get a thrill out of silken legs, it was something to write down in your little red book; for Anthony was woman-proof, except where Dolores Colquitt was concerned.

Brion Claire scrambled up after his sister, with Jim following. Breathless moments later the trio gained the top platform, barely large enough for them to stand on while Anthony lifted the tank's manhole cover.

INSIDE, SOLID DARKNESS met the eye; the darkness of a hell-pit. Even Jim Anthony's Hindu trick of widening his pupils did little good against such blackness; and he was compelled to use the tiny beam of his pencil flashlight.

As he sprayed the beam on the surface of the water inside the tank, an exclamation leaped to Susan Claire's red lips. "I—I see something floating! A big cork!"

She was right. The float drifted directly below the manhole, barely beyond reach. There seemed to be a string or cord attached to it, leading downward into the black depths of water.

Brion Claire's whisper was tremulous with excitement. "The Cask! We've found it!"

"I hope you're right," Anthony wedged himself perilously over the lip of the manhole, leaning far down until his fingers grasped the floating cork.

Susan clutched at his shoulder. "Be careful you don't break it!" her voice echoed hollowly inside the vast tank.

Her warning came too late, though. As Anthony pulled on the cork, the cord which was attached to it snapped apart soggily—and the lower length sank out of sight.

BRION CLAIRE UTTERED a smothered cry, half disappointment, half rage. He snatched the piece of cork from Jim Anthony's hand and stood for a bitter instant, staring at it as if this inanimate object were responsible for everything that had happened. "Damn! Damn the thing to hell!"

His sister seized it from him and flung it far across the roof. Then, sobbing hysterically, she leaned forward; pulled off one shoe, then the other. Young Claire tried to yank her upright but she eluded him; began peeling the sheer stockings from her slim legs.

"Susan, you fool!" he panted.

Her answer was unintelligible, muffled by the dress which she was already whisking over her head. Then she stood poised, erect, clad solely in brassiere and tissue-thin panties. Moonlight caressed her dulcet body; made it seem warm and sleekly inviting.

Jim Anthony reached toward her. "Wait!"

"Wait for what?" her tone was strained, harsh. "I risked my life in the jungle for that Cask. I took a chance of being murdered here in New York for it. And I'm not going to let a broken string stop me now!"

She made a sharp, clean dive over the lip of the manhole, her slender body slipping into the water with scarcely a visible splash. She disappeared under the surface.

Brion Claire moaned helplessly. "My God! It's all of thirty feet to the bottom… and suppose she comes up on the other side under that low top? There's hardly any air space… and if she doesn't have any strength left… *Do* something, Mr. Anthony! Help her! I can't swim, myself…"

"By the time you untie your friends, I shall be far distant," she said.

The millionaire criminologist was already stripping off his outer clothing, piling it in a heap near Susan's frock on the little platform. As he placed his coat on top of her dress, he noticed two long strips of printed paper, folded into compact packets and pinned inside the bodice of her discarded ensemble; and the pins reminded him of other sharp points inexorably coming closer to the heads of a pair of wax dolls which represented Dolores Colquitt and Tom Gentry. His droughts kept veering in that one ugly direction, picturing the peril menacing his fiancée and his friend.

Then, as Anthony turned back to the tank's open manhole, Susan Claire broke water; stroked herself toward the platform and reached up to grasp it.

"Any luck, sis?" her brother panted.

She shook her head, too spent to speak. "I... I didn't get deep enough..."

Anthony lowered himself into the blackness of the tank, his body superbly muscular in athletic shorts that weren't much more than a breech-clout. "Climb out," he commanded the blonde girl. "I'll take over."

He took a deep breath; flexed his arms. The long flat muscles of his shoulders rippled under sun-bronzed skin as he prepared to go under.

"No!" Susan gasped. "It's my job—"

Jim didn't hear whatever else she said, for the black water was already closing over him as he thrust himself powerfully downward.

WHEN HIS FEET touched the bottom of the tank he expelled some of the air from his lungs, reducing his buoyancy so that he could remain here and grope across the metal flooring inch by searching inch. If the Cask were on the bottom, it must be weighted; for under ordinary conditions a keg sealed with wax would float to the top.

Blindly the wealthy investigator began hunting. At this thirty-foot depth it wasn't an easy task. An ordinary swimmer might have difficulty in remaining this far under for any appreciable length of time; but Jim was no ordinary swimmer. His athletic prowess had been proven on hundreds of occasions—and now he called that prowess into play. From his Indian ancestors on his mother's side he drew a power of body which few men possess; and with the fighting heart bequeathed him by his hell-roaring Irish father, it made the perfect combination for the job at hand.

Foot by foot he traversed the bottom; and as the strain began to tell on him, his mind found an instant for admiration of Susan Claire. Whatever her faults, she had courage and nerve. A dive of this kind took guts, stamina; and there weren't many women who would have attempted it. She had, though; and she deserved credit for the try.

Anthony's lungs began to feel as if they were wrapped in an ever-tightening iron band. Deep in his ears there was a throbbing sensation overtoned by a humming buzz. This bothered him, for he knew what it meant; realized that sooner than he wished he would be forced to the surface for a breath of air. He circled half the tank, his long arms searching out in a wide arc, hoping to encounter an obstruction which would prove to be the Caribbean Cask.

But success eluded him. When he judged that he had completed half the circuit, he shot upward, aiding his comet-like progress by the sweep of his driving arms and the scissors motion of his legs.

It seemed forever before his head broke the surface and he dared to exhale the air pent up in his tortured lungs. Then he sucked in a deep, reviving draft of night; hooked his fingers on the edge of the platform at the brink of the manhole. There he rested, panting.

Above him, the Claires stared downward; their faces made white blurs against the darkness, and Susan's voice was strained with tension as she asked: "Did you f-find it?"

"Not yet. I've only searched half the bottom, though. We still have a chance."

"Let me go down this time. You're exhausted." She made a move to lower herself.

Anthony reached up, grasped her around the thighs and pushed her back onto the platform. Her flesh fell warm, velvety to his wet palms; the briefly intimate contact sent little thrills dancing through his veins. "No," he said evenly. "I started the job and I'll finish it."

Then he filled his lungs to the bursting point, exhaled and swelled them again, not so fully this time. Once more he sank down… down….

The present dive was a duplicate of the first, save that be turned to the left rather than the right when his soles touched bottom. And presently his groping fingers closed around a broken length of cord.

Savage elation hammered into his heart. He trailed the cord downward; discovered it to be fastened to something heavily metallic on the bottom—a chunk of scrap iron which seemed to be serving as an anchor. From this, the line was bent and knotted around a wooden object whose sides felt slippery, as if waxed. It was the Cask of Columbus!

Jim Anthony had come to the end of his quest.

CHAPTER IX

DEATH DROP

THE MILLIONAIRE CRIMINOLOGIST TUGGED at the improvised iron anchor, and he realized that it was too heavy for him to lift and carry to the surface. No swimmer in the world could accomplish such a task; it was humanly impossible. Therefore the Cask must be unfastened from the chunk of scrap metal; then he could stroke upward with it.

He attacked the binding knots which were corded around the wax-sealed keg; and as his fingers plucked desperately at these stubborn bindings, he again felt that constricting band closing about his mighty chest. The roaring was louder than ever in his ears, now, and little pinpoints of light jabbed at his eyeballs. Just as other pinpoints would soon be jabbing into the skulls of the Dolores-doll and the Gentry-image.

In silent fury he renewed his efforts on the knotted cord. It seemed that he would have to give up; that he could remain under water not an instant longer. And then, abruptly, the line gave way; trailed through his fingers.

The Cask was rising to the surface, shooting upward with a cork-like buoyancy. A bubbling blurt of air burst from Anthony's mouth as he followed it, kicking out with every last ounce of his splendid reserves. Any instant, now, this eternity would end; his head would break the surface and he could drink his fill of the air his tortured body demanded.

But instead, his skull smashed viciously into an unyielding solid. It was the tank roof. As he popped up from the water, he hit the metal covering a terrific blow; and it came near finishing Anthony for good.

Stunned, he sank like a stone. Roaring water filled his nostrils, his mouth; trickled into his laboring lungs. For one deadly second his muscles relaxed. It would be pleasant to let himself go; to let oblivion close over him. Then he could rest, sleep....

Idle thought of Dolores Colquitt and Tom Gentry snapped him out of this nightmarish desire for death. Rolling, regaining control of his paralyzed sinews, he fought himself back upward; broke the surface cautiously. And this time there was no brain-shattering concussion against the roof of the tank. He was above water. He was safe.

The Cask drifted by him, brushed him. He snagged it, swam toward the open manhole, summoned all his waning strength to grasp at the lip of the platform with one hand and pull himself up. And at long last he sprawled his length at Susan Claire's feet; shoved the Cask toward her brother.

Young Claire seized it, lifted it tenderly. "You found it!" he choked wildly. "You found our beautiful Cask!"

AS FAR AS Anthony could determine when his eyes regained their ability to focus, the keg wasn't very damned beautiful. Nor did it reveal many traces of antiquity. It looked more or less as he had expected it to look; crude in workmanship, coated with a smearing of wax, the curved staves held in place by broad, flat bands of copper. Despite its commonplace appearance, though, it represented life for Dolores and Tom....

The millionaire detective swayed upright, reached for his clothes. In the moonlight he resembled some bronze, pagan god—or an Indian warrior stripped for battle. He cast a sidewise glance at Susan Claire.

She, too, seemed like a living statue in her soaked brassiere and panties; a very dainty, very tempting statue brought to life by ancient magic.

"Get your dress on," Anthony told her brusquely. "We've got to get away from here. Fast"

She obeyed, donning her frock even more swiftly than Jim could wedge himself into his suit. Then she went down the rusty ladder along the outside of the tank, with her brother following and Anthony descending after them, carrying the Cask.

The Claires reached the graveled roof while Jim was still only halfway down. And then a snarling voice grated nearby, and a shadowy figure emerged from behind a chimney.

It was the hook-nosed Olaf Ericsen, a gun glinting in his fist. "Freeze, all of you!"

From the ladder, Anthony stared at the man. "What's the big idea? Was Lele afraid I wouldn't bring her what she wanted? Is that why she sent you after us?"

Hook-Nose grinned sardonically. "The hell with Lele. I'm on my own, pal. If that thing is worth so damned much to Lele, maybe I can squeeze some dough out of it for myself. Come on, hand it over."

"Sure," Anthony said. "Catch." And he hurled the keg with all his force, full at Ericsen's leering face.

The man's hands went up automatically to ward off the object which smashed at him. His gun was deflected as he tried to catch the Cask; and as he staggered under the impact, Jim Anthony leaped off the ladder.

THE JUMP WAS long, daring. From fifteen feet above the surface of the roof, the millionaire criminologist arrowed outward and down—and landed full on Ericsen's shoulders. Both men went tumbling in a heap, Hook-Nose taking the full concussion, breaking Anthony's fall.

The man moaned in pain, squirmed, shoved himself erect. One leg dangled queerly, incapable of supporting his weight. "My ankle… you've busted it… Gawd…."

His right hand still clenched the gun, although it hung loosely and unaimed. And as he lurched in an effort to steady himself on his one good leg, Susan Claire caromed into him; sent him spinning. A wild, panic-stricken oath bubbled on the fellow's flaccid lips as he went backward to the coping which rimmed the roof.

Anthony yelled a warning, but it was too late. As Ericsen struck the low coping, his feet went out from under him. Screaming hideously, he vanished over the parapet.

"My G-God!" Susan whimpered. "I—I've killed him!" And she flurried at Anthony; clung to him. "I didn't mean to shove him off the roof. I was afraid he'd sh-shoot. I acted without thinking—"

Jim's face was an impassive mask. "I'm afraid your motives don't matter now, as far as he's concerned. After a twenty story drop, he'll scarcely be able to accept your apologies."

"But I—I didn't intend to kill him; it was self defense! His life or ours!"

"Skip it, sis, and let's get out of here," her brother said grimly. "What's done is done. He wanted our Cask. Instead, what he got was death."

"Not your Cask," Anthony reminded him. "Mine. We made a deal for it, remember. A quarter of a million in cash, securities, and diamonds. We'll go to my penthouse and I'll pay you off."

As he picked up the wax-sealed keg and led the way down the concrete stairs from the rooftop, his mind was mulling over one problem after another. Of primary importance now was the necessity for eluding Trotter and his police. It was long past the midnight deadline which the homicide official had set for Tom Gentry's return to Centre Street jail; and, since that demand had not been met, New York would be teeming with cops on the lookout for Jim Anthony and his aviator friend. One of the most obvious places they would keep under surveillance would be the Waldorf-Anthony Hotel—and Jim had to run that police gauntlet, come hell or high tide.

But how?

By the time the automatic elevator lowered him to the apartment house lobby with the Claires, he had the answer. There was a pay phone booth by the deserted desk, into which the wealthy criminologist crowded himself. He dropped a coin, dialed, made contact with Doherty, the Waldorf-Anthony house dick.

Swiftly he issued instructions to his hotel detective, outlining what he wanted done. Then, ringing off, he returned to Susan Claire and her brother. "Everything's set," he told them enigmatically. "Let's find a cab."

THEY WERE MORE than two blocks away from Jim's hotel when they first heard the uproar. As their taxi drew nearer to the Waldorf-Anthony, the noise increased in volume—shouts, curses, the clatter of broken glass and the shrill beep of police whistles, the pounding of nightsticks on the sidewalk.

Consternation showed on Brion Claire's face. "A riot!" he exclaimed as he peered forward past the cabby's shoulder. "What in hell's name—?"

"Don't let it worry you," Anthony said. "It's a fake. Just a device of mine to distract the police so we can slip into the hotel without being seen."

"But that mob!" Susan gasped.

"Members of my Organization," the millionaire criminologist smiled; and there was pride in his tone. He told the hacker to stop; and then he led the Claires through a rear entrance to the building, past the mammoth kitchens and into the lobby. Nobody paid any attention to them as they scuttled into Anthony's private elevator.

Once in his penthouse, he moved directly to the wall safe in his library. Experience had taught him the wisdom of keeping large sums of cash on hand, for there had been many times when his unending warfare against crime had placed him in urgent need of ready money. This was one of those times.

From the safe he drew a leather bag, and into the bag he began stuffing wads of currency, a sheaf of securities, a double handful of loose diamonds. Presently he handed the bulging bag to the blonde Claire girl. "Take my word for it, there's easily a quarter of a million dollars here."

"I trust you, Mr. Anthony."

"Thank you. Now you two had better leave the same way we came in. But wait." His eyes searched Susan's. "Remember, you're Tom Gentry's alibi on that Wetzel killing. He'll need you, once I ransom him from Queen Lele."

She smiled wistfully. "I'll be in my hotel room. Tell Tom I'm ready to help him when he says the word."

Anthony watched as she and her brother stepped into the elevator. A full minute after the cage had descended, he picked up the phone; got Doherty, downstairs.

"The riot was swell," he praised the house detective. "Keep it going about five minutes more, then break it up. I'll be in the clear by then." He issued a few more orders, rang off, and pressed the elevator button to bring the car back to the penthouse.

WHILE WAITING FOR it to come up the shaft, he lifted the Cask which he had bought at such a costly price—and which, in turn, would buy the freedom of Dolores and Tom. The wax seals seemed to be daring him to break them open, so that he could examine the keg's contents. He resisted this temptation, though, because he remembered Lele's warning.

"The Cask must reach me intact, unopened," she had told him. He smiled crookedly now as he recalled the finality of her tone, the unveiled threat. She would get what she demanded, all right. Her property would not be tampered with—for the present. But later she might have a surprise coming!

Still smiling that curious, enigmatic smile, Anthony entered the elevator with the Caribbean Cask in his arms.

It was no trick to slip from the hotel unnoticed, for the spurious riot still raged around the lobby and front entrance. Jim beckoned a taxi on the side street, clambered in and gave the hacker Queen Lele's address.

CHAPTER X

CASK TANGLE

DURING THE PERIOD THAT the cab was rolling Jim Anthony across town, it happened that another Yellow was on its way to LaGuardia Airport, bearing a man and a woman who seemed to be in considerable haste. This couple kept urging their driver for more and still more speed.

Presently the man and woman gained their destination, paid their cabby and started up the ramp, pausing only to purchase a paper from a crippled newsboy. As the boy handed them the extra edition, he folded it with what looked like an unnecessary motion; a flourish which might have been a secret signal of some kind.

Then, as the couple started forward again, they were startled by the crowd that suddenly began closing in on them from every side. Ridiculously enough, the crowd consisted of fantastic elements—scrubwomen, beggars, porters, even a few men in tuxedoes and full evening dress. They milled like a stormy sea, yet they were weirdly silent as they impinged on the man and woman at the center of the human whirlpool. And the couple who were thus trapped found themselves being borne farther and farther from the airliner waiting on the field.

MEANTIME, JIM ANTHONY bounded up the front steps of Queen Lele's brownstone residence; thumbed the bell-push. After long moments the giantess herself opened the door.

At once her glance fell upon the Cask in the millionaire criminologist's grasp. "So you succeeded!"

"Yes. Here, take what belongs to you," he shoved the keg into her hands. "And give me what is mine—Miss Colquitt and Mr. Gentry."

She gestured him to the stairs. "There is no need for you to be impatient, Mr. Anthony. Walk ahead of me to my throne room. And by the way, I have you covered with a gun."

He did not break stride, but his broad shoulders twitched as he ascended the staircase. "So I bring you the Cask and step into a doublecross!"

"Not at all," she spoke behind him. "It is merely that I've heard of your reputation, your cleverness in time of stress. I take no chances with clever men, Mr. Anthony. There's the throne room ahead of you. Enter it, please."

He obeyed, coming to a halt in the room's center. "Well?" his eyes and his voice challenged the big woman.

Silken robes rustling, she circled him and moved toward the ebony altar with its flickering open flame, keeping her pistol aimed at Anthony's heart. "You will please stand very still," she said.

Then her sandaled foot evidently touched a concealed control switch, for the black altar started rising toward the high ceiling as if by some voodoo trick of levitation. Jim, staring, wondered if this could be an optical illusion.

Then he perceived that the altar rested on the superstructure of a small elevator device which was coming upward from an opening in the floor, pushed from below by a hydraulic piston; the kind employed in service stations for automobile lubrication racks.

And as the lower portion came into view, Dolores Colquitt and Tom Gentry were revealed side by side, strapped flat to a sort of flooring, spread-eagled on their backs. Helpless, incapable of the slightest movement, they lay with their heads directly below two dangling and sharp-pointed daggers which depended from the thinnest of strings.

The blades were so weighted that they would plunge point down if those fragile threads should break. Death would come instantly to Dolores and Tom if this happened.

A savage cry of rage welled gutturally in Anthony's bronze throat. Oblivious to the menace of Lele's gun, he launched himself forward. With a wide, sweeping arc of his arm, he smashed the two dangling daggers aside; broke their threads and sent them clattering across the room.

"Damn you—!" he faced the giantess. "I've had enough of this phony theatrical hokus-pokus. Drop that pistol!"

She backed off from him, the gun still raised, the Cask under her other arm. "Oh, no, Mr. Anthony. I am leaving now. By the time you untie your friends I shall be far distant. If you try to stop me, I'll shoot."

"I wonder if you'd dare."

"Try me and see," she taunted him.

He regained his poise; grinned sardonically. "What's the use? You won't go very far. And I advise you not to burden yourself with that worthless Cask. It's served its purpose."

"Meaning what?" her eyes narrowed.

"Meaning the keg is a counterfeit, rigged merely to bilk me out of a quarter of a million dollars."

LELE TENSED. "I know nothing of what you paid for the Cask. Nor does that concern me. I did not kidnap your friends for money. I kidnaped them to get back something which was mine." She drifted toward the door. "Now that I have it, I go."

"What's your hurry?" the millionaire criminologist drawled. "The New Orleans plane which the Claires bought tickets for has already gone."

"*What?*"

"You heard me. I saw the tickets pinned inside Susan Claire's dress tonight. Two tickets, mind you. Only two. That was when I realized they planned to skip with the money and leave you holding that counterfeit keg."

"You're lying!" the big woman shrilled.

Anthony lifted a shoulder, casually. "What can I gain by lying? I have my friends back, unharmed. The money I've lost won't break me."

"You're lying!" she repeated.

He grinned at her. "Too bad, after all the trouble you went to; the swell act you put on as a voodoo queen. Too bad a couple of cheap double-crossers should blow with the loot while you face a murder rap."

"I didn't kill anybody. I didn't!"

"We'll soon see," he said; and suddenly there was a bedlam of noise in the street below—the noise for which Jim Anthony had been waiting, sparring for time.

Lele dropped the cask. "Wh-what's that?"

"A mob. A mob of my friends, Lele. A vengeful mob, whipped to excitement by the knowledge of what you tried to do to me. I sent for them, Lele. Have you ever seen a lynching?"

The color drained from her face. "No! My God, you wouldn't let them— Listen, they're coming closer! I've got to get away. This can't happen to me—"

"I'm afraid it will happen to you unless you confess certain facts that I already know." He reached forth, took the gun out of her unresisting hand. "Will you talk, Lele?"

"I—I don't know what you w-want me to tell."

"The truth will satisfy me. The truth about how the Caribbean Cask came to be faked in the first place."

She cringed as the mob-sounds grew louder in the street below. "You knew it was f-faked?"

"Yes. Brion Claire's story tipped me off, although I didn't put my finger on it until later. You see, he went too far; told one unnecessary lie. He did it for the sake of buildup; but he made a bad mistake."

"Wh-what lie?"

"The part about an old Spanish priest prophesying the Cask would turn up in 1942, a transposition of the numerals 1492—the year Columbus discovered the New World. There never was a prophecy of that kind."

Lele seemed to sag inside her toga. "It was all Susan Claire's idea. She saw a newspaper article about the Cask of Columbus and decided to fake such a Cask, sell it to you. But she knew that you're shrewd; knew she would have to surround her scheme with a lot of trappings."

"So she hired you to pose as a voodoo queen and pretend to be chasing her brother and herself eh?" Anthony asked.

"Y-yes. I got a couple of men to help me put on my act. Susan drew that shyster, Wetzel, into the scheme. Through Wetzel she would contact Tom Gentry and meet you. Then she planned to appeal to you for help against me, which would arouse your interest in the Cask."

"Very neat," the millionaire detective grunted.

LELE QUAVERED: "IT might have worked, but Wetzel was a rat. He tried to cut himself in for the lion's share of whatever you might pay for the Cask. So Susan hired a gunsel named Raoul LaFie to kill Wetzel."

"And the shot was fired from a gun which Susan stole from Gentry, eh?"

"Yes. There was a reason for that. It caused Gentry to be arrested. Which would bring you back to New York in a hurry, as soon as you heard about it."

Anthony nodded. "I see."

"Then this gunsel, Raoul LaFie, got scared. He went to Susan's apartment, demanding more money. She and her brother murdered him with one of the voodoo pins we had made. They never expected you to walk in and find his body under her bed, though. When you did, the Claires had to move fast."

"They moved very fast," Jim growled. "They got Tom out of jail to make trouble for me with the police. They kidnaped Dolores so that you could demand the Cask in exchange for her freedom. That way, I was forced to buy the damned thing!"

Lele made a bitter mouth. "Sure you were forced to buy it—and to find it first. I suppose they were pretty cute, leading you up to the tank on that roof where they had it hidden under water."

"Cute enough, but I was wise to them by that time." Anthony broke off as a surge of footfalls sounded within the house. From the sound, a mob the size of a thundering herd must be coming upstairs. Babbling voices washed through the hallway like a vocal surf drawing nearer, nearer—

"Save me, Mr. Anthony! Don't let them get me!" Lele bleated hysterically. "Please!"

For answer, Jim yanked open the curtains of the throne room entrance; held up a hand. And at his gesture, the oncoming throng halted; fell silent. From the middle of the mob, three persons were thrust rudely forward.

The first two were Susan Claire and her brother. And the third was—Lieutenant Trotter!

Red-faced, apoplectic, the homicide official seemed on the verge of exploding. "Damn it to hell, Anthony, what's the meaning of this? I'm taking a look around the airport to see if maybe you and Gentry are on the lam, and all of a sudden this gang of hoodlums swallows me up, brings me all the way across town like I was riding a cyclone!"

"Not hoodlums, Trotter," Anthony corrected him. "Just some of my Organization."

"I don't care a damn who they are; I want—say, bigahd! There's Tom Gentry tied to that gadget. He's the guy I'm after! What the hell—"

Jim Anthony shook his head. "You don't want Tom. You want the Claires. Whatever else I may or may not be able to prove, I do know Susan Claire pushed a certain hook-nosed accomplice off a roof to his death. Deliberately. And her brother is just as bad. Take them away, Trotter, along with Queen Lele, here."

A LONG TIME later when the mob had dissipated and Trotter had been told the whole story, three prisoners were led away to the Tombs on the first leg of a journey which would end in the death house at Sing Sing.

And then Anthony smiled at Dolores Colquitt and Tom Gentry, who had long since been freed of their bonds. "All's well that ends well, I guess," he said. "You two are safe, I got my money back from the Claires, and the murders are solved. Could we ask for anything more?"

"Yeah," Gentry said ruefully. "I could ask for blinders the next time I see a pretty girl. And I could ask for a drink."

"What about you, Dolores?" Jim turned to his lovely fiancée. "What could you ask for?"

She said: "Just this, Jim, darling," and kissed him.

MURDER
BETWEEN SHIFTS

THE KILLING TOOK PLACE IN FULL VIEW OF HUNDREDS OF
PEOPLE, YET SOMEHOW JIM ANTHONY COULD NOT BELIEVE
THE EVIDENCE OF HIS OWN EYES. GRANTED THAT THE
FACTORY MANAGER HAD PLANNED THE KILLING, EVEN
THEN JIM FELT THERE MUST BE SOME EXPLANATION.

THE THIRD WARNING REACHED Jim Anthony shortly after supper. This time it was a .38 caliber bullet, an unfired cartridge in a small cardboard box. The two previous threats he had received that day had also been cartridges; the first a .22 target slug, the second a .32 dum-dum. But while the caliber increased with each successive warning, the messages were all alike.

These anonymous communications were typed upon narrow strips of paper, like ticker tape. Each one had been carefully wrapped around its accompanying bullet and they had all carried the same wording:

"Get out of Los Angeles or die."

Anthony was puzzled, but not frightened. He had no intention of leaving the west coast until his job was finished; nor did he intend to let anyone kill him if he could help it. The warnings served merely to put him on guard.

In consequence, his uncanny Indian sixth sense—a heritage from his Comanche princess mother—was alert to danger when he and his freckled aviator friend, Tom Gentry, set forth on a tour of the city's hot spots some time after midnight. They were seeking a man named Steve Ryerson; and presently, in a place called The Shed, they found him.

A few minutes later they also found murder.

THE SHED, WHICH was the name its owners had stuck up in front of the building before the dimout had shut off their neon signs, was a vast and barnlike structure almost the size of an assembly wing in an airplane factory. It was by far the largest in California's entertainment world, operating twenty-four hours a day in defiance of a state law prohibiting the sale of liquor after two in the morning; and it was so crowded that Anthony and Gentry had difficulty getting a table.

"What a joint!" the genial aviator exclaimed as he surveyed the mammoth dance hall. His face was flushed, not so much from the highballs he'd consumed as from the contagious excitement of this jampacked gathering of revelers. "Whew, I never saw anything like it in my life!"

Neither had Jim Anthony—and he had traveled to every corner of the globe. With his enormous wealth, inherited from his swash-buckling Irish father and doubled by his own financial wizardry, Jim had missed very little in his journeys; but never before had he witnessed a scene to equal the swaying mass of humanity which filled this tremendous cabaret.

"It's a safety valve, Tom," he said thoughtfully. "The safety valve of a people keyed up in wartime. But I'm not so sure it's a good prescription for taut nerves."

Out on the vast dance floor, people swirled to the music of two hot bands which alternated in furnishing jive rhythms. Unless you were a hep-cat, your life wasn't safe in that jitterbugging throng of people who apparently considered gymnastics to be more important than keeping step with the braying brasses.

The crowd was as motley in costume as in characteristics. Women in evening attire, with orchids or gardenias at their shoulders, danced with men who had just come from work in slacks and jackets. Percentage girls mingled with lady welders and rivet buckers, for this was the swing shift at play: the people who lived neither by day nor by night, but in that strange half-world which has grown up around a nation's war industry.

"You'll never laugh at me again," Wozniak said.

Tom Gentry's eyes glittered. "Finding any one guy in a crush like this is the same as picking a fly-speck out of a pound of pepper with boxing gloves on. You ain't going to locate Steve Ryerson this way, pappy."

"I've got to," Anthony made a grim mouth and snapped his hawk-like gaze over the crowd. "You know how important it is for me to talk to him."

Yes, Gentry knew; nor was he surprised at his sun-bronzed companion's tenacity. Jim Anthony's character had many facets—but above all was a bulldog determination to see any given task through to its conclusion.

A STRANGE PERSONALITY, Jim Anthony! One of the world's wealthiest men, he'd turned his superlative talents into many a curious channel. As an amateur criminologist, his skill at unraveling mysterious crimes had made his name feared throughout the nation's underworld; yet he was also a scientist, inventor, art collector, research engineer, and expert in aerodynamics.

His knowledge of aircraft construction was the reason he was in California now. For several years he'd owned a large interest in a Los Angeles plane factory; and recently, in his New York laboratory, he had developed a new plastic cargo airliner that could be quickly and cheaply made.

At first, government bureaucrats in Washington scoffed—until Jim demonstrated the ship's potentialities as a carrier of war cargoes safe from Axis submarine attack. Then, backed by surging public opinion, he'd practically forced the brass hats to award him a non-profit contract for manufacturing the giant plastic planes by the hundreds.

Naturally he turned the contract over to the Los Angeles concern in which he owned stock. The factory was headed by Steve Ryerson, a promoter rather than an engineer; and now that the plant was on a paying basis, Ryerson spent most of his time in various night spots in company with show girls and entertainers. This was why Anthony was now seeking him in The Shed.

Tom Gentry lighted a cigarette. "I don't know why you bother about the mugg, Jim. After all, things are running smooth enough. The plant don't need Ryerson as long as it's got Karl Wozniak as general manager. There's a guy that knows his stuff, even if he is a foreigner."

"Wozniak's not a foreigner," the millionaire scientist said. "He was born in Moravia, but he's a naturalized American citizen now. And he's quitting. He gave me his resignation today; plans to enlist in the army."

"What?"

Anthony nodded grimly. "He told me he couldn't take any more of Steve Ryerson's monkey business. That's why I've got to find Ryerson for a show-down."

THE INTERVIEW BETWEEN Karl Wozniak and Jim Anthony at the factory that afternoon had been brief, pointed. "I cannot go on like this, Mr. Anthony," the lanky, studious-looking general manager had stated flatly in the careful manner of a man who has mastered textbook English by diligent application. "I am finished. Let Ryerson employ a new whipping boy."

"What do you mean, whipping boy?"

"That is all I amount to as far as he is concerned. On the infrequent occasions when he comes to the plant, he finds fault with everything I have done. I might ignore that, perhaps, but there is something worse."

"Such as?"

"These night clubs and bootlegging dance halls are not good for our workers. I have suggested that we try to have the authorities move against them; but Mr. Ryerson rages at me whenever I mention the matter. Moreover, he sets a bad example by making his own headquarters in such resorts."

There was nothing priggish about this remark. It was delivered bluntly, as a plain statement of fact, with no hint of sanctimonious attitude. Wozniak wasn't against drinking and dancing because of any moralistic principle, he merely considered the swing shift liquor traffic as a menace to war-industry production and wasn't afraid to say so.

All the same, Anthony's sixth sense had tuned in on a hidden undercurrent behind the general manager's words; a feeling that there was something even deeper beneath the antagonism existing between Wozniak and Steve Ryerson. Wozniak had refused to admit this, though; and in the end, Jim realized he would have to pry the truth out of Ryerson personally.

Which was not as easy as it sounded, for Ryerson was a hard man to catch. He hadn't been near his home for three days, according to what his wife told Anthony on the phone; and he certainly hadn't seen fit to drop in at the airplane factory. Therefore it became necessary to search for him in the hot spots—and before this search began, Jim Anthony received the three threatening cartridges.

ALL THOUGHT OF those warning bullets vanished from the millionaire inventor's mind, though, as he stared toward an occupied table directly opposite his own in the crowded cabaret.

"Tom!" he whispered sharply. "We're in luck at last. There's Ryerson now! He was hidden by the dancers until just this instant, but now we've found him!"

Gentry followed the direction of his friend's gaze and saw a florid, fleshy man of middle age seated between two pretty girls, both expensively gowned.

"So that's Ryerson," the genial aviator muttered admiringly. "Well, you got to hand him one thing. He may have his mind on nothing but dames—but the dames he has his mind on are the kind you dream about on rainy Sundays! Come on, pappy, let's move in and wangle some introductions."

Anthony shook his head. "Take it easy. It's Ryerson I'm interested in, not his women. When I talk to him, I want his undivided attention. We'll wait until he leaves, then trail him,"

"Suppose he gives us the slip?"

Jim didn't answer. His gaze was suddenly riveted upon a spot across the room, where a lanky, studious-looking man was walking out on the dance floor. At the moment, the floor itself was deserted—both orchestras having blown themselves into a state of temporary exhaustion. And the approaching man was dressed so conservatively that he drew no notice.

Except Jim Anthony's!

It was the fellow's expression that awakened Jim's weird sixth sense: an expression of frowning concentration directed at the florid Steve Ryerson, who sat with his two feminine companions as if oblivious to any possible peril.

Anthony sensed that peril, though, even as his keen vision detected a suspicious bulge in the pocket of the lanky man. He was too far away to interfere or prevent what his intuition told him was about to happen. So he did the only thing he could under the circumstances.

He yelled.

"Wozniak!" his voice lifted thunderously. "Karl Wozniak! Don't be a fool!"

At the sound of Jim Anthony's commanding tone, an abrupt stillness settled over the vast, smoke-filled room. Even the drunks at the long bar seemed to know something was wrong, for they whirled in glassy-eyed silence.

Steve Ryerson's table was ringside, and the fleshy man twisted around to see his foreign-born general manager coming toward him on stalking tread, as inevitable and inexorable as death itself. Everybody in The Shed was staring now; and in the hush, Wozniak spoke tersely.

"I warned you, Ryerson. I told you that you were pushing me too far. You laughed. You called me a crazy Hunkey. Very well, perhaps I am crazy. But you will not laugh again."

With a swinging motion, he brought the gun from his coat.

Jim Anthony picked up a water carafe and hurled it, even as Wozniak pulled his trigger. The carafe struck the lanky man's elbow; jarred his aim. It seemed a long moment before a crashing explosion jolted the big room into echoing sound.

"Cripes!" Tom Gentry gasped.

Ryerson had come to his feet, no longer florid. Ugly pallor spread across his fleshy cheeks as he swayed, clutching the edge of the table for support. Then he toppled, and the two girls who had been with him screamed shrilly.

Karl Wozniak stood stock still for a split instant, looking down at his victim with disbelieving eyes. Then he pivoted; went plunging headlong through the nearest exit. And the crowd was too stunned to stop him.

CHAPTER II

DENIAL

JIM ANTHONY HAD ENGAGED a full floor in the Brentwood Apartments for his headquarters during his stay in Los Angeles, along with the services of a Filipino houseboy. But he had instructed the houseboy not to wait up for him; so when he keyed the front door open and saw light gleaming in the living room, he gave Tom Gentry a swift shove out of any possible line of fire. He was remembering the three bullet-warnings he'd received.

With equal swiftness he hurled himself sidewise, and a flat automatic appeared in his fist as if by magic. There was no need for the weapon, though. He realized this the instant he recognized the tall, thin, lanky man who stood before him.

"Wozniak!" he said tautly.

"Yes, Mr. Anthony. You will please forgive me for intruding at such an hour, but—but I had your servant let me in because I—I must explain to you what happened at The Shed." Despite the man's obvious nervousness, he still spoke with a precision usually found only in textbooks.

Anthony made a sour mouth. "There's nothing you can explain. You killed a man in front of more than five hundred witnesses. I don't think there's much to be said about it."

"But there is, sir. And that is why I have come here to ask your help. You see, I did *not* kill Ryerson."

Tom Gentry made a disparaging noise. "If you didn't kill him, then how-come he's so damned dead?"

"I wish I knew," Wozniak muttered. "Yet the fact remains that I am innocent. It is true that I intended to murder the man. But two things intervened. First, my pistol missed fire. Second, even if I had discharged the gun—which I did not—my aim would have been spoiled by the carafe you threw."

Anthony stared. "You claim you pulled your trigger but nothing happened? And then somebody else in the crowd shot Ryerson through the heart?"

"Quite so. Understand, I do not deny that I planned to murder him. I had warned him I would shoot on sight if he ever again went out with Mary Kilvaine. Tonight I learned that he had ignored my warnings—"

"So you went gunning for him."

"Yes, sir. But I did not kill him. And I do not wish to die in the lethal chamber for a thing I planned to do but failed to accomplish."

ONCE MORE GENTRY broke into the conversation. "Whale feathers! They found your roscoe on the parking lot. Its rifling checked with the slug they dug out of Ryerson's clockworks."

"That is impossible," Wozniak protested mildly. "Here is my pistol," he drew a .38 Smith and Wesson and extended it to Anthony. "Observe the cartridge in the chamber. It is defective. The mark of the firing pin is dented on the case, but the bullet was not discharged."

Jim Anthony confirmed this. Puzzlement slid into his narrowed eyes. "What about the 1914 model Webley automatic the police found on that parking lot?" he demanded. "It's the one that killed Ryerson. And it's registered to you."

"A British Webley? My God, I *do* own one of those! But it has not been out of its case in my flat for years."

The millionaire criminologist began pacing the rug. "There's only one possible answer— if you're telling the truth. Somebody stole the Webley from your apartment, shot Ryerson with it, then tossed it away. But how could

Though the caliber of the bullets changed, each warning was identical.

the murderer know you'd be in The Shed, or that your .38 would miss fire?"

"I cannot tell you that, sir."

"Did anyone know you were hunting Ryerson?"

"Why, yes. Mike Panama knew."

"Who's Mike Panama?"

"He is a Cuban, or perhaps a South American. He owns the cabaret. I had telephoned him, asking if Ryerson was there. He said yes, so I told him I would come to The Shed at once. But he could not guess I had murder on my mind."

"Suppose you tell me again about that," Anthony clipped out. "From the beginning. Including this Mary Kilvaine you mentioned. You say you want my help; but I can't give it to you until I have the whole story.

Wozniak licked his nervous lips. "It is very simple, sir. As you know, Ryerson was married. That happened very unexpectedly, about two years ago. At the plant we were not even aware of his engagement until he flew to Las Vegas one day and returned with a bride. The bride's brother was subsequently brought into the company as chief auditor."

"That would be Norton Pyle."

"Yes, and a very efficient man. One you can trust."

"Get back to Ryerson and Mary Kilvaine."

"Very well," Wozniak flushed. "Mary is a demure, beautiful—well, I happen to be in love with her, so perhaps I am prejudiced. But Ryerson wanted her, too. It made no difference that he was a married man. He dazzled her with expensive gifts, refused to let her alone even after I warned him to stop."

"She fell for him?"

"It seemed more like fascination, as a bird is charmed by a predatory snake. Norton Pyle also tried to interfere; after all, his sister was Ryerson's wife. But Ryerson merely laughed and continued to go out with Mary."

TOM GENTRY BURST out: "Cripes, maybe it was Mrs. Ryerson that creamed the guy on account of he was chiseling on her! Or what if the brother-in-law got sore and—"

"Thank you," Wozniak said gently. "Thank you for indicating your belief in my innocence."

Gentry did an immediate about-face. "Hell, bub, I didn't say you were innocent. With my own eyes I saw you pull down on Fatso Ryerson. So did plenty other people."

"The eye isn't always trustworthy, Tom," Jim Anthony remarked. Then he turned to the aircraft factory's general manager. "I want you to come into my lab for a paraffin test."

Wozniak stiffened. "You doubt my story, sir?"

"No, I just want to confirm it, is all. The test will show whether or not you've fired a gun tonight. If you're guilty, I'll turn you over to the law. Otherwise you can stay here in my rooms until I've looked into the case."

"But—but I cannot remain here, Mr. Anthony. That might involve you with the police."

"I'll take my chances," Jim smiled thinly. "Every cop in Los Angeles is on the prowl for you; but I don't imagine they'd think to look here. Besides, with Ryerson dead and you accused, it'll be up to me to run the factory temporarily. That means I'll want to consult you from time to time on technical details. So this is the best place for you."

"In that case," Wozniak held out his thin, work-hardened hands, "I am ready for any test you wish to make."

CHAPTER III

WIDOW IN NEGLIGEE

AS JIM ANTHONY TOOLED his big, cream-colored convertible coupé through the predawn darkness, he was sunk deep in reflection. Alongside him, the irrepressible Gentry gave vent to vocal bewilderment.

"Gosh, pappy, you could've knocked me down with a straw when that paraffin showed negative. I tell you, I'd have gone on the witness stand and sworn Wozniak browned Ryerson."

"He could have. You can rub certain so-called chemical gloves on your hands and possibly defeat the paraffin experiment. Still I'm inclined to believe Wozniak told the truth. His story was too screwy to be false."

"Hunh?"

"A guilty man would think up something more plausible. But an innocent guy relies on the truth even if it sounds like something out of an opium pipe."

Gentry settled back. "Yeah, I guess you're right. I don't figure what you hope to get from Ryerson's widow, though. You think you can slap a confession out of her, maybe?"

"At least I want to size her up." As he answered, the wealthy criminologist swerved his front wheels into the circular driveway of a rambling, ornate Spanish residence and came to a stop before the porch-like patio.

Despite the late, or rather early, hour, lights burned within the house; and when Anthony rang, the door opened almost at once. The man who stared out was the chief auditor of the aircraft factory, Norton Pyle—the slain Ryerson's brother-in-law.

Just now, Pyle's usual dapperness seemed somewhat frayed; his penetrating black eyes bloodshot. Even the waxed ends of his dark mustache, ordinarily twisted to spiked points, drooped as if with weariness. And his pleasant voice held a matching droop.

"Mr. Anthony!" he said. "You—I—I suppose you've heard the news about Steve?" He stepped aside for his visitors to enter the richly furnished living room.

Jim inclined his head. "That's why we're here. We were at The Shed when it happened."

"Were you? Funny I didn't see you. I was there too. Over near the bar. God, what a lousy thing to happen!" Pyle worried the ends of his mustache with nervous fingers.

"How is your sister taking it?" Anthony asked. "I was hoping to talk to her for a moment if I could."

The auditor hesitated. "Is it really necessary? Yvonne's been pretty brave, but—well, she cared a lot for Steve, even though you wouldn't call him the most faithful husband in the world. You can understand how this thing shocked her."

"I understand and sympathize. All the same, we've got one of the biggest aircraft plants in the world. And we've got a contract to fulfill; cargo planes to build. The country's at war, and one man's death mustn't stop us."

"It won't stop us, Mr. Anthony."

"No, I'll see to that! But with Steve Ryerson dead and Karl Wozniak a fugitive, it looks as if I'll have to take over. To do it, I'll need your help—and your sister's. She'll control Ryerson's stock now, and I want to be sure of her support."

FROM THE GREAT staircase in the main hall, a rich voice spoke in husky contralto. "You shall have my support, Mr. Anthony. That I promise you."

Both Jim and Gentry spun around; and the impressionable aviator suppressed a startled, admiring whistle. Anthony, too, felt a sudden tingling sensation when he beheld the regal beauty of the woman who came drifting toward him.

She was tall, almost as tall as Anthony's own six-feet-plus; and her sleek raven hair was marked by a startling white blaize from forehead to crown. Her face was like chiseled white marble, the features perfect, the eyes dark and heavy-lidded and mysterious. Against the pallor of her complexion, her sensuous mouth was a scarlet passion-flower.

"I am Yvonne Ryerson," she introduced herself simply; and she extended long, tapered fingers in a cool, graceful gesture.

For an instant, Jim Anthony was almost too stricken to take her proffered hand. As if hypnotized, his gaze was glued upon the perfection of her lush figure. She was clad in a gossamer orchid negligee that clothed her curves like a filmy cloud, hinting at the things it concealed and revealing far more than it hinted.

Anthony tore his eyes away from the dangerous allurement of her figure; forced a polite smile to his lips. "You're very gracious, Mrs. Ryerson. I can't tell you how much I appreciate your confidence."

"I'm sure it won't be misplaced. And you may call me Yvonne," her throaty voice was like a caress. Then she turned to her brother. "Mr. Anthony might like a drink, Norton. Why not take his friend along to help pour them?"

As Tom Gentry said later, he didn't need a brick chimney to fall on him; he knew when he wasn't wanted. All the same, he made a disappointed grimace as he followed Norton Pyle from the room. And then the millionaire criminologist faced the bereaved brunette goddess.

"What is it you want to tell me privately... Yvonne?"

Her red lips parted in a wry smile. "Was I as obvious as all that? It doesn't matter. I *have* got something for your ears alone. Something I want you to understand."

"And that is—?"

SHE DRIFTED CLOSER to him in an aura of expensive, heady perfume that seemed to seep into his very blood and ignite strange yearnings. "My husband is dead," she whispered. "Nothing you or the police can do will ever bring him back. I won't say I'm heartbroken. Steve treated me too shabbily for that. He neglected me, flaunted his other women in my face."

"He was a fool. Nobody but a crazy man would neglect a wife as lovely as you, Yvonne."

"Thank you... Jim. The fact remains that he *did* neglect me. I can't forget that. Now that he's dead, though, I bear him no malice. And yet, curiously enough, I can't bring myself to hate Karl Wozniak for killing him."

Anthony stirred, uneasy at her nearness. "There's some doubt of Wozniak's guilt."

"There is?" a peculiar glitter leaped into her dark eyes and then died as swiftly as it came. Just as swiftly, her voice dropped back to its husky register. "But that is the very thing I had wanted to talk to you about."

"Wozniak, you mean?"

"Yes. I'd like to see him cleared."

Anthony couldn't quite understand the pang of jealousy that stabbed through him. This Ryerson woman was like an intoxicating drug, filling him with dark emotions he'd never before experienced. It made him inexplicably angry to think she might be interested in Karl Wozniak.

Savagely he put down the feeling. "Why would you want Wozniak cleared?"

"I'm afraid you misunderstand me, Jim. When I mentioned Karl, I thought he was guilty. Now I'll make my statement more general. *Whoever my husband's murderer may be, I don't want him punished!* You see? I prefer the case to be closed, forgotten. Sending the killer to the lethal chamber won't bring Steve Ryerson back. And Steve got only what was coming to him."

"You mean you're asking me to—?"

"You have influence, Jim. I'm asking you to use it. Bring pressure to bear on the police department, the district attorney's office—*and have the investigation quashed.*"

"Is that your price for backing me with your stock-holdings in the factory, Yvonne?"

She swayed against him, lowering her voice to a husky whisper. "Let's not think of it as a business deal. Let's just say you're doing me a favor. You won't be sorry. There might be… this."

Then she wrapped her warm arms around his neck, and parted her avid lips succulently over his startled mouth.

A chaos of shocked thoughts seethed and churned through his mind. What sort of beautiful wanton was this, that she could offer her kisses to a stranger within a few hours of her husband's violent death? Was she clinging to him in genuine passion, or was she trying to bribe him into doing what she had asked? And if the latter theory were true, why was she so desperately anxious to have Steve Ryerson's killer go unpunished? What was the hidden motive?

He thought of Tom Gentry's casually-spoken theories: that Yvonne Ryerson herself had shot her florid husband—or that her brother, Norton Pyle, was the guilty one. In view of her present sultry tactics, either one of those suggestions might hit the nail on the head.

CERTAINLY SHE WAS driven by some urgent, impelling reason: otherwise she wouldn't do the things she was doing now. And yet it was hard for Anthony to be calm. For a moment he found himself forgetful of everything but her nearness and her desirable loveliness.

He crushed her in his embrace, almost brutally; mauled her until she gasped an inaudible protest that seemed almost a moan of ecstasy. Then, suddenly, he regained a measure of his self-control; thrust her away from him roughly and drew a deep, unsteady breath.

HE WAS JUST in time, for at that precise moment Norton Pyle and Tom Gentry returned to the living room with a tray of tinkling glasses full of ice, Scotch and soda.

Gentry handed Jim a drink—and a small paper cocktail napkin. "For the kisser, pappy," he whispered sagely, so that nobody else heard.

Anthony stared at him.

Tom winked. "On you, lipstick ain't so attractive."

If Pyle noticed any tension, though, he said nothing about it. Deftly the auditor drew the stalled conversation into impersonal channels. "The plant must operate. Cargo planes must be turned out faster and faster. Frankly, as far as I'm concerned, I'd like to see Karl Wozniak back on the job, running things—under your supervision, of course, Mr. Anthony," he added quickly.

The millionaire detective drained his scotch and soda; replaced the empty glass on its tray. "There's a chance you might get your wish," he said quietly; and he cast a significant look at Yvonne Ryerson.

A little later, dawn washed over the eastern mountain range; streaked the velvet sky with grey as Anthony and Gentry left the house and piled into the big cream-colored convertible in the driveway.

The freckled aviator was oddly lacking in his usual happy-go-lucky mannerisms. He said morosely: "You made hay fast, Jim. I take my hat off to you."

"Never mind that. I want to know something. Did Norton Pyle leave you even for a minute when you two were fixing the drinks in the kitchen?"

Tom frowned. "Come to think of it, yes. He had to see a dog about a lamp-post. Why?"

"Just this," Jim Anthony's voice was bleak as he extended a small cardboard box which he had found fastened to his steering wheel.

The box contained a .44 caliber cartridge, and the slug was wrapped in a length of ticker tape. On the tape a curt message was typed:

"Time grows short. Get out of town or die."

CHAPTER IV

TWO SCARED GIRLS

ROLLING THROUGH THE GREY tulle-fog of early morning, Anthony and Gentry were a long time silent. Finally, Tom asked questions.

"What about the Ryerson dame, Jim?"

"Nothing about her. She's dangerous, is all. And smart. She wouldn't be good to have for an enemy."

"Yeah, but did she croak her hubby?"

"I don't know."

"Did her brother do it?"

"I don't know that either—yet."

"Maybe you're more interested in Mrs. Ryerson than in whoever made her a widow, hunh?"

"I'm interested in clearing up the murder," Anthony growled irritably. He couldn't quite explain, even to himself, the peculiar effect Yvonne Ryerson had on him. Now that he was away from her he could view the matter rationally and wonder at the thrill he'd drawn from her kiss. That didn't help much, however. He was still at a loss to understand many things.

Tom said: "What's eating on you, Jim?"

"I've got an airplane factory to think about. Swing shift employes who drink too much… a general manager who's under the gun for a kill he may not have pulled. Something tells me there's a sinister undercurrent to this mess. I want to know what it is. I intend to find out."

For the first time in many minutes, Gentry grinned. "That's more like it! Now you're yourself again. You ain't Jim Anthony the inventor any more. You're Jim Anthony the criminologist. We headed any place in particular, pappy?"

"Yes. To see the girl who may or may not have been the cause of Ryerson's murder. Mary Kilvaine."

Tom came erect. "You know where she hangs out?"

"Karl Wozniak gave me her address when I was putting him to the paraffin test in my temporary lab. Here we are now," Anthony tacked

"Get hep, chick!" the gnome raged. "These guys
are reporters straight off the cob."

on as he drew up before an apartment house just north of Franklin.
"Come on, let's go."

There was a small lobby, but no night clerk; and nobody barred
their progress as they crossed to a small automatic elevator and rode
it up to the fourth floor. Then they came to the door they wanted, and
Gentry took the lead.

"Let me make the first play this time," he pleaded humorously.
"From what I saw of the two janes with Ryerson when he got blasted,

either one of them could be Mary Kilvaine and I'd be happy to put the shake on her." He knocked on the door.

Presently it opened—and Tom recoiled as if from an unhappy dream. The man who stood truculently on the threshold was absurdly short, not over five feet one, and his face was a wizened little monkey-mask marked largely by protruberant green eyes, like varnished flakes of emerald glass.

It was his costume that got you, though. He wore a weirdly patterned coat which might have been mistaken at first glance for a topcoat, since it draped down nearly to his knees. The patch pockets were oversize, the lapels exaggerated to the point of burlesque, and the padded shoulders winged outward to a grotesque width.

His matching trousers were equally fantastic. The waist band was so high that it came almost to its wearer's armpits, and the legs were so tight they had to be fastened along each seam from cuff to knee by means of zippers—yet the cuffs themselves flared like bells.

THE LITTLE APPARITION was in constant jerky motion as if to some unheard dance rhythm. His head bobbed, his feet tapped and he kept snapping his fingers like castanets. From his slit-like mouth came sounds which might conceivably have been interpreted as speech.

"Buckadiddle, buckadiddle, cha, *cha;* Biddleyump zing-zing, biddle-yump zing-zing, *cha;* What's fryin', Ryan? If you cats are cops, we've had some. If you're reporters, we don't want any. Take it on the scram, Sam. Blow, Joe. Do you dig me?"

Tom Gentry bleated: "Jeest, a maniac!"

The weird little gnome took exception to this—but violently. In one swift motion his left hand dipped into a side pocket of his coat and came out wearing brass knuckles. He swung these at the genial aviator's chin, leaping at least two feet straight up into the air in order to connect. Even so, the punch barely grazed Gentry's startled jaw, with just enough force to tip him backward.

"Dacka-loodle, dacka-loodle, chee, *chee!* You can't call me crazy, Daisy. I'll bounce you on your duster, Buster."

Tom, in the face of this dementia, backed away from a brawl for the first time in his life. He cast a harried and despairing look at Anthony, invoking help.

Jim acted. He grabbed the gnome, spun him around, seized a fistful of his lapels and held him off the floor at arm's length while the little fellow made wildly ineffectual swings. It might have gone on indefinitely, but a girl rushed to the door and put a period to the insane scene with two words.

She said: "Charlie, behave!"

Monkey-Face stopped trying to reach Anthony with his brass-bound fist. Still suspended like a pendulum in the wealthy criminologist's grasp, with his feet dancing a jig on empty air, he screwed up his wizened features in rage. "Get hep, chick. These guys are reporters straight off the cob."

The girl turned to Anthony. "Put him down, mister, he's harmless. Then I'll thank you to leave. We've got nothing to say to the press."

Anthony complied. Released, the little man jigged reluctantly back into the apartment, muttering under his breath and twitching rhythmically like a sufferer from some obscure nervous disorder, say St. Vitus' dance. Then the girl started to close the door, but Jim held up a hand.

"Wait a minute, please. Are you Mary Kilvaine?"

"No. I'm her room-mate. Florrie Sheffield. Good-bye now."

THE CRIMINOLOGIST STUDIED her— and liked what he saw. Florrie Sheffield was undoubtedly one of the two girls who'd been with Ryerson when that florid Casanova was murdered. You could recognize her easily enough, even though she'd exchanged her evening gown for a kimono of uncertain age. It would have been impossible for anyone to mistake her hair. It was the brightest red this side of a four alarm fire.

Her sea-blue eyes were direct, challenging; and she carried herself with a certain competent self-assurance which Anthony immediately approved. There was unveiled hostility in her stare, though, and a bitter twist at the corners of her ripe mouth; almost contemptuous.

Jim said gently: "We're not reporters, Miss Sheffield. I'm Jim Anthony—and this is my friend, Tom Gentry."

The anger died from her eyes. "Not *the* Jim Anthony? You mean you're that millionaire detective the newspapers are always playing up? The guy that invented the new plastic cargo plane?"

He nodded.

"Well, come in!" she breathed. "Why are we standing here in a tizzy?" As she conducted them into the modest front room, she cast a jaundiced look at the little gnome in the fantastic garb. "A fine Dopey Joe you turned out to be. Can't tell a millionaire from a newspaper buzzard!"

"Do I dig he's solid, chick? Can I riff he stuffs a blip of meters in his kick? So all reet, I make a mistake."

Florrie Sheffield turned apologetically to Anthony and Gentry. "In case you want that translated, he means how did he know you were okay, and how could he tell you were rich? By the way, he's my big moment. Around the jive dives they call him Zoot-Suit Charlie."

Tom Gentry blinked. "Is that a zoot-suit you got on, palsy walsy? With a reet-pleat, maybe?"

"Now you're sending," Charlie said. "It's the zootest set of threads on the coast. Made special for me. I wish I could think up some way to make it zootier. Buckadiddy, da. Buckadiddy, buckadiddy cha, *cha*." Jigging, he held out his right palm horizontally. "Press the flesh and no hard feelings. No, I didn't say shake hands. That's icky. The old corn. Do it this way."

He demonstrated by placing Tom's palm flat upon his own, then moving his wrist up and down with a hinge motion. The freckled aviator took part in this pantomime with the expression of one who walks in nightmare. It would be a long time before he recovered from his daze. Even Charlie's breath smelled funny.

MEANTIME, ANTHONY HAD drawn the red-haired Sheffield girl to one side. "I know what happened at The Shed. I was there; saw you and Mary Kilvaine with Ryerson when he was murdered."

A sharp breath pouted out her boyish breasts beneath the faded kimono. "Then—then you understand why Charlie's here. I wouldn't want you to think—"

"Yes, I know. You needed somebody to keep the reporters away. You two girls have probably had a tough time these past few hours. The police questioned you, of course?"

"And how!" she made a bitter mouth. "Mary especially."

"Do you think I might see her for a minute? There's something I'd like to tell her."

"We-e-ell, okay. I'll get her. But go easy, will you?" Florrie moved to a bedroom door just as a telephone bell tinkled. She opened the door, vanished, and a voice could be heard answering the phone: "No. I won't talk to reporters."

A moment later Florrie reappeared with Mary Kilvaine.

Tom Gentry gulped audibly when he saw her. Anthony, too, was impressed by Mary's fragile blonde sweetness. Her hair was like fine-spun gold, her face was a Madonna mask of suffering, and her dainty figure was exquisite in a shimmering chiffon negligee. In a way, she reminded Jim of a bisque doll—feminine perfection in lovely miniature.

When she spoke, though, her voice was brittle and jagged, as if edged with hysteria. "You wanted to tell me something?"

"Yes," Anthony said gravely. "I wanted to let you know Karl Wozniak may not have fired the murder shot tonight."

She flinched at the mere mention of the airplane plant manager's name. "Wozniak! It was his crazy jealousy that did all the damage. Now you try to make me believe—Why, I saw him with my own eyes! Saw him pull his g-gun and—"

"It missed fire on a defective cartridge."

"I don't believe that. I can't. Who are you, anyway?"

"Jim Anthony."

The blonde girl tensed visibly. "Steve Ryerson spoke of you just before he was k-killed. I remember now. He said…"

"Yes?"

She licked her lips. "He said he was afraid you were going to make trouble, now that you were in town."

"What kind of trouble?"

Florrie Sheffield broke in. "He didn't say. He acted as if he was sorry he'd popped off even that much. I didn't pay any particular attention to the whole thing. I don't think Mary did, either. Did you, honey?"

"N-no. It was right afterward that Wozniak sh-shot him."

"We're not so sure on that point," Anthony reminded her. "And it's a thing I'd like to clear up if I can. You see, the factory needs Wozniak—if he's innocent."

"Innocent!" the golden-haired Kilvaine girl curled her tremulous mouth downward. "I saw him shoot, didn't I? And I know what his reason was."

"Jealousy," Anthony agreed. "He's in love with you, and you were dating Ryerson."

Color came into Mary's cheeks, then receded. "He never could understand that. I'm not so sure I understood it myself."

"Meaning what?"

"Steve Ryerson wasn't anything to me, really. I mean I didn't actually care for him. He was like a—a drug. A habit I couldn't break."

"You didn't mind the fact that he was married?"

SHE FLUSHED AGAIN, briefly. "Mrs. Ryerson didn't count. Steve told me that much. His wedding was a sort of business arrangement, he claimed. It didn't stop his interest in me. Nothing could stop that! The one time I tried to break with him, he sent somebody after me; someone I'm scared of."

"Who?"

"Mike Panama."

Anthony's eyes narrowed. "The man who owns The Shed?"

"Yes."

"What was Panama's connection with Ryerson?"

It was Florrie Sheffield who answered this. She tossed her red hair like an angry halo of flame; laughed without mirth. "Ryerson was Mike Panama's boss. That's what the connection was. What's the use trying to hide it?"

"Suppose you make that plainer," Jim suggested.

"Okay, I will. Steve Ryerson was the real owner of The Shed. And several more swing-shift joints, too. Panama was just his handy man; the guy that fronted for him and ran the dives and sold liquor after hours."

"You're sure of this, Miss Sheffield?"

"Positive. Ryerson was a heel. He wasn't satisfied to be the president of a legitimate airplane factory. He had to take his cut out of a mess of other rotten grifts. Me, I'm glad the rat's dead. I wish I'd had the nerve to do it myself."

The millionaire criminologist let his face go blank, impassive. "What were some of Ryerson's rotten grifts?"

"I'll tell you one. That ought to be enough. He made hop-heads out of aircraft workers. Did you ever hear of reefers?"

"Yes, I have."

"Well, Ryerson controlled that racket in this town. He ran it through Mike Panama."

PRESENTLY, WHEN ANTHONY and his friend had left the apartment and returned to the big cream-colored convertible, Tom Gentry clucked his tongue. "Now, what the hell do you suppose made that red-haired cutie blow her topper that way? Cripes, she acted as sore as a picked blister!"

"She's got a very good reason to be sore," Jim said grimly. "Her boy friend is caught in an ugly trap."

"Zoot-Suit Charlie? What kind of trap?"

"A drug addict's trap. Did you notice his breath?"

"Yeah. It smelled funny."

"That's from smoking reefers, Tom. Marijuana cigarettes. The poor devil was a mile high. And I think we're beginning to get somewhere."

He was right. They *were* getting somewhere. A big black sedan slammed past them and gunfire chewed blazing yellow holes in the morning. It was damned inaccurate shooting, though. The convertible lost some glossy cream paint, but Anthony and his friend got out without a scratch.

CHAPTER V

MIKE PANAMA

FOR THE NEXT FEW minutes they lived in a blur of motion; a whirling nightmare of speed that would haunt Tom Gentry's sleep for months to come. Anthony slammed the convertible around in a vicious U-turn, mashed his throttle into automatic overdrive and sent the roaring vehicle in thunderous pursuit of the black sedan.

Under the hood of Jim's specially-built job there were sixteen power-packed cylinders; two vee-eight motors hooked in tandem in a design which he himself had blueprinted. The result was blinding, yammering speed which only a man of Anthony's superb strength could control.

But he was racing a driver who made up in trickiness what he lacked in horsepower. Moreover, the black sedan had a full three blocks' start—gained while Jim had been making his careening U-turn. And now the black car began cutting around corners like a rocket gone wild, taking the intersection curves on tires that squealed soprano protest.

Anthony clung grimly to the trail, breathing a silent prayer of thanks that there was no traffic on the streets at this early morning hour. And then, just when he was closing the gap, a motorbike siren shrieked behind him. Another yowling wail joined in as a second mounted cop took up the chase.

Gentry gasped: "Duck, pappy! Those rattlebrains are pulling their roscoes!"

The words seemed to cool the red, unreasoning rage that had filmed the millionaire detective's vision. He couldn't risk his friend's life by continuing this maniac pace, chancing a stray bullet from the pursuing motorcycle cops. Sooner than do that, he preferred to let the black sedan escape.

He took his foot off the throttle paddle; let the convertible slow itself against compression. Then the two motorbikes caught up, flanking him on either side. The officers had drawn guns and their eyes were flinty behind their goggles.

One uniformed man propped his mount on its parking spike and walked forward, swearing under his breath. "Drunk driving. Reckless endangerment of life and property. Excessive speed—we clocked you at ninety and you were going away. Let's see your driver's license."

The wealthy criminologist handed it over without saying anything. Attached to his case of identification cards were a pair of jeweled badges, one an honorary membership in the New York State Police, the other a Los Angeles Sheriff's Office star set in diamonds.

"Are you Jim Anthony?" the cop stared.

"I am."

"Let's smell your breath. Hm-m. If you've had anything to drink it's been hours ago. What cooks?"

"We were fired at. You can see the bullet holes for yourself. I was chasing the gunsel's car when you fell in behind."

"By golly, you're telling the truth! These *are* bullet holes! Say, you'd better roll on down to headquarters with us and give a report. Come to think about it, we had a radio call less than an hour ago to pick you up and ask you to come in."

Anthony's hawk-like eyes slitted. "What about?"

"Don't ask me. Aw, hell, I might as well tell you. Karl Wozniak was picked up in your hotel suite."

DOWN IN CENTRAL Station, Jim Anthony faced Lieutenant David Donaldson of the Los Angeles homicide bureau. Donaldson was big, beefy, inclined to be affable. It paid the police to be amiable with anyone as important as Anthony.

"But you were taking a long chance, harboring a murderer in your suite," the plainclothes lieutenant said chidingly. "That can get you two to ten in California."

"True. But first you've got to prove the man I was harboring is really a murderer," Jim smiled.

"Excuse me while I rectify
my error," Jim said.

Donaldson's cheeks reddened. "Dammit, at least five hundred witnesses saw Wozniak pull down on Ryerson! The case is open-and-shut. You know that."

"I don't know anything for sure. But I'm finding out plenty as I go along. I may get somewhere yet—if that black sedan doesn't catch up with me another time."

"Yeah, the black sedan," the homicide official worried his lower lip. "We'll investigate that, of course. You say you didn't see the license plates?"

"Sorry. I was too busy driving."

Tom Gentry horned in. "But look, pappy, I tabbed—" Then he subsided, wincing under the pain of a swift kick on the shins. He cast a hurt glare at Jim, which Donaldson apparently missed.

LATER, THOUGH, WHEN they had left headquarters behind them, Tom grew vocal in his protests. "Why didn't you want me to say I caught that sedan's number?"

"Because I prefer to settle that particular bit of nastiness in my own way," Anthony growled stolidly. "I think it's all of a piece with those four bullet-warnings we received. And when I crack down, I don't want any police interference. This is my own personal fight, now."

"Okay, keed. You know what you're doing—I hope. But I wonder who phoned in the anonymous tip that sent the law to our hotel to nab Wozniak?"

"Somebody who knew he was there, of course. Or at least somebody who guessed it."

"All right. Who, for instance?"

"He could have been shadowed to our place at the beginning," Jim pointed out. "Other than that, we have the two girls, Florrie Sheffield and Mary Kilvaine. And Zoot-Suit Charlie. We told them we'd talked with Wozniak, so any one of them could have figured it out that we were keeping him under cover."

Gentry nodded. "Yeah. For that matter, Steve Ryerson's widow could have doped it. Or her brother, Norton Pyle. That's a hell of a lot of suspects."

"Enough," Anthony agreed. "I'm not particularly interested in that angle at present, though. It's the black sedan I'm after. I want to trace that car—but secretly."

"How can you without the cops catching wise?"

By now, they were at the Brentwood Apartments. Anthony put his car in the basement garage, then steered his genial friend to the elevator. "I know a way. You catch some sleep while I set the machinery in motion."

"What about you? You could use some shut-eye."

"A bath and a drink will fix me up." Which was true. The millionaire criminologist's remarkable recuperative powers were a constant source of wonderment to Gentry—and to wrongdoers who happened to cross Anthony's trail. Jim was like his Indian ancestors in that respect. He could stalk his game for days on end, never tiring, never stopping until he ran his quarry to earth. Implacable was the word for Jim Anthony when his vengefulness was aroused.

IT WAS LATE afternoon when Tom Gentry awakened, showered, and wolfed a combination breakfast-supper. Then he sought his wealthy friend.

"Learn anything, Jim?"

"Plenty. I phoned a connection of mine in Sacramento and had him do a little private snooping in the Department of Motor Vehicles."

"He traced the black sedan that shot at us?"

"Yes."

"Cripes, pappy, don't keep me on the hook this way! What was the score?"

Anthony's smile was frigidly wrathful. "You and I are going slumming again, Tom. Right now. We're heading for The Shed. I imagine Mike Panama ought to be on the job by now."

"Why Panama?"

"It's very simple. You see, Mike Panama happens to be the registered owner of that black sedan."

THE SHED WAS indeed going full blast when Anthony and Gentry arrived there at dusk. And Anthony's second surmise had likewise been correct. Mike Panama was in his private office at the rear of the vast dance hall.

He stood up as the millionaire criminologist entered without knocking. Panama was a gross caricature of a man, so fat that it seemed impossible for him to have wedged himself into the tuxedo he was wearing. His hair was sleekly black, like the glossy pelt of a wet seal, and his face was a swarthy moon made of lemon colored lard.

His voice, too, was greasy and thickly accented, betraying his Latin-American origin. "What ees the meaning of these?" he demanded. "You deed not knock—"

Anthony said: "Excuse me. I'll rectify the omission now." Then he doubled his fist and slugged it home, full to Mike Panama's slobbery mouth.

CHAPTER VI

ESCAPE

MIKE LAY ON THE floor behind his desk, moaning. Tom Gentry lifted him, propped him in the swivel chair, and held him there. "Can I have a pop at him too, pappy? Just a little one, please? Why can't I have some of the fun?"

"Maybe, in a little while," the sun-bronzed criminologist answered sociably. "It depends on our fat friend."

Panama spat blood and seemed to shrivel in his dinner jacket. His eyes, deep in purses of unwholesome flesh, held murderous frenzy. "You—you weel not dare heet me again!"

"That's what you think. Do you know who I am?"

"I know. And I weel remember. When my men get feenished weeth you, there weel be a gravestone weeth the name Jeem Anthony on eet. Nobody pushes Mike Panama around and stays alive."

Jim nodded to Gentry. "Slug him, Tom."

"Hard?"

"Medium hard. I want him conscious."

The aviator made a show of spitting on his hands. Then, as he drew his right fist back, Panama started whimpering. "No, boys, no! Geeve me a chance—"

"Will you talk?"

"I do not know what you weesh me to say!"

"Then I'll tell you. I want you to explain why you tried to gun me down this morning."

"I deed not do eet."

"So okay. So you sent some of your hoods to do the actual job. You were behind it, though. Why?"

It was not pleasant to see the fat man cringe and tremble. He was like a quivering mass of panic-stricken jelly. "I was followeeng orders."

"Steve Ryerson's?"

Panama blinked stupidly and was silent; but his silence was a confession.

"Ryerson was afraid I might uncover something when I came to Los Angeles, wasn't he? That's why he had you try to scare me off with the series of warning bullets. Right?"

"You seem to know everytheeng. Why do you ask?"

"Because I'm trying to back-track Ryerson's crooked trail even though he's dead. I'm hunting a motive for his murder."

The fat man's swarthy features went grey. "You weel not peen that on me! Eet was Wozniak who keeled heem!"

"That's open to debate. Personally, I think Wozniak's innocent. His gun missed fire."

PANAMA SEEMED STUNNED at this bit of information. And Tom Gentry began to catch an inkling of what his wealthy friend was doing. Anthony was going from one suspect to another, letting them all know Karl Wozniak wasn't guilty. By such means, the criminologist hoped to smoke the real murderer out into the open; hoped the killer would betray himself—or herself—by some false move. It was damned clever strategy, Tom decided.

As for Mike Panama, the man's blubbery lips were beginning to writhe. "You are eensane, Meester Anthony! Wozniak ees your man. Look at hees moteeves! First, he was jealous of Ryerson because of that girl, Mary Kilvaine. And second, I theenk he knew Ryerson was ronneeng thees night spot."

"What's that got to do with it?"

"Wozniak is a fanateec. He theenk only of the airplane factory. He believes theese cabarets are bad for the workers. So he feegured we might close down eef Ryerson died. He was wrong, however! We weel *not* close down."

Anthony scowled. "Meaning Mrs. Ryerson will inherit the dives and keep them operating?"

"They weel operate. No matter who owns, them."

"And you'll continue to peddle marijuana cigarettes, eh?"

For an instant, Mike Panama seemed on the verge of complete collapse. Then he caught hold of himself, and a crafty expression creased his fat face. "Prove eet eef you can. Breeng the police. I challenge you. I even challenge you to prove I had anytheeng to do with the threats you received—or the attempt upon your life. You traced the black sedan to me. Bot I weel show that eet was stolen from my garage two days ago!" He settled back, smiling to himself. "Een fact, I reported the theft at the time. You are not dealing with a fool, Meester Anthony."

Tom Gentry made growling sounds in his throat. "This guy needs some more medicine, Jim. Shall I paste him?"

"No, I think we've got all we need out of him—for the moment. We'll leave now."

"When you leave, you had better go verree far away," Panama purred silkily. "Onless you like California so well that you weesh eets earth to cover your casket."

"I'll take that chance," Anthony said evenly. Then he and Tom backed out of the office, made their way along the corridor, came at last into the main part of the cabaret.

THERE, OVER BLARING swing music, Gentry spoke his thoughts into Jim's ear. "So now we got another possible motive to pin on Ryerson's widow and her brother. Either one of them might have bumped the guy, not because he was playing around with other dames but because they'd inherit his rackets."

"Perhaps so. Blackmailing leads to murder, lots of times."

"Hunh? Blackmailing?"

"Ryerson was blackmailed into that Las Vegas marriage; forced to install Norton Pyle as auditor of the factory."

The aviator made a gesture with his hands as if trying to capture something that eluded him. "I don't get it!"

"You were asleep today when I made my inquiries," the wealthy investigator smiled. "Remember I phoned Sacramento to trace Mike Panama's black sedan? Well, I also did some long distance calling to Las Vegas; checked with the city editor of my newspaper there. He dug some information out of the files for me."

"What kind of information?"

"Two years ago, when Steve Ryerson flew over to Nevada, he didn't expect it to be a wedding trip. He went to do a little gambling, have himself a fling. Or anyhow that's how I see it now."

"So what happened, pappy?"

"According to the newspaper files of that date, a man named Ryerson had a traffic accident while driving a rented car. A pedestrian was killed. But Ryerson won free on the testimony of two eye-witnesses who swore it was the pedestrian's own fault. Those two witnesses were Pyle and his sister Yvonne."

A gun sounded behind him as
Jim sprinted for the car.

"Jeepers! You think they lied to save Ryerson from taking a rap, hunh? And Ryerson bought their perjury by marrying the dame and giving her brother an important job!"

Anthony nodded. "It stacks up that way to me."

"No wonder the guy claimed his marriage was just a business deal! The two Pyles had him over a barrel, so they just moved in on him. Say, do you suppose they're hooked up with this Mike Panama slob? Were they the ones who forced Ryerson into the cabaret and marijuana grifts?"

"I don't know. Ryerson was a crook at heart, and he probably dipped into the rackets of his own free will. That part doesn't matter now, though. He's dead; out of the picture. I want to know who steps into his shoes as owner of The Shed and other similar dives."

"Why?"

"Because it will be a long step toward cleaning up such joints. The way they're running now, they interfere with war production—reduce the efficiency of the workers. But with the drug traffic stopped and liquor under legal control these cabarets can be a help rather than a menace. People need entertainment and recreation, Tom—as long as it's wholesome."

"Yeah. But how are you going to finger the new head man?"

Jim Anthony grinned engagingly. "That's where you come into it. You're about to start a honey of a fight."

"Me? I ain't mad at anybody."

"Then get mad. I want a look at Panama's office. I want him out of there and I don't want any of his hoods interrupting me. You furnish the counter-attraction."

LIGHT DAWNED ON Gentry and a cocky look of gleeful anticipation came into his merry eyes. By now The Shed was pretty crowded, not with swing shift workers however. The swing shift runs from four in the afternoon until midnight, and its employes live in a topsy-turvy world thrown out of synchronization by war demands. They play and dance while others are sleeping or getting ready to go to work; they sleep while their children are in school; and they labor during the hours when normal people seek rest or entertainment.

So it was now, at eight o'clock in the evening. The Shed's present patrons were those lucky ones who worked daytime and had their nights free. Tom Gentry elbowed his way to the long bar, picking a spot between two groups of men. One group wore North American Aircraft identification badges, while the others sported Lockheed buttons.

Tom trod hard on a North American worker's pet corn. The man, obviously a little tight, swung around. "Watch it, pal. You must have elephant blood, you walk so heavy."

"I should take talk like that off a North American jerk? Me, from Lockheed where it gives white men jobs?"

Somebody else, overhearing this, took up the cudgels. "What yuck says we ain't white men at North American?"

"Ask any Lockheed guy, chum," Tom said.

A fist was swung but Gentry ducked it, and the blow landed on a genuine Lockheed worker. Before you could blink, the two rival factions started swinging and the riot was on. Gentry crouched low, wormed his way out of the growing tangle and rested his shoulders against a far wall, watching the havoc he had touched off. In two minutes the scene before him resembled a retake of the battle of Gettysburg.

Bouncers were everywhere, trying to restore order with persuasive words and thudding blackjacks. Women screamed. Mike Panama popped out of his office and scrambled up on top of the bar to direct his men. Somebody christened him with a bottle of champagne and launched him into a spittoon. It was a tight fit, though.

THE DOOR OF Panama's office had a spring lock which snapped shut when the door was closed. Jim Anthony tried the knob, realized it wouldn't turn, and brought his prized steels from a secret pocket of his coat. With those steels he could force the cleverest lock ever devised; and he had no trouble with this one. The door swung open and Jim stole over the threshold.

The office held a desk, a row of steel files and a modern safe. Anthony opened the safe first, but it contained nothing except money. He was not interested. He turned to the files.

Their locks were easy prey to his steels. He pulled out bank after bank of drawers, riffling through stacks of correspondence and records, receipted bills, tax statements, employe insurance papers and social security blanks. Jim skipped these, but presently he found one thick manila envelope which seemed to contain what he'd hoped to find. He slipped it out, buttoned it under his coat and made for the door.

A hoodlum with a face like a movie villain was just staggering along the hallway hunting reinforcements for the mêlée which was being staged on the dance floor. He spotted Anthony.

"Sneak thief!" he yelled, and went for a shoulder-holstered gun.

Anthony swung from his shoelaces; made a bull's eye on the thug's jutting jaw. Then he stepped casually over his unconscious victim—and saw Mike Panama coming at him with two more snarling plug-uglies. The fat man screamed: "Burn heem down!"

Pivoting, the millionaire criminologist sped back along the hallway. There ought to be a rear exit, he thought. There *had* to be a rear exit! He burst through a tremendous kitchen like a ray of light, hit its back door and catapulted out onto a graveled driveway used by trucks to deliver liquids and solids to the cabaret. He raced down this curving path, skimmed along the side of the barnlike building and came at last to the front street—but by that time he knew he didn't dare go in the front door to get Tom Gentry.

Already Panama and his two gunsels were coming through the night, murder-bent. You could hear their footfalls crunching on gravel, lending emphasis to the proprietor's shrilly effeminate voice: "Keel heem. Don't let heem get away!"

Anthony's convertible was on the adjacent parking lot. He'd be a clay pigeon if he tried to reach it, however. He stared up and down the curb, hunting a taxi. There weren't any. The only car he saw was a clattery old coupé, its motor running noisily as it drifted slowly by.

Then a voice called from the coupé. "Mr. Anthony! Come on—quick!"

It was the red-haired girl, Florrie Sheffield, at the wheel. Zoot-Suit Charlie sat beside her, holding his door open. Anthony lowered his head and sprinted. A gun boomed and a slug sang its hornet song past his ear.

He gained the little car just as it surged into a second-gear blurt of speed; wedged himself inside, Charlie making room for him. The gnome jittered: "Buppadiddle, buppadiddle zing, *zing!* You're doing great, Gate." Then he looked at Florrie. "Out of this world, chick. Cook with ethyl."

She clashed into gear and tramped on the gas. Ahead lay the broad, dimmed-out highway to Los Angeles—a shadowy ribbon to be swallowed by whining tires. Florrie nudged her quivering speedometer up to sixty-five; held it there. "What happened?"

"Panama," Jim answered succinctly.

"That's bad. He'd ram us in the ditch and slit our throats." She cajoled an extra five miles out of the roaring coupé. "Look back. Are we being followed?"

"I don't think so. I don't see any headlights. But you can pull over and let me out. This isn't your party, after all. Why should you take risks for me?"

"Any enemy of Mike Panama is a friend of mine," Florrie said. She swept through Culver, made the turn under the P.E. tracks and straightened out into LaCienega; flashed across Pico and reduced her speed as she slanted toward Olympic.

Zoot-Suit Charlie twitched rhythmically. "You're a hot lick, chick. You're sweet molasses and Dorsey's brasses. But in the old groove, if you dig me."

She sighed wearily. "I'm hep. You mean we made it."

CHAPTER VII

SWING SHIFT PINEAPPLE

IN THE ANTHONY SUITE at the Brentwood, Gentry was sipping a rye highball, when Jim finally arrived. "Jeepers, pappy, I was about to send out a detachment of Marines for you. Where the dickens have you been?"

"Here and there. I see you got home okay."

The aviator smiled reminiscently. "Yeah. I was worried for you, though. I hung around until the cops put the riot out, but you must have scrammed in the meantime."

"Right. With Mike Panama's bullets urging me. Florrie Sheffield and Zoot-Suit Charlie pulled me out of a bad hole."

"What were they doing there?" Gentry's brows went up.

"It develops that they work in The Shed. Florrie's a percentage girl and Charlie's a spotter. He mingles with the crowd, and when he sees some jitterbug about to blow his top, he calls one of the bouncers."

"They were in the joint when I started my fight?"

Anthony nodded. "Yes. But it got too rough for them. Just as they were leaving, they spotted me and gave me a lift. They also gave me some pretty important information."

"What about?"

"Mary Kilvaine," Jim said soberly. "Believe it or not, she's a welder in our plant."

"A lady welder? That doll?"

"Plenty of nice girls are handling torches or bucking rivets these days, Tom. And nobody deserved a job more than Mary Kilvaine. You see, she's from the right side of the tracks. College and social background. Florrie told me the whole story while she was driving me home."

"I can't imagine that blonde Kilvaine babe in overalls!"

"It's a living," Anthony pointed out. "Her father dropped a fortune in one of Steve Ryerson's promotions up north, committed suicide and left her without a cent. She had to eat. And Ryerson certainly owed her something for what happened to her father. I imagine that was one reason he put her to work."

"But not the only reason," Tom said sagely. "Remember, he was on the make for her.—Say, do you suppose she held Ryerson responsible for her old man killing himself?"

"Possibly."

"Then maybe she deliberately played up to Karl Wozniak's jealousy, hoping he'd bump the louse. Which he tried, but his cannon missed fire. So then maybe Mary—aw, no. That's screwy. She just ain't the type."

THE MILLIONAIRE CRIMINOLOGIST'S teeth were white behind an indulgent smile. "You're learning, Tom. Never overlook a suspect no matter how remote."

"Nuts! I'd just as soon suspect the Secretary of the Navy. I wish you'd tell me what you found in Mike Panama's office. Or did you draw blank?"

Anthony withdrew the fat manila envelope from under his coat. "I drew aces. Panama inherits full ownership of The Shed in the event of Ryerson's death. Here's the signed agreement, as binding as a will."

"Holy Moses!" Tom breathed. "There's Panama's motive for bumping the guy! But can you pin it on him?"

"I'm not sure yet. But even if I can't get him for murder I can salt him away for peddling dope. It's all here in black and white: his volume of marijuana sales, his source of supply, his retail outlets. Our fat friend is washed up. I've got him where I want him, now."

"When do you figure to close in?"

"That will be up to the police. I'll hand them the evidence when I've solved the Ryerson murder case."

A frown wrinkled the aviator's freckled forehead. "It's all one and the same. The way I see it, Panama cooled Ryerson so he could inherit The Shed and the reefer racket."

"I wish I could make that stick, Tom. The trouble is, I have a hunch there was no connection between the killing and the marijuana grift."

"Well, hell's bells! That puts you right back where you came in. So now it's Mrs. Ryerson or her brother that drilled the guy on account of he was chasing around with other dames."

Jim said thoughtfully: "There's one person you haven't even thought of."

"Yeah? Who?"

"Florrie Sheffield. She's in love with Zoot-Suit Charlie—and Charlie's a narcotic addict, thanks to the racket Ryerson controlled. Natural red-heads have crazy tempers; you ought to know that because you're a red-head yourself. Isn't it possible that Florrie might have murdered the man who was responsible for her boy-friend's drug addiction?"

She looked like a visitor from Mars
in her wedding outfit.

Gentry put his disconcerted face in his hands and emitted a plaintive groan. "Why can't I think of things like that? Here I had Florrie pegged for a square shooter."

"Me too. I'm just pointing out the possibilities. When you come right down to cases, Charlie himself must be considered. A man might hate the guy who got him to smoking reefers—hate him enough to murder him."

IT WAS ELEVEN o'clock that night when Jim Anthony drove out to the aircraft plant. He put his convertible on the parking lot reserved for executives and department heads, close by the factory wing devoted to engine mounting. Entering through a side door, he was met by a blast of noise and activity.

Here was the final assembly line for the giant plastic cargo planes which he himself had designed. A tingle of pride surged through him as he saw the twin rows of gleaming ships, swarmed over by hundreds of men and women like so many intent ants. And presently a section foreman pointed out to him the person he wanted to see.

Mary Kilvaine looked like a dainty visitor from Mars in her denim overalls and her welding helmet with its blue glass vision plate. The sun-bronzed millionaire watched her for a moment, observing the sureness of her touch with the electric welding arc. Then, as she snapped off the blinding flame momentarily between jobs, he touched her shoulder.

She turned casually, unhurriedly, shoving the hinged mask up on her wavy masses of bright golden hair. "Yes, what is it? Oh-h, it's you, Mr. Anthony. You startled me." Her demure violet eyes strayed beyond him as if seeking something or someone, then back again. "Where's your friend?"

"Tom Gentry? I left him home for once." Jim decided that the genial aviator must have made quite an impression on her. "Could you spare me a minute or two?"

"Well, this is a production line," her softly modulated tone reminded him. "There'll be another cowling mount for me to spot-weld in a little while."

"I'll try not to take long. But there are a few questions I'd like to ask you."

Her smile was vaguely unhappy. "I'll do my best to answer if I can."

"Thank you. This may shock you, but did you ever hear Florrie Sheffield say she hated Steve Ryerson enough to kill him?"

"Wh-why, no. Are you accusing her of—?"

"I'm just checking up. I had a long talk with Florrie a while ago. Mike Panama was gunning for me, and she and Zoot-Suit Charlie risked his wrath by helping me get away. I'm wondering why she told me certain things. Such as your father's suicide."

The girl's Madonna-like face clouded. "So now you suspect *me* of the murder," her voice was almost chiding.

Anthony denied this. "Not at all. I don't even think Florrie meant to imply such a thing. She probably thought it strange that you could be friendly with the man who'd caused your father's suicide—if she thought of it at all."

"Strange? But I've already said that myself. Ryerson fascinated me somehow. It's one of those things you can't explain. Maybe fear was mixed up in it, too. Not fear of Ryerson himself, but of the men he controlled. Men like Mike Panama."

"You accepted this job from Ryerson," Jim mused. "Was that because of fear, too?"

"No. It was a matter of money. He offered me more than the prevailing scale, perhaps because he felt he owed me something. I accepted. But I could have worked for Douglas or Vega or Lockheed—any of them. I went to welding school and prepared myself. If you think I was taking charity, you're wrong."

THERE WAS PRIDE in this girl, and self-confidence. You could sense her innate good breeding, her patrician acceptance of things as they were. She wasted no time complaining about the cards life dealt her, but played them for what they were worth. Jim Anthony liked that. He liked the girl herself. Even in her denim working clothes she was dainty, subtly feminine. Her nearness stirred him in a curiously poignant way, not at all comparable to the seething turmoil Yvonne Ryerson had aroused in him with her kisses and her almost exaggerated ardor.

He wrenched his thoughts away from such comparisons. "How do you really feel about Karl Wozniak, Mary?"

"I guess you'd call it passive," she said frankly. "I'm sorry for him because I think he cares for me—and I can't return his love. He had no cause for jealousy, though. I told him many times I'd never marry him."

"But you'd like him cleared of the charge against him, wouldn't you?"

"If he's really innocent, yes."

"I think he is. And we need him here at the plant. A man of his abilities shouldn't be in jail." Another engine cowling came riding down the overhead trolley of the production line, and Mary Kilvaine reached to adjust her mask. Anthony's time was up for now, he realized. "May I talk to you later? I'll be here for at least a couple of hours. Until one, probably."

"I go off shift at midnight. You can come to the apartment if you like. I'll look for you at one-thirty, say?"

"Thanks. It's a date."

NORTON PYLE LOOKED up from his desk as Jim Anthony strode into the office. Some of the auditor's haggardness was gone; his penetrating black eyes were clearer, his spiked mustache jaunty again. "Hello, Mr. Anthony. I've been expecting you."

"How did you know I was coming?"

"My sister wanted to see you on a business matter. She called your apartment and Gentry said you were headed this way. So she came here to wait for you. She's in the office that used to be… Steve's."

The millionaire criminologist repressed a frown of annoyance. Tom Gentry talked too blamed much. The way things stood, plenty of people might still be entertaining a desire to remove Anthony from the scene—permanently. Mike Panama and his mob, for example. By now, the fat man had surely discovered certain damning records missing from his files. And if Mrs. Ryerson had so easily obtained information from Gentry concerning Jim's whereabouts, others might have equal success.

But none of these thoughts showed in the sun-bronzed investigator's expression. His face a stolid Indian mask, he said: "I'll go to your sister. Thanks for telling me." Then he made his way to what had been the factory president's office.

"You wanted to see me, Yvonne?" he asked, closing the door behind him.

Steve Ryerson's widow came toward him, undulantly, her every movement a fluid poem of grace. She wore clinging black to match her hair; glistening pearl ear-pendants to complement the startling white blaize which streaked that sleek raven coiffure.

"Yes, Jim," she purred. "I did want to see you. And to say I ought to be angry with you."

"Angry? Why?"

"Because you didn't keep your promise. I asked you to bring your influence to bear; to quash the investigation of Steve's murder. You didn't do it. The police have been hounding me with all sorts of questions."

"Maybe you overestimate my influence with the law."

She put her hands on his shoulders. "I don't think I overestimate anything about you, Jim Anthony. I think you can do anything you set out to do. The fault is mine because I failed to persuade you." Her ripe lips parted, and her voice dropped to a sultry whisper. "What does it take for me to get you on my side? How far must I go?"

He was thrilled, unreasonably, by her touch. "How far would you want to go?"

"All the way to hell—or heaven—with you." Then she kissed him, and this time there was a hundred times more feline fervor in it than there had been in that other kiss, back in her stately residence. Perhaps this was because she knew they were really alone, now, with no chance of interruption. There had merely been promise, before.

Her mouth was a hot scald upon his own, and her vibrant body strained against him, demanding his caresses. There was primordial passion here, stark and raw. Her glowing dark eyes stripped her thoughts naked before him; her breath was gusty fire on his cheek—

From somewhere outside the plant a hellish blast of shattering sound erupted, deep-throated in its detonation, shaking the very earth with its insane roar. That savage explosion jarred Jim Anthony back to reality, even as the factory's disaster siren ululated to a high-pitched scream.

Jim hurled the brunette woman away from him, so hard that she tripped and sprawled backward to the floor. He paid no heed to the symmetry of her silken legs. He turned, catapulted out of the office.

Presently he learned the ugly facts. Someone had planted a bomb in his cream-colored convertible. Then a youthful parking attendant, drawn by the automobile's unusual lines, had sat under the wheel as youngsters will—just for the pleasure of pretending to drive the great Jim Anthony's car. The kid had touched the starter. He died instantly and very horribly.

CHAPTER VIII

DEATH IN A ZOOT-SUIT

CAPTAIN FLOYD SPELLMAN, THE head of the homicide department, took personal charge of this investigation. "You think the pineapple was intended for you, eh, Mr. Anthony?"

"That's rather obvious. The parking lot boy saved my life at the cost of his own."

"Got any idea who planted the bomb?"

"No. Not yet."

"Who knew you were here at the factory?"

"Any number of persons," the millionaire criminologist said wearily. "I can't give you a list because I don't know. You had better check with my friend Gentry at our apartment. He seems to have been rather free with the information."

Across the office, Yvonne Ryerson's face went so pale that her scarlet mouth seemed like a splash of blood by contrast. "I don't like the implication of that. *I* phoned Mr. Gentry and found out you were coming here to the plant. Are you trying to say I prepared that sort of welcome for you?"

Her brother chimed in bitterly. "Or me, for that matter? You think I arranged to blow you up when Yvonne told me you were coming for an inspection?"

Anthony's voice was as stolid as his tanned face. "I make no accusations, Mr. Pyle. That's for the police to decide."

"Yeah," Captain Spellman growled. "You two keep quiet. What about this Mike Panama? Did he know where to find you?" he asked Jim.

"I wouldn't know. He could have."

"This evidence you've just turned over to me. If Panama got wise you'd lifted it out of his office, that would be a motive, don't you think?"

"A very good motive." Jim Anthony looked at his wrist watch, and its hands made a vee indicating twenty past one in the morning. He felt curiously tired—a sensation to which he was definitely unaccustomed. The thought of Mary Kilvaine, waiting for him to call on her at one-thirty, aroused him from this dark torpor. "I've told you all I know, Captain Spellman. I wonder if you need me any longer?"

THE MAN HESITATED. "Well, I guess not for a while, anyhow. I'll call Donaldson at headquarters, have him put out a dragnet for Mike Panama. And we may learn something from the wreckage of your car—the type of bomb, possible fingerprints and so on. Not that there was much left of the machine. Or of the guy that died in it. Yes, you can go."

"Thank you."

"Stay where I can reach you, though."

"I'll do that."

Yvonne Ryerson came to her feet, gracefully. "Wait a minute, Jim. Maybe I can take you somewhere—if the captain is finished with me."

"I'm not," Spellman snapped. "Sit down."

She cast a look at Anthony, half irritated, half amused, all of it spurious. She was acting a part, but doing it well. "Can't you do something about this, Jim? I mean, after all, there's no necessity for—"

Jim said dispassionately: "Sorry, Mrs. Ryerson. I never interfere with the police."

His voice was as flat as a horizontal surface, but he knew she had caught his meaning. He'd called her Mrs. Ryerson rather than Yvonne. He'd told her she could expect no help from him, in this or any other matter.

He had done these things deliberately, seeking to penetrate the invisible armor she wore—the veneer with which she concealed her actual thoughts and emotions. And he succeeded. Into her dark eyes a flame leaped: an uncloaked malignancy, a blazing hatred, the fury of a woman whose body is scorned and whose schemes are flouted.

Her enmity was out in the open, now. And it broke any last remaining spell, any charm or hold she might have had on him. Jim Anthony didn't feel tired, suddenly. His shoulders squared, as if somebody lifted a weight off them.

MARY KILVAINE OPENED her door to his knock. She was wearing the gossamer negligee that had adorned her dulcet body when Jim first met her, twenty-four hours ago. Was it really only twenty-four hours? It seemed much longer. It seemed as if he had known the golden-haired girl always.

This meeting was not like last night's. It differed in many ways. Then, Florrie Sheffield and Zoot-Suit Charlie had been here. And Tom Gentry, too, had been along. All told, the scene had been pretty damned hectic.

But now Jim was alone with the fragile, diminutive blonde girl; and she herself was less distrait, less edgy. Her bisque-doll loveliness brought a catch to his throat, and the touch of her hand extended in welcome warmed him even more than her smile.

"Come in, Mr. Anthony. Tell me what other questions you want me to answer."

His lips quirked upward at the corners. "There aren't any more questions."

"Then… why are you here?"

"I'm afraid I can't put it in words very well. Were you ever very tired, and then suddenly saw something that seemed to refresh you and rest you and make you new again? A flash of summer sky, a reflection of the sun on open water?"

"Y-yes. Things like that have happened to me. A very, very long time ago. So long ago I can hardly remember."

"Then you know why I'm here," he said. "You're a mountain brook in the sunlight, a cool breeze on the desert night." He was silent, looking at her. "Restful. And very beautiful."

Two spots of red stained her cheeks. "Funny you should… talk that way to me. I mean… we don't know each other. I like it, though. It makes me feel sort of light and gay, inside. Gayer and lighter than I've felt in years. I wonder if you can understand that? Probably not. You don't know my background."

"I know enough. You weren't made for sadness, Mary. You were made for laughter and music. And happiness."

"Laughter and music don't always mean happiness." Her violet eyes became remote, and he guessed she was thinking of the kind of music Steve Ryerson had brought her: brassy swing jitterbug jive, merriment as empty as an idiot's smile.

He caught her mood; and then, just as quickly, it was gone. He thought some of his heart went with it. She was self-contained again, and efficient, and quite sure of her emotions. "There's nothing in the flat or I'd offer you a drink. I can't even ask Florrie to go buy something. She isn't here."

"Where is she?"

"Working at The Shed, most likely. You said you had a talk with her there this evening."

"Not exactly," he showed his teeth. "Remember I told you we had some trouble with Mike Panama? Florrie, Charlie, and I left together—in a hurry. She might not go back."

"I remember now. Was the trouble very serious?"

He nodded. "We weren't sure if Panama saw us all in the one car. If he did, he might take steps."

"You—you don't think Florrie's in d-danger?"

"I hope not. But you never can tell. Somebody planted a pineapple in my car at the factory a while ago. It exploded prematurely; killed a parking boy."

"Oh-h-h, n-no! You—you're joking!"

"I wish I were," he made a grim mouth.

"Yes. Jim's here with me," she said.

FEAR DRAINED THE color from her delicate oval face. "But—but why? Why should anyone—?"

"It was an attempt to get me. The parking kid's death was accidental."

"But *why?*" she repeated dully.

"Somebody's afraid of me. Afraid I'm about to close in on the Ryerson killer. Afraid of what I know, of what I might find out. Murder's a queer thing, Mary. One leads to desperation, and desperation leads to more killings."

She came close to him, trembling. "You make me scared when you talk that way. Scared to—to stay here alone."

"There's room in my suite. You'd be safe there." He grinned crookedly. "I'm not propositioning you."

"I know you're not. That's why I'm going to accept your offer, Jim. Wait here. I'll dress." She left him; scuttled into her bedroom and closed the door.

It was funny, he thought, how the idea of Mary Kilvaine under his own roof made him as nervous as a high-school boy on his first date. He lit a cigarette, smoked it in short, staccato puffs. The phone behind him jingled shrilly.

From the bedroom came the blonde girl's voice. "Will you take it for me?"

"Of course." He moved to the instrument; uncradled it. "Yes?"

Silence. Then: "Is Mary there? This is Florrie." Excitement put high, driving overtones into the sharp voice.

"She's dressing, Florrie."

"Call her, please. But quick."

Anthony went to the bedroom door and knocked. "Florrie Sheffield wants you, Mary. She sounds upset."

"All right. Coming. Don't look, though." The golden-haired girl opened the door before Anthony could avert his gaze, and he felt a sudden leaping of his pulses. She wore leg make-up in lieu of stockings, the creamy fawn-colored stuff artfully applied to shapely tapering contours. Brief pink underthings hugged her rounded form. She hadn't had time to put on her dress.

Dutifully the millionaire criminologist stared the other way. It wasn't cricket to play Peeping Tom. He found himself wishing he weren't quite so chivalrous about such things.

Mary picked up the phone. "Yes, Florrie? You *are?* What? But is he sure of... yes, that was Mr. Anthony. He's here with me. I think he would... Of course. All right. Right away." She hung up and turned around. "Jim!"

He judged it would be okay to look at her, since her voice gave tacit permission. He pivoted slowly, savoring each instant of anticipation before his eyes finally drank in her sweetness.

But she seemed oblivious to his admiring stare. "Florrie wants us, Jim."

"As much as I want you, I wonder?"

"Please don't say things like that... now."

"How can I help it?"

"You must. Florrie needs us at once. She—"

Anthony strode toward her like a man walking in the shadow of a dream. He put his arms around her, very gravely and gently. He drew her close, and he kissed her on the mouth. She tried to push him away with both hands, forgetting the lack of a dress. He looked, and was not ashamed to look again. She whimpered a little and didn't fight off his next kiss. She accepted it and then laughed jerkily.

He released her. "Sorry, Mary."

"Skip it. You're a man. Men are all alike. Will you listen to me n-now or do I have to think about struggling to keep you in your place?"

"Sorry, Mary," he repeated woodenly.

She made a tiny, helpless gesture. "Don't keep saying that, Jim. Maybe I liked what you did. Maybe I wanted you to kiss me! We haven't got time to think about things like that, now. There's Florrie."

"What about her?"

"She's with Zoot-Suit Charlie in his apartment. They've found out something about Steve Ryerson's m-murderer."

"Mrs. Ryerson? Mike Panama? Norton Pyle?" Jim listed them one by one. "Or Karl Wozniak?"

"She didn't say. Charlie wants to tell you personally."

"Get dressed, my dear. I'll call a taxi."

The apartment was on the rear lot of a large house, over a double garage. Hollywood has lots of these. They afford cheap rent to movie extras and bit players and the screen-struck kids from Keokuk who jerk sodas and take car-hop jobs at drive-in sandwich stands, hoping to be discovered by some major studio director. Two or three shabby, plainly furnished rooms, usually, with a porch no wider than an overhanging balcony and an open stairway leading down to the garage driveway. One is like the next, and Charlie's was like all of them.

Nobody answered, though, when Jim Anthony knocked on the upstairs porch door. Mary shivered against him in the darkness. "Wh-why do you suppose—?"

He drew his steels from their concealed pocket; used a Hindu trick he had learned years ago in India, widening the pupils of his eyes by conscious effort until he could actually see in the thick gloom. He applied steels to the lock. The lock turned and the door whispered open.

Stygian blackness loomed beyond the threshold, but the wealthy criminologist's uncanny vision penetrated it. He put out his arm and brushed the golden-haired girl back. "Stay on the porch, Mary. This isn't for you to see."

"What—what do you mean? What is it?"

"Stand back, I tell you."

"No. I want to know." She ducked under his arm, groped into the room, found the wall switch and clicked it. A floor lamp on the far side glowed to life. "Oh-h-h, my God!"

Florrie Sheffield and Zoot-Suit Charlie were stretched out on the threadbare carpet, clasping hands like two children who'd fallen asleep after a hard day's playing. It was a very permanent sleep. Both of them had been shot through the head.

Anthony saw a phone, lunged for it, dialed it. "Is that you, Tom?"

Gentry's genial voice was explosive. "Yeah. Cripes, I've been hoping you'd call. I got news."

"Pass it. Listen carefully. I want—"

"I can't pass it, pappy. We got a visitor. Guess who?"

"I'm not interested. Pay attention to me."

"It's Karl Wozniak," Gentry blurted. "He's here. Just ankled in. He pulled some kind of screwball crush-out, so he says. Hour or more ago. Ducked and twisted around, finally wound up here. He figured you might need help running the plant."

The wealthy investigator rasped an oath. "God help fools and little children and guys named Wozniak! Okay, so he's with you. So you can take him along on the job I've got for you."

"What job, Jim?"

"I want you to find Yvonne Ryerson and her brother. Pyle may be at the factory; I don't know. Mrs. Ryerson could be anywhere. But locate them. Fast. And take them to Mary Kilvaine's apartment. Wozniak too. Understand? Hold them there until I show up. Don't miss."

"I catch, pappy."

AS JIM HUNG up, Mary came toward him; dry-eyed, tearless but with little choked sobs welling in her throat, lifting and lowering her dainty breast. "Norton Pyle. Yvonne Ryerson. Karl Wozniak. It was one of them?"

"It's got to be."

"Poor Florrie. Poor Charlie. If they'd only told us over the phone when they called. At least we'd have known for sure, even though they d-died the next instant."

"Florrie didn't make that phone call, Mary."

She stared at him. "But I heard her voice. I don't think I know what you mean."

"Somebody impersonated her. The call was not more than ten or fifteen minutes ago; we hurried right over."

"Well?"

"Those bloodstains have started to coagulate. Harden. Death struck almost an hour ago, my dear. Quite a while before your phone rang." His eyes were hard, tense. "I think we may have been lured into a trap."

Suddenly her unnatural composure broke and the tears came. "Oh-h-h, Jim… Jim…."

He put his arms around her. He was holding her that way when Mike Panama walked in with a gunsel behind him. Panama looked at the corpses on the floor, then at Anthony and Mary.

"Thees ees nice," he said smoothly.

CHAPTER IX

SWING SHIFT SHOWDOWN

WISELY JIM ANTHONY'S BLEAK, hawklike eyes surveyed the fat man and the fat man's gun and the fat man's broad-shouldered torpedo. It wasn't possible to jump them from all the way across the room unless you wanted to stop a bullet with your forehead. And there was Mary Kilvaine to consider, too.

"It's your dice, Panama," Jim said. "Roll them."

"I theenk you have rolled them for me, Mr. Anthony. Eet saves me the job I came to do." His glance flicked toward Florrie Sheffield and Zoot-Suit Charlie clasping hands in death.

"Slog heem, and freesk
heem," the big man said.

The criminologist grinned without mirth. "That's funny. Very funny. You're considering a frame, of course. With me in the middle for these two kills."

"Ees pretty good, no? First you rob my files. Then you make getaway with thees girl and her jitterbug."

"So you saw Florrie driving me away."

"Sure I saw. And I see you put me in hole weeth the coppers. You blow the wheestle on me. Mike Panama takes that from nobody. Mike Panama goes hunteeng for girl and jitterbug who help you to scram. Mike Panama burn them down eef he find them. I don't find them for long time, though. Finally I theenk to look here in jitterbug's apartment. So they are already keeled for me."

"Meaning you haven't been here before?"

"Ees correct. Eef Mike Panama keel these people, would he return?"

"Maybe you would," Anthony said. "Maybe you'd come back and put the finger on me."

"That ees happy accident. Eet make me feel glad—for me. But sorry for you."

"How will you trade, Panama?"

The fat man's heavy lids blinked lazily. "Trade?"

"You say I blew the whistle on you, put you in a hole with the police. Suppose I tell you you're wrong?"

"Mike Panama ees not wrong. Mike Panama have a grapevine to headquarters. The heat ees on Mike Panama."

"The heat, maybe. But no concrete evidence to make it stick. I have that."

"The papers you took from my files? You have not yet turned them een?"

"Right," Anthony lied—and hoped he made it sound truthful.

Panama held out his left hand, the one that didn't have a gun in it. The palm looked moist, greasy. "Geeve me."

"How will you trade?"

"When Mike Panama hold tromps he ees not eenterested een tradeeng." He turned to his gunsel. "Slog heem, Bull."

BULL CROSSED OVER to Anthony and punched him in the mouth, an ugly, jolting blow that rocked the millionaire's head far back. A trickle of blood wormed down Jim's chin from his split lip, but no sound escaped him. His eyes glittered, though.

Panama held his hand out again. "Geeve."

"I haven't got the envelope with me."

"Slog heem, Bull. And freesk heem."

Bull did both, very efficiently. His fist struck high on the criminologist's cheekbone. His fingers delved into pocket after pocket. Presently he turned around. "He's clean."

"He has a gon?"

"He did have." Bull grinned and displayed the flat automatic he had lifted from Anthony's armpit holster. Anthony was silent, waiting. Mary Kilvaine whimpered a little.

The fat man sighed. "So I keel you without the papers. That ees very sad."

"It wouldn't have to be sad. You could trade."

"What ees thees trade?"

"Miss Kilvaine's life and mine for the manila envelope."

"You theenk you could trost me not to bomp you after you've geeven me the envelope?" Panama asked through a belly-chuckle. "You are not afraid of a double-cross?"

"It's the chance I'd have to take. Maybe your insides are whiter than your skin."

Panama seemed to take this as a compliment until he thought it over a second time. Then he wasn't so sure. "I might play ball weeth you. Tell me where the envelope ees."

"I won't tell you. I'll show you."

"Slog heem, Bull."

Bull slugged him. Anthony grinned woodenly. "Keep it up. Let me know if it buys you anything." He licked fresh blood off his puffed lips.

"Maybe eef we work thees girl over," Panama mused. He reached out, hooked fat fingers in the front of her dress and yanked. The dress tore open and she moaned. "Maybe eef I geeve her to Bull for hees play-toy, hah?" he suggested.

Bull breathed sharply. "Now, boss?"

Anthony said calmly: "So I'll watch. So you still won't get the envelope."

"Jim…!" Mary said. Her voice was stricken and her violet eyes wide with unbelief. "You wouldn't… let him…" Her shoulders shook.

The millionaire criminologist tried to tell her with a look that he didn't mean what he was saying. He wasn't sure she understood his glance, but he couldn't help this. "Sorry, Mary. There isn't much I can do, is there? I can't stop these rats if they go for you."

"You c-could… tell them wh-what they… want to know."

"I'll show them. I swear I won't tell them."

"Kees the girl, Bull."

Bull put his mouth on Mary's lips, noisily. His hands mauled her shoulders.

Panama was looking at Jim Anthony. "Steel stobborn about eet, meester?"

"Still stubborn about it."

"You weel queet what you are doeeng, Bull. I theenk we make a trade. Thees guy holds one tromp, after all. A very leetle tromp, wheech he weel soon find out."

Anthony's battered lips curled up at the corners. "You mean you'll let us live until you get the envelope. After that—"

"Ees accordeeng to how I feel about eet when you geeve me the papers. Maybe I keel you, maybe not. You said you weel take thees chance. So now you get your weesh."

ANTHONY DROVE PANAMA'S sedan, with Mary sitting beside him. Panama and his gunsel were in the tonneau where they could keep their captives covered. Mary made a small frightened sound when Jim stopped in front of the apartment house where she lived. She seemed suddenly to comprehend the millionaire criminologist's strategy, and the swift glance she gave him held forgiveness for the way he had stood calmly by while the fat man's thug defiled her lips with kisses. She knew, now, that Jim had never had any intention of letting it go beyond kisses. He had bluffed, and he had won a slim chance for both their lives.

"Thank you," she whispered softly.

He got out of the car and took her arm, steered her into the building with Mike Panama and Bull close behind, their pocketed guns ready to blast at the first false move. All four went up to Mary's floor; approached her door.

Tom Gentry was waiting in a corridor alcove, unseen, as they passed. The freckled aviator chuckled as he stepped forth with an automatic in his fist. He said happily: "Shall I blow their kidneys out, pappy?"

Panama's fat face turned mustard color and Bull merely froze in his tracks, stupidly. Gentry came up from the rear and disarmed the fat man and his gunsel.

"So you led us eento a trap," Panama said. "Next time I weel know better than to cross swords weeth Jeem Anthony. Ees moch too dangerous for a dope like Mike Panama."

"There won't be a next time," Jim promised him evenly. Then he looked at his freckled friend. "You gathered everybody together, Tom?"

"Yep. They're all in the apartment. I already had Wozniak; I told you about that. So I went out to the factory and found Yvonne Ryerson and her brother still there, being quizzed by the cops. I had to bring the cops along, of course. Captain Spellman and Lieutenant Donaldson, the homicide bright boys. It took a lot of talking to persuade them. Then I figured you might need me, so I hung around in the hall. Neat, hunh?"

"Very neat," Anthony said. He opened the door, gestured Panama and Bull inside, then Mary Kilvaine. He and Gentry followed. A gasp went up from those who were already in the little front room. The party was complete.

Lieutenant Donaldson choked: "Look, bejeest! Look who he nabbed!"

"Nice work, Mr. Anthony," Captain Spellman said. "Now tell us which we want."

The wealthy investigator surveyed the gathering. Karl Wozniak stood in a corner, tall, lanky, studious-looking, his eyes glittering with interest. Norton Pyle was nervously working on the spiked points of his mustache. Yvonne Ryerson looked beautiful and bored—on the surface. She was all tension underneath, though.

"So you broke out of jail," Jim said to Wozniak.

"Yes. I was apprehensive about the factory—"

The criminologist turned to Norton Pyle. "How are your books, Mr. Auditor?"

"Bring in a certified public accountant and see for yourself," Pyle's white teeth flashed. "I've got nothing to hide."

Yvonne Ryerson drawled purringly: "Don't you want to say something to me, too, Jim? Or am I a stepchild?"

He ignored her, just as he ignored Mike Panama and his gunsel. "I'll wind this up in just a moment," he told the two homicide officials, Spellman and Donaldson. "There's one more thing I have to do." Then he strode across the room, opened a side door, vanished over the threshold and closed the door after him.

THE BOUDOIR WAS unlighted but his Hindu eye-control permitted him to find the phone. He uncradled it, dialed 1190 and then hung up. In about ten seconds the bell jangled shrilly.

Somebody answered on the living room extension. Anthony pitched his voice staccato. "Hello, slick chick. This is Charlie. Zoot-Suit Charlie with a floy, floy. Biddleyump, zing. Biddleyump *cha!* Haunting you, baby. I'll always haunt you, darling. You shouldn't have killed Florrie and me. We wouldn't have squealed on you, ever. Buppadiddle, chee. Buppaddiddle che-*chee!*"

In the front room, Mary Kilvaine screamed horribly and dropped the phone and fell to the floor, writhing. "I did it. I did it! *I did it!*" Then she broke into keening, mindless laughter; the mirth of the hopelessly insane.

Jim Anthony came out of the bedroom. "She was psychopathic," he said regretfully. "I couldn't stand the thought of sending her to the lethal chamber." It was his first and only mention of the decision he had faced and made. In his hands had rested the golden-haired girl's fate: death by execution, or forever in a padded cell. He had chosen the padded cell for her, and he had deliberately driven her unstable mind over the ragged edge, into the happy forgetfulness of permanent insanity.

CHAPTER X

SWING SHIFT HARVEST

S **TERNLY ANTHONY FACED HIS** listeners. "I knew Mary was guilty when we got the purported phone call from Florrie Sheffield. Mary asked me to take it here in the living room. Yet she had an extension in her boudoir. I remembered that from the first time I ever visited this apartment and heard her refusing to talk to a reporter on her bedroom telephone."

"But look, pappy—" Tom Gentry burst out blankly.

"It's an easy stunt to call your own phone by dialing 1190, hanging up and waiting for it to ring back. That's the telephone company's testing number; automatically returns your own call. I knew Mary was impersonating Florrie's voice from the boudoir, just as I imitated Zoot-Suit Charlie a minute ago. I wondered why. So then Mary and I went to Charlie's apartment. He and Florrie were almost an hour dead. It explained everything."

"You mean she faked the call to alibi herself?"

"Yes. I'd already told her, at the factory, that Charlie and Florrie were in danger from Mike Panama. So she killed them, hoping Panama would be blamed."

"But why did she kill them?"

"She was afraid they knew too much. Afraid they were aware that she was the one who murdered Steve Ryerson at The Shed. She hated Ryerson, who had caused her father's suicide. It was a psychopathic hatred, the hatred of an unbalanced mind. She worked on Karl Wozniak's jealousy; tried to make him do her killing for her. An accident prevented this. Wozniak's gun missed fire.

"But Mary had Wozniak's other gun, a Webley she'd stolen from his apartment for emergencies. She had it in her purse, with a napkin wrapped around the purse. When Wozniak failed, she fired. Purse leather and linen napkin stopped any possible powder burns on Ryerson's chest—made it seem as if he'd been shot from a distance."

Captain Spellman said: "She's the one who put the pineapple in your car at the factory?"

"Yes. She was afraid I was closing in—because Florrie Sheffield had told me about her father's suicide. Don't ask me where she got the bomb. Maybe she'd had it a long time, thinking maybe to use it on Ryerson if her other schemes failed. Anyhow, when she went off duty at the end of her swing shift trick, she put this explosive on my car's starter circuit—and a parking kid died. Then it came Florrie's turn, and Zoot-Suit Charlie's. They were killed for what they'd said, what they guessed, what they knew. When Mike Panama walked in, later, it was coincidence."

The swarthy fat man stood up. "Een thees case, then, I am een the clear, hah? I can go now?"

Lieutenant Donaldson handcuffed him. "Yeah, you can go up to San Quentin for peddling reefers. Anthony gave us the goods on you, pal. Hours ago."

Yvonne Ryerson drawled: "You're good, Jim. Plenty good. So what happens to me? And my brother?"

"You two blackmailed yourselves into a soft berth," the millionaire criminologist answered levelly. "But the man you blackmailed and married was a rat. If your brother's accounts are in order, I can't see what I can do to you. I'm not sure I care to do anything."

"You can buy out my aircraft stock," she recognized the disinterest in his voice and knew she could never again tempt him with her lush body. "Norton and I have no reason to stick around, now. Not with a million dollars to spend."

"I'll buy it—if Karl Wozniak approves."

The factory's general manager stared. "What have I to do with it, Mr. Anthony?"

"I'm installing you as president. It's the job for you."

Wozniak bowed formally. "I will not betray your trust in me, sir. And... thank you."

They took Mary Kilvaine away, then. Took her on the long, one-way ride to an asylum from which she would never return. Nor would Jim Anthony ever forget the shrill emptiness of her maniac laughter... or the warm young sweetness of her lips, the one time he had kissed her. That kiss had been good-bye; he had known it even then. And its poignant memory would remain always.

CAULDRON
OF DEATH

NEVER HAD JIM ANTHONY ENCOUNTERED A MUDDLE LIKE
THIS. THE MAN WHO APPARENTLY HAD TRIED TO KILL HIM
HAD EVERYTHING TO LOSE BY HIS DEATH! THE MAN WHO
HAD APPARENTLY KILLED MCQUAYDE MUST HAVE BEEN DEAD
WHEN MCQUAYDE WAS MURDERED! NOTHING MADE SENSE!

A S A PROFESSIONAL AVIATOR, Tom Gentry's flying career had carried him to many a dirty corner of the world. Yet there was an expression of humorous distaste on his good natured freckle-specked face when he traced his initials on the film of grime which covered the hotel desk where his friend Jim Anthony was signing the register. The expression deepened when he surveyed the resulting soot on his fingertip.

"You'd think they might use a dust cloth once in a while," he complained as he and Anthony followed a shabbily dressed bell-hop toward the ancient elevator across the lobby. He glanced at the frowsy furnishings, the lights that could have been brighter with a good application of soap and water. "If this is supposed to be the best joint in town, I'll take vanilla."

Jim Anthony, millionaire scientist, sportsman, criminologist, and newspaper owner, grinned as he stepped into the creaking cage. "Rose-ville has two other top notch hotels, Tom."

"Then why didn't we go to one of 'em?"

"Because they're all alike. This one's no better and no worse than the others."

"You call this top notch?" Gentry sounded aggrieved.

Anthony's chuckling smile irradiated the sun-bronzed sternness of his features and flashed across the mask of stoic reserve which had been bequeathed him by the blood of his Comanche Indian mother. From his Irish soldier-of-fortune father came his warm laughter. "You're getting soft, Tom."

"Who, me?"

"It would seem so. When a little honest dirt gets under your skin, it's time to toughen up."

"You mean it's time to scrub up with Dutch Cleanser."

Jim chuckled again, then grew grave. "You can't make steel without soot and smoke. Blast furnaces are the same, wherever you find them. And they're damned important today. They've got to be kept going every hour of the twenty-four. There's a war being fought—a war to the death. The soot you're yelling about means that steel is being produced at full capacity. Be glad of it."

The genial aviator had to admit this was true; but the Grand Roseville Hotel's carelessness annoyed him just the same. A town this size ought to support something better, he contended. After all, it wasn't a country village; it was a city of a hundred and fifty thousand population.

ROSEVILLE! THE NAME itself seemed incongruous to Gentry when he thought about the narrow, cobblestoned streets which ran from the banks of the muddy river back to the rising, mine-scarred ugliness of hills dotted with flame-belching foundries. As far as Tom was concerned, a better name would have been Grimetown.

And yet it differed in no respect from the cities flanking it both to the north and south. All along the Ohio River valley from Pittsburgh south to Wheeling, steel was king; and the night skies were always

Deliberately he hurled the
man the length of the room.

cherry red from the big blast furnaces turning out a constant stream of war material for fighting men. Steel was the watchword, the war-cry.

Jim Anthony had been here before, many times. He was accustomed to these dull, drab, smoke-stained cities that seemed to crouch under the never ending pall of soot. He was used to the roaring mills and foundries and a sky stained bloodily crimson like this one glowing over Roseville tonight. It was a new experience for Gentry, though, and the aviator was definitely not happy about being here.

Presently he would be a lot less happy than he was now, but he didn't know it at the moment. This was probably fortunate for his peace of mind.

Anthony tipped the bell-hop who led them to their two-room suite, and the shabbily dressed boy departed. Then Gentry moved to a window, pushing back bedraggled curtains which no laundry on earth could ever make white again. "Br-r-!" he said. "That red glare gives me the creeps, I don't see why you couldn't have picked a cleaner burg for your investigation."

The millionaire scientist answered indulgently. "Roseville happens to be where young Tyler Hunt has worked out his new alloying process. You wouldn't expect them to move a blast furnace all the way to New York so I could check the method."

"No," Tom admitted. "I wouldn't expect that. But—" He never completed whatever he'd intended to say, for just then the whole upper pane of the smudged window fell in against his chest with a shattering clatter.

Gentry jumped backward, yelling. But his movement was not as rapid as that of Jim Anthony. The millionaire pivoted as lithely as a jungle animal, leaping across the room in one long flowing blurt of motion. He clipped his freckled friend as he went past, knocking the aviator, flipped the light switch and plunged down. Then he reached the far wall, the room into darkness, dropping to the floor as he did so.

"Tom!"

"Yeah. I'm here."

"Hug the carpet! Are you okay? You weren't hit?"

"Not that I know of. What do you mean, hit?"

"By the bullet, you idiot!" As he spoke, Anthony whipped his automatic from its shoulder holster and made for the shattered window, crawling Indian fashion on his belly. Not until he reached the sill did he raise himself.

SCARLET SKY-REFLECTION SENT a hint of glow into the room, but not enough to enable a normal man to see clearly. In this respect, Jim Anthony wasn't a normal man. Years ago, while studying in the Orient, a Hindu yogi had taught him a certain ocular trick; a control of the pupils of his eyes by conscious will. Mastery of it gave Jim the uncanny ability to see in almost solid darkness, like a cat.

He employed the method now; perceived that Gentry had dropped to the floor, and that the worn green carpet by the window was littered with shards of broken glass. Suddenly there came a pinging sound from the opposite wall, and a shower of plaster rattled down from a small hole which hadn't been there an instant ago.

"Cripes!" Tom whispered. "What was that?"

"Another little token welcoming us to Roseville."

"A slug, you mean? Through the busted window?"

"Right."

"But I didn't hear a shot!" Gentry muttered.

"Somebody's using a silencer, probably on a rifle with scope sights adjusted for night work." The millionaire criminologist edged side-wise out of the line of fire, then lifted his head at a corner of the sill while screening the rest of his body behind the casement. He peered out, grimly.

The window of this third floor room overlooked the dingy and narrow main street of the city. Directly across from the hotel there was a three story building with a flat roof guarded by a waist high masonry coping. The shots had apparently come from that roof, with the rifleman concealing himself behind the coping as he took level aim at the hotel window.

But although Anthony waited and watched silently for a good ten minutes, nothing else happened. It was quite obvious, he concluded, that the unseen marksman had gone.

CHAPTER II

HELL-BLAST

JIM STOOD UP, REACHED out cautiously, and pulled down the roller shade. Then, still keeping away from a direct line with the window, he crossed the room and clicked the wall switch. "Okay, Tom. You can get up now."

Gentry slowly pushed himself to his feet, unhurt except for a slight trace of blood from a nick on his freckled cheek where a flying sliver of glass had scratched him.

He blotted this with his handkerchief. "Maybe I need a new calendar, pappy. I didn't know today was the Fourth of July, did you?"

"For us it could have been doomsday," Anthony's voice was icy with repressed anger. "Those shots were much too close for comfort."

"You said it! I guess somebody here in town don't love us, eh? But who? And how did he know we'd be in this particular room at this particular time?"

The wealthy investigator's sun-bronzed face displayed no emotion, but his hawk-like eyes glittered. "That's what I intend to find out. There's been a leak somewhere."

"Got any ideas?"

"Well, I wired the hotel for reservations, which is one possible angle. That might have tipped off our unknown reception committee. And I notified the young metallurgist, Tyler Hunt, that I was coming to inspect his new steel alloy process."

Tom shook his head. "I don't get it. Why should the natives treat us like ducks in a shooting gallery? You ain't got a secret enemy in Roseville, have you?"

"Not that I'm aware of. Let's go down to the lobby and have a talk with the desk clerk."

THE TWO FRIENDS left their dingy suite and made for the jerky elevator; rode it down to the main floor. As they emerged from the cage, Gentry said: "Maybe the new alloy you came here to look at is the reason somebody tried to use you for a clay pigeon. Suppose some guy don't want you to inspect it?"

"That hardly makes sense. The Government asked me to make a report; but even if I'd been killed, they could send someone else in my place."

As he spoke, Anthony made for the desk. The lobby proper was much the same as it had been a while ago; two traveling salesmen were hanging around the telephone switchboard, kidding the bleached blonde operator. The shabby bell-hop drowsed on a bench. But the desk clerk wasn't anywhere in sight, nor did he appear when Jim rang the rusty tapbell on the counter.

At the tinkling sound, the switchboard girl twisted around, her movement dismissing the two traveling salesmen. They sauntered away and the girl stopped chewing her spearmint long enough to remark: "I can ring the manager for you if you want. Baldy ain't comin' back, I don't think."

"Baldy?"

"The night clerk. Baldy Parker. He got a phone call and left in kind of a sweat, like he had ants. He said for me to watch the desk the rest of my trick."

Anthony smiled down at her. "I don't suppose you'd know what his phone call was?"

"How would I?" she started to look offended, then changed her mind when she saw his ingratiating grin and the ten dollar bill he'd drawn from his wallet. "We-ll, maybe I did leave my key open by accident, sorta. You understand I don't make a habit of listenin' in on conversations, but—"

The man was fat, but there was an atmosphere of power about him.

"Strictly an accident," Jim agreed politely. He folded the ten-spot into a compact square and dropped it casually so it landed in her lap. "The call?" he prompted her.

She worried her chewing gum. "It was kinda screwy. A man's voice told him *you'd better scram, it's gonna happen.* So then Baldy rung off an' got his hat an' blew."

"I see," Anthony's smile was fixed, affable—and completely counterfeit. "Thanks a lot. Oh, by the way, I wish you'd do me a favor. Have the manager switch me to some other suite and get the bell-hop to move our luggage. My present quarters have too much exposure."

"Sure, mister."

A moment later, at the lobby's entrance, Tom Gentry made a sour grimace. "There was the leak, pappy. That lousy clerk tipped somebody to your room number. He probably gave us a front suite so the guy with the rifle could do his stuff."

Jim nodded dourly. "No doubt about it. But who was the rifleman? That's the question. And there's only one way I know to learn the answer."

"How?"

"We'll go have a talk with Jeff Stanton. He knows Roseville inside out."

THIS STANTON TO whom Anthony referred was editor of the Roseville *News-Press,* a paper which the millionaire detective owned as part of his nation-wide chain of dailies. Jim had inherited these newspaper properties from his father, along with a multitude of other varied investments including mines, factories, one of New York's greatest hotels—the Waldorf-Anthony—and the New York *Star,* a journalistic giant which formed the keystone of his newspaper empire.

The income from any single one of these holdings would have made him wealthy beyond measure. Totaled up, they spelled riches of staggering proportions; the Anthony fortune was one of the nation's largest. With such a background, Jim could have been America's biggest spendthrift and playboy had he been so inclined. Instead, he'd spent his formative years in the acquiring of an amazing education in every branch of the sciences and arts—and in the development of a superlatively muscled body skilled in all conceivable forms of athletic prowess.

Thus equipped, he had then turned his fine mind to the study of criminology, until finally he had become an amateur detective of international fame. The very name, Jim Anthony, was sufficient to strike terror into the heart of any lawbreaker great or obscure; for when the millionaire investigator turned his attention to a crime mystery, you could depend on it that the guilty person would eventually be brought to book for his misdeeds.

So it was in the present instance. Somebody had attempted to murder Jim and his aviator friend for a reason which at the moment was hidden from view. Therefore, this unknown somebody must be captured and punished. In Anthony's mind the thing was inevitable; it represented a problem he had to solve—and when such a problem confronted him, his bulldog tenacity never permitted him to stop until he had fathomed it.

Standing at the curb outside the Grand Roseville Hotel, he hailed a rattletrap cab and gestured Gentry into it; followed the freckled flyer into the tonneau and said to the hacker: "Take us to the *News-Press*, please."

The jehu nodded, clashed his gears, sent the taxi clattering forward through the night. And as the noisy vehicle jounced along the cobble-stoned street, Jim Anthony was plunged in somber silence. From his Comanche princess mother he had inherited a weird sixth sense which functioned in times of danger, warning him whenever he ventured toward peril. This curious sixth sense was working now, filling him with an uneasy premonition of evil, seeming to foretell dire events ahead.

He made no mention of this to Tom Gentry, though. He hadn't the slightest idea what form of jeopardy lurked in the immediate future, despite his inner conviction that something ugly was going to happen. From past experience he knew his hunches were never wrong; yet there was no use worrying the carefree aviator any more than necessary.

The Roseville *News-Press* was the least impressive of all the Anthony journalistic properties. It had belonged to a company from which Jim had purchased a big Pittsburgh daily, and had more or less been thrown in with that deal. Still, it was a link in his national chain; and it had given employment to its staff throughout the depression—which was the principle reason he'd kept it running. Now, with steel booming, it stood on its own feet as a solid investment.

In another year, if it stayed on the profit side of the ledger, the millionaire criminologist planned to erect a new building to house it. Currently it operated in a dilapidated structure on a side street, a grimy and dingy two-story affair that looked just about ready for condemnation by the building inspector.

THIS APPEARANCE OF frowsiness was emphasized by the street itself, which was blocked off by wooden barricades and red lanterns. Like most such towns, Roseville was built upon a honeycomb of old abandoned mine tunnels long since exhausted of ore. Every once in a while one of these forgotten stopes would cave in, taking the street with it. This had happened here, causing the block to be barricaded against vehicular traffic. Beyond the red lanterns, a sunken hole yawned bleakly.

However, the sidewalks were safely shored up for pedestrians. The cabby dragged his brakes. "End of the line, gents. From here you walk—and be careful you don't fall down the pit." He pointed a calloused thumb. *"News-Press* entrance is halfway up the street. You can't miss it."

Tom Gentry made a disparaging noise. "No lights in the windows. A fine thing. Looks like a morgue!"

"After all, it's an evening paper," Anthony told him mildly. "The staff works daytime; goes home when the last edition rolls off the press at the supper hour."

"Then maybe we won't find anybody there."

Jim shrugged. "I've got an idea Stanton will still be at his job. He makes a habit of staying late. Come along."

"Ain'tcha forgettin' somethin'. Cap?" the cab driver inquired. "I show forty cents on the clock."

"Sorry," Anthony apologized. "I intended for you to wait, but I'll pay you now if you prefer." He pulled his wallet, hunted for a dollar bill—and thereby saved his life.

Dead ahead, the *News-Press* building lurched, quivered and came apart. Cracks opened in the brickwork and the windows bulged outward in shattered chunks a split instant before the hellish explosion thundered through the night. Sheets of blinding flame erupted from the structure, and a deafening roar yammered at Anthony's eardrums with sickening concussion.

He shouted a warning at his aviator friend, knocked him flat behind the taxi so that its tonneau would offer protection from a sudden rain of debris. "Wh-what was that?" Tom yowled.

The millionaire criminologist's mouth was a thin-lipped line of rage. "A bomb," he said. Once more his uncanny sixth sense had called the turn.

CHAPTER III

SMASHED CRUSADE

LONG BEFORE THE LAST fragment of wreckage had stopped dropping from the sky, Jim Anthony was racing toward the broken newspaper plant. "Faster, Tom!" he snapped over his shoulder as the dazed Gentry panted behind him. "People may be trapped in there! We must see!" Licking tongues of flame were already stabbing upward within the ruined building. The two friends charged through the wrecked entrance. "Watch the wall, pappy. It might fold!" Tom warned.

"We'll risk it," Jim's voice was cool as he went plunging across what had been the business office. Now it was a chaotic confusion of scattered furnishings and files. There didn't seem to be anybody in this shambles, though. Anthony made certain by triggering a beam from his pocket flashlight, a miniature electric torch of his own design whose candlepower was far brighter than any ordinary commercial flash.

Guided by the bright ray, he turned to a staircase that led upward to the editorial rooms. The stairs were twisted as if by a giant hand, the joists bent and splintered; but the treads supported his weight and Tom's as they ascended.

"Holy smoke, what a mess!" Gentry gasped at the top of the broken stairway.

That was an understatement. Once the barnlike city room had contained orderly, regimented rows of desks; but there was no order to the scene now. Desks, chairs, and tables had been tossed like so much matchwood; typewriters were insanely scattered, Paper lay everywhere, some of it beginning to burn.

The worst of the wreckage was at the far side of the long room. Here had been a row of glass partitioned offices for editorial executives, but the glass was gone and the partitions leaned drunkenly. A cavernous hole in the floor indicated where the actual explosion had erupted, directly by the door of the largest private office.

Anthony lunged toward this. He circled the hole, catapulted into the partitioned cubicle and presently reappeared with an inert burden: a mangled figure which once had been a man. Behind him, fire began to flicker and swirl.

"Who's that?" Tom Gentry bleated.

"The *News-Press* editor, Jeff Stanton—what's left of him."

"Alive, Jim?"

"A trace of pulse. Feeble. Got to get him out of here. Flames are gaining headway. This'll be an inferno in another minute." As he spoke, Anthony carried the injured editor to the sagging stairway and picked a path downward as easily as if he'd had an infant in his arms rather than an unconscious adult. Gentry followed but made no offer to help because he knew it wasn't needed.

At long last they gained the outer street.

ALREADY A CROWD was collecting, drawn by the blast and by the leaping fire. At the mob's fringe a short, slight man dressed in conservative grey serge seemed to be struggling with a girl much taller than himself; a girl who apparently wanted to race into the burning building. Others of the thickening throng milled uncertainly on the opposite sidewalk, prevented from coming any closer by the yawning black chasm of the collapsed street where it had caved into the mine tunnel below.

Anthony stretched his limp burden on the pavement; made a swift examination. The newspaper editor wasn't a pleasant sight. His suit was charred, torn; his face a gory horror. Jim searched for heart action; found none.

Acrid smoke stung Jim's nostrils as he straightened up, and in the distance he heard sirens wailing, coming nearer. Then someone flurried at him, clutched his arm. It was the girl who had been struggling with the little man across the street. Now she'd freed herself, skirted the black maw of the collapsed mine pit and gained the *News-Press* side.

"You saved him!" her voice was throaty, husky, with just the slightest trace of slurring accent. "You rescued Jeff Stanton—that was wh-what I wanted to do!"

"You knew he was in his office?" Anthony asked.

"Y-yes. What happened? How is he?"

Jim's eyes were somber. "He was murdered."

IN A LITTLE while the fire apparatus arrived, and pumpers began smashing rhythmic tons of ineffectual water into the blazing newspaper plant. An ambulance carried Jeff Stanton's body away; and now Anthony and Gentry braced themselves at the fringe of the jostling crowd, restrained by a fire-line cordon of police.

Between Jim and his friend stood the girl who would have risked her life in an effort to save the *News-Press* editor. Her face was a white, tense mask wet with unashamed tears.

Anthony touched her shoulder. "We may as well go. There isn't anything else we can do."

She turned to him, and for the first time he caught a full look at her features. Her eyes were deep purple, ever so slightly slanted, and her wide-apart cheek bones were high, prominent. Against the scarlet blossom of her generous mouth, her complexion was flawless. She wore her sleek dark hair in a page-boy bob, stressing the Slavic oval of her face; and she couldn't have been older than twenty-four or so. A

While he was paying the driver,
the explosion sounded.

draped skirt flared from her hips, again proclaiming the Slavic strain which sometimes produces women of amazing beauty.

"I must stay," she said simply; and once more the millionaire criminologist was struck by the rich throatiness of her voice. "I seem to be the only staff member here."

"You work for the paper?"

"I write a daily column; local interest stuff. I'm Pola Valska." She made a bitter mouth. "I guess that's finished, n-now."

"Why should it be?"

"The *News-Press* hasn't been showing much profit. It's really owned by a wealthy New Yorker named Anthony, and I imagine he won't resume publication after what's happened—the plant smashed, the editor k-killed."

"The paper will continue, Miss Valska," Jim said quietly.

Her purple eyes grew big, dark. "How do you know?"

Tom seized this chance to edge into the conversation. "Let me introduce my friend, baby. You're talking to Jim Anthony." He added hopefully: "And I'm Tom Gentry, in case you care."

Embarrassed color reddened the girl's cheeks as she stared at the millionaire newspaper owner. "I'm stupid, sir. I should have recognized you; I've seen your picture often enough. I—I guess I'm not thinking very clearly."

Anthony made a gesture dismissing her apology. There was something vibrantly alive about this Valska girl; something that drew you to her like an invisible magnet. She was quick, intelligent—and appealingly feminine.

"I'm Jim to my friends, without the sir," he told her unaffectedly. "And I'd hardly expect you to recognize me under the circumstances. Stanton's death hit you pretty hard, didn't it?"

"Y-yes. I'm a Hunky, born in a shack behind the slag dumps. He made a newspaper woman of me, gave me the breaks. He was the whitest man I ever knew."

"He'll be avenged," Jim promised.

"You intend to carry on his campaign?"

ANTHONY'S BROWS PULLED together. "Afraid I don't know what campaign you mean, Miss Valska. I came to Roseville to inspect a new alloy developed by a research metallurgist named Tyler Hunt of the Acme Foundry."

"Oh-h-h," she sounded disappointed.

Jim studied her. "Can you think of anybody who mightn't want me to see that alloy?"

"No," she answered promptly. "The whole town would like young Hunt to put it across. He's a nice kid; hasn't an enemy in the world. Roseville would welcome anyone who'd take an interest in his method."

Anthony showed his white teeth. "I was welcomed, all right—by a bullet through my hotel room window. Then came this bombing. It, too, may have been meant for me after the rifle shots failed. In another minute I'd have been in Stanton's office to get what he got."

"Heavens!" the girl whispered. Then she shook her head in puzzlement. "I can't believe you were the bomb target. Jeff was the one they were after."

"They?"

"His killers, whoever they were. It's all hooked in with the campaign he was getting ready to spring. He'd spent two years gathering evidence. The documents were in his office safe—which wasn't fireproof," she turned down the corners of her full, ripe mouth.

"What was the nature of the campaign, Miss Valska?"

"A clean-up. Anti-gambling, anti-tenement. He didn't tell me the details. Didn't tell anybody. He kept a tight mouth, collected his material slowly, filed it until conditions were ready for the blowoff. That would've been soon—if he'd lived."

Tom Gentry let out a yelp. "There's the answer, Jim! By coincidence, you hit town just when the poor guy was getting set to tear off the lid. Somebody figured you were here to help him, so they beat you to the punch!"

"You may be right," the wealthy detective's tone was thoughtful. "But if Stanton was murdered by his underworld enemies they made a bad mistake. Because they're *my* enemies, now."

Even as he announced this quiet challenge, Anthony heard his name being spoken through the surging crowd that milled all about him. He whirled; saw two people making for him, a man and a girl. It was the girl who had called to him, and presently she and her companion reached the spot where he stood.

Simultaneously with their arrival a weird thing happened. Pola Valska vanished as completely as if the earth had opened up to swallow her!

CHAPTER IV

DEATH SENTENCE

FOR A LITTLE WHILE, neither Jim Anthony nor Tom Gentry noticed the uncanny disappearance of the girl with the purple eyes. They were both too busy with the pair who had just approached and accosted them.

Anthony recognized these newcomers at once, having met them before on several previous visits to the steel town. The man was Cabot McQuayde, a former Boston attorney turned newspaper owner. He published Roseville's only other daily, the *Clarion*, and there had long been a friendly rivalry between his sheet and the *News-Press*. He was in his forties, at a guess; a dapper, crisp looking man, the color of whose eyes you could never quite determine because they seemed to change from grey to green to blue as often as he changed his editorial policies.

It was the girl who gave Anthony a start of surprise, though; or rather, it was her presence with Cabot McQuayde—for she was Karen Stanton, sister of the murdered *News-Press* editor. Why, Jim wondered, should the slain Jeff Stanton's sister be running around with the owner of a competitive newspaper?

She thrust out a hard, brown little hand. "Hello, Mr. Anthony. I didn't expect to find you in Roseville, let alone here at the scene of the—the accident." Her voice was as firm as her handclasp, betraying no emotion.

Which was characteristic of her, the millionaire criminologist realized. Karen Stanton had nerves like steel wire, a fact which she had demonstrated often enough in national golf tournaments all over the country. Match or medal play, her game was of championship caliber and her name was one to conjure with on the toughest courses in the land. It was quite evident that she carried over into her private life the icy, unshakable qualities that had won so many golfing trophies.

Even so, it seemed queer that she could be so collected, so utterly self possessed, when her only brother had lost his life less than thirty minutes ago. Even her vigorous handshake rasped on Anthony's sensibilities while he was unwillingly admiring her trim little athletic figure, the bright coils of her hair, the elfin piquancy of her sun-tanned features.

Gravely he introduced her to Gentry, who was visibly impressed. Then Cabot McQuayde cleared his throat, spoke diffidently.

"I, er, met Miss Stanton at the hospital while she was, er, ah, identifying Jeff's body. Poor fellow. Nasty accident. Can't imagine how it could have happened." As Tom Gentry remarked later, he sounded like a Harvard professor.

They reached the opening and saw the red glare of the sky above.

Anthony frowned. "I don't class bombs as accidents, Mr. McQuayde."

"Bombs—?"

"That was what killed Stanton and wrecked the *News-Press.*"

"Well, er, ah, I must say this is distressing news!" the man's eyes seemed to flicker, change color. "I, er, I had better return and inform my city editor. You will, ah, forgive me for leaving so precipitately, I trust?" Then he looked at Karen Stanton. "My, ah, er, offer still holds, my dear. Let me know."

THE MILLIONAIRE CRIMINOLOGIST watched him speculatively as he wormed his way through the jostling crush that jampacked the narrow street. For all McQuayde's impeccable tailoring and courtly manners, there was something repugnant about the fellow; a slimy quality you sensed instinctively.

"What offer did he mean?" Jim asked Karen Stanton.

"The use of his *Clarion* plant to print the *News-Press* until we get new equipment. A newspaper courtesy," she answered without hesitation. "He'd have done it even if he weren't engaged to me, I'm sure."

Gentry twitched. "You're going to marry that guy?"

"Yes. Why?"

The freckled aviator seemed on the verge of blurting that he didn't like the color of McQuayde's teeth, but he caught himself in time. "Nothing," he answered lamely. "I'm just disappointed, is all. Every time I meet a beautiful wren, she's already spoken for. That is, I mean—" he flushed hotly.

Karen's smile was brief; faded into seriousness. "Thanks for an outspoken compliment." She looked up at Anthony. "You said it was a bomb that killed Jeff."

"Yes."

"Then he was murdered." Her lips thinned. "Stepan Koblick will pay for that. I'll see to it."

"Stepan Koblick?"

"Yes. My brother's one and only enemy in Roseville. The man Jeff was out to smash if he could."

"Tell me about him," Anthony said gently.

She shrugged. "There's not much to tell. Koblick's a Hunky—a Serb, I think. He runs all the gambling in town; squeezes the miners and mill hands out of dimes and quarters they need for food and rent. There's even talk that he controls the holding company which owns the tenements and shacks, although nobody's ever proved it."

"Sort of a crime czar, hunh?" Gentry interposed.

"Jeff thought so. And yet Koblick's popular with the workers; has the labor vote in his hip pocket. When you say labor vote, you say it all. There's no other kind. Jeff was a fool to think of bucking that big a man, I suppose. Maybe I'm a fool, too, for wanting revenge."

Jim Anthony's grin was almost wolfish in the fire-glow. "Then you've got a partner in foolishness, Karen. I'm going to fight it through with you. If Stepan Koblick is guilty, he'll be punished. And I think we'll have more help."

"From whom?"

"From Miss Valska, here." The millionaire detective turned to speak to the *News-Press* columnist. It was then, for the first time, that he noticed she had vanished.

Her unseen, unheard disappearance filled him with a knife-sharp stab of premonition. "Tom!" he rapped out. "Where did she go?"

"Damned if I know, pappy. She didn't pass me, so she couldn't have gone this way."

"Then the only other direction was through the fire lines!" Jim pivoted, bashed his way to the police cordon. His voice rose above the crackling roar of flames, the throb of pumper engines, the excited chatter of the crowd. "You!" he singled out a police sergeant. "Did you see a girl go this way? A girl in a gabardine suit? Purple eyes, tall, striking?"

"That sounds like Pola Valska, bub."

"Right. You know her?"

"There ain't a cop in town that don't know her. She didn't go by here. I'd of saw her if she did."

As if hypnotized, Jim Anthony's gaze slowly turned toward the yawning, sunken black orifice in the middle of the street, where it had collapsed into an abandoned coal stope. Both reason and instinct told him what he would find at the bottom of that sinister hole....

SOMEWHERE IN ROSEVILLE, in solid darkness, a telephone tinkled softly. Out of the darkness a hand lifted the instrument from its cradle and a voice spoke into the transmitter. "Yes?"

"Two reports for you, boss," came over the wire.

"I'm listening."

"Well, Stanton's private safe is a total loss. It was red hot when the fire laddies hit with a stream. Cracked it wide open. It was a tin can."

"The papers in it?"

"Not a trace."

"Good. What is the second report?"

"This guy Anthony and his pal. Looks like they're beating a lot of gum with Karen Stanton. You want we should do something—while she's got them on the spot?"

"No, not yet. Not until we see which way Anthony moves. But I *have* got a job for you."

"Yeah boss?"

"Baldy Parker. The hotel clerk. He is no longer useful to me; and he knows too much. You know what happens to men when they are no longer useful?"

"Sure. They get bumped."

"Very good. Bump him." The connection was softly broken.

TOM GENTRY SAW his sun-bronzed friend approaching the sunken pit in the middle of the block. He excused himself to Karen Stanton and pelted around a policeman. "Jim! What cooks?"

"I'm hunting Pola Valska," the wealthy detective said bleakly. "She didn't pass you; she didn't get by the cops. She couldn't go flying through the air. Therefore—" he edged closer to the hole, moving carefully.

Tom gasped: "Cripes, you think she's down there?"

"She could have gone in no other direction." Anthony went to his knees over the pit's jagged brink; sprayed light downward in a brilliant stream from his flash. The drop was sheer; at least twelve or fifteen feet to a glistening surface of roiled water seeping into the stope from the tonnage being pumped at the burning *News-Press* building. How deep this water lay, he had no means of knowing. That was the chance he had to take.

He swung himself over the edge; let go. He dropped.

The splash of his landing was matched by another as Tom Gentry came plunging down beside him. Then they both stood upright, thigh-deep in swirling seepage, surrounded by the gloom of the abandoned mine drift. The air was dank and foully moist; rotted wooden supports leaned crazily, some of the timbers completely splintered where the tunnel roof had collapsed and carried the street surface down into this subterranean place. In the beam of Anthony's powerful electric torch, two beady little eyes glittered as a swimming rat circled desperately.

The millionaire criminologist stabbed light to right and left, along the eerie distances of the underground cut. The world overhead seemed weirdly remote, the noises of the fire apparatus curiously muffled. Then, as Anthony's flash-beam bored along a slanted rise to the right, he stiffened.

There was a narrow shelf running there from where he stood; and sprawled on this shelf lay a girl in gabardine, an ugly blue bruise above her temple.

He'd found Pola Valska.

CHAPTER V

BLED BRAKES

THE GIRL'S PURPLE EYES opened as Anthony chafed her wrists. "It—it's y-you—!" she whispered, struggling herself to a sitting posture. She swayed dizzily.

"Yes. Tell me what happened."

A shudder racked her shoulders. "I d-don't know. I was standing there near y-you. The crowd was jostling us. I saw Miss Stanton and Cabot McQuayde coming. Just as they reached us, I—I was shoved, tripped. I g guess I must have hit my head when I landed. I have a vague recollection of crawling a little distance; then everything w-went black." She plucked at the flaring drape of her skirt's hem, drew it down to cover the tapered loveliness of her legs.

Tom Gentry, who had been raptly staring, blushed and turned away guiltily. Anthony, though, had no time for the appreciation of feminine charms. "I want to ask you a question, Pola," he said grimly.

"Y-yes?"

"Do you think you were deliberately pushed into the pit?"

"I—I don't know!"

"Did you recognize anyone near you at the time? Anyone connected with Stepan Koblick, for instance?"

She drew a sharp breath. "No. Wh-what do you know about Koblick?"

"Jeff Stanton's sister has been telling me the position he occupies in Roseville's underworld. Apparently Jeff's clean-up campaign was to be directed at Koblick. Were you aware of that?"

"I guessed as much," the girl admitted. "And it worried me. Stepan Koblick is a dangerous enemy. The mayor takes orders from him. So does the police chief. Even Lawrence Rosewater's influence has never been enough to win an election from the Koblick machine."

"Rosewater? That name sounds familiar."

"It should be. Roseville was named for his grandfather. Lawrence is president of the chamber of commerce; full of civic virtue and reform ideas. A little fellow; you may have seen him trying to hold me when I wanted to go into the burning building. He was afraid to have me risk my life."

"In love with you, Pola?" Jim asked shrewdly.

She flushed. "Well, y-yes. Pathetically, because he isn't my type. I don't like stuffed shirts."

Tom Gentry's eyes applauded this. "Sure you don't, baby. I never did trust these professional reformers. Lots of 'em put pennies in the collection plate and swipe millions in graft. Do you suppose this Lawrence Rosewater guy is the real brains of the town's underworld? I mean, would he have any reason to bump off Jeff Stanton?"

The Valska girl's lips curled upward in a wry smile. "That's fantastic. Lawrence would cross the street to keep from stepping on a bug."

"Then you think he ain't connected with Koblick, hunh?"

"I'm sure of it."

Jim Anthony studied her quizzically. "You were tripped into this pit around the time Karen Stanton and Cabot McQuayde reached us. What's your opinion of McQuayde?"

"You m-mean, do I think he tried to kill me?"

"Just tell me what you think of him."

SHE WAS THOUGHTFUL. "He's got a pretty good paper in the *Clarion*. I'm not sure I'd trust him very far, though. He always seemed— well, devious. And it struck me as odd for him to be engaged to Miss Stanton when he publishes a rival paper. Jeff didn't like it much."

"Jeepers!" Gentry burst out.

"Maybe that's an angle, pappy! Jeff Stanton didn't want his sister to marry this McQuayde character. So McQuayde bumped Jeff with a bomb, getting rid of him and the *News-Press* all at one time!"

Pola Valska shook her head. "I don't think so."

"Why not?" Tom demanded.

"It's too drastic for a man like McQuayde. He was going to marry Karen anyhow, in spite of Jeff's disapproval. After all, she's of age. It's her privilege to choose her own husband."

"Yeah, but—"

"And there's business enough in Roseville for two dailies," Pola went on. "No, I'm afraid I wouldn't suspect McQuayde any more than I'd suspect Lawrence Rosewater."

"Which brings us back to Koblick," Anthony mused. "I think I want a little talk with that gentleman. Can you take me to him?" he asked the girl.

"Gladly." She shivered despite an obvious effort not to.

Jim noticed this and was at once contrite. "Forgive me for keeping you down here! You need rest—and a doctor to attend to that bruise on your head! Come along."

"This whickey is loaded with yellow phosphorus," he said.

He half-guided, half-carried her along the narrow ledge at the side of the dark tunnel so she wouldn't get her gabardine outfit wet by wading through the swirling waters of the drift proper. Presently they were directly under the gaping hole formed by the collapsed street overhead.

Here, using his powerful flashlight, the millionaire criminologist spotted a rickety old ladder partially projecting from the muddy flood. He seized it, raised it, found that it was long enough to reach street level. Above him glowed a ragged patch of night sky, as red as fresh blood.

IN A BARREN second floor room of a filthy clapboard building that masqueraded under the name of hotel, a bald man cringed on his sagging and dirty bed; stared at the visitor who had just entered.

"No, pal. Nix!" he whined. "You can't do this to me!"

"Sorry. Orders from the boss."

"Please! I been on the level, ain't I? I done everything I was told. I put the Anthony guy and his friend in that front suite. I ducked under cover so the SPOS can't run me through no wringer. I don't shoot off my face—"

"Sorry, Baldy. Orders from the boss."

"Oh—no—don't—!" the cringing man bleated. His outcry was suddenly drowned in a liquid gurgle as a glittering knife licked like a thirsty metal tongue across his fat, flabby gullet. He went backward on the grimy pillows, and a spreading wet stain turned those pillows from grey to scarlet—matching the night sky that glowed over Roseville.

THE *NEWS-PRESS* BUILDING was a gutted mass of embers within four stark walls when Jim Anthony, Pola Valska, and Tom Gentry ascended to the street. Already the throng of onlookers had thinned to a few stragglers, most of the fire apparatus had left, and a lone police-man stood guard in place of the recent cordon. Nobody even noticed the trio who emerged from the abandoned mine tunnel's maw.

The girl smiled wistfully at her rescuers. "I'm quite okay," she tried to assure Anthony. "Barring a headache, I'm afraid I'll live. You want me to take you to Stepan Koblick's headquarters? I have a car."

"No, Pola. You need rest, sleep," the wealthy detective said firmly. "And don't forget, an attempt was made on your life. Probably because someone thinks you know too much about the clean-up campaign Jeff Stanton was about to launch. They may strike at you again; you'll be safer at home, under cover."

Her purple eyes were steady, unafraid, and she squared her shoulders in a defiant gesture. "I've never run away from danger, Mr. Anthony... Jim."

"Then this is a good time to start. I'll drive you wherever you live; then I'd like to use your car for my visit to Koblick. I'll return it later, of course."

"That won't be necessary," her smile was warm, friendly. "I can pick it up tomorrow morning at the Grand Rosedale if you put it in the hotel's garage. Besides, what use would I have for it tonight when you're practically ordering me to stay home? You're my new boss now; I have to do what you say."

Anthony decided it was very pleasant to boss somebody as attrac-tive as this dark-haired Slavic girl. A tingling thrill coursed through him when she took his arm and pressed herself close to him, leading him toward the next block where she'd left her little roadster parked.

It was an old but well kept Model A, painted bright red, its upholstery spotless. Jim drove, Pola Valska sat in the middle and Gentry sandwiched her from the other side. En route to her modest apartment, she gave detailed instructions about the location of Stepan Koblick's headquarters.

Later, after she'd been dropped off, the genial Gentry whistled admiringly. "What a woman!"

"Very lovely," Anthony admitted. "By the way, I think we're being tailed. Those look like the same headlights behind us I saw while we were taking Pola home. Check, will you?"

Tom glanced back. "A car there, all right. Can't tell if—*hey*, watch it, pappy! You almost threw me out on my elbows when you took that turn on two wheels!"

"Hang on." Grimly the millionaire mashed his throttle all the way down; sent the roadster roaring forward at right angles. He yammered around another intersection, turning to the left, tires screeching protest as they smoked across rough cobblestones. A narrow alley bisected this block and he aimed for it, drove down its perilous length at breakneck speed.

The freckled aviator let out a strangled cry as they thundered out into the adjacent street. A right turn followed, then two more to the left, the little car rocking and jouncing with savage momentum. "Jim, this ain't a plane! It's just an auto!"

But Anthony refused to slacken his headlong speed until he'd made a figure-8 circuit of four more city blocks. Then, scowling, he slowed down. "See if we've lost the guy."

"Not a headlight in sight, pappy. Cripes, nobody could have stuck with us unless they'd been welded to our rear bumper!"

"Good!" Jim breathed. And he drew up before a long, low, one-story building of discolored brick which abutted upon an ancient slag pile at the crest of one of Roseville's steeply tilted side streets. "This is Koblick's joint. Come along."

The two friends piled out of the car, made for the brick structure and entered. Shortly afterward a shadowy figure skulked out of an opposite alley and approached the parked roadster, crawled under it. Muffled hammer-sounds echoed metallically, and presently the shadowy shape stood up; strode off into the night.

CHAPTER VI

HUNKY'S HANGOUT

S **TEPAN KOBLICK'S DIVE WAS** a combination bar, dance hall, and gambling hell. The dance hall and bar occupied the big front sector of the building, music furnished by a juke box constantly dinning brassy swing as drunken puddlers and miners plied it with nickels. Dancing girls mingled with sweating men whose broad, flat faces were stained with the ineradicable grime of mines and steel foundries.

Behind this room of whiskey-induced gaiety lay the gambling chamber, almost as large. There was nothing fancy about it, however. No carpets covered the bare boards of the floor, and there were no drapes at the black-painted windows. The walls were of plaster, tinted a sickly yellow that reflected harsh light from dangling, unshaded incandescents.

To compensate for this lack of glamor, the gambling equipment itself was remarkably complete—and expensive. The four roulette tables operated wheels as fine as Anthony had ever seen. There were several crap layouts, well patronized. Other miners and steel mill workers hovered around blackjack games, birdcages, a wheel of fortune, and something you rarely saw in eastern gambling establishments—a faro bank.

At one side were a series of blackboards faced by three rows of seats, like a school room. The comparison was incongruous, for this was no hall of education. The blackboards were covered with chalked race entries left over from that afternoon; it was one of the biggest bookie layouts the millionaire criminologist had encountered in a long time.

A man in dirty slacks and a sweat shirt with Roseville A.C. lettered front and back sat beside the door, a dented derby tilted over one eye. He squinted at Anthony and Gentry as they entered, the dead cigar that made a dimple at one corner of his hard mouth jiggling up and down as he spoke.

"Want something, pals?"

"Yes, if Stepan Koblick's around," Jim said.

"Where the hell do you think he'd be, out drinkin' tea at the country club?" The sweat-shirted one jerked a thumb toward a door at the left. It was marked *Roseville A. C. Office.*

As Jim and Gentry approached this, the good natured aviator made disgusted sounds. "Athletic club! The only dumb-bells around here are the customers. I bet there ain't a square game in the house!"

Tom hadn't realized that the office door was slightly ajar, and that his words had carried. He knew it, though, when the door was suddenly yanked open from within and he found himself facing one of the biggest, queerest-looking men it had ever been his misfortune to confront.

THE FELLOW WAS a veritable giant, fat and yet somehow giving no impression of pudginess. You sensed that there were iron-hard muscles underlying the layers of obesity; muscles capable of savagery and destruction when aroused. His hair was startlingly yellow, almost golden, curling tightly to his thick round skull like a matted cap. His eyes were big China-blue discs wide with an appearance of perpetually sad astonishment, and his nose was a mere button lost in the red expanse of his face.

He wore a loud butternut suit with wide blue stripes, and his bulging paunch stretched the fancy checkered material of a vest that belonged on a circus barker. Across this blinding waistcoat drooped what might have been a dog chain except that the links were of solid gold; and a round golden medal dangled from the center of the chain—a religious medal.

When he spoke, his voice held rumbling thunder, like a basso profundo in a third rate opera company. Curiously, though, there was no anger in this deep rumble; but rather a plaintive quality to match the sadness of his surprised blue eyes.

"Who say there no square games in Honest Stepan Koblick's place, huh? Who tell lies like that?" he demanded.

For once in his life, Tom Gentry was willing to eat his own words for the sake of avoiding an argument. "Skip it, mister. I was only making conversation, was all."

"Me, I no like this conversation stuff. You lose money here, she's your hard luck, you bet. But you no say game not on level. Is a lie, see? You win, I no squeal. You lose, you keep mouth shut. You want make me feel bad, huh?"

Anthony stepped forward. "We didn't come here to discuss the honesty of your layouts. You're Koblick?"

"Sure. Honest Stepan, me," the giant tapped his gorilla-size chest. "Who you? What you want?"

"A little talk. I'm Jim Anthony."

The millionaire criminologist scarcely expected his name to register, but the big fellow fooled him. "Ho. So you Jim Anthony! No look different from other guys."

"What did you expect?" Gentry asked truculently. "Superman?"

"Hah. Is joke. Expect Superman, see nobody but guy named Anthony." Koblick's laugh could have been either merriment or contempt; there was no way of telling. "Come in." His barrel legs carried him back around a scarred desk and he settled into what was quite obviously a specially built chair. It creaked vigorous protest to his weight. "Sit down."

Jim ignored the invitation; remained on his feet. "Have you any idea why I'm here, Koblick?"

"You tell. I listen. No got time to play guess games."

"All right, I'll deal my cards face up. My newspaper plant was bombed tonight; destroyed. The editor was killed—Jeff Stanton. Maybe you knew him."

"Sure. She's honest guy, that Stanton. Sorry when I hear he die. Make me feel bad."

"Oh, yeah?" Gentry muttered.

The big man's sad, surprised eyes regarded him without rancor. "Oh, yeah. You no make fun of Stepan Koblick or she's yank your arm off, beat you on head with it. You think I can't, hah, do you, maybe?"

"I don't doubt it," Tom said hastily.

"Is better. That Stanton is good fella. All time try do something for Hunkies. Want them to live in good house, not shack for high rent. Give Hunky people the breaks. Let Hunky girl Pola Valska write stuff in paper. Now Stanton all dead to hell. No, heaven I think maybe," he fingered the medal on his watch chain. "Me, I say little word for his soul. So what?"

"So it's going to be too bad for whoever killed him," Anthony flung down the quiet gauntlet.

KOBLICK CHUCKLED WITHOUT sound, his whole body seeming to jiggle with this unvoiced mirth. "You think I blow him up, hah? Sure.

"Freeze, you murderer!"
she commanded.

Everybody think of Stepan Koblick when bad thing happen. So she's okay; sometimes they right. Not this time, though."

"You don't know anything about the bomb?"

"Not any thing. Why I kill Stanton? She's nice guy."

"You've already said that. But he was getting set to launch a clean-up campaign."

"Clean-up? What is this clean-up stuff?"

"Graft, perhaps. I'm not sure. Gambling, very likely." Jim's eyes were cold, direct. "That would have affected you."

Koblick's grin showed teeth too perfect to be real. His dentist was an artist. "What I care? Clean-up no touch me. The mayor, the cheese of police, the voters—all take orders from Koblick. Hunkies gamble, get square deal. Go broke, Koblick lend them money. They Koblick's friends."

"In other; words, you own Roseville."

"No, just own Hunkies. Somebody make trouble, throw Koblick in jail, Hunkies tearing jail apart and string up trouble maker on lamp post. Clean-up stuff in newspaper, hah! Most my boys, she can't read nohow."

Tom Gentry scratched his chin. "You know, pappy, this guy's got something there. He's too solid to have been scared of Stanton; and if he wasn't scared, he wouldn't have any reason to kill him."

"Your pal, she's smart fella," Koblick brightened.

Anthony reverted to first principles. He stared at the gambler. "All right. Assume you weren't after Stanton."

"Is good talk, now. Now you getting sense."

Jim fired a verbal shot in the dark; watched to see what reaction it would bring. "Maybe you were after me instead of Jeff. Your silenced rifle missed, so you tried to bomb me at the *News-Press* and Stanton got it by accident."

"Hah?" Koblick's China-blue eyes widened. "Why you say thing like that, make me feel bad? What for I try kill you?"

Anthony fired his second barrel. "Perhaps you didn't want me to inspect Tyler Hunt's new alloy."

In response to this, Koblick looked genuinely shocked. "That's completely ridiculous!" he snapped without the slightest hint of accent. For an instant his guard had slipped, revealing that his English was perfect when he wanted it to be. He recovered immediately, though. "Jim Anthony, she's talk like screwball!"

The millionaire criminologist grinned bleakly. "You can drop the phony brogue, Koblick. You've given yourself away. What kind of game are you playing? You're no Hunky."

"All right, my friend. So I fake my accent. So you were clever enough to trip me up. Is that a crime?" the fat man's tone was silken.

"Not in itself. It indicates you're not as straight as you pretend to be."

Koblick's head wagged. "Wrong. I shoot square, whether you believe it or not. And I *am* a Hunky—although most of it got rubbed off at college. The accent is part of my stage dressing. It keeps the other Hunkies from thinking I've gone high hat."

"Very interesting," Anthony said ironically.

Anger flared on the gambler's florid face but he controlled it. "I don't want to quarrel with you, Mr. Anthony. You represent money to me. Big money."

"Do I? In what way?"

"You've come here to inspect Tyler Hunt's alloy. If you happen to approve it, the government will buy the process. So then I make a fortune."

"How?"

"Because my money financed young Tyler Hunt. I paid for all his experiments. I get half his profits. Therefore I have every reason for wanting you alive—at least until you turn in your report to Washington. Chew on that a while."

"And suppose I don't believe you?"

KOBLICK AROSE, WENT to his office door, opened it and peered into the gambling room. "Hey!" he called. "Kid! You come. We have little talk." He was using his accent again.

A studious looking youth moved promptly from one of the roulette tables where he'd been watching but not participating in the play. He was thin, threadbare, wore thick-lensed glasses. But his hands looked hard, capable.

"Yes, Mr. Koblick?"

"This guy, she's Jim Anthony. Tell him your name, kid."

"Why—why, I'm Tyler Hunt. I'm honored to meet you, sir," he stammered to the wealthy criminologist. "You can't imagine what it meant to me when I got your wire saying you were coming to inspect my alloy. Do you plan to look at it soon?"

"Very soon," Anthony said gravely. "Is the process entirely your own?"

"No, sir. That is, Mr. Koblick financed me. He owns a half share."

The fat man chuckled sourly. "Hah! What I told you?"

For once in his life, Jim Anthony was stumped by a paradox. Here was a man, Stepan Koblick, who might have had a motive for trying to murder him—and for actually succeeding in the murder of Jeff Stanton at the *News-Press*. Stanton's forthcoming reform campaign would have been that motive. Yet diametrically opposed to such a theory was Koblick's investment in the Tyler Hunt alloy process—whereby the fat man stood to gain a fortune only if Anthony remained alive!

The pattern was insanely jumbled. Was Koblick friend or foe? There was no way of telling, at the moment. And even as Jim tried to decide, hell broke loose in the gambling room beyond the door of the office. Men shouted, a woman screamed—and a pistol shot cut across the uproar.

CHAPTER VII

DEATH'S NEAR MISS

AT THE SOUND OF that gun-blast, Anthony and his freckled aviator friend pivoted in unison; dived toward the door. But Stepan Koblick, for all his size, was amazingly quicker. From where he had been standing, he was a good three steps nearer the doorway; and he gained it just ahead of the millionaire criminologist. He ripped it open with a hand that almost wrenched out the knob by its roots. "Hah!" he rumbled.

Pell-mell confusion reigned in the gaming chamber. Women and men were huddled at the far side of the room, motionless, tense. The fellow in the sweat-shirt and battered derby crouched ludicrously, gulping at the remnants of his cigar and swearing bitter oaths under his breath.

The man responsible for this tableau was stalking forward through a wispy curl of gunsmoke, the acrid cordite fumes drifting around him. He was small, clad in conservative grey serge—the sort of person you might see in a crowd and promptly dismiss from your memory. His face, now strained and working, was utterly lacking in notable characteristics; the face of a Joe Doakes, anonymous, unimportant.

But the automatic in his fist made up for all the qualities he didn't possess. It gave him equal stature with anyone else in the room, made him the situation's master. Even the warning bullet he had pumped into the ceiling seemed to have borne a tangible authority far out of proportion to its .32 caliber.

"I want Pola Valska," he said shrilly.

Then Jim Anthony recognized him as the one who'd struggled with the Valska girl at the scene of the *News-Press* explosion—the man who'd tried to restrain her from plunging into the bombed structure when she had entertained the idea of rescuing Jeff Stanton. In brief, he was the frustrated reformer and president of Roseville's chamber of commerce, Lawrence Rosewater, whom Pola had described as a stuffed shirt.

STEPAN KOBLICK MOVED stiff-legged toward the little man as if contemptuous of the gun he grasped. "Ho. You come here, look for trouble, yes?"

"I want Pola Valska."

"You think you bust up gambling, wreck Koblick's roulette wheels like last time." Which was news to Anthony. He hadn't known that Rosewater had ever carried out single-handed raids on this gaming room.

"Where's Pola?" the little man shrilled.

Koblick kept moving toward him. "You no remember warning, eh? You no remember Koblick she's tell you to stay away from here or you be sorry."

"Hey, boss," the man in the derby bleated. "Don't blame me for lettin' him in. He had that gat. When I tried to stop him, he blasted at me.

"You shut mouth," Koblick said, and the derby wearer subsided. "You Rosewater. You drop gun or I'm make you eat it."

A hint of panic slithered into the little reformer's eyes at his giant enemy's inexorable approach, although he held his ground.

"I want Pola," he repeated unsteadily. "I've got news for her. I just heard a police radio report that her cousin Baldy Parker has been found murdered in a rooming house. His throat was cut. She's got a right to know."

Hearing this, Tom Gentry clutched at Anthony's arm. "Jeest, Jim! Baldy Parker—wasn't that the name of the desk clerk at our hotel, the guy that lammed?"

The millionaire nodded, watched grimly.

Koblick was still closing in on Rosewater. "Why you look for Pola here, hah?"

"I saw her car parked outside as I drove by on my way over to her apartment. Where is she? Let me talk to her."

The fat man's two great hands flashed out. One of them closed around the automatic, plucked it from Rosewater's grasp as easily as pulling a weed out of the ground. The other seized the reformer's skinny throat and clamped there, viselike. "Koblick she's warn you. Now Koblick she's break your neck."

Indian file, they followed the perilous cat-walk.

Tom Gentry yelled a protest; sailed at the giant and tried to drag him off his victim. Koblick's vast shoulders shrugged as if flicking away an insect—and Tom went careening backward like a stone from a slingshot. He tripped and fell sprawling to the floor, dazed, scarcely knowing what had happened to him.

Then Jim Anthony took a hand in the game.

He lunged at Koblick, and a well directed fist blow smashed the fat man's grasp from Rosewater's throat. Rosewater sagged, stumbled sidewise, made strangling noises as he rubbed his bruised gullet. Meanwhile Koblick whirled on Anthony and the two of them came to grips for one mighty instant of combat.

But this time Stepan Koblick had encountered an adversary worthy of his mettle. Jim grinned as he met the gambler's ponderous attack; wrapped his arms around Koblick's barrel torso and got his fingers locked together at the bigger man's spine. He applied savage pressure.

Slowly, inevitably, Koblick was bent backward despite every ounce of strength he employed to break that crushing hold. His breath began to wheeze out of his chest, and his sad, surprised blue eyes bulged stupidly—as if he couldn't quite understand the vast riptide of pain pouring through his bones, his sinews. Then, suddenly, the millionaire criminologist made a lightning shift. He caught Koblick and deliberately lifted him off his feet, raised him high in the air—and hurled him the length of the long room!

LIKE A GIANT missile, the gambler went catapulting across a roulette table; crashed jarringly against the furthermost wall with an impact that shook the building. He dropped in an inert heap, quivering, stunned, semi-conscious. And a concert of gasps went up from the onlookers who had witnessed the astounding spectacle of Stepan Koblick, Stepan the invincible, bested and cowed and whipped by a man he outweighed a good hundred pounds.

You could almost taste the electric tingle that filled this silent room as the spectators began to stir and whisper to themselves. Koblick had been beaten. Koblick had lost face among his fellows. Koblick had been toppled from his throne; his hold upon his followers had been broken.

And as the giant gambler lurched groggily to his feet, he apparently realized this. For a moment his blue eyes mirrored the crafty depths of his soul; revealed that he knew he'd met his master. Then, shrewdly, he did the one thing any man in his position could do that might be calculated to snatch a small measure of victory out of utter defeat.

He staggered to the wealthy detective and threw an arm around his shoulder. "This guy, she's Jim Anthony!" he announced. "She's my friend, see? Jim Anthony lick Koblick. You take good look. Koblick, she's Jim Anthony's pal. Something bad happen to Anthony, watch out. Koblick tear somebody apart."

"And that's what I call political strategy," Tom Gentry said with unwilling admiration. "As some wisenheimer once remarked, if you can't lick 'em, join 'em!"

Anthony, though, was not too impressed. He realized that the fat man might be playing a game, acting out a part. This offer of friendship was all very well in public; but in secret it could easily mask a knife in the back at the first opportunity. From now henceforth, Jim knew he must stand constant guard against any such chance.

But his expressionless, sun-bronzed countenance revealed no hint of his actual thoughts. He pulled away from Koblick's heavy, encircling arm. "We'll leave now. Come along, Tom. You too, Mr. Rosewater."

The little reformer's lower lip pouted sullenly. "Not until I see Pola."

"She's not here. She's safely at home."

"But her roadster—"

"I borrowed it. That's why it's parked out front." With which terse explanation, Jim gestured Gentry and Rosewater from the gambling dive and followed them. Nobody made any attempt to interfere with their departure.

OUTSIDE ON THE grimy sidewalk, Anthony faced the colorless president of the chamber of commerce. "I wonder if you can spare me a few minutes? I'd like to ask you some questions."

"Why—why, gladly, Mr. Anthony. Only too pleased."

"Thanks. Suppose we go to my hotel. Here, get in, I'll drive you," Jim opened the roadster's door.

Very promptly, Rosewater backed off. "Oh, no. I—I have my own sedan here, you see. No use leaving it. I'd only have to come back and get it. Suppose I follow you, wouldn't that be much better?"

"All right." The millionaire criminologist wedged himself under the small car's wheel; Gentry piled in alongside him while Rosewater walked across the steeply slanted street to a four-door Buick.

Many blocks distant, at the lower end of the street's long hill, the river could be seen like a wide band of tarnished silver in the moonlight—a silver ribbon touched with faint tinges of pink from the cherry glow of the sky where it reflected the fires of dozens of roaring blast furnaces up and down the valley. Anthony got his motor going, backed away from the curb, dropped into second gear and shifted easily into high as the roadster gained immediate momentum on the downgrade.

Its speed increasing with each revolution of the tires, the little car began to rattle and jounce on the cobblestones. Jim touched his brake pedal to keep the vehicle under control—but nothing happened.

He pressed harder.

"What's the matter, pappy?"

Anthony slammed the pedal all the way down. The roadster's speed increased instead of diminishing. He grabbed for the emergency; yanked it tight. It did no good whatever. The speedometer wavered up to forty—fifty—fifty-five—

"Cripes, Jim, take it easy!" Gentry yelped plaintively. "It's a straight-away drop to the river!"

The sun-bronzed millionaire knotted his fists on the wheel. "Somebody realized that fact. If this car's got hydraulic brakes, they've been bled dry of fluid. If the brakes are mechanical they were disconnected. Hang onto your hat, Tom. We're going for a one-way ride!"

CHAPTER VIII

POISON—TWO KINDS

IT LOOKED FOR A while as if that one-way ride would end in death, with the roadster plunging headlong into the river. Like an invisible fist, gravity tugged the little car downward with cannonball velocity. Now there were but four blocks intervening between the hurtling vehicle and the unguarded waterfront. Three. Two....

With strength that almost ripped out the transmission, Anthony slammed the gear lever into second; let out his clutch. The motor howled protest as its compression formed a brake; but it was insufficient. The speedometer still registered almost sixty.

Then, in the last block between himself and destruction, Jim spied a long stretch of high curbing at which no cars were parked. This was the miracle he'd been hoping for. He jammed his wheel hard over, angling toward that curb. "Hold on, Tom!" his voice rose above the whistling of the wind around them. "This is it!"

Then his right front tire bounced into the curb with an impact that almost tore the steering wheel from his grasp. The tire's side wall caved in with an explosive bark and the inner tube collapsed in fragments. Anthony snubbed ruined rubber hard against the high curb, friction sending up rancid smoke and hot sparks.

It took delicate handling to keep the roadster from leaping up over the sidewalk and turning turtle; but the millionaire detective gauged the desperate maneuver accurately. With grim purpose he scraped along the curbing; and then, at long last, he had control. Shuddering metallic protest, the little car screeched to a stop less than ten feet from the riverbank.

THIRTY MINUTES LATER, Anthony and Gentry were in their suite at the Grand Roseville, with Lawrence Rosewater as their ashen-faced guest. The colorless president of the chamber of commerce had followed their headlong flight down that tilted street; had picked them up as they piled out of the disabled roadster at the foot of the murderous incline. Now he'd brought them to their hotel rooms; and he was still shaken from the experience of seeing them plunge toward the river.

"My God!" he mopped his pale forehead. "I thought y-you were both doomed. How you ever managed to get Pola's car stopped I'll never know. It was like a—a nightmare!"

Anthony nodded his agreement to this, but his expressionless Indian features betrayed nothing of what he actually thought. In his mind he was casting up accounts, reckoning the possibilities. They seemed endless.

Three distinct attempts had been made upon his life since he had arrived in Roseville a few hours ago. But of those three, only one could be counted as having really been aimed at him directly. That was the silenced rifle which had whispered two shots at his window.

Definitely, those bullets had been intended for him. He wasn't so sure about the other occasions. For instance, the bombing of the *News-Press* plant might have been meant for Jeff Stanton rather than himself. At least, Stanton was the one who'd died in the blast.

Then there was the sabotaging of the brakes on Pola Valska's roadster. Maybe Pola herself had been the intended victim. Maybe somebody had recognized her car standing in front of Stepan Koblick's gambling dive and jumped to the conclusion that Pola was inside. Maybe the breaks had been disconnected with the idea of plunging the girl to a watery death.

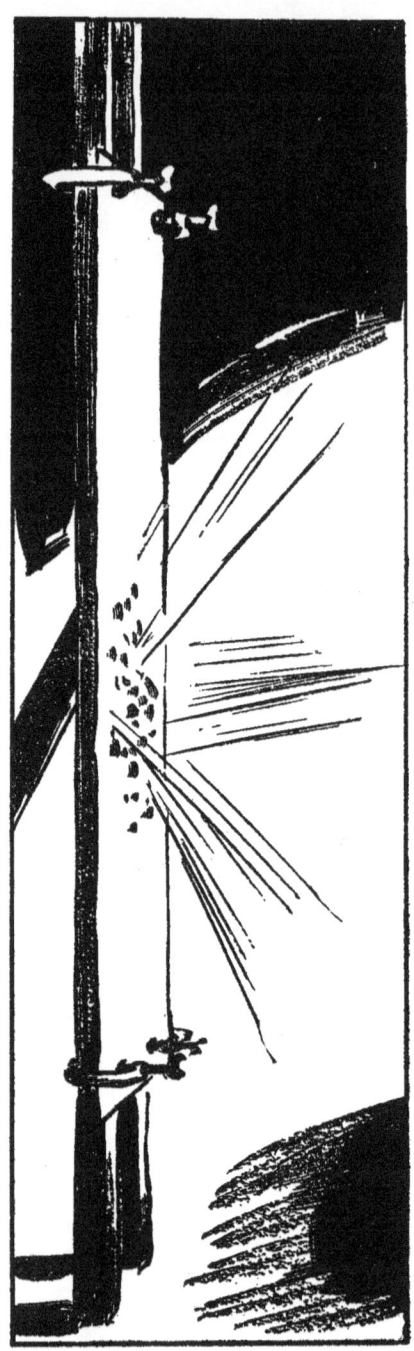

The millionaire criminologist cast a veiled glance at Rosewater. The colorless little reformer was in love with Pola; and she had rejected him. The jealousy of a spurned suitor sometimes leads to murder; and certainly Rosewater had been under the impression that the girl with the purple eyes was in the gambling joint.

Moreover, the little man had been unwilling to ride in the roadster later, when Anthony invited him. Could that have been because he knew it had no brakes? Or had it been due to his plausible excuse that he had his own car there?

JIM'S THOUGHTS SEETHED and churned; his intuitive sixth sense kept telling him that the essential clue had already been disclosed to him— if he could just remember it, put his finger on it. So many things had happened in the past few hours that he felt curiously confused, unnaturally unsure of his ground. The sensation was definitely disturbing because he wasn't accustomed to it. Ordinarily his keen mind cut straight to the heart of a problem; but tonight his perceptions had been blunted and dulled by too great a piling-up of event on event. Had there been a hidden connection between all the night's happenings, or were they all unrelated coincidences?

One thing was certain: two men had been murdered within the past few hours—Jeff Stanton at the *News-Press* explosion, and a treacherous hotel clerk named Baldy Parker. And Jim Anthony himself had narrowly escaped death on three occasions. All of which added up to—what?

"What I need is a drink," he said sourly. "Ring for the bell-hop, Tom. Ask him to bring us some Scotch."

The genial Gentry snapped his fingers. "Boy, am I a dope or am I a

Not one of the heavy slugs penetrated the armor-plate.

dope? I found a bottle on the table when we came in. Here it is. Look. There's a card attached to it. *Sincere compliments of Cabot McQuayde.*"

As he spoke, he broke the seal and pulled the cork. "Where's some glasses?" he went on. "I guess we could all use a couple of snifters, huh?"

"Not me," Rosewater held up a deprecating hand. "I never use the stuff. Don't mind me, though. You two go ahead."

Tom found two tumblers in the adjoining bathroom, came back with them and started pouring. But Anthony halted him. "Hold it a minute."

"Why, pappy? Ain't you thirsty? You said—"

"I've got a hunch." From his luggage, Jim extracted a black kit of his own special design; a flat leather container packed with certain scientific apparatus without which he never traveled. Into a miniature glass test tube he poured a few drops of the Scotch, sniffing it. "Faint odor of garlic," he commented.

"So what?" Tom's voice sharpened.

For answer, Anthony selected from his kit a tiny vial marked Sulphuric Acid and let four drops dribble into the test tube. He next drew from his kit an electric heating element of his own design, its plate no bigger than a silver dollar. He plugged this into an electric outlet on the wall, resting the flat-bottomed test tube on the hotplate. Now he inserted a fragile, hollow rod of pyrex glass into the tube's length, corking the mouth of the contrivance. "Wet a cold cloth for me, Tom."

Gentry obeyed and the millionaire scientist wrapped the wet cloth around the projecting hollow glass rod, which was like a bent sipper straw used by patients in hospitals when they drink liquids while in bed. "Turn off the lights."

Tom plunged the room into darkness. The Scotch in the test tube began to boil over the electric hotplate; steam came up in the glass rod, to be condensed by its wrapping of cold wet cloth. Tiny flashes of light flickered in this condensation, like toy lightning.

Anthony clicked the wall switch, and his eyes were hot with anger. "That was the Mitscherlich test. This whiskey is loaded with yellow phosphorus—a deadly poison!"

HIS WORDS SEEMED to stampede Lawrence Rosewater's nerves into jittery panic. "Good God! Then Cabot McQuayde sent you the bottle in order to m-murder you!"

"So it would seem," the millionaire criminologist spoke grimly. "But why?" Then his hawk-like eyes bored into Rosewater's. "You've lived here all your life, haven't you?"

"Y-yes. The town was founded by my grandfather. I t-try to uphold the family traditions, keep Roseville as it ought to be. I've done a rotten job, though." He made a bitter mouth. "President of the chamber of commerce! By rights I should be mayor, boss, richest man in the city. Then I could clean out the vice, the gambling, the bloodsuckers like Stepan Koblick. Instead I'm just a stuffed shirt, a professional reformer everybody laughs at." He sneered in self-contempt.

Anthony felt almost embarrassed to hear the man stripping his soul bare this way. "Aside from all that, Mr. Rosewater, what can you tell me about Cabot McQuayde?"

"Not much," the little fellow's gaze flicked toward the poisoned liquor bottle and back again. "He was a lawyer before buying the *Clarion.* He handled the deal when I lost most of my inheritance."

"How do you mean?"

"I owned a lot of Roseville in those days. Downtown property; block after block of cheap residences."

"Tenements and shacks?"

"Well, yes," Rosewater flushed. "Although I'd hoped to clear them all away, some day, and build decent homes for the miners and the mill workers. It was a dream I got from Jeff Stanton."

Anthony tensed. This corroborated something Stanton's sister had told him tonight. "So Jeff was interested in housing projects for the men, was he?"

"Yes, and that was where I made my blunder. I dabbled in the market, hoped to make a killing so I could tear down the shacks and erect decent homes. The depression caught me short. I had to sell my real estate, piece by piece."

"All to one buyer?"

Rosewater shook his head. "The deals were all separate, individual. Not that it made much difference. Over a period of years, most of the property was bought in by a holding company; a dummy organization."

"Who are the stockholders?"

"Nobody ever knew. I've always thought Cabot McQuayde had a hand in it; he took care of the original sales. But all he'll say is that the company is owned by a group of eastern investors. I only know rents were raised gradually from year to year; until what little the workers save from their gambling at Stepan Koblick's place, they're forced to pay out for living quarters. It isn't a pretty set-up."

"Get it, Jim, that makes it all clear!" Tom Gentry exploded excitedly. "Jeff Stanton was going to use the *News-Press* to smoke out the owners of this rent-gouging landlord company. He'd gathered evidence showing who the owners really were. So they bumped him to shut him up!"

Anthony nodded. "I think your guess comes pretty close to the mark. When we find the top man of the holding company, we'll have a line on that bombing."

"Find him?" Tom said. "This bottle of Scotch is enough to hang it on Cabot McQuayde. Why else would he try to poison you unless he was scared you might carry on Stanton's campaign?"

THE MILLIONAIRE CRIMINOLOGIST started to answer, but the words never left his grim lips; because just then a thunderous pounding sounded at the door and a voice rasped: "Open up in there. This is the law." Jim sprang to the knob, turned it—and admitted a florid, beefy man in uniform of greasy blue serge, two of its brass buttons missing from the stained tunic. The man wore a cap with the word *Chief* lettered on it, and his tarnished badge repeated that legend. He had a gun in his fist.

"Your name Anthony?"

"Yes."

"Got a guy named Gentry here?"

Tom said: "That's me. So what?"

"So you're both under arrest, palsy walsy. Don't get lippy or I'll soften you up, see?"

Anthony waved the aviator quiet. "What's the charge, do you mind saying? And where's the warrant?"

The police official's bulldog jaw jutted truculently. "Listen, my friend. This is Roseville, not New York. You ain't got any influence here, see? So don't start givin' me no legal double-talk. On the kind of rap you're facin', I don't need no warrant. I take you in and you'll like it."

"The charge, please," Jim said patiently.

"Okay. You admit you and your buddy was in a brawl with Stepan Koblick tonight, don't you? No use denyin' in, on account of I got too many witnesses. You pushed Stepan around."

"And what if I did?"

"He was a big shot in this town, mister. Mighty big. He had a lot of friends, includin' me."

"Well?"

"So he's been croaked. He kicked off with a dose of gun poison in his guts—and you're gonna be mighty lucky if you don't get lynched for slippin' him the chill."

CHAPTER IX

ESCAPE

THE CELL WAS CRAMPED, dank, verminous. Anthony and Gentry had been booked on suspicion of homicide, fingerprinted, and locked up despite Lawrence Rosewater's most desperate protests.

The little reformer had pleaded all the way to police headquarters, shrilly insisting that he could alibi the millionaire and his aviator friend. "They weren't out of my sight a single instant from the time we left Koblick's place!"

"Oh, yeah? And you went there yourself with a rod; did some triggering. Maybe *you* creamed him." Whereupon Rosewater was also booked and confined in the same cell with Gentry and the criminologist.

Now the three of them stood behind bars, surrounded by the jail's midnight gloom. The only light came from a bare bulb far down the silent corridor; and there wasn't even a turnkey on duty to observe their pacing of the cramped space.

Presently Tom muttered: "So now what happens, pappy?"

"I do some investigating."

"By remote control or did you smuggle a crystal ball in here with you?"

Anthony's smile was bleak, almost sinister. "I smuggled something better than a crystal ball." And from a secret pocket of his coat he withdrew his prized steels. They were instruments of his own devising, and with them he could pick the cleverest lock ever built.

"Boy, you're going to spring us!" Tom said gleefully.

"Not us. Just myself. You and Rosewater will stay here as a coverup. Make a dummy of your coats and put it on the top bunk in case a keeper should look in and count."

Rosewater's lips worked loosely, and his face looked haggard. "A very good trick. But suppose the Hunkies form a lynch mob and come here to d-drag us out?"

"I'll be back before that can happen, if it happens at all," Jim shrugged. Then he set to work on the lock of the barred door; and in a moment it clicked open. He slipped out into the musty corridor, shut the door after him, and sped away as noiselessly as an Indian warrior stalking game in the forest.

THE BUILDING WHICH housed the Roseville *Clarion* was newer and far more modern than that of the *News-Press* which had been destroyed. And, unlike the *News-Press* earlier this evening, its windows gleamed brightly with lights, indicating furious editorial activity; for Cabot McQuayde's sheet was a morning daily whose staff worked during the night hours in order to roll it off the presses in time for dawn delivery.

Anthony entered through a side door and moved unobserved toward a staircase leading upward. He got past the city room without being seen; stole along a dim hallway until he reached the office he was hunting. Frosted glass on the door bore the lettering: Cabot McQuayde, Publisher.

Through the frosted glass panel a beam of light could be discerned, flashing to right and left, then at last coming to rest. From its movement, it couldn't be an ordinary bulb. It was the ray of a flash-lamp.

That seemed damned queer. McQuayde himself couldn't be in his office or he'd have switched on his desk light. Therefore the person on the other side of the door was an intruder; possibly a burglar!

The wealthy investigator's hand stole toward the knob, tested it without sound. It was latched. He cast a swift glance up and down the hall, saw nobody, and used his steels on the lock. But a mischance made him fumble ever so slightly; just enough to cause the veriest whisper of metallic noise.

He cursed silently as the flashlight winked off within Cabot McQuayde's room. Footfalls pattered, died away. Jim's sixth sense, alert and warning, dinned a premonition of evil into his heart. He twisted the steels and the lock surrendered to his deft manipulation. Like a wraith he slid over the threshold into ominous thick gloom.

Employing his Hindu trick, he dilated the pupils of his eyes—just in time to keep from stumbling over a sprawled figure on the floor. Tension gripped him as he recognized the supine man lying there.

It was Cabot McQuayde, his throat cut, the blood still welling from that gaping wound. The newspaper publisher was past all human aid, though. The murderer had done a thorough job—and a hideously recent one. McQuayde's flesh was still life-warm to Anthony's touch, although there was no trace of pulse.

ON THE OPPOSITE side of the office there was another doorway, standing ajar. Unquestionably the intruder with the flashlight, who must also have been the killer, had escaped by means of this second exit at the sound of Jim's approach. And the reason for the murder was quite apparent when the millionaire's penetrating gaze cut through the darkness to behold a bank of steel files whose drawers had been unlocked and opened, their contents scattered as if by some desperately hasty hand.

Obviously the burglar had been prowling those files when the ill-starred McQuayde entered and caught the culprit red-handed. Before the publisher could make an outcry, he had been knifed to death.

And now Jim Anthony found himself confronted by an ugly dilemma. If he hurled himself in pursuit of the prowler, what would he gain? Already his quarry'd had time to make a getaway; and to raise a commotion would merely reveal that Anthony himself was here in the office when he was supposed to be in a prison cell. He might even be accused of McQuayde's killing.

Yet if he remained silent, the guilty person would escape completely....

"No!" the millionaire detective whispered to himself. "There will be no escape! I'll see to that—when the time comes!" Then, with grim speed, he moved toward the files and began examining them minutely.

What had the intruder been searching for? And had it been located before Anthony spoiled the game? That was what he had to find out; and his fingers moved unerringly through drawer after gaping drawer while his abnormally keen eyes inspected each envelope, each document.

After what seemed an age he found a manila folder marked *Realty Holding Company.* It was splotched with sealing wax, closed against prying. Without hesitation Jim broke these seals and began studying the folder's contents.

The story thus unfolded sent an electrifying shock through him. No wonder Cabot McQuayde had ceased to be an attorney and had acquired the money with which to buy the Roseville *Clarion!* He had obtained his funds from none other than Stepan Koblick—for services rendered, and probably some blackmail had been mixed in with it. Hush-payments.

The complete answer was in the manila envelope. *Stepan Koblick was the sole stockholder of the Realty Holding Company!* Over a period of more than ten years he had bought up parcel after parcel of Roseville real estate, some from Lawrence Rosewater, some from other sources. And McQuayde had been his front man, the purchasing agent for the dummy corporation!

This, then, was the evidence which Jeff Stanton had spent so long and painstaking a time gathering. By one means or another, Stanton must have finally unearthed the truth. And he had been on the verge of spreading that truth all over the front page of the *News-Press* when the bomb killed him.

That campaign, had it appeared, would have been sheer dynamite. It would have torn Roseville inside out, for the Hunkies would then have been informed that Koblick, their ostensible friend, was really the man responsible for the high rents they were forced to pay. The game had been deep, clever. Koblick gouged his hard-working victims on rentals, then took away whatever they had left by means of his gambling games. He could afford to run honest games on that basis; could afford to loan money to the workingmen when they went broke—loans which probably drew exorbitant, even usurious, interest!

SO JEFF STANTON had been slain in order to prevent his using what evidence he had found. That placed the crime squarely on Stepan Koblick's doorstep. And the murder of Cabot McQuayde was cut from the same evil cloth, for McQuayde had been in on the deal; had known its secret ramifications. With matters coming to a head, he too had been wiped out to keep him from talking.

There was only one flaw in the entire chain; one weak link. Stepan Koblick was dead; had been murdered more than an hour ago. How, then, could he be held responsible for McQuayde's killing? On this single factor, Anthony's entire theory collapsed like a house of cards. Koblick was a corpse—and corpses can't go around cutting throats!

If ever a case had become a nightmare tangle, this one had. A sense of angry futility filled Jim Anthony as he considered it. Everything pointed to Stepan Koblick's guilt from start to finish. Who but Koblick could have feared exposure by Jeff Stanton's coming campaign in the

News-Press? And who but Koblick would have assumed, erroneously, that Anthony had come here to Roseville to assist in that campaign?

The fat gambler had been the only one with a motive for the attempted killing of the millionaire criminologist—and for the successful killing of Stanton as well as the hotel clerk, Baldy Parker. Koblick was the only one who could desire McQuayde's removal because of what he knew.

Yet Koblick himself was dead! Therefore he couldn't be responsible for this latest crime. Jim's thoughts raced around and around like a crazy carrousel, always returning to this one fantastic point. It had to be Koblick—but it couldn't be Koblick!

And then, in one blinding flash of inspiration, the wealthy detective hit upon the solution. Savagely he pawed through the manila folder until he found the document he was looking for: the last will and testament of Stepan Koblick, drawn and executed by Cabot McQuayde in his capacity of attorney, adviser, and general legal handy-man to the gambler.

That will contained the answer; but before Anthony had an opportunity to read it, hell broke loose around him. Somebody entered the office, switched on the overhead light, saw McQuayde's corpse and spotted Jim standing there in front of the bank of looted files. The newcomer opened her mouth and emitted a piercing scream. Then she delved into her handbag, whipped out a pearl handled automatic.

"Freeze, you murderer!" Karen Stanton said.

CHAPTER X

UNDERGROUND

ONLY AN INSTANT AFTER that first shrill outcry, the yellow-haired girl regained full control over the incipient hysteria which had apparently seized her when she'd first seen the body of her fiancé. Now she stood firm and glacier-cold with the gun in her capable little sun-browned hand, as outwardly nerveless as she might be on some golf course with a championship depending on her next move.

But Anthony knew she was overwrought beneath her calm exterior. He could tell by the twitching of a tiny muscle in her lovely cheek. She was like a splendid thoroughbred, tautly reined by the restraint of her own indomitable will power. And her eyes held glittering menace.

In that tense moment she reminded Jim of her slain brother. More than once he had seen Jeff Stanton wearing this same determined expression when, as editor of the *News-Press*, some problem had arisen demanding courageous decision.

But it was a fantastic twist of events that such high courage should be so utterly misdirected now. "Listen!" the wealthy criminologist rapped out. "Surely you can't be foolish enough to think I killed McQuayde!"

"What else can I think? Raise your hands."

Jim moved with the desperation of necessity. Should he be captured here he'd be in an ugly jackpot; his escape from jail would be held against him as prima facie evidence of wrongdoing. Every effort would be made to convict him of the murder of Cabot McQuayde, since he was also under another homicide accusation in the death of Stepan Koblick.

What he needed was an alibi to confound the blonde Stanton girl's unsupported word as to his presence in this office. Such an alibi might hold against her charges—provided that nobody else backed up her statement that he'd been here. In brief, he had to get away before she gained the backing of additional witnesses.

And witnesses were coming in answer to her one penetrating scream. He could hear footfalls in the corridor, advancing, growing louder. And as the sounds increased, Anthony made his desperate move. He launched himself forward, knocked the automatic out of Karen's hand before she could guess his intention; before she had a chance to pull the trigger.

"You little fool, I'm trying to solve the murder of your brother and your sweetheart! You want to block me completely?" Then he wheeled and went catapulting toward that door on the other side of the room—the door through which an intruder had escaped just a few short moments ago.

IT LED INTO an ante-room and thence to a rear passageway. He sped along its dim length, found a back stairs, and plunged downward at blinding speed which was all the more astonishing because he made no sound as he fled. As noiselessly as one of his Comanche ancestors hurtling through a silent forest, he went flashing down the gloomy steps, past the ground floor and onward to the basement, which housed the *Clarion's* big sextuple rotary presses.

Sheer luck had grouped the pressmen at the forward part of this basement where they were busy receiving curved, cast metal plates from the stereotypers and preparing to latch those plates onto the press rollers. Hence they didn't see Anthony as he flitted to the rear.

He spied a door which looked as if it hadn't been used for a long time; made for it, opened it and lunged over its threshold into the blackness of a tunnel. As he closed the door behind him, he dilated the pupils of his eyes; perceived that he had entered one of the myriad abandoned mine stopes which formed an underground honeycomb beneath the streets of Roseville.

He saw, also, that the city had made some use of these long neglected subterranean passages. Water mains, sewer pipes, electric conduits and telephone cables ran through the labyrinthine maze, taking advantage of excavations and drifts and bores made years before. With his instinctive sixth sense, the millionaire investigator quickly oriented himself as to directions; began putting distance between himself and the *Clarion* plant.

His loping, tireless strides carried him forward at steady speed; and his abnormally acute vision guided him safely through the darkness. He was following a main phone conduit now; saw and passed a big branch-off panel where scores of wires separated from the main line, with a testing instrument hooked in. Mud began to suck at his feet and he slogged through slimy ooze where water had recently lain.

Grim satisfaction filled him as he realized he had come in the right direction. Overhead a pinkish glare suddenly revealed that spot in front of the gutted *News-Press* structure where the street had collapsed into the deserted mine. The rickety ladder still stood where he had last left it; and he ascended its rough rungs to emerge at street level.

His surroundings were bleakly deserted; his newspaper building loomed stark and shattered, its four walls enclosing masses of charred rubble. Like a wraith, Jim cut through block after grimy block of forbiddingly black alleys; until presently he had reached his goal—the Roseville jail.

FIVE MINUTES LATER, completely unobserved, he gained his own cell, picked the lock, and slipped inside.

"Cripes, pappy!" came the choked whisper of Tom Gentry. "You took a hell's own time getting back here! Where've you been?"

"Places." Jim made for the lower cot of the tier on the opposite side of the barred room. "Need a blanket to wipe this mud off my shoes." Then he stiffened. "Where's Rosewater?"

"Gone."

"Gone—?"

The freckled aviator nodded. "He got sprung less than two minutes after you left. Don't ask me how come; I wouldn't know. That greasy chief of police showed up and told him he was turned loose. So Rosewater thanked him and beat it."

"Was anything said about me?"

"Not a word. I sweated blood for a while, though. We had a dummy rigged on the top bunk and I was scared any minute the chief'd get wise. But Rosewater kept his mouth shut and I said you were asleep and we got by with it." Gentry narrowed his eyes. "Why? Did something happen? I mean, after Rosewater pulled out, did you run into something?"

"I ran into plenty. Cabot McQuayde's been killed. And Karen Stanton caught me standing over his body."

"Oh-oh!" Even as Tom voiced his dismay, footsteps and voices sounded in the jail corridor, approaching the cell. "Boy, here comes trouble!"

The genial flyer was right. Jeff Stanton's diminutive, athletic blonde sister was pattering forward with the police chief at her side; and the girl's tone was shrilly vindictive as she said: "I tell you I saw him with my own eyes. You think I could mistake recognizing a man like Jim Anthony?"

"You must've, Miss Stanton," the chief growled uneasily. "He ain't been out of here since we nabbed him. I'll take a paralyzed oath to that." Then he reached the cell door. "See for yourself. Here he is." He pointed through the bars.

Anthony stepped forward. "Hello, Karen. What brings you here? Is anything wrong?"

Her kissable lips curled in contempt, but her eyes grew large with startled puzzlement. "Y-you—she breathed. "How did you get back so quickly?"

"Back? I'm afraid I don't understand," he answered steadily, injecting a hint of surprise in his voice. "You talk as if you had an idea I'd been somewhere."

"You *have* been somewhere. To the *Clarion* building. Don't pretend you weren't in Cabot's private office less than fifteen minutes ago."

"Cabot McQuayde? Does he claim I visited him?"

Embittered, frustrated fury flared in her glance. "He can't claim anything. He's dead. You know that as well as I do. You k-killed him."

"I think you're making a mistake," Anthony retorted levelly. "You say McQuayde's been murdered? That's ugly news Karen. I can say only that I'm genuinely sorry to hear it. But you're wrong in accusing me, my dear. A man can have no stronger alibi than the fact that he's been locked tightly in jail at the time any stipulated crime was committed."

The police chief wagged his shaggily unkempt head from side to side like a bewildered bear. "Yeah, Miss Stanton, the guy's right about that."

"But I saw him!" she stamped her foot.

"Have you corroboration for that?" Jim asked her.

"You know I haven't."

He surveyed her mildly. "It must have been a case of mistaken identity, Karen."

"That's a lie!"

"Here, here, now, Miss Stanton," the chief said. "After all, he couldn't be in two places at once. You was just seein' things, is all. I don't blame you for bein' upset, with your sweetie in the morgue along with your brother—not to mention Stepan Koblick, although I guess *him* gettin' croaked don't mean too much as far as you're concerned. All the same, somebody's gonna take the rap." He cast a jaundiced look at Anthony through the iron bars of the door. "Probably you, pal."

HE WAS WRONG about that, though.

After a while he persuaded Karen Stanton to leave the corridor with him; apparently talked her into going home, for she didn't return any more that night to renew her accusations. In fact, nobody came back to the cell until a good two hours after sooty dawn had broken the following morning.

Then the chief of police showed up with Lawrence Rosewater and Pola Valska. Pola's purple eyes were bright with excitement, and she clutched a legal looking document in her hand.

"Mr. Anthony... Jim!" she exclaimed. "You're free!"

CHAPTER XI

CAULDRON OF DEATH

TOM GRASPED THE BARRED iron door and gave an excellent imitation of a monkey in a cage—a large and very grateful monkey. "What a woman!" he said, grinning boyishly at the Slavic girl. "How did you work it, babe?"

She waved the document. "Mr. Rosewater and I worked like beavers the whole night through until we finally found a judge who was willing to issue a writ of habeas corpus." Then she turned to the millionaire criminologist and smiled wistfully. "Y-you wouldn't expect me to let my new boss stay in jail any longer than was necessary, would you, Jim?"

"Thank you, Pola," he touched her hand briefly when the door had been unlocked and he emerged from confinement. It was queer, he thought, how the mere contact of her soft fingers upon his own could send such a tingling thrill through him. There was something electrifying and vibrant about her, something that struck deeply into a man and disturbed him emotionally.

Gentry, watching, sensed this; and his boyish grin faded. Always it was the same old story. He fell for a dame and she never even realized he was on earth. Not as long as Jim Anthony was anywhere near. Jim was the guy who got the play. Tom sighed enviously, without jealousy, and lapsed into wry silence.

Meantime Pola was talking excitedly to the wealthy detective. "Did you know you have a date this morning? Tyler Hunt is expecting you at the foundry to examine his new alloy. I took the liberty of telling him I'd bring you there as soon as I arranged your release."

"Very good. We may as well go at once and get it over with," Anthony agreed. "All of us," his eyes included Gentry and Lawrence Rosewater and even the police chief.

Then, outside the jail building, a new and uninvited guest joined the party. Karen Stanton came racing up, bitter protests forming on her lips as she addressed the brawny, slovenly police official.

"You're turning Anthony loose!"

"Yeah, Miss Stanton."

"You can't. I won't have it. He's a murderer!"

The chief's shaggy head wagged lugubriously. "Listen, lady. A writ is a writ, see? When some fool judge signs a paper to spring a prisoner, the prisoner gets sprung whether I like it or not. And whether *you* like it or not."

Tears brimmed in the blonde girl's eyes and spilled down her lovely, healthy cheeks. They were angered tears rather than sad ones; the tears of an unrequited desire for vengeance. She whirled on Anthony.

"All right. You won't get out of my sight a single instant until I've brought you to justice," she said tonelessly. "I intend to follow you, haunt you twenty-four hours a day until you break—and pay for your crimes."

HE BOWED SLIGHTLY. "Very well, Karen. Would you care to ride with us out to Acme Foundry to meet Tyler Hunt? That's where I'm going at the moment."

"No!" her upper lip lifted scornfully. "I wouldn't get in the same car with you if my life depended on it!" And she turned, got the door of her own little coupé open; slid under the wheel and sat there tensely, waiting.

Pola Valska led her companions to a taxi standing across the street. Its driver looked vaguely familiar to Anthony; and so did certain deep dents on the cab's battered hood.

"Hiya, Cap," the jehu grinned. "This ride's on me. You never did get your sixty cents change back out of that buck you gimme last night when the *News-Press* blowed up. Remember? And anyhow, a pal of Pola's is a pal of mine. Hop in."

Jim let the others precede him: Pola herself, then Rosewater, and the police chief, and Gentry. For himself he took one of the jump seats. They got under way—and Karen Stanton trailed them in her coupé.

AT THE FOUNDRY and rolling mill, the path to Tyler Hunt's metallurgical laboratory led over a high, narrow catwalk far above thundering machinery and a raw red hell of molten steel which was being poured out of blast furnace caldrons into vast shaping containers, whence the glowing metal was fed into giant rolling presses which compressed it and hammered it into long flat sheets of armor plate.

Indian file, with Pola leading, the group moved along the perilous catwalk with hellish din and inferno heat rising below them. Presently they reached their destination.

Tyler Hunt greeted them at the door to the room in which he conducted his experiments. He looked much the same as he'd appeared last night at Stepan Koblick's gambling dive—painfully thin, his clothes threadbare, his eyes studious behind the spectacles he wore. His handclasp was firm and competent, though.

"This is a real honor, Mr. Anthony," he said with a trace of nervousness. "I—I hope I can succeed in convincing you that I really have something in this new process."

Then he surveyed his other visitors as if a little stunned by the thought of making a demonstration before so unexpectedly big an audience. He seemed particularly surprised at the presence of Karen Stanton and the chief of police, although apparently he was acquainted with them both. Lawrence Rosewater didn't bother him, evidently; and as for Pola Valska, he looked genuinely pleased to have her there. He even thrust out his hand to the taxi driver, who'd tagged along to see the show.

"Hello, Sammy. When are you going to sell your cab and come back to work in the foundry?"

"Aw, you know me, kiddo. Sooner work for myself."

Hunt crossed the room. "Well, Mr. Anthony, I may as well demonstrate what I've got here." From a table he picked up a sheet of metal which resembled aluminum in appearance and seemed not much heavier. "Feel this."

The millionaire hefted it, nodded, and passed it to Tom Gentry, who remarked: "Gosh, almost as light as balsa wood! What is it, tin?"

"No, it's steel. My kind of steel," Tyler Hunt smiled indulgently. "Now watch."

He placed the piece in a big cold press cutter and sheared off a two inch strip. "Notice how it works cold."

"Excellent," Anthony approved.

THE YOUNG METALLURGIST took the strip to a drill press; drilled a hole in it. He then attached the upper end to a heavy clamp, and began hanging weights on the lower end by means of the drilled hole. Gentry's eyes popped as the weights were added one after another. "Why don't it buckle?" he demanded.

"Because of its tensile strength," Hunt told him. "Now for its resistance to compression stress." And he placed a small bit of light tubing into a press; applied hydraulic pressure. The metal withstood an amazing amount of poundage.

Jim Anthony's eyes were friendly. "Most satisfactory."

"Thank you, sir. And now, if you'll permit me, I'd like to illustrate the alloy's qualities when used as armor plate. My demonstration is rather spectacular, almost theatrical—but very effective."

As he spoke, he led the group into an adjoining chamber; a long, narrow room where a sheet of the alloyed steel stood at one end. This sheet was at least four feet wide, six high, braced by several clamps along either side. At the room's opposite end stood a submachine gun with a full drum of cartridges.

"You will please all stand behind that large metal shield at my left, the one with the bullet proof glass observation plate," the young metallurgist requested. "Once in a while we get a bad ricochet."

His visitors complied. Then Hunt seized the machine gun and began blasting a savage stream of slugs at his demonstration alloy plate. The weapon's thunderous chatter was deafening, and the sound of bullets bashing against impervious steel sent shrilly whining echoes over the explosive stutter of the gun. Presently the burst was stilled, and Hunt pointed.

His light, thin steel armor plate was dented in a scattered pattern; but not one of the heavy slugs had penetrated.

"I'm convinced," Anthony said as he stepped from behind the safety shield. "This is the best thing of its kind I've ever encountered; and I'll recommend it in my report to Washington when you've given me your formula and cost-checks."

"I—I'm very grateful, sir."

The millionaire criminologist held up a hand for silence. "I have something else to take up, now that I've completed my investigation of this alloy. There is a matter of four murders here in Roseville, all of which occurred last night. The first was Jeff Stanton, my editor at the *News-Press*. The second was a hotel clerk named Baldy Parker. The third was Stepan Koblick. And the fourth was Cabot McQuayde, publisher of the *Clarion*."

"Whom you yourself killed," Karen Stanton said bitterly.

"No, Karen. You're quite wrong about that, as I'll show you in a few minutes. First, though, let me take up those murders in sequence. Jeff Stanton was bombed to death because he had unearthed certain evidence and intended to run a newspaper campaign based upon what he'd learned."

"Well?" Karen said steadily.

"Jeff, I'm convinced, planned to expose the real owner of the Realty Holding Company which was guilty of extorting fabulously high rents from the workmen for the shacks in which they lived. I firmly believe Jeff knew that owner and was going to unmask him."

The chief of police growled: "Name the guy."

"Very well, I will. He was Stepan Koblick."

"Gosh, pappy!" Tom Gentry said. "You mean—"

Anthony disregarded the interruption. "Next we come to the murder of the hotel clerk, Baldy Parker. He was killed because he'd taken the orders of someone higher up; placed me in a certain suite where an attempt could be made on my life with a silenced rifle. Baldy Parker was then murdered so he wouldn't be able to name the person who'd bribed him."

"Keep talkin'," the police chief rasped.

JIM NODDED GRIMLY. "As for Cabot McQuayde, he was the lawyer who handled Stepan Koblick's secret real estate transactions. He was murdered because he knew too much. He caught someone looting his files, searching for the Koblick dummy-company papers, and he was stabbed by this burglar."

"What about Koblick hisself?" the chief demanded.

"He was a crook, a cheat; a man who pretended to be a friend of the workingmen when he was secretly squeezing them of every cent they owned. I can't say I regret his death; he deserved what he got. But he is the key to the riddle."

"How so?"

"He was murdered; which cleared him of guilt in the other killings. Who, then, could have profited? There's only one obvious answer. Somebody will inherit Koblick's estate; his realty holdings, his gambling dive, his interest in Tyler Hunt's alloy. That heir, ladies and gentlemen, is the murderer."

For the first time, Lawrence Rosewater managed to speak. His voice was squeaky as he said: "What heir?"

"The person to whom Koblick willed everything he possessed. A person who knew about the will—and also knew about the campaign Jeff Stanton was preparing. This person is avaricious to the point of blood-lust. The campaign would have wrecked everything; so Stanton was bombed. Efforts were made to kill me because the guilty one thought I might undertake the cleanup in Stanton's stead. We have the picture clearly before us, now."

"What heir?" Rosewater repeated shrilly.

Anthony faced him. "You're in love with Pola Valska, aren't you? You asked her to marry you and she refused."

"Wh-why, y-yes."

"Did she give you a reason?"

"N-no."

"Then I'll tell you why she couldn't marry you. *She was already married to Stepan Koblick. She inherits everything—Watch her, Tom!*"

EVEN AS HE yelled the warning, Jim Anthony realized he was too late. The girl with the purple eyes had sidled toward the door; and now she called a command to the taxi driver.

"The machine gun, Sammy."

Sammy gulped, grabbed the weapon, tossed it to her. She waved its menacing muzzle in a flat arc. "Back, all of you."

Shaken with astonished fear, everyone in the room staggered toward the rear of the long, narrow chamber. Karen Stanton whimpered softly in her throat.

But there was one in the group who showed no terror. That was the millionaire criminologist. "Sorry, Pola," he said evenly. "You won't get away with it. You're through."

"That's what you think."

"It's what I know."

"You'll die with the knowledge, then," the Slavic girl said in her throaty, deadly voice. "All of you are going to be full of bullet holes in another minute. And I'll merely report that I'd been invited to test that steel sheet with this gun; that its trigger tripped by accident and killed a roomful of people."

"Will anyone believe your story, Pola?"

She laughed. "When I inherited Stepan Koblick's holdings, I also inherited his influence. That's why I killed him. I'll own this town, now. The mayor, the cops—everything. Sure they'll believe my story. I'll make them believe it." She laughed again, unpleasantly. "Me, a girl from the wrong side of the tracks—Queen of Roseville!"

"My God," Lawrence Rosewater gulped. "And I wanted her to b-be my w-wife!"

Pola sneered at him, then turned her eyes back to Jim Anthony. "Tell me how you found out."

"Koblick's will named his wife as his sole heir. It didn't say who the wife was; but at least I knew the guilty person was a woman. Then I thought of certain blunders you'd made."

"Blunders?"

He nodded dispassionately, his face expressionless. "First, you claimed that you'd been tripped into that open mine tunnel by the *News-Press* plant. But actually you went down voluntarily, by means of a ladder which you then pulled in after you. When I found you, later, with a self-inflicted bruise on your forehead, there was one thing that should have told me you were lying."

"What?"

"Your gabardine suit. Had you actually fallen into the tunnel you'd have landed in four feet of water. You'd have been soaked. *But your clothing was dry!*"

She grinned. "That was bad, wasn't it?"

"Yes, although I couldn't put my memory's finger on it until a long while afterward. There were other mistakes, though. For example, the sabotaging of the brakes on your car. *Nobody else but you knew I was going to drive that car to Koblick's joint.* Then who else could have followed me there to disconnect the brakes?"

"Very clever," she applauded mockingly.

ANTHONY BOWED. "AND when I first borrowed the roadster, you'll remember telling me you could pick it up later at the garage connected with the Grand Roseville Hotel. Which meant that you knew the hotel I'd selected for my headquarters. *You were responsible for the silenced rifle shots.*"

"Did you link me to the poisoned whiskey?" she taunted him.

"Obviously, when the other pieces fell into place. Putting McQuayde's name on the gift card was a nice frame; but I wasn't fooled. And finally, I happened to do some exploring of the mine tunnels during the night. I saw a lineman's testing phone hooked up to a main trunk, near the *News-Press*. That must have been the one you used for secret communication with your henchman, this taxi-driver named Sammy. That was why you pretended to fall down the pit in the first place, I suppose—in order to instruct Sammy to murder Parker, the bald hotel clerk."

The girl's purple eyes darkened and her finger grew taut on the trigger of the submachine gun. "Good guessing, Jim Anthony. Give my regards to the devil."

In that last split instant before the weapon began vomiting out a spray of death, Jim acted. He lurched sidewise, grabbed up the big sheet of lightweight bulletproof steel. "Back behind that observation screen everybody!" he roared. Then he advanced full at the hail of slugs Pola Valska hurled at him.

SCRAMBLING DESPERATELY, KAREN Stanton and Lawrence Rosewater and Tyler Hunt and Tom Gentry and the police chief dived for shelter. Only Sammy, the cab driver, was caught unprepared. Ricochetting bullets slammed him backward and he fell to the floor, dead before his corpse came to rest. Meanwhile Anthony advanced toward the murderess.

Chattering slugs bashed, at his shield, tried to wrench the sheet of metal out of his grasp. He clung grimly, bracing himself to the constant shock of impact as hot lead smashed against the unyielding alloy.

And then Pola Valska's submachine gun clicked empty.

She screeched, hurled the thing away from her, turned and went racing from the room. Like a beautiful she-fiend, the girl hurled herself out upon the catwalk which ran above the foundry far below. Red hell-glare from open caldrons of molten steel sent crimson reflections upward, staining her the color of blood.

And as she catapulted onward, she missed her footing—just as a blast furnace directly beneath her was tapped of its white hot, liquid steel contents.

Her scream was hideous as she toppled. There was a bright and blinding white flash under the catwalk; a splash of molten metal and a single puff of acrid smoke.

Pola Valska had vanished as utterly as if she had never existed.

ON THE PLANE headed back to New York, Tom Gentry gave vent to a vast sigh. "I could've gone for that jane, pappy. To think she was such a hellcat! Br-r-r! It gives me the creeps!" Then, abruptly, he brightened. "But this Karen Stanton, now. *She's* really a dish."

"She's quite lovely," Jim Anthony admitted.

The freckled aviator chuckled. "Right! And did you notice how she looked at you when she apologized for her accusations? Maybe we ought to go back to Roseville some time, Jim. If you ain't interested, I could maybe pinch hit for you, sort of. Hunh?"

"Roseville is behind us," the millionaire criminologist answered moodily. "I think I never want to see it again."